THE MAID SILJA

*the history of the last offshoot
of an old family tree*

By

F. E. SILLANPÄÄ

Translated from the Finnish by
ALEXANDER MATSON

Cherokee Publishing Company
Atlanta, Georgia

Library of Congress Cataloging-in-Publication Data

Sillanpaa, Frans Eemil, 1888-1964.
    (Nuorene nukkunut. English)
    The maid Silja: the history of the last offshoot of an old family tree /
by F. E. Sillanpaa; translated from the Finnish by Alexander Matson.
        p.   cm.
    Translation of: Nuorena nukkunut.
    Reprint.
    ISBN: 978-0-87797-280-8
    I. Title.
PH355.S5N813   1989
894'.54133--dc20   89-70847
                                                      CIP

Manufactured in the United States of America

ISBN: 978-0-87797-280-8

Cherokee Publishing Company is an operating division of the Larlin Corporation, P O Box 1730, Marietta, Georgia 30061-1730

THE MAID SILJA

Fallen Asleep While Young

DEATH came to Silja, a young and beautiful country girl, a week or so after Midsummer Day, when summer is still fresh and new. In view of her station in life, she died a fairly decent death. For although she was but a fatherless and motherless farm-maid, with no other relatives either, to whom she could turn for aid, and although she had had to be cared for by others for some time, at least she had not been dependent on charity. Thus her life escaped even that slight tinge of ugliness. On the Kierikka farm, where she was then in service, a tiny room adjoined the bath-house. There she was allowed to take up her quarters and thither her food was brought, the scantiness of which was well justified in that she never ate it all. This humane treatment was in no way due to any special love for their fellow-men on the part of the Kierikka family, but rather to a kind of shiftlessness; the farm was in general not very well managed. Perhaps they had Silja's savings in mind. At any rate she had plenty of good clothes, which of course became the perquisite of the person who nursed her. The mistress had already shown a tendency to borrow Silja's clothes.

Silja, taking after her father in this, was particularly neat in her habits; she made that wretched hovel quite pretty. From it emerged the faint coughing that sounded through the ramshackle window as far as the grass of the yard, where the drab-faced Kierikka children spent their days. It was one of the little things that, with the grass and flowers, went to the making of life that summer in the Kierikka farmyard.

There, towards the end of her days, the girl was able to taste the incomparable joy of solitude. As her mood, accord-

7

ing to the wont of consumptives, remained light to the end, this spring solitude was an admirable balm for her somewhat excited love. She was solitary only so far as human beings were concerned ; sympathetic company, speechless, it is true, but all the more devoted, she had in abundance. The relative sunniness of the room and the twittering of the swallows nesting in the bath-house eaves gave her finer instincts admirable material for the creation of bright and happy fancies. Dread visions of death kept away until the end ; indeed she hardly realised that it was the death so often heard of in life that now came to her. Death itself came at a moment when the speechless delights of her surroundings were at their tenderest and strongest. It came in the morning, just before five, the crowning moment of the sun and the swallows. The newborn day further chanced to be a Sunday, and at that hour there was nothing in the surroundings to spoil it.

Seen from the moment of death, the life of Man is like a brief, petrified vision, a kind of symbol evoking melancholy. Thus, Silja was twenty-two years old ; she was born yonder, a score or so miles to the north, and during her life she moved ever farther southward. From the incorporeal image that death always conjures forth as it were in the air near the scene of its presence, from that picture all inessential features are shed, until one might almost declare all patterns of human fate, in the light of that moment, to be pretty much of like value. In the after-death image of this maiden, which, to be sure, there was no one to absorb with his consciousness so early that Sunday, there was not much to shed. From its secret timeless beginning onward, the whole of her being, as life went by, had grown harmoniously together. A pure unbroken skin held it with elastic bonds in its own dark fastnesses, whence, to the close-held ear of a lover, had carried the beating of a heart, and his seeking eye caught a reflected glance. During her life she had not had time to be much more than a human being who smilingly fulfilled her fate. All that concerns Silja, now lying dead in the Kierikka bath-house, is for the most part ravishingly insignificant.

True, in the distance represented by the time around her birth, events are dimly discernible in which natural Fate moves on a bolder scale, having to set the luck of this dying breed on a new foundation for its closing phase. For Silja, be it re-marked, was the last of her family. The extinction of such breeds of small fame is indeed observed of none ; yet in the process are repeated the same melancholy main features as in cases of greater consequence.

The Father

THE summer-morning death of Silja, that lonely figure left to her own resources, may thus be seen as the end of a long chain of events that we can regard as beginning thirty years earlier, when Silja's father Kustaa inherited the Salmelus farm. It was not a big estate, but the family had held it beyond all memory, at any rate since 1749, the year from which the parish register began ; that was a known fact. The reputation of the early masters had of course been forgotten, but probably most of them were the best of the dwellers in the tiny community. The finest strength of the family flourished at its highest during the rule of Kustaa's father. Its growth was imperceptible : rumour knew of no specific acts, either good or bad ; yet to humbler toilers the gable windows of Salmelus spoke the language of an ever prouder dignity. There was something peculiarly dignified even in the fact that only one son was born to him, which sole child seemed nevertheless to thrive. During the whole of his childhood he was allowed to live as he liked. He looked on the entire farm as a big playground, where he sauntered, humming and smiling, into boyhood. " The young master of Salmelus " and many another such phrase caressed his ear and mind, little as he pondered over their meaning. The unvarying dignity of his parents educated him in a manner unperceived ; hardly anyone had ever heard the master or mistress counsel, let alone punish him. So he grew into a big, smiling youth, who had inherited his slightly beaked nose from his father and the colour and expressions of his eyes and hair from his mother.

Doubtless the parents nurtured many silent hopes in regard to their son, but they could not, of course, speak to him of them. The mother was sometimes inclined, when the talk turned to the rest of the world, to explain her own views to the boy, but these attempts ended in a mild argufying and joking, which revealed as in a flash the strong ties of natural affection. The mother was left with the feeling that the boy was what she was, and the father's heart warmed in secret when he saw this. Two centres formed in the boy's mind, around which the incidents of his character settled : one was a kind of unconscious honourableness, honesty, a word he was unaccustomed to hear, the other a strong feeling that Salmelus was something eternally lasting and independent of people, something in which all that happened was as natural as breathing, something that led people instead of being guided by them.

Growing up in this way young Kustaa experienced the funeral, first of his mother, and very soon afterwards of his father. His mother died in the spring while the ice was breaking up, his father in the autumn of the same year.

Immediately after his mother's death, Kustaa sensed that life at Salmelus had been badly shaken for the first time in his experience, that it had taken a new course, from which it was hardly likely to return. Nor could he have said whether the turn was for the better or the worse ; the reviving glory of the spring mingled with the gravity of death and a change in life that might lead whither ? Clearly something more had happened than the departure of a single person ; those who remained were not as before even in the beautiful sunlight.

It was a strange summer. Kustaa returned from taking the horses to pasture. In the midst of the familiar evening glow he shuddered unpleasantly : looking affectionately at the house, he had forgotten that his father lived, was still alive. As though loneliness personified had come to meet him as he stood there at the pasturage gate ... Hilma, the young kitchenmaid, sat on the porch steps gazing with dreamy eyes at the horizon. An incident usual in the extreme : the farmhands were at supper and the girl was there to help if anything ran short at table. A hundred bright summer evenings may be superficially as alike as the tickets in a lottery. But in one is the great prize ; solemnly exciting, as the threat of thunder at bedtime. Kustaa was compelled from a fairly long distance to approach the sitting girl straight across the yard. The girl might have risen and slowly, in perfectly normal fashion, gone in. But she did not do so. She sat there, calmly letting her face reflect her beautiful melancholy mood, her half-swooning glance seeming to demand the familiar young man's recognition of it. To a young man who had lost his mother the mood and glance of the girl were very sweet. He had to place the reins on the wall of the porch where the girl sat. He stretched out over her shoulder to hang them up. . . . There, on that summer evening, were Hilma and Kustaa, coming companions in fate, parents of jointly begotten children. There was no getting rid of that evening by ignoring it.

On the contrary, the consequences of that moment led far and, from the very beginning, in different directions too. It was not long before the old master noticed how matters stood. He tried his best not to see it, but young love that has not yet led to any act fills the whole house with its peculiar throbbing. It issues from each movement and speech of the lovers, even from their silence. In this respect the note of a soft and very modest humming has all the force of a mighty roaring. Impossible, however, for the master of Salmelus to think clearly and simply of matters which his nature abjured. Thus, he now pondered chiefly on the extent to which the death of the mistress had altered the life and atmosphere of the farm, on how much of the loss was inevitably absolute or strove to be compensated in strange forms. . . . The master of Salmelus felt an unpleasant twinge when he found that his meditations had brought him up at the most distasteful of all distasteful minor details : that the girl was a poor servant. "Not that, I didn't mean that," and it seemed to him that this fact, on the contrary, gave to the girl a trait of some alien nobility. Yet the old man sensed in those tiny, ever more frequent incidents something else, the first faint grins of a coming mockery. All unconsciously an old familiar path had been lost, the ground underfoot was now plainly unreliable. And at this rate it would be night before the path was found—if it ever was found again.

The old master was suddenly aware that nothing had been arranged on the farm after the death of the mistress. How had it been possible to go in this fashion? Why, it was as though she who had been escorted away in the spring had not been needed. The master meditated in his room and felt at the same time what he did not desire to feel : how somewhere at that very moment some mocking force of nature was causing two hearts to palpitate, both of them really guiltless. So much the harder, then, this germinating fate, seeing that both were so innocent. The master pondered and gazed at the dark August alders and the cut fields. Martta would have to be invited here. Perhaps she could slightly remedy the change by a new change.

He wrote a letter to his sister and set off that same evening to post it. At the post office he was given a letter containing an invitation to a wedding, three parishes away. He came home at dusk and, speaking of the wedding, said to Kustaa : "I suppose you will have to go there, I don't feel strong enough."

Kustaa consented, in reality blissfully. It was a light task for him now to set out on such a convivial journey. On his departure eyes gave solemn assurances on both sides, and at his destination Kustaa Salmelus was a bright and handsome wedding guest.

He felt greatly refreshed by the wedding. Happiness, accumulated during absence, had not evaporated; it now flooded his being, and all through the last stage of his return journey he was visited by the most delicious moods. Happiness led him a downhill track; even at a distance no difficulties loomed. His luck was indeed good, for at a bend in the road a woman came artlessly from a cottage by the roadside and even more artlessly entered into conversation with him. Kustaa learned one thing and another from her without any show of curiosity on his part, for what more natural than that he should be in no hurry on his home-coming from a wedding that fine evening. The master's sister had come to Salmelus to take charge of the household, and had said at once that no two women were needed in the house if she was to be mistress, and that very day she picked a quarrel with Hilma, whereupon the master had gently told Hilma to look for a new situation. So that Hilma was now back at her home in the backwoods.

" Was that so ? Well, goodbye then. Goodbye, goodbye."

Kustaa did not even think of what he had learned until he was out of sight of the cottage. Neither did he look behind him and see the cottar's little girl creep cautiously after him, and, seeing him turn off along the backwoods track, speed off home again. Not until he was on the track leading to the cabin where Hilma lived did he sit down at the roadside to rest and savour his mood, which had greatly expanded these last few days and now seemed to be turning really bright. All he saw was the trees of the forest, and nothing was farther from his mind than the rule of a household, present or future. To the after-languor of a wedding visit joined easily the light atmosphere of childhood, which in reality had never faded from his mind. He had known Hilma ever since he was a child—actually he was coming home from distances far remoter than the scene of the wedding. The calm warm weather lent to the falling evening a sense of fullness and absence of haste. Long, long hours would pass before he, some time that night, would go to Salmelus, to his own room. As to the mind of a child, the hours before him loomed long and delightful. The private room of a young man is dear to him because of its willingness to wait.

The fullness of life almost oppressed him at the moment when the cabin came into view. Was it not a weekday in summer and had not so much occurred latterly; and was it usual for the heir to Salmelus to walk there as he was doing, dressed in his Sunday clothes? The road and gate-posts seemed to view the approaching visitor with surprise, but the face of the mistress of the cabin revealed some anticipated joy; in it was the same gleam as in the eyes of that old woman by the roadside. Luckily, Hilma was not in the cabin.

" I heard as I was going home that Hilma had left us, so I came to see her."

" There's no room for two mistresses in the same house, we do know." Hilma's mother fussed softly with coffee for the visitor.

" It looks as though Hilma isn't at home."

" Aye, what if your trouble was for nothing?"

" She's out yonder, in the bakery chamber," burst from the youngest sister. Kustaa had the sensation of having called at an envious neighbour's as he came down the steps and smiling, with calm footsteps, crossed the yard to the bakery.

The chamber was a tiny old room with no other view from its windows than the hop-poles and between them a glimpse of field and lake; of the rest of the homestead no sign.

16

There, in the greenish twilight of that low-ceilinged room, he found Hilma. The same girl as on the porch steps at Salmelus, yet not the same. Here the girl was in her own atmosphere, her bosom beat unoppressed by fear, the faint ransom of shame was here a delight. Their love, which hitherto had known neither word nor act, knew both that night.

Kustaa Salmelus—afterwards Silja's father—walked every path of his life with smiling eyes.

Since then years have passed by the dozen, enough for such matters to be forgotten, especially as it was much later that events occurred at Salmelus which here as elsewhere are the real things, things concerning the farm and property.

Yet that autumn was enough to set tingling the minds of the lowly people who, in their confined circumstances, are so greatly in love with the customary. And what, to tell the truth, was there unusual in this event if not its background and the property and chattels involved. The women of the cabins almost suffered from their lack of proper words to describe it. It was an unpleasant, unsettling disturbance of the subconscious foundations of their existence. If a roistering farmer's son had tried to reach the bed of a cottar's daughter by night and been admitted, that would have been a refreshing event in the life of the backwoods. Nothing to worry about for her who could sue a farmer for the support of a child. If all went well, a farmer could pay quite an enormous sum to keep the matter relatively dark. But that was not Kustaa's way, the instinct of the women was annoyingly clear on that point. This phase of the matter, however, faded from memory long ago. The chattering wives have been borne long ago, all admirably silent, from the backwoods to the village church and lie, thoroughly forgotten, in the grassy lines of the common graves. Someone may still know enough to say that the dead wife of that dead master of Salmelus who moved away was born in the cabin yonder, but no one is left who could make a right good tale of it.

The old master of Salmelus lay awake that night until Kustaa came home. It was about two in the morning when he arrived. The boy came on dancing feet, and the father needed to hear or see no more than that to know everything.

The man who arrived at the old house in the moonlight scarcely thought at that moment of the important changes his father and aunt had carried out there. The old master understood it perfectly. He grasped that if the boy had thought at all of such remote matters, he would certainly have been grateful to them. He heard Kustaa getting ready for bed ; although the sounds carried faintly, he seemed to read from them the happy state of mind of the mover. When no further sound came, the old master felt himself finally alone, alone with the utter vacuity of his recent arrangements. Though not even to himself would he admit that he had tried to arrange matters with an ultimate motive.

When an old man stays awake in the small hours thinking such thoughts, it is apt to go ill with him, particularly if he can reach no strong redeeming decision. His grip on life relaxes, and in the same degree he feels the clutch of death. In the silence of the waning night the master of Salmelus remembered his wife in a specially serious fashion. Up to then his instinct had been that there were two to remember her, and everything had been easier, more loving. Now, suddenly, the inner meaning of things had changed. A spasm shot through the left side of his breast with such pain that the pipe nearly fell out of his hand. He put it quickly from him and began hastily undressing himself that he might be ready in bed, if haply—his sleep were to be long.

Three had formed a whole; when one was torn away, the others fell away lifeless. Continuity was no longer possible; even the farm became a thing unsubstantial to the man aware of the proximity of death. All that still had being was the picture of the dead mistress and the memory of her with those solemn traits that are and remain in every case the living core between husband and wife and become evident to them only at moments of great gravity. Whether he would see another day was of no importance. In a deeper sense, no morrow could ever dawn for him again. His defeat was complete, although no battle could be said to have been waged.

After that night the old master was graver than ever and extremely reticent. He moved about as before, but spoke so little that the men sometimes found it difficult to guess what they were supposed to do, as Kustaa too was inclined to a similar silence. Everyone knew quite well what was happening, but strangely enough the closest spectators found little to say about it. Even Kustaa's excursions were known, but how to tease him about them was somehow a problem.

Once a cottar happened to explain his errand to the master while Kustaa and a few other men were near. The old master said hardly a word, only smiled very faintly and looked at Kustaa. " What do you think ? "

Kustaa blushed and smiled, but simultaneously a look of helpless pain came into his face. " What have I . . . ? " He walked away and nearly cried.

Later that evening in Hilma's room, he aroused the girl's attention by his passionate caresses and silence.

" What's the matter with you ? " she asked.

The man only stared before him and his jaw quivered.

" Tell me, it will make it easier," went on the girl.

" Father is getting so weak."

These were Kustaa's words and the girl found no other

answer than silence and a lapse into non-existent thought. Kustaa laid his head on one side of her breast as a tired child leans on its mother. There he liked to linger, in the mood and the attitude in which the repose of a child and the oblivion of a man are at their deepest.

The master's room at Salmelus and Hilma's room at the cabin. These were the poles of Kustaa's life, between which he moved, in his mind a vague majestic sense of waiting. When he arrived at the one, the other faded entirely. At home he sometimes found himself longing for his mother. On such occasions a soft melancholy drew down his male mind to the safe level of a child's mind.

So wore on the fine weather of the late summer. The weather grew damper, threshing-barns smoked. One morning the master of Salmelus was seen to go to the barn, as usual. From the woodstack he took an armful of split cordwood, threw it over the threshold into the barn and after what looked like a pause, moved clumsily in himself. Martta, his sister, saw this, and as by chance she had happened to watch Vihtori's entry into the barn, so, without thinking of the matter, she continued to stare in the same direction for some time. The morning was colourless and insipid: one of those stray moments of life when even a busy person may suddenly, startled, become aware of the dread weight of time. This happened to Martta, who became conscious at the same time that she had been staring a long time with wide-open eyes at the barn. But no smoke came from the barn, nor did Vihtori reappear through the door. Not the slightest sound came from any part of the farm. Martta rose and looked around her: the clock showed an unexpected hour. Where was everyone?

She went out and stood on the kitchen steps. The opening of the barn gazed at her, black and relentless, seeming to prolong this strange moment of time. What had happened to the

20

world ? It would be foolish to walk over to the barn ; nevertheless she went. " I came to see what you were dawdling here for," she thought of saying to Vihtori. No sound came from the barn, not even when she was near it. And when she peered over the threshold, she saw Vihtori, dearest of her brothers, lying on the floor with his arms straight along his sides.

Thus that day began with the morning and throughout its course seemed to thicken as evening drew nigh. Usually a sense of relief attaches to the death of an old person, but it was not so in this case. Kustaa had not had a downright talk with his father since he was a child—a childhood that had continued until his mother's death. Now his father had silently drawn away from him, leaving unsaid what he might have had to say to the man. And he who thus withdraws in silence, withdraws a victor.

That evening Kustaa set out rather early for the backwoods.

" What kind of a man are you ? Your father still warm and you after women. Do you know, boy, why your father died ? "

" I'm thinking Hilma will have to be told," Kustaa answered his aunt.

" I suppose you mean to bring that person here, now that— "

" I don't know. It was you who drove her away."

" I did not drive her away, but I do know that she will not come here so long as the one who drove her away is aboveground."

Kustaa knew exactly how matters stood, yet the conversation made an unpleasant impression on him. If his father's silence had been effective, neither were the words of his father's sister ineffective. Kustaa lacked one quality : he did not know how to be ruthless. There lay the key to his fate, even later, when material misfortunes befell him.   He was susceptible to poison.

Hilma was to him what she was, irrevocably all that a wife, good or bad, is to a man ; yet the words of this old unmarried woman had their intended effect.

It was not Hilma's fault that she did not know how to approach her sweetheart in these matters, that she was compelled to stop at silence, and affected meditation.   Nor did she sin by so doing.   She was indeed Kustaa's bride now, but otherwise she was only Hilma, a young and childish backwoods girl, who had been in service at Salmelus—and in her own way had been more skilful than any other.   She had known enough to look a man in the eye on that distant summer evening and hold her ground when he bent over her to hang up his reins.   By that act she had arrived then at Kustaa's side and remained there.   She had confirmed her act by the manner in which she received Kustaa when he came to her room on his return from the wedding.   During the whole of that long evening and night all that had happened had been a further growth and confirmation, sufficient to all eternity, of what had already begun.

So that to kill what had then been born was more than any poison could now do.

Hilma did not come to Salmelus while the old master was above-ground.   Not until the third day after the funeral, after the last guests had gone, did she come, faintly shy, yet quite sure of herself and not in the slightest afraid of old Martta.   A young maiden, who was however in secret already a wife, as such Kustaa saw her now in the old farmhouse, which at that moment began to live again in the rays of a powerful and, now, calm love.   Kustaa had not invited Hilma to come, she had been guided by her own sure instinct.   Such a coming is more precious than the most precious assurances.

22

Martta was silent in the kitchen when Kustaa went there, and gave no answer when he asked for some refreshment for the visitor. Kustaa began foraging for himself, but as Anna, the dairymaid, happened to come in at that moment, he asked her to continue. At that Martta burst into an angry weeping in the midst of some small task. Anna made no move, only stared angrily, she too. Kustaa said to her, smiling, but gravely : " Will you do it, Anna ? "

Without a word in reply the girl set wrathfully about obeying him.

Kustaa insisted on keeping Hilma overnight. He made the bed for her in the guest-room with his own hands. Hilma smiled her calm smile, rather shy of the familiar imposing interiors and even of Kustaa, who was the master of all this and as such inevitably strange in some ways.

Far away in the distance was the summer day of Hilma's departure, a fair memory with its delicious excitements. Now it was late autumn when Hilma a little clumsily said good-night to Kustaa on the threshold of the dignified old room. She understood why Kustaa did not follow her into the room. Sleep was slow in coming, but it was good and peaceful in the dark silence, which in a matter-of-fact tone, as though to itself, seemed to be recounting the events that had occurred on this farm, all unfamiliar to her, but pleasant to see in nightly visions like these. She vaguely awaited Kustaa about midnight, but did not feel disappointed at being left alone until daybreak.

During the morning Hilma stayed in the inner rooms, but in the kitchen old Martta angrily prepared to leave the house. When Kustaa saw his aunt's swollen eyelids, he felt a distasteful pity for her. It was as though the old and spiteful woman were not alone, beside her seemed to stand something invisible, something old and harsh, against which one wanted to

rebel, although instinct said that it had the weight of generations behind it.

Kustaa inquired as tactfully as he knew how, whether there
had been any arrangement about wages.

"I have never been a paid servant in all my life, and am
not now."

After this slight thrust Kustaa began to feel that the victory
was his when he went to the back room, where Hilma sat in
her Sunday clothes and smiled. He had the upper hand of
Martta, but even then the day was a strange mixture of Sunday
and weekday, happiness and something else. He ought to be
picturing to himself how Hilma would soon be moving in
here, to become—the mistress. Soon this childish sweet
maiden, to whom all oppression of mind was as alien as sin
to an angel, would be his altogether; in these rooms, with
nothing to be ashamed of, without Martta, without anyone
. . . He had not gone to Hilma in the night . . . all this was
somehow too gentle, crushing in its softness.

The stable-hand came to ask whether he could be spared to
escort Aunt Martta, as she had asked him and was waiting.
Even the stable-hand looked bad-tempered and downhearted,
as though he too had an angry retort ready for an opportunity
to use it. When, a little later, the couple drove out of the gate,
with Kustaa and Hilma looking on from the window, Kustaa
had a feeling that there was something shameless in that
moment into which he, and still more the backwoods girl
beside him, had been drawn. The house was definitely
emptied of something that had always been there, but was
scarcely likely to return. Something of which departing
Aunt Martta was only a vague, tiresome relic. It had gone
now, but in the walls of the house remained a spirit of permanent bliss. Kustaa felt clearly that that evening, the colour
of life just then, would henceforward continue. To this he

had come with Hilma, who understood nothing of it all; who, like a faithful dumb animal, went where he went, awaiting his sign to give him everything she, a woman, had to give. More than at any other moment Kustaa would have liked to lean his head against Hilma's breast in the deepest oblivion of all. But it ought to happen in the tiny dark bakery-chamber at Hilma's home, with all that this deserted home stood for forgotten—though here the house was, it too like some helpless being that not even a stranger would coldly ignore.

Kustaa was perhaps born to take leave of things, but was unable to leave them. He hardly noticed the crossroads before him: that a path would have led him away from the broad flat road to deep, peaceful, homelike lands. He set off along the broad road, taking with him the weaker of the two.

The dairymaid came to ask what was to be cooked for supper, and who was to cook it. She had no time.

This question of supper made the first steps along the new road deceptively delightful. Hilma had to take her old place in the kitchen, but in a new frame of mind. Again the girl beamed her brightest rays. She enjoyed enormously the contact with familiar things. Here and there alterations had been made since her departure in the summer; now it was all the more pleasant to wipe out this alien touch from some shelf of the cupboard. Supper was prepared, the farm-folk came to eat. A merry cottar took the edge off the atmosphere of self-consciousness by cracking a few hearty jokes about the new mistress, whom he avowed he had missed.

Among the rest of the eaters, especially among the women, a different mood reigned. There were glassy stares and a continued sullenness. And when the same cottar, after resting a few minutes on top of his supper, took his dinner-bag and remarked : " Suppose I too had better go and give my missus a hug," no one made any answer.

Hilma saw nothing of these moods around her. Her womanhood throbbed at its strongest. It was beautiful to have such a very good reason now to stay here another night —why, she had been here since daytime yesterday. And she was more than convinced that her darling beloved man would not leave her to spend the whole night alone.

She went of her own accord to make her bed, again in the guest-room. Was it not evening ?

When Kustaa went into the kitchen the next morning, while Hilma still slept, Hilma's mother sat there. With fawning mien she inquired about her daughter—surely the old aunt hadn't eaten her, as she had not come home. And hearing that Hilma was still in bed, which she had of course already heard from the maids, she began playfully insisting that it wasn't for a mistress to dawdle like that in the morning ; the farm would soon be sold up. The maids would have a fine lot to say about her.

" I'm not going there until she's gone. What business had she to come here ? " said Hilma from her bed to Kustaa.

She got up, however, and went into the kitchen, but Kustaa did not show himself again to Hilma's mother.

In the afternoon Hilma said : " I suppose I'd better go and fetch some of my clothes. Are you coming with me ? "

" Perhaps it's just as well that you go alone. The boy can drive you there."

It was twilight before Hilma returned and began setting out a few small objects in the guest-room. With unconscious feminine unscrupulousness she took permanent possession of the room. Kustaa had to come there to visit her, as he had done in her bakery-chamber. And from that day onward she stayed at Salmelus—until her departure eight years later, with Silja, the only child left to her, on her arm. But before that much had time to happen.

True, it was only slowly and by small stages that everything happened. The big clock marched steadily and gravely across the hours of life, minute by minute, holidays and weekdays, through calm and storm. Seen from the clock they look fairly much alike, but if one moves away from the clock and begins to live them, one discovers that they have other dimensions than mere length. Each of them, however, has to be lived by those still in life, and for each minute account must be rendered at least in that the following minute begins from it. It does not begin from emptiness, nor can one elect to begin it from some pleasant past minute.

Thus the young couple at Salmelus lived their life. As they became accustomed to what had been set going, it became, imperceptibly, as the clock marched ever onward, the fundamental colour of life. There was no reason in the beginning to picture the onward flow of years, that was a capacity they had exchanged, during that summer and autumn of wonders, for the glow of the moment.

The wedding was held in all privacy. Hilma's mother came indeed twice to Salmelus to persuade the young couple to celebrate their wedding at Plihtari, at the bride's home, according to custom. But on neither occasion would Kustaa allow himself to be drawn into a conversation with her, and Hilma on her part said that Kustaa could do as he liked.

" People will begin to think the marriage was before the wedding," grumbled Tilta, Hilma's mother.

" It was," said Hilma with a provoking smile.

" Well, then, it doesn't matter where a couple like that is married, if anywhere—perhaps there won't be any wedding."

27

The mother-in-law's visit ended drily; even the coffee seemed to stick in the woman's throat, and her goodbye was said in a queer whinnying tone. Three weeks, however, had elapsed since the banns were read in church, so that something final had to be done about it. The following morning, while still in bed, Hilma seized Kustaa's hand and said:

" Listen, we shall simply have to see a parson. My clothes are beginning to feel tight."

" Let's go then," said Kustaa, and jerked his hand away with playful ferocity.

A little while later he returned to the room and said:

" Aren't you ready? The trap is waiting."

Hilma had only reached the stage of combing her hair, but she hugely enjoyed this early joke. The comb stopped at first, then began to move at a busier rate.

" Am I to be married to-day? "

" Aye, and I too, I suppose," Kustaa said playfully.

In spite of everything the day denoted an extraordinarily blissful rise to Hilma. Although the banns had already been read, it was impossible for Hilma to regard herself as other than a girl, whose fate had been what it had been, but whose life was nevertheless sweet and sheltered in the protection of yonder reticent, smiling man. Now she was to be a wedded wife. A wife—Hilma pondered over the word as though it was the first time she had heard it.

Behind a black horse with tinkling bells they drove to the Rectory. On their return later in the day the master soon found an opportunity of saying to the maid: " Ask the mistress."

The supper was richer than usual. There was a white cloth on the table and a few glasses of spirits were served, as the custom had been on festive occasions when the old master was alive. And during the next few days the cottars' and

28

labourers' wives who came to the house were received with more ceremony than usual until all of them had shared in the festivity. The cottars' women returned home on different days by their own paths, thinking of the new and rather strange conditions on Salmelus Farm.

The early winter then passed quietly and peacefully. No one disturbed the young couple ; in the absence of other heirs no division of the estate had been necessary. The young mistress went about her tasks on the wintry paths of the yard. An old man from the backwoods would chance to pass the house. Seeing the mistress he would stop, stare with his eyes and bedraggled mouth, and then go on his way, to tell those at home all he had seen on his travels. The blessed state of the mistress of Salmelus was obvious even from the road.

" Ah now, there's a girl who knew her way. How the Plihtari crowd will riot there ! Tilta knows what she's about. Funny how some people have all the luck. . . . "

Kustaa was sometimes treated to the sight of the ill-mannered pause of such ancients, and guessed its import. He heard remarks too. One evening, when the stable chaff-boxes were found to be breaking up, the master said good-humouredly, without further thought :

" We'll have to ask old Plihtari to mend them."

He felt as though he had said a good word for his wife in the hearing of all these men. One old cottar, however, flashed out, as though airing some secret fury :

" Devil take it, we don't need any master-worker from Plihtari for that." And as he lifted the box into the manger he swore at the horse.

" Is Vuorenmaa angry with Plihtari about anything ? " Kustaa asked the other men.

" It's not worth anybody's while to be angry with a rag like him," muttered Vuorenmaa, who had heard the question.

Kustaa hammered a shade too loudly at the tub beside him, but said no more. The men finished their tasks and hurried away. Vuorenmaa was last and absent-mindedly made as though to blow out the lamp.

"I'm stopping," said Kustaa, and struck the tub a loud blow.

"Stop, damn you, for the rest of your life, if you like," hissed the old man and bounced out of the stable.

Kustaa put out the lamp and followed him.

In the kitchen the men were already at supper and Hilma, too, was busy there, to Kustaa's eye very much as she had used to be while in service. The present kitchenmaid Loviisa, Vuorenmaa's daughter, had seated herself beside her father, the mistress was alone beside the range.

"What are you standing there for? Loviisa can do the waiting," said Kustaa in a strange voice and went past them into the inner rooms.

The hands went on eating without a word, and Hilma remained where she was. A tense atmosphere could be felt in the farmhouse that evening, though no one knew whence it spread.

When the men had risen from their meal and gone out, the cottars to their homes and hired men to their quarters, Kustaa came into the kitchen again, where Hilma still was, now alone with Loviisa. The girl was clearing the table and the mistress seemed to be waiting for an answer to some recent remark.

"Old Vuorenmaa was in a great temper. What's happened to him," said Hilma as Loviisa went on with her work.

Kustaa looked at the girl's back and then at his wife.

"I don't know what it was about—the old man snapped at me too. Doesn't Loviisa know?"

Kustaa went out, moved about the yard for a while and returned to the kitchen.

"His daughter Eeva's in the family way, I hear. That's what he was full of, I suppose," said Hilma.

"Yes, and it's Iivari Plihtari's doing," said Loviisa and jerked at some object with unnecessary violence.

The married life of Hilma and Kustaa moved steadily onward. Their conversation that evening, after they had withdrawn to their own room, did not lack serious turns and long silences. The Plihtari crowd, Hilma's family, grew in significance each day that passed. Kustaa no longer had the feeling of being alone with Hilma, not even in these late loving hours. The farm and its inhabitants, cottars with their daughters, Plihtari, and Hilma, Plihtari's daughter, were all here now. At one moment Kustaa would be shocked at the run of his thoughts : was he alone amongst all that ? And since when ? Perhaps since that evening in the little room at Plihtari, when Hilma had not known what to say to him. . . . Were the two evening hours, then, all there had been to it : one here on the kitchen porch and the other there, on his return from the wedding ?

Yes, there was something else. In the movements of the woman with him in the room was none of the shyness of the slender cottage girl, nor need there be. That swollen waist held something untouched by these other things. Kustaa looked and looked as though he was only just now aware of his wife's state ; a warm passion unknown to him before filled his blood and spirit. The loss of all that had been at Salmelus before denoted only an emptiness, the weight of which had again been heavy this evening. But from this winter would emerge the spring and then summer ! living did not stop, it only had to be sheltered. The moment began to take on nearly the same colour as once before on a summer evening on the porch. Hilma's soft sobbing had stopped, the last repartee had been forgotten. Driven by his awakened strong passion, Kustaa crossed over to his wife and hugged her. Hilma's eyes were still bright with moisture as she said :

" Not so hard—you might hurt the boy."

At such moments only the walls of the little room and familiar objects, some of them from Plihtari, from Hilma's former room, encompassed them. They slept like unconscious children, but in the morning, when they awoke, the farm with its workers, the cottars with their daughters, the Plihtaris, were with them.

In the kitchen might be Tilta Plihtari, looking marvellously modestly and humbly at Kustaa as he went by. It would then come out that they were short of money, at home. Hilma would say the words. And when, later in the day, a worker happened to ask for his wages, the master would be a bit short of money—in hand, of course, for there was plenty loaned out during the old master's time. On such days it was as though the traces of Tilta Plihtari's morning call still remained in the house. Kustaa's countenance changed as he spoke to the worker who had come for his wages : red of cheek he looked at Hilma, who ought to know and understand. But on Hilma's face was that special absent air that Kustaa had sometimes seen on it before. Now for the first time he saw it at a moment when they were not alone.

Money, aye, what was to be done about money ? He would have to call in a few loans. Kustaa spoke as though to himself, but both the worker and Hilma were permitted to hear. And it was not long after that a debtor came of his own accord and paid back a loan.

" I heard that you were thinking of giving me notice about that loan, and hurried to repay it."

" I've never said a word about you."

" Ville Kivistoja said that the master had threatened to give Korkeemäki notice to repay, one day when he hadn't the money to pay for the woodcutting. But he's such a rattle that there's no trusting what he says."

This event, too, gave rise to a nocturnal conversation between the couple. There was money, however, in the cashbox now, and it was not to be loaned out again. The five hundred marks that Iivari Plihtari got from them before Christmas could hardly be called a loan. The master of Salmelus did not even dream he would ever get it back. Unpleasant, however, the whole matter.

It began to occur ever oftener that when one of them, Kustaa or Hilma, accidentally mentioned the Plihtaris, the conversation led sooner or later to a minor discord. Kustaa showed with increasing clarity that he did not like his mother-in-law's visits ; when she sat, honey-sweet, in the kitchen and with obvious pleasure addressed her son-in-law in the presence of the servants, Kustaa would say something, as though in answer, to the dairymaid who drank her coffee apart from the rest. Nor did Kustaa show any special regard for Hilma in this matter. Whoever liked could see the shuddering rise of the man's gorge at such moments, and the young dairymaid would be disconcerted by the needless favour shown by the master. As though she—and this chance kitchen company, on whose side even the mistress appeared to be on those occasions—had unwittingly, by her mere presence, been a source of irritation to something that ought not to be irritated.

In the field and sheds Kustaa would occasionally come on the men in the midst of some coarse tale, which they would break off with a couple of mysterious remarks on his arrival, as though to spite him. " Who said that—or did that ? " asked the master openly to get into contact with the spirit of the gathering.

" The girl in the story," the answer might be ; or : " the boy when he came home from market." And no other explanation followed, until the master happened to be standing apart from the others with an old cottar, who told him in a fawning tone that it was Iivari Plihtari's adventures that they were joking about.

After such experiences Kustaa would be silent as he laid himself down beside his wife. Hilma sought and pressed his hand, but there was no answering pressure, only the lifeless calluses of palm and fingers, to her touch. The dark silence grew heavier, and under the common quilt both tried to prevent their breathing from being heard. The wife found it harder ; her state made her breath come quickly, and agitation made her pant softly. When she turned, a quivering sigh broke from her, and suddenly she seized her husband's arm and amidst her passionate sobs a whisper could be made out that tended irresistibly to become a cry.

" Why are you always so sulky ? You knew well enough where I came from when you took me. And there's no need for you to see my folks here if you don't want. I haven't asked mother to come here. I'll tell her to keep away. And none of the others have been here."

"They haven't, but their fame has," answered Kustaa harshly.

Hilma seemed not to have heard his remark. She continued to cry and to press ever closer to her husband. Finally Kustaa could not help trying to make some comforting gesture with one hand. But at that the sobbing woman broke into full lamentation.

" Oh, why has it come to this ? Why has my life got to be spoiled for such things, when I've never done or been like that ? "

Her woman's body felt as though warmer than before and slightly clumsy as she nestled under her husband's shoulder.

34

Realisation of this softened the man's temper as it had some-times done before. Her last sentence, too, claimed his atten-tion : the thought had never entered his mind that Hilma, Plihtari's daughter, might have had her adventures before she came to Salmelus. By Hilma's remark he knew now that on that point at least he need fear nothing : Hilma seemed en-tirely unconscious of what had happened between them : and that was the surest of all guarantees. Tenderness gained the upper hand in his mind, and he caressed his wife as he had used to do when she was unwed.

Followed hours of silent and loving rest, but in the morn-ing they awoke earlier than usual. The look in their eyes seemed to remind the other of something, and then, in low tones, they began to converse.

Hilma now spoke to her husband for the first time in earnest about her brother Iivari, with whose very latest doings she seemed to be well acquainted. Eeva Vuorenmaa had probably been delivered of a child by now, and the child was Iivari's, there could hardly be any getting away from that. The Vuorenmaas, however, were said to have let it get about that if Iivari would definitely agree and was able to pay Eeva five hundred marks, they would not go to law. But it would have to be done before Christmas, or else he would get the writ as a Christmas present. But how could Iivari be expected to own such a sum—unless he could borrow it somewhere and work off the loan little by little with odd jobs.

Kustaa acted as though Hilma had put a direct question to him or appealed to him outright.

" You ought really to go there to-day and get all the facts straight," Kustaa said as he got up to dress, and by the gentle-ness of his voice he let her know that he would not mind her resting awhile yet. And Hilma remained in bed, warmed by his attention, though she had no need of rest. It was good,

anyhow, to think over the weeks still before her and her preparations, those done and those still ahead.

The earth was frozen, but the winter's snow had not come
yet. The road from Salmelus to Plihtari was in good condition even for a bad walker, so that it was only with faint pro-
tests that Kustaa allowed Hilma to set out on foot. It was nice
to watch her move along the road, away from the house, on a
known errand. Hilma walked rather heavily, but still with so
much elasticity that the sight warmed the heart of her husband.
To Hilma herself the journey brought a powerful joy unexperienced by her before : it was only now that she had the
feeling of approaching her former home as the established
mistress of a farm.

The air that rushed to meet her as she opened the cabin door
felt unfamiliar too for the first time, and for one moment a
feeling flashed into her mind that she was on an unnecessary
and badly planned errand. Her mother had paused in a
strange attitude in the middle of the floor and was looking at
her daughter as at some mysterious intruder, taking in with
bold directness and at great length the swelled contours of her
body before saying :

" Been sacked by some old aunt again ? "

" What makes you think that ? " It was all the daughter
could say.

" I was only thinking that the mistress of a farm as big as
yours would have had no need to walk all that way in your
state."

" And I thought that it would be nice walking on a dry
road, as I was in no hurry. Old Granny Tonttila told me
that a fair amount of walking would be good for me."

" Is it Granny Tonttila's advice you're following these
days ? Well, she's known how to advise her own, as two of

them have brats for no other known reason than that self-same advice."

"Soon there'll be two of yours as well off as hers. One's got his squalling already, I hear, and the other's not far off, as you can see."

It was no more than might have been expected of Tilta, yet the very air of the cabin seemed more disgusting this time than ever before. It gave, however, an easy lead for the errand on which she had come. Iivari himself was not at home, probably after squirrels with his gun.

"No, he's not, he's at Kyntöhuhta hearing the prices at market, so's he can send his squirrel-skins," said the youngest sister irritably.

"Aye, then there'll be something for Vuorenmaa's daughter to lay her hands on," grumbled the mother, this time at her son.

Not until old Plihtari, the father, came on the scene, hooked his axe on a peg, threw his mittens on a rafter and got the necessary hold of the subject, did the talk lose its edge. Old Vuorenmaa had personally told him that they would be content with five hundred marks; he had objected that it was rather a lot, but the old chap had started harping on rich sons-in-law and all kinds of things.

Hilma's little sister listened with her high forehead drawn into deep wrinkles as the grown-ups arranged the matter.

"Kustaa can lend it well enough," said Hilma in a thin adult voice and so that all of them could note her use of that Christian name. "But Iivari'll have to pay it back."

"I'm sure he wouldn't take it as a gift. Who knows whether he'll consent to borrow it?" said the father amicably.

Hilma was really grown-up as she discussed the matter in brief phrases. Even the mother let fall a gracious remark, and when at last old Plihtari set out with his horse, no less, and rattling cart to take his daughter to Salmelus, there reigned at the moment of departure a real clannish spirit in the house, of the kind that comes seldom, but when it does come is exceedingly familiar to all, warm, like a nourishing breath. It remained hovering over the mother, sister, and the air of the cabin and accompanied the married sister as she sat beside her father behind the familiar small horse. Only when Salmelus came into view did Hilma lose her confidence. The gable windows of Salmelus were like a seeing eye, and Hilma felt as though in some way she was there, behind those windows, and had never gone from there, though she was now sitting beside her father. To enter Salmelus now gave her almost the same feeling that entering the Plihtari cabin had given that morning. The blissful happiness she had known a moment ago made the place seem strange to her. With painful effort Plihtari's little mare, driven by the old man, drew its load up from the storehouse hollow to the kitchen steps.

The master and mistress debated this time with old Plihtari in the inner rooms. The farm-hands might think and say what they liked. They had plenty to say. Some of them passed fairly straight hints to old Vuorenmaa. Eeva's chances of getting her baby its due, one of them said, were very good, judging by the big pile of cakes that had gathered below the old mare's hindquarters at her hitching-post.

"The Devil and all," said old Vuorenmaa, spitting angrily.

Kustaa knew well enough that the clearest and surest way would be for him to give the money to Vuorenmaa; and if it had not been for the recent incident in the stable he might have done so. It was impossible now. He gave the notes to his flushed and voluble father-in-law, knowing as he gave them that they were gone for ever and doubting the outcome.

During Plihtari's slow leavetaking Kustaa vanished and did not reappear in the house until he heard the rattle of the departing cart. He understood Hilma's festive mood, which on that cold day of early winter illumined the whole house, but could not help being irritated by it. Somehow it made him feel more alone than ever, in spite of his wife's evident efforts to draw nearer to him. Hilma tried by her gestures and glances to reveal that there was no need for Kustaa to bother about that, or about anything else. And she succeeded. That evening they could still forget their worries of the day.

The Plihtari family then kept away from Salmelus until, on the day before Christmas Eve, Hilma's young sister appeared, with an invitation to Kustaa and Hilma to come to Plihtari some time during the holidays. The invitation was reasonable enough, as the young couple had not once been together to the wife's former home. When Kustaa, on his way to work in the morning, saw his sister-in-law on the bench in the kitchen where his mother-in-law usually sat, he nodded affably and even shook hands. And when Hilma told him her sister's errand in the girl's hearing, he answered in the same mood : " Yes, let's go during the holidays. But, have you got anything in the way of a Christmas gift to take there ? "

But at the same moment an unpleasant memory awoke in his mind : the words Christmas gift reminded him of Vuorenmaa and of the " Christmas gift " Vuorenmaa had threatened to give the Plihtaris, of whom there were again two in the kitchen. Let one of them into the house and at once there were two.

Kustaa went into the cattle-yard and hoped that when he returned, his wife's sister would have gone.

Vuorenmaa happened to be working there just then at some little winter-day job set for him by the master. Faintly sullen in appearance, as usual, he glanced now and then towards the kitchen door, as though expecting someone. When the Plihtari girl finally appeared, he left his work without hesitation and went to talk to her. The conversation did not last long. Vuorenmaa came back to his work, to where the master was still standing.

" I asked the girl what young Plihtari means to do about his child, but she didn't know. Christmas is near enough now, so that perhaps it's best to set the sheriff on the job."

The master said nothing, and Vuorenmaa went on with his work. When at last he cast a side glance at the master he saw the familiar threatening flush on his cheeks. For all his age Vuorenmaa was still a man, and in his prime no one had dared to lay hands on him. With the young master of Salmelus, however, it had happened to him more than once that against his will he had had to speed up his work while the master stood beside him, gripping him, or so it felt, by the neck. Or else he had to get quickly out of the way, as on that day in the stable. Something like that was in the air now, so long as the master remained silent.

" Hasn't Iivari been to see you about some agreement ? " came at last the master's voice as though from somewhere behind his throat.

" He—has—not." Vuorenma let the words come one after the other as a winning card-player plays his last cards. Obviously the man knew everything.

The master turned away as though to search for something in his pocket. He turned back again and asked in an ever thinner voice :

" Will five hundred be enough for Eeva ? " Not until he had uttered the words did he see how much deeper he had sunk : he had never even discussed the matter before with Vuorenmaa, or the sum.

Vuorenmaa gave a harshly worded assent, and the master

turned away again. When he turned once more to speak, he had to clear his throat, first softly, then loudly.

"You can leave your work early enough for you to get to the sheriff's in your working time, to hear what he has to say."

The master then went his way in earnest. At any rate, his last word had been an order to his cottar. But how alone he was.

From this began the first act done by Kustaa without the knowledge of his wife; perhaps it was also the beginning of his outward misfortune. But, as we have hinted before, order had to be made out of disorder, whether by the course of life itself or by its humble agent is a matter of indifference, if one takes the wide view. Kustaa may have thought, who knows, that he only wanted to spare Hilma a distressing agitation, her pregnancy being nearly at its end. Somewhere, however, at the back of his thoughts was the feeling that he was punishing somebody; certainly also himself.

It was easy for Kustaa to get away to the village, what with Christmas preparations in the air. He found so much to do that the time passed almost unnoticed to late evening. When he left home Hilma submissively suggested that he might bring something for the Plihtaris. To this Kustaa said nothing. At the village he was seen to go first of all to the sheriff's; from there he called at the tanner's and then went to the shop, where, very slowly, he made his purchases. The horse stood for hours on end at the hitching-post, and the clumsy scrolls of the embroidered date on the Salmelus sleigh rug hung over the back of his sleigh. As it was rare for Kustaa to leave his farm, one and another of the customers at the shop came to shake hands with him. He saw old Vuorenmaa approach the shop—look at the old fellow, coming right to the village in his resiny working clothes. The master of Salmelus began to make his departure and reached the shadow of the doorway just as the cottar entered. There were those in the shop whose eyes took on a new gleam, especially after Vuorenmaa had paid for his purchases out of a fairly big wad of notes, which anyone could see had not been long in the old man's pocket.

Half an hour later the sheriff and his wife gazed on the young farmer who, for the second time that day, was setting out from their yard. They admired the fine flush on his cheeks, his slightly arched nose and his valuable rug. They spoke, too, of the matter that the master of Salmelus had arranged that day through the sheriff. The matter had resulted in a document now in Kustaa's pocket, attesting that: "I Kaarle son of Sefania Vuorenmaa, on behalf of my daughter Eeva, a minor . . . received . . . undertake full responsibility that no money in respect of the child will hereafter be sued for from Iivari Plihtari . . . event of death her assigns shall not be required to repay . . ."

This document Kustaa Salmelus thus kept secret from his wife. For all that on his return home he was calm and gave a full account of his purchases to his wife. True, he had not known what to buy the Plihtaris, but perhaps Hilma would find something suitable at home. And if Kustaa henceforward was rather inclined to absent himself, there was nothing in that to awaken Hilma's surprise ; it was inevitable that in their intimate relations, for the time being, Kustaa would gradually have to draw aside.

They paid their Christmas holiday visit to Plihtari, although Kustaa knew as they set out that the journey would not end well. And as Kustaa is as central a figure in this story as his future daughter, towards whom the story is shaping, and as this visit denoted a decisive turn on the path to which this last male descendant of his family had been brought, the visit should be described in full.

42

. 2 .

PLIHTARI was an old homestead on the edge of a sparsely-populated backwood settlement ; a characteristic winding forest road led to it, marked in summer by the raised roots of trees and the cow-tracks that thickened into muddy patches with greeny-yellow pools at the halts formed by gates ; in winter by the deep ruts of wood-loads and bunches of hay accumulated at the gates. A generation ago it had been a prosperous homestead, but the present Heikki had allowed it gradually to deteriorate. To some extent this was due to the expiration of the former lease ; the tenant having fattened, the owner naturally made the terms of the new lease harder, and as Heikki Plihtari was a simple, good-natured fellow, he was incapable of leaving the place, but agreed to a curtailment of his usufruct rather than have his rent raised. But just as much it was due to something wrong in the way the household was ruled. Heikki had married, or had been snatched by, Tilta, one of the notorious Karjaharju girls, and the handling of one of these would have been task enough for a harder man. Along with her there came into the house a certain un-rest and commotion, a groping, grasping spirit. Whatever was gained thereby, Tilta regarded as her work and especially as redounding to her honour ; what was lost, of that Heikki heard sufficient. Tilta bore three children, of whom the oldest, Hilma, although taking more after her father, mild and silent, succeeded after all so marvellously in becoming mis-tress of the old and respected Salmelus estate ; quite as though there never had been a half-ruined Plihtari and the girl had burst into bloom there out of the air.

And now in answer to an invitation, she drove beside her

husband along the wintry road. The day was a Sunday between Christmas and New Year's Day. Hilma was in a rather
inspired mood, for they had even been together to church that
day, as on some pleasure trip. The smile of the man too sitting beside her was more expressive than usual, as though
his wielding of the reins was some jolly task, the import of
which would be revealed later. A pretty visiting load in every
way.

At their destination, the Plihtari cabin, they were expected,
but the moment never comes there when everything would be
ready to receive anyone. During these Christmas holidays
quarrels have been even more frequent in the cabin than usual,
and now the old man in particular fumes and grumbles, without really knowing at whom. He it was who took the money
and in some measure he is guilty of its shrinkage, though he
never intended as big a hole in it as that. All he had wanted
was a new bell for his horse-collar and a set of winter harness,
and he was sure that at a pinch Vuorenmaa would have agreed
to wait for that bit even until after Christmas. But then Tilta
took her share and finally Iivari himself took some, and in the
end the sum was not big enough to be worth while taking to
Vuorenmaa. Iivari and Tilta side with each other ; with her
connivance the son has been at the barrel of strong ale that
was not to be tapped until the Salmelus couple came, and now
he mocks at the whole matter.

" Stop that jawing, you scoundrel," roared the old man at
his son with really astonishing vehemence. The son stood up
and began, cursing, to explain that he had never begged anything from the master of Salmelus, and God help him, never
would ; if a man like me isn't good enough to be his wife's
brother, he can do without, and I'm not going to feed any
brats of Vuorenmaa's daughter. At that, however, paternal
instincts began to awaken in good-natured Heikki. He roared

44

louder, but the son only seemed to brace himself up, and the mother was about to intervene—when all at once the tinkle of an unfamiliar sleigh-bell sounded from the stable corner, the arched neck of a bay filly came into view, followed by two familiar faces at the back of a sleigh. A moment later Heikki was already holding the reins ; Iivari had slipped round the porch and out of sight.

He was allowed to go in peace, even to stop and listen how humbly Tilta and Heikki received their visitors ; no one took any notice of him, Iivari. His self-confidence swelled as he trod the narrow path through the snow towards the cellar. From the cellar door he sank into the dank mild depths, smelling of damp stone, fumbled through a series of familiar actions, until the friendly noise of strong ale running into a can answered from the darkness.

" Yonder in the little room there's our old man now, father —hm—and then that young Salmelus, who's like a father even to father—ah—and then our sister, stuck up, she too— Ah-h—" So ran Iivari Plihtari's thoughts as in the darkness of the cellar he sipped the drink that had been strictly decreed was to be saved for the master of Salmelus. And the more he drank, the sicker he became alike of Plihtari and Salmelus and Vuorenmaa, each in his own sphere, and he decided to go somewhere else, to the neighbouring villages, not to return until the visitors could be expected to have gone. He made sure the tap of the barrel was closed, locked the cellar door and, without thinking of what he was doing, put the big key in his pocket. His temper ran high, yet for the length of a furrow he advanced half running.

Inside, the visitors had been led into the little room, newly heated, and Tilta was to bring coffee and cake there while Heikki mulled ale. It was not long, therefore, before the loss of the key was discovered, and the fact that Iivari, too, had disappeared, though no one thought at first of connecting the two. Fierce, whispered quarrelling, bustling and the sound of searching carried through the wall, whereupon Hilma went to see what was the matter. The drive to Plihtari had flushed her slightly thinned face to real beauty, and she wore a new dress, straight and ample, made especially for her, as for gentlewomen in her state. She was a fairly imposing sight as with her arms behind her back she stepped into the empty centre of the living-room floor, like any other guest from a guest-chamber.

It was Hilma, too, who first began to suspect that the key might be in Iivari's possession. And after a few ejaculations and a protracted aimless searching, the hosts were ready, as though defeated in their efforts to keep Iivari out of it, to accept the theory. Hilma begged that the door might be left alone until the boy came, surely he would not be long; but when Tilta firmly declared her intention of having the potatoes for soup out of there within an hour, Heikki went off without a word to the cellar and broke open the door. Soon ale foamed in the tankard and old Heikki was able to lead the talk with his son-in-law in the direction he wanted. An old man like him didn't need much before both his voice and his speech grew soft. Heikki described matters, and the mother and daughters delivered the side-remarks demanded by the fashion of the family. The old man's account stretched over the whole evening and only ended in the living-room bed, into which he collapsed in a noisy slumber at nine, fully clad. By that time it had been clearly explained how it would actually have been foolish to thrust all that money on the Vuorenmaa crowd, when it wasn't even said that the child was Iivari's.

" Yes he is it's father," broke in the fourteen-year-old sister at this point.

"You shut up," roared the mother in answer and then went on to say that they hadn't taken out a writ after all, in spite of their threats to have it served as a Christmas present, and that was why Iivari was now so joyful that he'd taken the key.

"If he took it," interjected the youngest of the family.

"Yes, perhaps it was you," whinnied the father in an attempt at a joke.

Kustaa, too, had sampled the excellent ale with a relish—Tilta Plihtari was so skilful at brewing that she was often fetched to brew guest-ale on the big estates. In honour of her son-in-law she had now brewed according to her reputation, for which purpose she had had to make a new breach in the notes obtained from Kustaa, and Iivari had not had time to draw more than a couple of quarts from the cask. The fine flush on the cheeks of the master of Salmelus gradually turned into a dull red, and at last he too was delivering a similar endless, though rather vaguer, speech to that of his father-in-law. He related to Hilma's mother Tilta how he had been thinking over that matter of Iivari's and come to the conclusion that if his father and mother had been alive to advise him, he, though the matter did not concern him, Kustaa, or his wife, the slightest bit, he would have had to do something for the sake of the family name, and so in the end he had paid up after all. To this the mother-in-law did her best to explain that even if the money they got had not been put to that purpose, it had not been wasted, not much of it. Anyone would feel ashamed to visit a son-in-law like him with old tattered harness like theirs had been—folk might have taken them for a pack of gypsies—and so on, beyond Kustaa's understanding just now.

And so matters became no clearer until Iivari, returning home, made them plain. His manner of explanation was such as to bring the newly-formed bonds between the parties to their final and irremediable strain. Snap they might, but only after a series of deaths.

Old Heikki was thus already speechless in his bed at nine, and Tilta's meal, for which the potatoes had been brought through the same broken door as the ale, was at last ready for Hilma and Kustaa to enjoy. They ate in solitude in the little room, and by now Kustaa was explaining to Hilma all that about the advice his father and mother would have given him. Then the first sounds of the brawling of approaching drunkards were heard, soon to resolve themselves into a babble of speech, after which the noise of Iivari groping clumsily into the cellar could be heard even in the room. He did not stay there long; soon doors banged, first the porch-door, then the living-room door, where arose the commotion that might have been expected.

Tilta's reproachful whispers alternated with Iivari's ever louder opinions. " Our ale isn't going to be drunk by that Salmelus lot. It's surely Kustaa Salmelus's own brat, as he's paid both me and Vuorenmaa's girl now—ho-ho-hoo—oh God save us—is that parrot-beak still here with his woman ?''

Even Heikki could be heard awakening in his bed and trying to yell some command, but he was soon silent again. Then Hilma rose from table and rushed into the living-room. Kustaa stayed where he was, but cocked his ears, and soon he heard something that made him get up and go into the living-room.

He came at the right moment to see, and experience, an event that remained the only one of its quality in his whole life. Was that well-dressed pregnant woman really his wife, and the drunken man who at that same moment pushed the woman so that she staggered helplessly against the corner of the stove, was it his wife's relative, her brother ? Whatever

48

they were, Kustaa Salmelus, for the first and last time in his life, now did violence to another man. A dreadful nausea gripped the whole of his being as he felt his fingers twist into the collar of that—Iivari, was that his name?—so that the side of his forefinger lay along the man's flesh. They were bent somehow over the oven-side bench, some brand-new harness dangled between them, and Kustaa came to his senses to find two women shrieking prayers into his ear. His grip relaxed of a man whose face was dark-blue and from whose one hand a big iron key, from the other the tap of a barrel, had fallen to the floor. He saw old Plihtari standing behind him in solemn anger, as though the old man had just quelled him. Somewhat confused, Kustaa laughed aloud and said: "Now the Salmelus family is going." He saw Tilta and Hilma trying to revive their still unconscious Iivari, and dashed hatless towards his sleigh.

Kustaa did not properly awake until on his homeward journey in the sleigh, while skilfully avoiding a bad stump he had noted on his arrival, he saw his wife sitting beside him as though half-asleep, looking slightly bored. Before them shone the moon, newly risen. Kustaa remembered everything, and refrained from opening his mouth. He was again midway between Salmelus and Plihtari. Was his father still alive there where he was bound? No: not even alive. Matters were bad.

In the yard Hilma got out of the sleigh and went, she too wordless, inside. Kustaa settled the horse in the stable, and when he arrived at the bedside, Hilma lay there turned away and seemed to sleep. A long quivering sigh, however, showed that she lay awake.

· 3 ·

WHEN people say that so-and-so lost his farm, they are not as a rule referring to any specific event that was directly responsible for the loss, unless the question is expressly of the hauls made towards the end of the 'sixties. In those years of helpless famine many a resourceful farmer laid the foundations of the material prosperity which enables his son even to-day to walk idle and rich, especially if the " old man " had the sense to eject his chief tenants before newfangled protective legislation came into force. In those years, towards the end of the famine, farms were sometimes sold by the provincial authorities for unpaid taxes of no great size, and if one of these far-sighted farmers had the coin, naturally he went and bid for the threatened estate rather than lend the money to his oppressed neighbour, who was unable to do more, perhaps, than read a few chapters of Luther before trying to sleep.

And sometimes a fever wiped out the folk on a farm so well as to leave no importunate supplicants for help, beyond perhaps a half-witted old pensioner. The tale might be embroidered to any length—recalling off-hand phases of it as one views the half-educated landowners who pry even to-day for the chance of a good bargain in land and then turns one's gaze to some taciturn, wizened old labourer in whose features one seems to descry a certain dignity, only to hear that he is the former master of such and such a farm.

These matters are in a class by themselves and link up with the history of the country, with the great joint trials of the nation.

The everyday, less noticeable cases, however, are sometimes much more mysterious in their hidden causes. On

50

many farms sickness can strike down the cattle, children, the wife, twice in succession ; an April wind can wipe the tender rye-shoots off the soil and an August frost freeze the sap in the half-ripe ears of summer corn ; fires can occur or a neighbour for whom the master has entered into security fail ; and still the farmer remains on his land. But the next generation, son or son-in-law, can be swept away, though nothing of the kind befall again. On the contrary, in the 'nineties, the time with which we are concerned just now—the rule of Kustaa and Hilma at Salmelus lasted fairly exactly that decade through —it might happen that the first symptom of decay was an outwardly swift rise in wealth and consequence. The results of the forest sales of those times are well known ; it is easy to imagine that type of old rustic swaggering with his money in some town tavern. Now that the debris of those fellings has rotted where it lay and new trees await their fate at the forester's hands, the sole relics of those sudden accessions to wealth are a few stone granaries on insecure foundations and those raw-looking " best room " windows with two bare upright panes and a third laid crosswise over them, which remind one especially of the leather money-case of a forest-buyer of the period. A pot of money obtained by the drawing of a crow's-foot tempted the farmer to show himself modern, and that none might fail to see it, he altered the old dignified six-pane windows of his best room to the kind in his brother's home in the suburb of a town, that same brother who made a definite pauper of his country brother, and so on. . . .

The last hereditary master of Salmelus sold no forest and did not change the old greenish window-panes of his house. And although to Kustaa, on his return from that Christmas-tide visit, the instinct of centuries of landowners whispered that his life and situation were not what they should have been, his straightforward nature, in which, to be sure, was also a strain of high-minded obstinacy, was wholly unable to grasp that he was the master who was to lose Salmelus. Even afterwards, when the enormous bulk of the master of Roimala already grunted its satisfied appreciation of the Salmelus lands, Kustaa could not have named any specific act by which he or his wife could have occasioned the loss.

In the morning Kustaa awoke first, lit the lamp and then looked at his wife, beside whom he had slept this as other nights. Hilma seemed to be sleeping more heavily than usual; her face was half turned away, and its lifeless expression was directed elsewhere, as though to some other life, as one gazing at it from afar, well able to understand its meaning. The quick breathing of the sleeper seemed to affirm its entire innocence of what the face revealed. The heavy womb discernible under the counterpane was like the touching relic of some catastrophe.

A strange blight lay on the man's awakening consciousness. Why should he feel like this, growing worse as moment by moment memory returned. We were at Plihtari, with the sleigh . . . didn't I stable the horse . . . ale and food . . . well, now I made the trip we spoke about . . . and there's the daughter who still followed me from there . . . aye, I am fastened to her, she is mine, mine . . . aye, what can rightly be the matter with me. . . .

Kustaa remembered how old Heikki Plihtari, that loose-kneed ancient, had been the last to stand on the cabin floor, as though he had vanquished them all, even Kustaa, his son-in-law. . . . Why, it was as though he had become the old man's son. . . . Was that what his relations with Plihtari had become. . . . Plihtari's worthless old tenant still fathering it over him here, in this early morning hour, in this old room at Salmelus, all through that daughter of his sleeping there who . . . was firmly anchored here and . . . It was the

52

same room as before, although for long now its atmosphere had not resembled that of the former guest-room; sweated and breathed to exhaustion as the air was. Nor was there any longer the familiar coughing of his father beyond the door ... I live on the farm alone now, with no one to support me ... and there sleeps that ...

Hilma did not awaken even now. Perhaps, while the night wore on and her husband slept, her own agitation had continued, until but a while ago she fell asleep. Kustaa dressed himself slowly; it had to be done, seeing that it was morning, and early winter working morning. On such mornings a farmer rises on awakening, no matter what his night was like. If he is undisturbed in mind, no gazing on a wife for him, for his wife will have risen before him and awakened the maids, whose sleep never ends of itself. A happy farmer has no thoughts as he draws near to his stable in the morning twilight and hears the familiar whinny of his own hack. The men follow him and know their work.

But at Salmelus on that particular morning neither maid nor mistress was yet awake, and there was no sign of the men; and the master tried to think as he trod the stable-path.

He went into the stable and carried out his usual tasks: lit a lamp, shovelled out dung and curried his horse. Then he put the harness on its back. As he busied himself it seemed to him as though some other person was following through his eyes what he did, trying to guess his intention. As a matter of fact he had no intentions, but—he had to go somewhere. The men's soiled sleighs stood outside the stable where they had been left the last weekday; they would be driven off again after day had broken on their old tracks, no master needed for that. Or really—a good deal was needed, but now the master was off to the distant back-meadows to fetch hay. That too was a man's job and very suitable for a master between holidays. The best time to set off would be a couple of hours later. But an early bird . . .

As he drew fast the collar of his horse, Kustaa paused a little, as though thinking together with his horse. The morning was a silent moistish winter morning, so still that the rumbling in the horse's stomach sounded clear and sharp, and when the horse shook off the last vestiges of stable warmth, the clatter of harness and the shafts made a great noise.

Just then the maid Loviisa went past near enough to see what the master was about; she saw the cage for the hay and would thus be able to tell the mistress where he had gone. From the porch she still looked back, then went shivering inside and could be seen lighting the fire. The master felt that he could set off. Unnecessary to go in again to say anything.

Kustaa let the horse take its own pace. It was still so early that he would reach the meadows before dawn. Standing in the sleigh a man could well sink into thought of any depth. The road wound on, a deep furrow across fields, pasturage, forests. A single pair of tracks; the space between them gave the width acquired by an ordinary farm sleigh through the centuries. His son's sleigh would fit, if one might say so, the ruts left by his father's.

Kustaa thought of what he would now do. He had a general feeling that he had to get rid of something. What it was he could not discover, it only felt good to drive off into the wilds. The snow-embedded forest made a man forget the worries he had acquired with his fields. Such moments of oblivion were to be had here at any time, although the thoughts attached to the cleared land always won in the end and took up their everlasting round.

To escape, and never see again or need to remember at least that male being whose throat his hands had recently crushed and for whom he could not, at that moment, think of a name. But as he imagined, standing in the sleigh, such an escape, at once there rolled up so much else that seemed to depend on that male being. The Plihtari homestead and its inhabitants, the daughter now probably awakening in the room at Salmelus, with no companion beside her for the first time since she became mistress of the house. Aye, and Salmelus too, the whole farm, even those who had bequeathed it to him: mother and father; all became joined to that dim idea of escape, in the end even he himself, as though he would have had to escape from himself too. And then that which would soon be born. For the first time Kustaa now thought of that too, directly and bluntly. But even from that, thought led straight to the same sore point, irresistibly. Kustaa's gorge rose: that male being was just dashing Hilma against the corner of the stove when he intervened. Or, his intervention came too late; had not he seen his wife's body fly against the stove. And now afterwards he had the feeling that he had not received proper restitution from that being, and never would. Such things had to be avenged on the instant.

The image of Iivari Plihtari continued to grow in Kustaa's consciousness; powerless the snow-clad forest to help him any longer. As the morning advanced that too became shorn of charm. Iivari Plihtari, that drunken brutal clod, had laid hands on his wife heavy with child, his wife, who was also— oh!—a sister, its sister. More and more entangled everything; ever greater the disgust that swelled in his breast. Kustaa was unable and ashamed to think the matter out, but somewhere at the bottom of his mind he felt that that man had attacked his unborn child too and not only his wife. By his act the man had in some way thrust him, Kustaa, from his strange throne, vaguely envisaged as yet, of fatherhood. He was almost aghast at his own state. Even to fare in this direction seemed vain ; the road seemed to be saying : you can drive along me for all I care, but that's all the help you'll get from me. You'll have to turn back anyhow.

Kustaa's road led past Vuorenmaa's cabin, a matter he had not thought of when he set out. The road went rather steeply downhill just there, so that he drove past at a trot. But on his return with the load the horse walked all the slower. For that matter, the young master of Salmelus no longer found any particular grudge in his mind against Vuorenmaa. On the contrary, something new and refreshing seemed to attach to the man at that moment. Old Vuorenmaa was indeed a man and had always been one. He had always been on good terms with Kustaa's father too.

On the return journey the horse stopped of its own accord at Vuorenmaa's well. Kustaa drew water for it, and seeing faces at the window he deemed it the right thing to go in. He was very thirsty.

The old man stood in the middle of the floor, looking as though he was just about to depart, and cast a sharp, somewhat doubtful eye on Kustaa. It turned out that he was just going up to the farm, was he maybe very late, seeing that the master had already done so much ? No hurry at all, these holiday times. Vuorenmaa could have a seat on the load, with the master. Easier for an old man to travel lying down than upright.—Aye, that's right, one had to lie down anyway when the end came.

From the adjoining room came the sound of a cradle rocking ; the cradle was moved at intervals, after which the sound was fainter for a time. Then it stopped altogether, and Eeva came into the living-room, pale and with her clothes thrown on anyhow. Kustaa asked for something to drink. The mother asked Eeva to fetch it. But it would have to be mulled first.

The ale came; the visitor noted that it had fermented to perfection. Short sentences were exchanged, words that sought for openings and were charged with hidden meanings, until at last it was possible to speak outright. And once that point was reached, there was much to say. Even old Vuorenmaa gave his idea of matters at great length, as he saw them, and he was not to be misled, poor as he was. Finally he spoke standing up and then began firmly demanding that they should go to Salmelus; he, anyhow, had to go, the master could do as he liked. And he pulled on his gauntlets ostentatiously, crossing his thumbs loudly.

Kustaa did not leave. His horse stood at the gate all that winter afternoon. Someone who went past recognised it, and marvelled, recalling the relations between Vuorenmaa and Kustaa. Hard words were being exchanged there, he would wager. The matter· was wonderful enough, however, to make a detour to Salmelus necessary, to mention the news in the kitchen. And an hour later an old woman's jaw was wagging there: " It was the master of Salmelus all right, I know his horse, I do, and Vuorenmaa's woman was fetching in ale from the cellar. Easy for them to brew ale now, after all the money Eeva got. And the master of Salmelus is the right man to offer a head-full of it to . . . "

Hilma too heard. Without a word she went back into the inner rooms. It was growing dark. Meanwhile Kustaa felt at home in the Vuorenmaa cabin. Warmed by the ale, he talked with the women, with Eeva too, for hours; old Vuorenmaa had carried out his threat and disappeared. Eeva, the daughter who had had a child, sat quite primly alone with the master of Salmelus while her mother was out on some necessary task, sat and conversed patiently, though firmly, skilfully keeping the master's rather slowly advancing argument on the right track. No reason why there should be any quarrel between these two, the master and Eeva, two people, if one might say so, in a similar relation to Plihtari. Kustaa offered the wife payment for the ale, but the woman refused it. " We keep no tavern here and no other loose life either, even if that girl yonder did happen out for a bit of bad luck. . . . Is it true what people are saying, that master had already given the money once to Plihtari and that they spent it on themselves, so that master had to pay it twice over ? To be sure, it was only Iivari who had said so, but he was shouting it yesterday all over the village and then bragging about all kinds of things. . . . "

At this point Kustaa seemed to wake up. He stared at the tankard a moment or two, then swallowed its contents and said goodbye, but no more. With composed features he went out of the door, fumbled a little over the unfamiliar steps, gave his horse more water and then climbed on to the load. The midwinter day was over in the backwoods.

It was over also at Salmelus.

" Has this farm any meadows so far away that it takes a whole day to get there ? " Hilma asked her husband when he came into the house. It was the first time Hilma used this tone. During the day one thing and another had occurred on the farm which the master ought to have attended to, and the mistress had had to act and worry over them to the best of her ability. Money too had been needed, and Hilma had not been able to find enough.

As the woman did not cease complaining, Kustaa said in a tired voice :

" Are there any new children to pay for at Plihtari ? "

This too was probably the cruellest word ever spoken by the man to his wife.

"Who knows," answered Hilma. "This last one may well be part yours, as your time passes so quickly with that bitch."
58

Kustaa's expression grew suddenly sharp; he seemed to attack her with his glance. But in the wife's eye was a faint mockery. She was not alarmed, but stood sure of herself and arrogant behind the shelter of her unborn child. Kustaa saw the two of them as though arrayed against him. He was aghast. In his own house he was living as in the house of an enemy.

From such a situation there is never a complete escape. Sad that love should always begin at its highest, purest level, so that often its only course can be downward. Between man and wife it is like an organism of whose veins and tissues some, once broken, can never heal again. The wisest course would be to keep it outwardly rugged and bare from the very beginning. And for a man the very wisest thing would be to seek a wife beyond three forests and seven lakes.

Already during that winter one and another neighbour had his attention drawn to matters in the management of the Salmelus farm that had been done differently during the reign of former masters. Repairs that ought to have been done, a fallen board from the outer lining of the house, a sloping gate-post, were left undone for ever longer periods. In the fields work that ought to have been done in the autumn was left to the spring. Even ditches were left undug. All this became apparent during the succeeding years; no need to recount single details.

Nor was Fate very promising in regard to the continuation of the family line.

In its own way the day when Hilma lay down on her first childbed was a high point in Kustaa's life. The mistress had risen in the morning as usual and sat beside the kitchen table, weakly guiding the household work as well as she could, mostly giving way when the maid offered a contrary suggestion. " Do as you like, I haven't the strength and don't know enough." And by a gesture that had become customary she slightly raised the hem of her dress to observe once more how swollen her ankles and even her calves were.

'Suddenly her glance seemed to dissolve, she stood up, but remained leaning on the edge of the table. Loviisa saw her fingers clench. " Mistress, what's the matter with you ? Shall I fetch master ? "

When the master came, the mistress had already gone into the bedroom and stood in a strange half-leaning posture at the door. Since that Monday their relations had been what one might expect them to be. They had been kept private, however, and no dispute of any consequence had taken place in the presence of others. No one from Plihtari had been to Salmelus. Kustaa had kept mostly to the fields and yard, and even in the evenings little had been said. The nearer Hilma's time came, of which she herself had only a vague idea, the more insignificant Kustaa felt himself beside her, whatever her behaviour. Gradually, too, the memory of that moment at the Plihtari stove faded, though sometimes, when they lay silent in their common bed, there came over him that loathsome feeling that someone of such and such name had as it were violated his secretest fatherhood. Kustaa no longer awaited his heir, as one might have expected, knowing his strong male feeling at the time from which his expectations might properly date. Now he merely existed in a situation created for him, unconsciously fending off certain dreadful flashes from his mind. Lest they should crystallise into definite hopes.

Now, as he entered that room of many memories, he felt a new warmth gush through his being. It flowed towards the wife, who in her strange posture seemed to be appealing to the protective instinct of the male. He went across to his wife and without noticing it put his hand on her shoulder and

60

asked her some trifling question. She turned her face to him, and the man was astonished at her expression. Her face had the appearance of some part of her skin that it was impermissible for him to be looking on in such fashion.

"Will you go and tell Granny Tonttila that I sent for her. Tell her to try to come without the whole village noticing it at once, and there's no need to send any word to Plihtari. Go now—oh!"

This was the day, then, that had been ordained, this day was to be the day of days, a day the old farm had not experienced since the birth of its master. Outwardly the news of the beginning pangs of the mistress weighed down the atmosphere of the house, but inwardly it aroused a solemn excitement. The young maids, girl-children of their mothers, felt as though their worth had been increased that day by the state of their mistress. Supreme power over the household was wielded by Granny Tontilla, who gave directions and commands, and who, although usually a good-natured person, would now look no one in the eye, but said her say as it were off-hand. As the day wore on her expression became graver.

The master kept to outdoor work, trying to arrange that there would always be something that he could do alone, now in the woodshed, now in the storehouses, now in the barns. Even to the latter place his feet led him, although once he was there he could not remember what it was he was supposed to be fetching. He opened the door—and there before him was the place where his father had been found, stricken by death. The son stood calmly, with vague eyes. Was it for this he had walked as far as the barns? His brain projected a realistic vision of his father on the right spot on the floor, but the ghost seemed to be sleeping its own sleep before the fireplace and had nothing to say to the son. At least it did not blame him for anything.

Kustaa sat down on the threshold of the barn, half outside of the building; it was as though he felt most at home here after all. He had a clear view of the house from where he sat, even of the window behind which was Hilma, Hilma, whom he had brought here and made. Kustaa had a very vague idea of the process of birth, but he suspected that to it attached, besides pain, blood and other matters that had to be decently spirited away. In it all was something that aroused a man's loathing ... and to it all joined again ... again all that of a little while ago, foremost Iivari. The picture of Iivari seemed to float somewhere nearer to the bedroom, its expression saying that if it came to that, he didn't mind being mixed up in this either, but he wasn't going to bow down to Kustaa's topboots. ... And beside it was the mother ... and then the drive to fetch hay ... and over there was now being born that which had become mixed up ... ah ... The dreadful thing, kin to a hope, was again trying to rise right to the level of conscious thought. Kustaa wailed in spirit, cast himself wholly into the barn and without thinking of what he was doing took his stand in the middle of the space where his father's body had lain. He stood there as though listening to something. Slowly his mind resolved into a state resembling that of a little boy, and so he started off towards the house again.

A search had already been made for him. Everywhere in the house an unfamiliar petrified stillness. The maid Loviisa came out of the bedroom with deliberate slowness and an attempt at silence. "Would the master go in," she said queerly. The master went.

Granny Tonttila's face was in a curious sensitive twist. She seemed to be crying without tears. These few days Kustaa had felt himself a stranger in his own rooms; at that moment the feeling was at its strongest. Everything in the room was different from what it had been. The bed had been moved to form a passage between it and the wall, and it was there that Granny Tonttila stood. Hilma lay in the bed, pale, with eyes listlessly shut, nor did she open them as Kustaa drew near. The finest acts of affection and the meetest words of love of which that weak and humble woman had been capable, now came into the man's mind in one general impression that included them all. At such a moment the measure of affection left in a man for his wife is shown to him, shown every bit as exactly as if he were to go to a cupboard and count the money in his box.

" No human aid could help thee, and never will unless God helps too," said Granny Tonttila faintly.

And as she spoke the old woman turned her gaze to a bundle placed across the foot of the bed. Kustaa too looked, emptiness in his eyes, for he sought nothing. In the opening of the bundle the purple, lifeless head of an infant was visible.

Kustaa could not indeed think of it as a child, still less his child, nor that it was lifeless. When he finally understood, a curious mood descended on him. No despair, not an inkling of sorrow. Even Granny Tonttila's attention was awakened, so that her own mind withdrew for a time from its agitation. She noted for the first time that Kustaa resembled his father, who never showed any agitation in any circumstances. Granny Tonttila had helped to bring Kustaa into the world and since then had regarded him as her boy. Now, before her eyes, this Salmelus boy took on the apparition of staid middle-age, as in certain weather one can follow the growth and development of a cloud against a wall of sky.

But, even in the innermost depths of Kustaa's mind, neither despair nor sorrow could have been found at that moment. His face showed that which moved invisible within him, but its nature was unguessable. He felt a quite special sense of liberation that had begun out there on the barn floor and now reached its height. Actually his expression as he looked upon his dead child resembled the expression one can imagine dwells on the face of a victorious duellist at the moment when his opponent's seconds tend a collapsing body.

Kustaa turned once more towards Hilma, who had revived so much that she was conscious of her husband's presence. A very faint red had risen to her cheeks ; Kustaa took note of it as a sleepless person waiting for morning notes the first reddish rays in the air of his room. And now Granny Tonttila witnessed something she had never seen before among country people in her professional capacity. The husband bent down towards his wife and pressed his cheek against the woman's brow. It was Kustaa's own individual caress that he had earlier often bestowed on Hilma. He did it now in the presence of a third person, that moderately good old woman. He felt his cheek warm Hilma's icy forehead.

Something returned—not to what it had been, yet to some measure of permanence, and thereafter remained in the main unaltered. It was repeated years later in outwardly similar circumstances when Hilma, once more recumbent in weakness, was giving up her own spirit to death. The marriage of Kustaa and Hilma was now what it was.

To many other things the day and the moment brought a certain stability. Husband and wife were thereafter more alone together than before ; the rest of the world withdrew to its natural distance. During the next few years some flickering touch of feeling at odd moments could recall the first period of Hilma's wifehood, the time when she, though unmarried, was already Kustaa's wife, so distinctly that even Hilma observed it and told her observation to Kustaa.

The Plihtari family of course still existed, Iivari, the old man and the others, and sometimes showed a tendency to make family calls at Salmelus. But since that first still-born child, Hilma's attitude towards them was in some way more passive than before. If she happened to hear of their doings, she no longer drew them into as close connection as before with her own family life. Iivari spent, as a matter of fact, a good deal of time in lumber camps outside of the parish during those years, and did not consequently come into direct contact with Kustaa. And since that moment of mutual recognition at Hilma's childbed, Kustaa perceived a change in his own mental attitude towards his wife's scapegrace brother. Now and then he dreamed indeed a dream that set his spirit on edge even after he had awakened : seeing that dead child of his in a dream he invariably identified it in some way with Iivari, in the fainting state in which Iivari emerged from his hands on that occasion in the Plihtari cabin.

· 4 ·

So far as this story is concerned, the next few years could be passed over briefly and the reader brought straight to Silja, the youngest child of the marriage and the only one to live for any length of time. The married life of Kustaa and Hilma had now become settled, but it no longer brought them the cheerful strength needed to run the farm. Hilma had not had much of it to begin with, child as she was of a feckless backwoods cabin, with no heritage of such strength in her blood. It was as though the status of Salmelus had dropped a rung lower during the first conflicts of their married life, and as the years went by it began to resemble one of those medium-sized farms with a large family, the master of which only just manages to scrape through with his children and taxes. Even from this level, however, the couple managed to descend another rung, outwardly to about the one from which Hilma had come.

Something had come back beside that unhappy childbed, but—much was gone for ever. However well everything had turned out and even if that unhappy visit to Plihtari had never been made, much would in any case have altered. Hilma was no longer the fair young girl who had set Kustaa's mind on fire and provided him with the highest flowering festival weeks of his youth. What then now, after all those calamities! There were all kinds of after-rites that left behind them an impression which this simple woman was unable to efface from her husband's mind quickly enough by her own efforts. The man went his way, wondering at the events thrown in his way by life, and struggled. . . . Struggled without thinking of help from his wife in this battle.

66

About two years later, without any special fuss, a boy was born to them, who was christened Taavetti, which had been the first Christian name of Kustaa's father. Two years later came a girl whom they named Laura, that too an old Salmelus name.

Two sentences suffice to relate these events, but the years in question contained much more. Never in all his life-struggle was Kustaa Salmelus at a lower ebb than during the time between the births of these two children and the years that followed. His characteristic smile often vanished altogether during those years, without any compensating flashes of manly anger as had been the case when he was younger, during his years of level strength when surrender was not even to be contemplated. Now there was much that it was vain to quarrel with, that slowly bore him down without arousing him to open opposition. In some curious fashion everything in the household grew slacker and thinner, and a day came when the master of Salmelus signed a note of hand in the room of the master of Roimala, as during his childhood many a homespun-clad topbooted farmer in difficulties had done in Kustaa's father's room. He well remembered those old cabin-dwellers and backwoods farmers, red with embarrassment and nervously restless, on whom his father enjoined the importance of paying their interest regularly. It had been one continued recollection of his father and his boyhood, the gradual calling-in of these loans. Now the master of Roimala, a prosperous stout man, one of the leaders of the parish, stroked his side-whiskers and warned Kustaa that he wanted his interest on the appointed day. He then made a rumbling noise in his throat and nose and began to speak of the approaching election of Electors for the Farmers' Estate of the Diet, strongly recommending a certain Elector—who was later elected and helped to send the master of Roimala to the Diet. For that matter, without the support of the Salmelus vote.

The master of Roimala was elected to the Diet, and once there he sponsored a proposal for draining a lake in the parish, or for a government subsidy towards the cost of the work. His bill passed. Now the Roimala estate and another farm recently bought by Roimala gave largely on the lake, so that it was only natural that their owner should go to some trouble to secure the support of the gentlemen of the Diet for his plan. But the matter also concerned the interests of other farms ; certain lands belonging to Salmelus faced the lake too. And the owners of these farms were now called upon to contribute a certain sum towards the amount needed over and above the subsidy. Roimala was the guiding spirit of the plan and everyone grasped that it would be carried out as he wanted it to be and also that someone would benefit by it—at any rate Roimala himself.

Kustaa's domestic life was just then at its lowest. The children were ailing, often really ill, and had to be rocked in the cradle most of the night. The guest-room at Salmelus, where a cool unbreathed air had once greeted the visitor and which by the merest chance had become the bedroom of the twain, although a more homely room, the old master's, was available beside it—the guest-room was now filled day and night with the smell of babies and drying cloths. It was no pleasure to a man to go there in the evening, especially when his wife was constantly bewailing some pain or cough.

Kustaa never bought drink for the house, except for some celebration, and these were rare at Salmelus. During those years, however, it happened fairly often that Kustaa would drink to intoxication while out in the village; somehow he always happened to be there where liquor was flowing, the worse matters were at home the oftener. Once he drank himself nearly into a helpless condition. This was after the meeting at which the shareholders agreed about the cost of draining the lake and paid their shares. The meeting was held at Roimala. Salmelus and another farmer with very little land lacked cash and regretted their inability to pay, whereupon the master of Roimala offered to lend them the money. Notes of hand were written, and Roimala gave an acknowledgment that the lake-money had been received ; no money changed hands. While drinks were being handed round an old farmer who had been a good friend of Kustaa's father took Kustaa aside and said a few words of warning with regard to Roimala. " You ought rather to have sold some of your timber," the old farmer said.

" I'm not going to start selling forest ; my father was always against it," said Kustaa.

" Your father may have been that, seeing that these notes of hand were the other way round with him to what happened to you just now."

When Kustaa awoke in the morning he had no clear impression of how he had come home. But this he remembered, that in Roimala's desk there were now two notes of hand written by him, Kustaa. Hilma was still in bed, not asleep, though she did not move even when she saw Kustaa dressing ; she had the air of one pondering over some painful matter. One of the children lay beside her, the other could be heard crying in the kitchen. The maid was trying to soothe it, the hour was therefore late enough for the maids to be up, though both master and mistress were still in bed. Kustaa was so out of countenance that he was unable to make up his mind what to do. He hardly answered old Vuorenmaa's civil question.

Such was the life of the twain in their prime. It began to look as though after the two children now alive, no third child was to come to Salmelus. But the time came for that too—and it was Silja, the only one to reach maturity, who was then born. The origin of the girl's existence is related to an event that was one of the happiest in the now fairly joyless life of Hilma and Kustaa. The mood of the two on that occasion resembled in surprising degree the first period of Hilma's wifehood, the time when a love out of the ordinary so bravely expelled the old traditional spirit from the guest-room at Salmelus. Hilma and Kustaa were invited to a wedding on the same farm where Kustaa had been when Hilma was driven away from Salmelus. The farm was three parishes away and they had to spend the night there; ultimately they spent two nights. Both were marvellously rejuvenated during the days and nights they were away from Salmelus. For that matter they had hardly slept a night together elsewhere since the nights in the bakery room at Plihtari during their first summer. The wedding was a grand one and the festivities lasted three days; between meals there was dancing and ale. Even Kustaa Salmelus danced. On the night of the wedding he could not persuade Hilma to more than a square dance, but the next day Hilma too dared polkas and mazurkas. It was an unusually merry wedding. In the big house were many rooms, one apiece for couples from a distance, whilst the young people slept on large common beds on the floors of the company rooms. Skylarking and giggling could be heard from these rooms up to dawn, but it did not disturb the married couples in the bedrooms, some of whom, inspired by the spirit of jollity, slept in the first close embrace for long.

Even after their return to Salmelus the festive mood of Hilma and Kustaa continued. Hilma in particular had shed years; she whispered the fact in her husband's ear on their first night again in their everyday bed. " It's just like old times, do you remember ? We'll see whether it ends in the same as then."

As the sun sometimes looks backward, gilding the tops of the forest with a sudden beam before setting, so for Hilma and

Kustaa the wedding formed a break in their life that was like a gleam from better days. The workaday life of the farm with its difficulties soon withered the brief after-love of the two, but there was one thing it could not stop. The union of two living human cells, growing apace and acquiring at the right periods certain shapes, began more and more to resemble a human being. No one saw it, for it was hidden in the womb of the woman, bound to her by a throbbing cord.

And birth came again to Salmelus, for the fourth and last time. At a certain unpredicted moment the embryo, that had eagerly moved its limbs for some months, began a new series of movements. It turned its head in the direction it was to take, then its shoulders and finally its trunk and limbs—until it had wholly emerged into the light of day ; the umbilical cord snapped and a girl-child began its life, of which at that moment no one could say with certainty more than that which applies to all life : that it would end in death.

Just then, to be sure, no one thought of death. The birth had been an easy one, and although Hilma was very tired, she was calm and happy when Kustaa came to her bedside. Curiously enough, the family atmosphere resembled that attending a first birth, one that has turned out happily. It was an evening in spring, and the sunbeams awakened an illusion of happiness in the old room as Granny Tonttila fetched the coffee specially brewed by her for this occasion. It was strong and clear, intended to refresh the exhausted mother. The child had already been bathed and slept peacefully in its fresh-smelling basket when Kustaa bent down to examine it. The father's smile was at its brightest. Even the pale older children seemed nearer to him that day.

After a few hours the child awoke. It was put to its mother's breast and at once began suckling fiercely. It lived. The father gazed at it and forgot his cares.

Cares he had in abundance. He had been compelled more than once to ask Roimala for a small additional loan to pay his interest. Roimala did not refuse. Sharp-sighted neighbours began to guess whither relations between Roimala and Salmelus were tending.

" The best thing Kustaa could do indeed would be to sell his farm and buy a smaller one, the distaff side of his family being weak-like—he'll lose it to Roimala anyhow in the end, so it's no use Kustaa's beggaring himself for Roimala's benefit." So spoke certain staid farmers among themselves, and sometimes, over a glass, even to Kustaa.

Poor, indeed, was the living on the farm, as in any big household whose mistress is growing weaker. It sapped Kustaa's energy too; if it had not been for that darling youngest child, it is very likely that Kustaa would have done the trick and sold his farm. But the girl, christened Cecilia but called Silja, grew and prospered and knew nothing of adversity. She had large gentle eyes with beautiful eyelashes. The colour of her eyes, almost black at first, turned gradually into a pure brown. In her features was a hint of her father, and certain old people declared that she resembled in quite special degree Kustaa's mother in her youth. Strange how the two older children were outshone by the youngest, whom everyone addressed and treated as Kustaa had been treated when he, an only child, was the apple of the eye of the dignified master and mistress of Salmelus.

As it turned out, the life of the two other children, Taave and Laura, never came to denote much, to anyone. They moved about together hand in hand, silent and slightly timid, as though each saw his or her main support in the other. Until the time came for them to depart, when, after lying ill side by side in the same bed, they died, one a couple of days before the other. Their sickness was an extremely infectious

72

epidemic that laid low a very large number of the parish children within a few weeks and is sometimes mentioned even now, after the elapse of decades.

Silja did not fall ill, though she had been allowed to move freely in the sick-room. More than one of the people on the farm and its visitors remarked that one would see what happened to that youngest. Kustaa was reticent, but his soft smile began to reappear. As adversity grew until it finally reached its present exceptional stage, the man, now past middle age, began to divine, somewhere at the bottom of his consciousness, that in all this he had been carrying out some preordained task. It seemed almost as though past generations nodded to him as he moved in such thoughts and by their gesture wished to say that to be sure the farm, the inheritance, would have been good to keep and increase, but as matters have turned out you must remember that there is something in a man, the retention and increase of which is more. And as though to seal the matter, that invisible nod seemed to include in its circle the girl-child who by that time had begun to seek the hand of her father in her toddles.

Difficulties on the farm increased. Most of the hay made in the previous summer had rotted. First it had been gathered in too fresh, and self-combustion had begun, so that it had to be carted out anew to dry. Then, just as the hay was ready to be stored in the sheds, a sudden rain made it wetter than it had been while growing. The master was not at home, and so— A master ought not to have too many errands outside of his farm. The part of the hay that was finally dried was not worth much. Good oat-straw, it was said, would be better, which is true. But that year more straw had to be used than usual, and the result was that during the most critical period of the spring, just when the children too lay ill, the state of the Salmelus cattle became serious ; the cows began to develop softness of bone and the horses grew thin. Kustaa had done his best to economise with grain, but now the dairymaid threatened to go unless she was given something to feed the cattle. Cows, however, cannot be fed on grain alone, but must have some green fodder.

Thus there was distress on both sides of the yard-fence. Kustaa moved about like a sleepwalker. Hilma took to her bed ever oftener, and her face and the way her clothes hung on her showed that she was not doing it without good cause. An expert stranger could have concluded with entire confidence that not many more cuckoos would fall to the lot of the mistress of Salmelus to hear. Even Kustaa sensed that for Hilma and him there would be no more weddings like that one a while ago, three parishes away.

Kustaa went one day to see the old farmer who had been a great friend of his father's and who had once warned him. " Can you lend me some money, seeing that you warned me about getting mixed up with Roimala," Kustaa said openly.

But the farmer explained that much as he regretted it, it was impossible, so willingly as he would have helped Vihtori Salmelus's son. " You see, I'm an old man and according to the laws of dust my time is short. It's no good me moving even an inch from the road I have trodden in the days of my strength, the road your father too trod, or I'd soon be walking about on the same errand that brings you here. I am not rich, but I have my living, and in the hardest times God has helped me, as I have helped myself. You are caught so tight in Roimala's net that even for that reason it wouldn't be right for me to meddle in your affairs. You, dear boy, have done certain deeds on the path of your life that it isn't for me to judge, and for that matter I haven't heard anything of you that would be unbecoming in a man—on the contrary I have caught a glimpse of your father in your doings. But "—

and here the aged farmer nodded his white head—"your father was a sturdy farmer who knew his job, and at your best you're only middling good. There's something gentleman-like in you that comes from your mother's side, well I know it, and I am quite sure that even if it goes ill with you in this world, your eternal welfare is in order."

He spoke as he had often had to speak, during his many years as an alderman, to some young inexperienced judge on his first circuit. As an old man he had to end up by dwelling on the future life. Not that he was grown sentimental, for he knew what practical advice to give his friend's son. He now repeated his advice about selling timber, but Kustaa explained that Roimala had a mortgage on the farm and that the agree-ment was that even if Kustaa were to sell a single tree the money would have to be given to Roimala in payment of his debt. The debt was now so large that a good deal of forest would have to be cut before there would be enough left over to help Kustaa out of his present fix, and that was something he was not prepared to do, and even that would not bring in anything at once.

"Aye, aye, aye, aye," said the old alderman. "I see, I see everything. He's got his eye on the sawmill, it's in a bad fix just now, soon ripe for harvesting, that blade too, aye, aye . . ."

Kustaa hardly heard the old man's conclusions, so rapt he was in the critical position of his own farm. Not until the old fellow began talking again of Kustaa's affairs did he wake up and take an interest in the conversation. "So much I do know about your affairs that you are not quite a pauper even now. The question is, do you know how to sell your farm to the best advantage? Aye, there's no need for you to start, for as you are now placed and even with an eye to the future I can't see any other way out. Roimala means to get it, everything shows that, but—let us see whether that czar is going to get it for nothing. I know your farm well, both the lands and the forest, and I tell you—I've been thinking over the matter before this—if Roimala does not pay you—so and so much, well—I will."

The last words came with conscious weight and were followed by a dignified snort, as though the old man had been standing up to deliver a speech and then sat down.

This valuation of his farm was the only benefit Kustaa gained by his visit. He was in sore need of money—the cattle were crying for fodder and the farm-hands for wages. All that was left to him was—to drive to Roimala.

Even Roimala, however, was unwilling to lend this time, but began, he too, enumerating the mistakes Kustaa had committed during his life, doing it in a much coarser manner than the old alderman. Roimala emitted mighty grunts and had a coarse name for everything connected with Kustaa's youthful visits to Plihtari. " The only heir to a farm as big as yours gets out of such matters by paying—even boys from worthless backwoods cabins manage that sometimes, so I hear—ha-ha—as you well know. . . . "

Up to this point Kustaa had blushed. Now he paled and his teeth met. This was the moment of his deepest degradation, and what was he to do ? He stood up ; Roimala too was silent and slowly hoisted his mighty carcase into its well-known backward curve. Again Kustaa felt himself entirely alone. At that moment the only thing near to him was his own male spirit. The shadow of that big-bodied man seemed already to lie over Salmelus ; what Kustaa had to do was to try to save what he could from that shadow as quickly as possible, his wife, two sick and one healthy child, servants, cattle. It was not worth while losing one's temper over the man, who was again stroking those side-whiskers of his, a man too old and helpless for anyone to lay hands on him. Kustaa laughed, he too, with one corner of his mouth, a gesture he had never made before. Then he said :

" Take the whole farm, for that is what you want."

Roimala's eyebrows rose, as they sometimes did in church when the parson, forced thereto by his text, had to say something touching the destruction of soul so easily brought about by earthly mammon. Well, well, so the man was already offering his farm.

" Yes, it may well be that you are not the right man, as you are now fixed anyhow, to manage a farm, and I'm well able to buy it and manage it too. . . . But—ahem—we can't talk of such things without toddy. Mother, will you send us some hot water and sugar," shouted the master through the crack of the door in a voice that forced Kustaa to laugh, though a deep disgust at the hypocritical warmth of the words and tone was near to turning his stomach.

The toddy tasted well to Kustaa Şalmelus at that moment. Now that he had gone so far, he might just as well go on sitting here. He was on his guard, however, and only surrendered outwardly. Roimala acted in as fatherly a fashion as he knew how ; he spoke in almost the same tone as he had used in ordering the hot water. He tried to offer different prices on different conditions, now for the farm alone, now for the farm and movable property, now for the farm and part of the movables. It was on the latter basis that the sale was finally settled. Kustaa was not quite sure what kind of a bargain he had made, but as Roimala had agreed to pay him a good deal more than the sum mentioned by the alderman as a lowest limit, he shook hands to seal the bargain. Roimala counted out a deposit, and a day was appointed on which the deed of sale would be drafted.

Kustaa felt no regret, even in the morning. Hilma, on her part, staggered about with a shawl over her head, nursing her sick children. Seeing money she revived somewhat and began getting ready for a trip to the village—there was wheat flour to be bought and the house had run out of coffee. The trip was made.

There was also, however, the future to be planned. Best move to town and start something there, was Hilma's opinion. To this, Kustaa's only answer was the news that Roimala had granted them the right to these two rooms and kitchen up to the autumn, if they wished to stay. In his own mind Kustaa had already decided that he would not stay a day longer than necessary, but would take the first opportunity of securing some smaller place farther south. Strange how he was drawn southward. He had so much money over that he knew he would be able to pick up some cabin and a patch of land.

Roimala had his own proposal ready in that matter too. On his backwoods lands there was a cabin that he was prepared to sell. Or he might perhaps lease it with a bit of land. "You would be a kind of watchman for my timber," said Roimala. Kustaa said nothing, but went out of the room at Salmelus where Roimala was sitting ; he had "dropped in to look at this third farm of mine." As he went away through the yard he said to Kustaa :

"I had a good look at those rooms and made up my mind that you won't need the back one, as the one next to the kitchen is so roomy. And anybody can see that you'll soon be less one bed-full, they're that bad, the girl and the boy. . . . Aye, and let's see . . . keep an eye on that corner of the forest next to Plihtari, those 'in-laws of yours have been using it as their own, but seeing that I made a bargain with you for the farm as it stood, what I mean is that it will be your loss like, if anything's taken away there."

Kustaa let the man talk and cough in a self-important manner. And then Roimala was off again. Kustaa went off too, into the house, where " one bed-full " was indeed sobbing out its last breaths. The boy died that same day, the girl kept them waiting for her end the whole of the next day.

In some way life was again high and solemn, as it had not been for long. There was no lack of anything ; the cattle got their fodder, the humans their food. Even a faint touch of luxury was not lacking. Hilma had retained a juvenile fondness for pancakes, and now she fried them, thin and greasy, so that they almost crumbled in the hand. Even the maids got their share ; the whole population of the farm lived in a state of joint expectancy. One period of waiting, to be sure, was over ; the little boy and girl who had always been together, now lay side by side on boards in the store-room, their pinched bodies blue with frost. Little Silja was as well as before. Enwrapping all life was again, now perhaps stronger than ever, that quite special atmosphere of happiness that had made itself felt for the first time at Salmelus when Hilma Plihtari finally settled down there, when the old aunt departed —from that day to the marriage. At other times, too, the same feeling had occasionally embraced everyone on the farm.

For Kustaa luck was favourable in that quite of itself, a new and in his opinion suitable home appeared for them. The sheriff told Kustaa about it when the deed of sale was signed, having heard of it by chance. It was two parishes away to the south and was in the market for a curious reason that the sheriff related over the coffee at Roimala. " You go and look it over," he advised Kustaa. And Kustaa, who had learned to trust the sheriff, followed his advice on this occasion too, making his inspection and closing the bargain on the same trip.

Everything went on excellently now, matters once having begun to do so. Kustaa arranged his movables carefully, setting apart those articles which had to be left to Roimala and those he intended selling by auction. He then arranged for the sale to be held a fortnight later, on a Monday, following the burial of the children on the Sunday.

The time of waiting for the funeral and auction was a time of peaceful and deep rest for the whole family and the farm-hands. On the pretext of fetching a piece of timber Kustaa drove through his backwoods, as on a farewell visit, for it was there after all that his dearest memories centred. Some related to little adventures of his boyhood on occasions when he had been allowed to accompany the labourers to those distant sites and had been able to eat from a dinner-pail like a full-grown man. On these farewell rounds he passed Vuorenmaa, that too the scene of an adventure on a misty December day at the time that first still-born child came. The memory of that birth brought a curious pang, and this time he refrained from going into the house, though he watered his horse at the well.

Hilma made a few visits, the nearest on swaying feet, those farther off in the trap—as they still had the horses and hardly any work for them. She paid one visit to her parents at Plihtari, and the visit troubled Kustaa not at all.

Then came a day when the joiner brought the children's coffins ordered from him and the bodies were laid in them and dressed out. The baptismal robe had been preserved and was now used for the dead girl ; thin as she had become, it was not too small for her. " Let her take the baptismal dress with her, no more children of mine will be baptised, and other people's children are nothing to me," said Hilma with a dim smile when one of the servants made a timid reference to that side of the matter.

During those days little Silja was a kind of outside being whom no one knew how to treat in a natural manner. Kustaa carried her in his arms, oftener than ever before. Even outside the house the master was seen carrying the thickly-clad girl. He was heard to talk to the child in a lively manner, which the farmhands found solemn in some strange way, but at the same time touching too. The master had never been heard to chatter like that before, either to children or others.

The appointed days drew nearer. After the lapse of centuries a turn was occurring in the history of Salmelus.

When he sold his farm, Kustaa dispensed with his regular hired hands, who were taken over by Roimala and had latterly been working on his farm. It happened therefore that when the dead children were taken to the grave it was Vuorenmaa, with the usual expression of slightly ill-tempered gravity on his face, who drove the hearse. Kustaa drove his own sleigh with the family in it. Hilma was very tired and it was not particularly wise to expose Silja to the sharp late-winter wind, but someone had to escort the poor dead.

This was in fact the last time that the couple drove from the Salmelus estate as master and mistress; already the next day the auction was to take place. There they now drove, and that was about all they had accomplished by their marriage. They drove almost as once before, many years ago, to Plihtari, on that Christmas holiday, a little before the birth of the first child.

Now both were much older; in Hilma hardly a trace was left of the features with which the young master of Salmelus had fallen in love. She now looked like any cottar's wife, some of her teeth gone, the others dimmed, like her hair. During her mistress-ship she had not even put on the usual flesh of her status, but the delicious softness too of her girl-hood had vanished and given way to angularity.

In Kustaa's face and figure, older as he had become, the inherited marks of race were indelibly visible. On this journey they seemed clearer than ever. A woman who, in her youth, had looked with favour on Kustaa Salmelus, and perhaps hoped that he would return her glance, was among those in the churchyard, standing apart from the rest. She was able to see Kustaa in profile, and her heart was moved and warmed when Kustaa stood bareheaded during the service.

She saw Kustaa again as he walked up the aisle in the church, erect and with his head in a familiar pose, and sat down in the Salmelus pew. A slight mist rose before the eyes of many acquaintances as they looked at the couple : the calm man, on whose face was always the finest shadow of a smile, and the weary woman, of whom no one could really say a bad word, only that that body too has probably done what she could, but from whom could a Plihtari girl have learned the skill demanded of a mistress of Salmelus.

Nor did the little girl escape notice, as she toddled, the only survivor, between her parents, tending to ask a little too loudly what everything was, for it was her first time in church. A brown-eyed girl with a well-shaped head, in which one could note resemblances to her father and mother. A pity the child was not able to grow a little older in the family house.

The child was suddenly heard to ask in a high-pitched voice where Laura and Taave had been left : why hadn't they come into church, were they still in their coffins ? The whole congregation was as one family at the moment when the child's words vibrated in the air. Then the organ began humming and gave little Silja an impression she remembered all her life. Surely in her fading consciousness the same music accompanied the twittering of the swallows on that early morning when she died in the bath-house at Kierikka. Now, however, she was alive and could not quite understand why Laura and Taave were not alive too. On the way home she still demanded, as they passed the churchyard, that now, at any rate, they ought to be fetched from there. Her mother said that they had gone to Heaven and would never come back any more. Silja pondered over this in silence all the way home. She could not understand what good all that grandeur was if they were never to have the chance of telling anyone about it.

No funeral feast was held, except for the people on the farm. Roimala chanced to join in unbidden—he might have come, of course, on the strength of his ownership. As it happened, he had an errand. He said that he had expected to find a good many people there. He was collecting signatures to a paper that was to be presented to the Czar and was a petition asking that the rights of Finland should not be violated. Kustaa understood what it was about and had indeed heard of it before somewhere, though the matter now seemed rather irrelevant. He routed out, however, an ink-bottle and pen and began writing his name. Hilma too came into the room and said : " Haven't you had enough of Roimala's papers ? " The visitor told her, slightly ruffled : " This is no paper of Roimala's—and for that matter Kustaa had not had any worse experiences of Roimala's papers than of Plihtari's papers." Whereafter he trumpeted his nose on a familiar note.

Sunday afternoon passed quite ordinarily ; a sunbeam travelled along the floor of the living-room as it had done during the centuries the pine building had stood. The smoky-red rocking-chair for two, with its back-rest of two skilfully carved lyres, stood exactly where it had stood before, over the hollows in the floor worn by the rockers and the feet of sitters. The clock ticked on the back wall, the almanack hung from its nail beside the window, a special faint smell was in the air. Yet everything was different in that the prevailing peace had in it the expectation of a coming unrest, like waiting for the execution of a death sentence. Even Roimala asked Kustaa as a round-off to his farewell:

"Well, you'll be beginning to-morrow at nine, I suppose?"

"Nine's the hour announced," answered Kustaa, his eyes smiling. Hilma went staggering away from them with a grumbling remark that remained inaudible.

The auction was unusually well attended and the auctioneers had thus an adequate sounding-board for their quips. Here and there an old fellow had had a glass too much and made rude remarks when some homely object, a garment or article, was put up for sale. Iivari Plihtari, for whom the day was of course a kind of festival, behaved in similar fashion. Joking remarks were addressed to him now and again, and he was quick to retort. The crowd knew perfectly well that Iivari would not take offence.

This was the last time the brothers-in-law were face to face. On this occasion the meeting led to a brief encounter. Kustaa went away for a moment and in his absence the auctioneer took his joiner's bench and tools and offered them for sale. Kustaa had meant to keep them; now his only resource was to bid for them—against Iivari Plihtari, who was bidding for them in earnest.

"What do you want a joiner's bench for—I'm told you're looking for a job as farmhand," said Iivari, and was rewarded with a delighted crowing by his like.

Iivari raised his bid until it was nearly more than a fair price. Kustaa at once raised his, being determined not to part with his bench.

"Are you sure you can answer for your bid?" shouted Iivari.

This was going very far, but among the crowd were still enough spectators with mouths cruelly agape, ready to bite at any quip thrown to them by Iivari Plihtari. They continued to crow.

Kustaa blushed slightly; his faint smile thinned almost to extinction. The joint feeling among the honourable element in the crowd had now gained in weight and was on Kustaa's side, on the side of the man who had escorted two children to the grave the day before and now had to leave the family estate. The roar awakened by Iivari's words quickly died down when Kustaa answered:

" Well, I have a small claim on you, I believe."

Everyone recalled that event many years ago, which had after all impressed itself deeply on the local mind, to the shame of Iivari; a minor shame perhaps, but still a shame and not a merit. The joint mood of even such a crowd as was then assembled fluctuates easily; the moment it was spoken, Kustaa's remark further revealed the manliness shown by him in sticking to Plihtari's daughter, and not trying to buy her off, though it might have been better for him if he had done so. The whole of this sympathy for Kustaa now compressed itself into the frame of his half-compulsory exile from his lands when he hinted at the considerable sums he had paid on behalf of that rascal Iivari, paid twice over. Up to that moment no one had ever heard Kustaa refer to them by a single word.

" Well, keep your muck then," said Iivari and turned away with a boastful gesture, trying to find some support for his words in the glances of those nearest to him. But now the crowd's sympathies were all on Kustaa's side, and Iivari stood alone. One aged throat emitted a bellowing laugh, but it was aimed at Iivari.

It was almost as though the bench had become dearer to its owner after that encounter. During the first few months in his new home he used it very often. Partly because the household, in its new shape, needed all kinds of articles that had not been worth carting from the old home, partly because he had begun to turn out farm implements for his new neighbours, who soon learned to know him as a skilful and reliable man. At Salmelus there had been a large stock of seasoned timber which lay unutilised under the rafters during those years of trouble, part of it placed there by Kustaa's father. Kustaa did not sell this wood, but took it with him.

Hilma wept on their departure. A feeble thin crying, the submission of a weak person to the unavoidable. She wept over the cows and other animals given over to strangers, over the cat left on the farm, the cat that the children had let in and out of the door in winter—yes, and she now wept over her dead children, left behind in another parish; almost she wept over the sole remaining child in her lap, big-eyed, long-lashed Silja. Weakly crying she left the house to which she had come on a certain autumn day with her young heart full of a bliss that somehow seemed unnatural. At a time when the strong spirit of the old master and his unspoken thoughts had still filled the air of the farm. Into that air, in a manner unnatural, had come the young, insignificant cottar's girl with her own knowledge and preferences.

She now departed, thin, angular, with tearful eyes. At a corner of the road her mother, Tilta Plihtari, and her younger sister, had come to witness her departure. Both of them had of course grown older as the years passed, but age had not altered the general tone of their appearance much. Now, as before, a mocking word seemed to hang, ready to fall, at one corner of Tilta's mouth; the head of the youngest had the same sage tilt as before; almost one expected to see it trembling a little already. Neither had the courage to come boldly forward. Old Vuorenmaa was still the driver; he drove the loads, whilst Kustaa himself drove the sleigh with the family. On Vuorenmaa's face was an expression of stern gravity. Instinctively he too felt that at this moment he represented the last vestige of the old Salmelus times.

The farm was left behind, and soon the backwoods road leading to Plihtari was passed. Up to this, Hilma's weeping had been silent, now she broke into a fit of sobbing, for in her heart she knew that she would never walk that road again, that the journey begun along a strange road would carry her to ever more unfamiliar scenes and ultimately to the wholly unknown.

Kustaa neither did nor said anything to her, merely adjusting little Silja's cap, for the spring wind still blew. Not that there was really anything to adjust in the cap. The day was in no wise hard to bear for Kustaa. He had fought out his inward battles long ago and knew whither he was bound; he felt himself freer to-day than for a long time past.

Hilma went on sobbing until the forest became less familiar. Vuorenmaa, coming on behind, swore unnecessarily at a horse. The fellow was getting so old that his jaw felt inclined to shake and his eyes to fill with tears at the cross-roads when he saw Hilma begin to sob and remembered all that linked these two fates with the road, remembered too his own connection with the two here and those at the end of the road.

The forest through which the road now ran was part of the Salmelus lands. Kustaa would scarcely have thought of it if he had not seen men at one spot felling a tree. They were Roimala's men, some of them formerly in Kustaa's service. They had cut down a mighty drooping spruce and were lopping off the boughs. Seeing the procession on the road they stopped working and stared stupidly at the sleighs, remaining standing there long afterwards, as though the episode had ended too soon.

At that part of the journey Kustaa's peace of mind was slightly shaken; it was as though he was again staring absently through the barn doorway at Salmelus, at the place where his father died. He thought for a moment or two of his own death and of how and where it would happen. Hilma had calmed down again, and old Vuorenmaa had given the horse its own head. The day of removal was passing, the destination drawing near.

. 5 .

MATTERS turned out so well that little Silja received no conscious impression of her arrival at the new home. She slept soundly all through the last part of the journey, and did not awaken even when she was carried into the house. The departing inhabitants had heated the stoves to a festive glow in honour of their departure, and the heat was now welcome owing to the length of time the doors had to be open while the furniture was being carried in. Silja slept on the living-room table in her travelling clothes until the bed had been warmed after its exposure to the air.

The next morning the first thing to greet her awakening eyes was the sun, which now let its golden ray play on the floor of this new and wonderful room. Father and mother were there, looking just the same as before. But father was now busy planing beside the side window and mother was peeling potatoes near the range, which had been fitted into the side of the heating stove. No Taave or Laura, they had been left there in the graveyard, or they might have been left in the store-room, which wasn't anywhere here, that she could see. Beautiful curly shavings were starting up under father's plane—was this the living-room then ? Never before had Silja awakened to see her father working at his bench. It was one of the marvels of this day. Mother's knife moved skilfully round the potatoes—could this be the kitchen, and had mother begun to do Loviisa's work ? Most wonderful of all, however, was the sun and this light that came from three windows ; in the old home the two windows had been in the same wall, and there were only doors in the other walls. And still more wonderful that father and mother were busy in the same room when she awoke.

So happy all this was. To be sure, mother was coughing as she peeled the potatoes and looked anxious as usual. But Silja knew quite well that when she should climb down from the bed and go to her mother, her mother would stop working and hug and pat her, and father would stop planing and turn his smile to where she was with mother. Later, father would be sure to lift her on to his arm and carry her outside, where the marvellous light on the floor came from.

This situation was Silja's first fully clear impression, one that remained in her memory throughout her life. She remembered, too, that her father did carry her on his arm all over the grounds of the new house and talk to her, the whole time, sometimes putting her down to make something funny of snow, which he would throw at her, trying to make her laugh. All this Silja clearly remembered ; what she did not remember was how she came from the bed to her father's arm outside.

The child did not remember it for the reason that when she climbed out of bed, her mother had not petted and hugged her as sometimes before, but with the same worried look that Silja had observed from the bed still on her face, had begun to dress her.

An anxious-looking woman peeling potatoes—that was the last impression gained by the surviving child of its mother. Hilma lived, indeed, for some time afterwards, but her life was such that the subconscious part of the child's mind retained no impression of it. When the ice on the lake near by began to be in such condition that careful farmers no longer drove across it and the foolhardy were giving their horses a ducking, Hilma Salmelus, as she was called in the new locality, took to her bed, from which she was never more to rise. This fatal illness of Hilma's was another significant

90

period in Kustaa's life, his last trial, in its own way the deepest depression in the curve of his life, as that evening in Roimala's room had been, when the sale of his farm was finally settled. Only in the present case there was nothing humbling, rather was it in the nature of a decisive turn in Kustaa Salmelus's path of purification.

The man had once laid his reins on the porch of his old home over the shoulder of a young and fair servant-girl and by that act was drawn very close to her. Now the local woman called in as help saw the newcomer Salmelus press his cheek against the forehead of his dying wife. The wife was still fully conscious, and smiled as well as she could at her husband. The strange woman who witnessed this scene could not divine everything that went to that smile.

Silja was toddling outside at that moment. She too was living through a new experience. From the lake came a strange uninterrupted tinkling, rattling, roaring, and occasionally a real frightening sound. The noise seemed to come from quite near. It affected the girl so that she was hardly aware of anything else. Even the removal of her mother's body was unnoticed by her. Not until late evening was she told that mother had gone the way of Taave and Laura at their former home. Just then, however, it was more important for Silja to be told quite clearly what the tinkling and rattling was that had sounded the whole afternoon from the lake. Father explained it to her as he put her to sleep—this time in his own bed. "You see, when summer has gone, it gets cold, ever colder and colder, until all the flowers and butterflies die and the lakes freeze up. That lake of ours froze up too last autumn. Then the sun begins to climb higher again and everything becomes brighter and warmer. That makes the ice melt in the lake, and as it melts and disappears it makes that tinkling and rattling."

The father saw that his only child, his only one in every sense now, was asleep. The child had fallen asleep while he was talking of flowers and butterflies. It was as though she had wished to follow those dear friends of hers along their easy road of death.

. 6 .

THE spring wore on. Kustaa Salmelus lived in his cabin, lived and grew older; but he was now free from much that had weighed down his spirit. This weight had been borne by him so long that he could not have said when it originated, only that behind it all glowed the memory of something happy and strong: the golden solitary days of his youth. Solitary they had been indeed, they too, and in that respect his days had never changed; it was only that the gold had worn off the days of his later adult life until now, when he was nearing old age.

The spring advanced, and life rose and grew in Nature. Silja, too, seemed to be growing at a quicker rate than before under the eyes of her father. She had to be found new clothes, her worn winter clothes were beginning to resemble the mottled earth reappearing from under the snow. The child had to be found something new and more colourful—as flowers arose in the grey aftermath of winter in the home brushwood. A visit had to be paid to the village sempstress, and the best time for that was Sunday morning. There was laughter and mild joking at their destination, and the faces of all wore a kind expression while the little girl was being measured. In some small degree it was due to the special circumstance that so staid a father gave the orders. " Yes, think, the poor child lost her mother as soon as they moved here," the talk ran on the sempstress's porch when Kustaa and Silja had gone, " but the father is greatly attached to the girl." And then everyone recounted the little they knew of the newcomers. Some one said that they had lost their farm three parishes away, but another speaker argued that he didn't look like a ruined man, wasn't he living on his means—moreover he had heard that the man had only grown tired of farming after his wife became ill and his children died and all sorts of little worries came, and had wanted to take some little place like this.

Meanwhile Silja and Kustaa stepped out along the road, making their observations of nature and telling them to each other.

" What makes the lake there so ali /e, like lots of little bright animals on it ? " asked the girl.

" Those are little waves running on it, like this "—Kustaa described the motion of a wave with his hand, " and for one moment the wall of every wave is like a looking-glass that catches the sun. Wait till we get in and I'll show you."

They went into the cabin, Silja humming and tripping ahead and the father behind like an instructive big brother. The mirror was taken from its peg beside the window and father had to show how the lake's surface glittered. He was forced to smile, however, and laugh at his pupil, and soon to take care that the mirror did not fall or was not dashed against the wall. The play of the sunbeam was so hugely exciting to Silja that it was vain to speak to her of waves in connection with it. Unwearyingly the child flashed the beam along the walls, the floor, the stove, and her mirth overflowed when the idea struck her of flashing it on her father's coat, then on his chin and lastly in his eyes, so that he had to shut them and turn his head away. . . . And then on to the leg of the bed and the joiner's bench, and again on to father.

Kustaa could not help wondering at the child's joy. Without thinking that it was so, he sensed something touching in the matter, in that the child had never before played with a sunbeam. There had never happened to be a looking-glass and the sun together in the same place. By now her play was going so far that he had to forbid it. The girl had begun to wave the mirror behind her back, and it would soon be broken.

So they lived without serious troubles. The father spent most of his time at his joiner's bench, except when he was cooking their meals. Kustaa would have no stranger in the house if he could by any means be without. When he was in need of help he would fetch Miina from the other end of the village, Miina, who lived entirely on odd jobs. In the village were an old farmer and farmwife who had known the Salmelus family a long time back ; there may even have been a blood-tie, very remote, between the families. The mistress of that farm often sent Kustaa and Silja part of her baking, especially after Kustaa had made her a neat low rocking-chair, in which it was unusually pleasant for her to rock her old body.

The first summer passed of Silja's and Kustaa's life together. The child became acquainted with many kinds of birds and still more kinds of flowers. She saw boys fishing. They wore big hats and had the legs of their trousers rolled up. They walked along the edge of the lake and looked with a stranger's eye at the neatly dressed little girl standing on the top of the bank. Each of the boys had heard talk in his own cabin of the new tenants of that house, the old man and the little girl who bothered so little about other people.

Harvest-time came. The friendly farmer asked Kustaa to help in the fields, and Kustaa went. He had to take Silja with him and leave her at the farmhouse. There were the children of some of the other reapers, including the two of Miina's, the woman-of-all-work. They had no father, Silja was told.

" Did he die and was he taken to the grave at church like mother and Taave and Laura ? " asked Silja of her father at dinner-time in the farmyard.

"I suppose that's what happened," said Kustaa with a smile,

but refrained from turning his smile on the other men lying in the grass. Instinctively he observed the same shades of behaviour as he had done in the days of his masterhood.

" He's not in any grave, but hopping about over yonder in Kokkinen's fields this very day," remarked the loose-mouthed tailor, who had climbed down from his table while the harvest hurry was on and taken to the sickle.

In the old days Kustaa Salmelus would have risen and without a word gone into the house, by which the men would have known that " the old man didn't seem to like that." But he was no longer anybody's " old man," only one of a group of reapers in another farmer's yard. Where could he have gone until the bell rang for him to go to the fields ? He had to stay where he was, and the child with him, waiting for the moment when the girl would be left until supper-time with those " fatherless " children. A moment of distasteful annoyance—when Silja, hearing the tailor's words, persisted that they had a father after all. Kustaa remarked, in a suitable tone : " Well, that tailor seems to know something about it," and added to Silja in a voice that made her obey him, " and you'll ask no more questions."

Silja walked silently away, but did not join Miina's children at once. Nor did the men say anything. Their impression of Kustaa Salmelus had been enriched by a little, but effective feature. Rather soon after dinner, the reapers drawing nearer to the house, the children went out into the fields and for the rest of that day Silja remained near her father.

The summer passed ; soon the smell of smoke spread from the threshing-barns, and on the window-sill, right before Silja's face, appeared a lively little bird, peering into the room with its head on one side. "It's a tomtit," said father, and brought meat and bread crumbs, which he spread on the sill. Pickysoo — pickysoo — pickysoo — tee — tee — tee — heard

Silja, and hardly was father in the room again before the tom-tit was at its former place and pecking eagerly at a bit of meat which it held between its claws. The bird became a new all-winter companion for Silja. Silja looked on it as the same bird, as there was very seldom more than one on the window-sill. If two did happen to fly on to the sill, Silja was sure the first was the " right " one.

· 7 ·

LITTLE Silja sailed the sea of her life, leaving ever farther behind the shore whence she set out. Her senses developed, their circle of observation widened. Every impression sent through them by the life around her to the storehouse of her consciousness remained there, though some of them sank at once into such distant recesses that the keeper of the storehouse, the human being that was Silja, would never when grown up believe they were there; though they failed not to exert their influence even from their secret hiding-place.

During this first conscious winter there was one such hiatus. For over a week Silja's tomtits could cry their "pickyṣoo" as eagerly as they liked around the house and strut however livelily and peer in at the windows, without those delicious crumbs appearing on the sill. The living-room was silent; no child's face appeared at the window; and even the man moved cautiously. In the circumstances even a tomtit could be excused for remaining sitting disconsolately on the sill for a long time. Not until the moon rose did it move to its customary roost in the attic. During those silent days and nights too, Silja was in the house. On this night she is just awakening. She does not know when she fell asleep. It feels almost as though she had never existed before, familiar as the objects looming through the darkness seem.

Silja is dreadfully hot and her mouth very dry, but she is unable to ask for anything. It is dark, but near the window it is light, a special kind of white light, as though something very big, invisible to her eye, were looking into the room from the top of the house. So much of the light flowed through the window that the apparition sitting beside the table before the window showed up clearly against it. At the same moment a loud crack sounded, as though all this white silence had only been there to give one a chance to wait for some such sudden noise. Silja gave a start, as did that human apparition by the window. It turned towards her, Silja, lying in bed. It was father; the child recognised it now that it moved. Father came and touched her forehead and breast, then took a mug from the table and, holding up Silja with one hand, let her drink from it.

The child sank into unconsciousness again and the man sat down in his former place. He cannot sleep, now that the child is so bad. He wonders whether he will lose this one too. The man tries to envisage his solitude; such thoughts run easily, as though speeding along the moonlit snowdrifts outside. He would be left quite alone, as he always has been. For him too it would be death, as he had earlier died to so much. The child over there is his only tie with life.

Ever more agitated grows the mind of the solitary night watcher. The child's breathing is hardly audible; now and then she gives a slight moan, her body trying in its exceeding weakness to give voice to its pain. Hidden deep in the body is the tiny soul, deep in the shadow of the fevered body, and yet it feels an immense cold. It believes itself to be lying in the big living-room at Salmelus, as whose heiress it was joyfully conceived and happily born. But it is there quite alone; the door has been left open, snow flies through the crack, and with the snow glides in a big cat, not the house cat, but a stranger. It is big, almost the size of a dog, and of terrifying colours, yellow and green in its eyes and the gap of its mouth. It mews spitefully, as though it too was cold, then seeing the child, balances for a moment on its paws as though preparing to spring on a mouse or a straw and jumps straight on to the moveless child, sits on her chest, licks its own chest and purrs. It is heavy, so heavy; it settles down to sleep, a dread weight. Then it rises and begins to stretch itself, straightening its paws, and at each movement the claws sink into the child's breast; then it begins to whet its claws, as though awakening on a fence.

By this time the father had lit the lamp, sat down beside the bed and crossed his arms. A wave of love, long and low, flowed into his male heart at that moment. He did not touch the child, as he could see that the crisis was on her, yet with a sweeping strong movement he drew her into the depths of his embrace, closer than by any arms of flesh. Prayer filled his mind, though he sought not words. He saw the child living, ripening, growing to full maturity, beautiful, fair, but retaining the same soul that now burned in fire. The vision was a hope, a passionate prayer, in the realisation of which the father now unconditionally believed. He remembered some of his own bad deeds and had the feeling that the child's fever was burning the dross from him, the father, too.

Morning drew near. The father felt the child's forehead and chest and found them perspiring freely; his hand came away quite wet. Unused to sickbeds, all the father could do was to leave the child in peace and cover her still more closely, lest in her perspiration she should feel cold. He tucked eagerly at the bedclothes with a faint impression that the mother, a woman, was somewhere beside him. He lit a fire in the range and hunted out clean clothes for Silja, in order to be able to change her linen when she awoke. He put the coffee-pot on the range and brewed strong coffee to keep himself awake. Everything was well, the child's breathing was more regular; warming a nightdress over the range he considered the best way of substituting it for Silja's damp nightdress. He might give the child a drop of coffee.

All this he did. The fever had left the child, so quickly that the father was anxious. But after Silja had drunk her drop of coffee, she was so far revived as to talk already clearly, almost merrily. Her tiny sentences were as full of hope as the rising day. Soon it would be summer again—even if she were to die then, she would not have to stay in the cold storeroom, would she? Silja remembered her tomtits too, and asked about their crumbs. The father laughed, realising that he had altogether forgotten to feed those pets. Almost at a run he made haste to do so, and was soon able to tell the girl that their table was spread, all she had to do was to wait. " The birds went away so as not to disturb you with their chirping while you were ill. They're sure to come back soon when they hear that you are better. Try to keep very quiet now, for fear the fever might rise again."

The birds came very soon, and the child wanted so much to see them, that Kustaa was forced to take her carefully up in his arms and carry her to the window. Silja looked and laughed, her constricted chest giving her laughter a strange hoarse note. The child's breathing became rapid again. Kustaa heard a faint panting beside his ear and hastened to carry the child back to bed.

That same day the mistress of the friendly farm, knowing how matters stood in the house, came to see the father and child and bring the sick child some suitable food. She found the two inhabitants of the house asleep in the same big bed, in which they slept at night. Silja lay, half on one side, beside Kustaa, whose arm was wound so skilfully round her neck that few mothers could have slept so well beside their child : so thought the good-natured farmwife to herself before proceeding to arouse them.

Kustaa had the feeling, after that illness, of having been given the child a second time. Silja's convalescence was a blissful time ; looking at the child without her knowledge, Kustaa would often pause to think what would have happened if he had really lost her. However, as she did recover, she was surely intended for something in this world. And Kustaa keyed his mind again and again to that particular state of hope that was like a long, perfect prayer, though the pure-minded man would never have thought of calling it that. To this state of hope was invariably attached an invincible belief in the realisation of the hope, while deeds and thoughts of his own that conscience had sometimes condemned would recur to him.

When she was fully recovered, Silja again began to grow and mature, quicker it seemed than before. Now and again she would wander beyond the confines of the house, a matter that kept Kustaa on the alert, as he did not want her to stray about the village in the same way as Miina's children. It was difficult, however, for Kustaa to explain to the child in words everything she was not supposed to do, and consequently Silja sometimes erred in her outings. She would go off on a Sunday afternoon with Miina's children to a reaping-bee near the cabins on the edge of the village, where life was very pleasant and full of fun and new to Silja, until Kustaa's voice would be heard calling from the bend of the road. At that everybody would stop working, and all eyes would watch Silja's passage from the merry harvesters to her waiting father. That was a severer punishment than any hiding, not that a hiding ever followed. The father took his daughter by the hand, and so they would walk through the evening shadows on the leafy road, soft and muddy in places. The mud scrunched between her toes as she walked on regardless of where she stepped. So, without a word, they came home. Silja went straight into the house with her muddy feet, but her father fetched a bucket of water, brought it into the house, and his first word was to tell Silja to wash the mud off her feet.

As the girl grew up, such more or less serious incidents occurred, owing perhaps in part to Kustaa's inability directly to teach the girl.

Then came the time when Silja had to learn to read. Kustaa brought home a new a—b—c book from the village shop as gravely as any other purchase and began teaching her the alphabet and spelling. In this the father was near to lagging behind. One of the village girls with whom Silja had been much together sometimes visited her just then, and the girls whispered together over the a—b—c book. After such visits Kustaa noted that Silja knew things in the a—b—c book that he had not taught her, even things that he himself did not rightly understand. Kustaa felt almost as though she had again been on some forbidden excursion.

Silja went to a couple of ambulatory classes and then to the elementary school in a village about a mile away. She was in the last class when an event occurred one spring Sunday that was unlike anything else that had happened between father and daughter. The day was a warm, thawy Sunday. Kustaa lay as was his wont on the bed and Silja idly thumbed her lessons. As she had plenty of time she looked at and read things that were not in her home lessons and occasionally spoke a word or two to her father. If it was only a remark Kustaa made no answer and did not open his eyes, but if the child asked him something, he moved his eyelids and in time gave some kind of answer. Silja turned the pages of her Bible history, which had a map of Palestine as frontispiece. It gave rise to many questions :

" Is there really a Jerusalem—and Bethlehem, even to-day ? "

" Of course, if they are on the map."

" Why is it called the Holy land ? "

And there began a long discussion, during the course of which Kustaa found his own knowledge very deficient. He remembered, however, as they talked of Jerusalem, that there was a long account of its destruction at the end of the hymn-book ; his mother had sometimes made him read it out on some such languid Sunday at Salmelus as to-day. Kustaa got up from the bed, went with eager steps to the corner shelf and took down the big hymnbook. Silja watched him with curious eyes as he searched for the page. Having found it he placed the book before her, pointed with his middle finger at a passage, and told her to read it aloud. He himself returned to the bed and resumed his recent position.

Silja read, and wondered to herself that all this was in the hymnbook—" Then at the Emperor's command Vespasian went to Galilee, where dwelt many people, and plundered and ravaged the land so sorely, that of murder, robbery and fire there was no end. Then were many Jews killed, at one time fifty thousand strong picked fighting-men, besides women, children and other men. The enemy pitied neither young nor old, neither women with child nor babes in their cradle. Vespasian sent six thousand young men to Achaia to dig across a cape. Thirty thousand Jew warriors were sold into slavery, and fifty thousand broke their necks, in their despair dashing themselves down from high places in the mountains. . . . Then he took their town Gadara, and with his lieutenant Placidus killed nearly thirty thousand of the fleeing inhabitants and took two thousand prisoner ; those who escaped threw themselves into the River Jordan, and the river bore their dead bodies down to the Lake of Pitch, known as the Dead Sea."

The girl's voice ran on in the Sunday peace of the room. The father lay on the bed and listened as the girl went on reading, now and then stopping for breath in the wrong places, until she had reached the end : " Wherefore let none believe that the punishment of sin lies not in wait in the doorway ; for verily it shall go with the godless as with Jerusalem. This we must consider in all truth and impress on our hearts, repent us of our sins and turn to knowledge of the true Christ. Amen."

Having come so far, Silja rapidly turned over the remaining pages and from the end of the book, as though to free herself of something, read the last hymn in a singsong note as she would some child's jingle. Then the wooden covers of the book closed with a bang.

The father lay without moving on the bed, as though wishing to deepen the impression left by the reading. But Silja's cheeks were a hot red ; she pranced up and down the floor, helplessly, as one trying to remember what she had to do. In the yard the silence of a Sunday thaw continued. Noon was long since past, but there was still abundant light and glamour in the air, on the ground and in the treetops. Silja took a shawl for her head, watching whether father would have anything to say. But father was still lying in the same attitude on his back with his eyes closed, his head bent slightly back, so that Silja could see the under side of his chin, his curving nostrils and the hollows of his eyes. The sight was curiously unfamiliar to her just then. As though to flee from it, Silja rushed into the yard and with no thought of where she was going, slid on her skis down to the bank and on to the ice.

On the melting snow the light girl sped quickly as on a forbidden path. The loose snow had already melted from the surface of the lake, and on the ice her skis skimmed still easier. In one place water showed, only a narrow bridge joining the ice sheet of the middle of the lake to the shore ice. Across this bridge Silja skilfully guided her skis, the fever born of the reading still in her veins. Soon she found herself confronted by a hole in the ice. She stopped and listened for a moment to the measured beat of the blood in her ears, to which was joined another sound, the one she had listened to on the day her sick mother vanished from the house. The sound was now fainter, but came from somewhere quite close. It seemed to whisper an accusation in her ear. . . . The bridge over which she had recently skimmed had collapsed. Fear entered the child's mind; she hurried landward, but there too was water, brownish after-winter water. The ice beneath her was moving. In the rattle of the ice and the beat of her heart she now seemed to distinguish her father's warning voice. What would happen to her now? She was unable to cry out; her body only crouched a little and her face contorted into a fit of weeping. Along the road came a couple of Sunday idlers, who stopped to watch. Silja shouted and tried to fix her glance on the house windows through the trees on the bank.

The ice-floe moved slowly, but relentlessly. The men left the road and made for the shore, at a slightly quicker pace than they had been walking. They had almost reached the water's edge when Kustaa Salmelus dashed past them, bareheaded and coatless, in his eyes a queer flickering flame. Before the walkers could guess his intention, he had jumped on to the ice-floe, the edge of which broke under his first step, but held under his second, so that he was able to stride on to it and seize the girl. He took her up in his arms and jumped back. But the intervening space had meanwhile widened so much that he came down in open water. He succeeded, however, in throwing the girl clear, so that only one of her boots was wetted.

Kustaa sank to his armpits in the water before he could get a firm enough hold of the ice-crust on the shore to enable him to draw himself on to dry land. The two villagers hardly got beyond a thunderstruck stare. In the eyes of the man fighting to regain dry land was still the same alarming glow that had been in them when he ran to the shore; the men drew back a little, vaguely afraid he would strike them. But Kustaa rushed up to Silja, and his first act was to seize her by the hair and shake her severely. The girl uttered no sound, only stared at her father with terrified eyes.

"So that's what you found to do," he muttered. His jaw trembled violently. Gradually, however, he seemed to wake up and look around him. He began pushing the child towards the house.

The old mistress of the neighbouring farm had been rocking gently in her little chair and had witnessed the whole incident. It was over before she had time to lever herself out of the chair. She knew, however, what she had to do. Waddling over to the cupboard, she took out a bottle containing spirits and pieces of camphor, called the maid and gave brief orders. "If Salmelus doesn't happen to have any medicine in the house, he's a dead man. Run across with this and tell him to take a big dose."

The girl snatched her shawl and went. The old mistress too put on her outdoor things and set out for Kustaa's cabin. The maid met her halfway and said that Salmelus had carried out her instruction at once.

Kustaa was in his underwear when the old farmwife came into the room. His cheeks were flushed and the glow in his eyes had turned into a dull shine. He talked incessantly about how he woke up in that bed and without knowing anything rushed to the shore, quite as though he had been told in his sleep that the girl was in danger. In the cup on the table was still a little of the camphor and spirits mixed with coffee. Kustaa emptied it into his mouth and went on with increasing warmth : " I was so muddled that I laid hold of the child's hair, and I still feel a bit dizzy, though it was a fine thing that you sent me this, or I don't know what would have happened to me."

The old farmwife was not quite sure what was going to happen to him even now. Was his present extravagant condition due to the spirits or the accident? To make doubly sure, the woman mixed another dose and advised Kustaa to swallow it and then go to bed. She examined Silja too, and being convinced that no harm was likely to come to her, went off with slow dignity along the road she had come. As she drew homeward she smiled at the couple : how cosily she had found them lying together when it was the girl who was recovering. The old woman's heart was very warm.

The day faded into evening. Kustaa lay on the bed and Silja sat beside the window. Her father's wet clothes hung near the range, and Silja's boots lay upturned near the stove. No words were spoken. To Silja life felt very strange now, and not only because of the incident in the daytime. The morning when she had read aloud from the hymnbook seemed immensely distant. The man, too, breathing in the bed was quite a different being from the one who had shown her the piece about the destruction of Jerusalem. This man had seized her by the hair and had then told the old farmwife about it as though telling her something wonderful. Against her will she laid note once more to the under part of her father's jaw and the hollows of his eyes.

Kustaa did not contract any direct illness as a result of his wetting ; the following day he went about his work as usual and sent Silja to take the camphor bottle back to the old farmwife. But the strange softness of mood that had come over him after the rescue of Silja seemed to continue. During the next few days he told everybody who chanced to be within hearing, in an ever merrier tone, how he had been so agitated that he " even laid hold of that girl's hair." When, by this chatter, he finally made Silja too smile, he looked curiously happy.

. 8 .

THE spring came when Silja would have to pass her Confirmation class. From Kustaa's dwelling to the church
the distance was about six miles, so that he had to find
lodgings where she could sleep on weekday nights. There
were many girls in the same situation ; they lodged in groups
in the village houses and assembled in the evenings on the
bridge and the quay, conscious of the clumsy remarks and
coarse bursts of laughter from boys of like age and a little
older. Some of the girls already felt a strong inclination for
such company. They gave back as good as they received.
And even the minds of the shyest were moved by certain
hitherto dimly perceived matters. They were on the threshold
of maidenhood. The summer that now unfolded from day to
evening in the open spaces around the church, was to be their
first summer of liberty, during the course of which many were
already to experience why they had been born women.

When Saturday evening came they could be seen happily
trudging away along all the roads leading from the village.
At cross-roads they stopped and chattered a while before
parting, in that, too, resembling older women in a faintly
ludicrous manner. For the boys of Confirmation age, partings at cross-roads were of a very different character : bold
impertinences were shouted at boys from other hamlets ;
stones flew, and sometimes, on suitable occasions, a group
would be chased, when blood flowed freely from noses that
had tended to tilt too far skyward in the churchyard and on
the village paths in the evenings. There no one had dared to
fight for fear of the constable and the curates.

The girls walked as became young women ; a few of the

farmers from the most distant hamlets had left their trip to the village to Saturday afternoon, and now the daughter would be perched up on the trap beside her stout father on her way home for Sunday. Cries were exchanged between the girls too, between those on foot and those driving, but these cries were merry and decently worded. The evening rays seemed to rejoice in the flashing of eyes and the gleam of teeth.

On one road Silja Salmelus walked homeward, first with two companions, then with one, and after the departure of this last friend alone. Her father could see her coming nearer. He stood beside the wood-pile and chopped fuel for the bath-house. Silja came, cast an open glance at her father, but said no word of greeting as she passed him on her way inside. The strokes of Kustaa's axe echoed and the billets crackled ; it was a delightful Saturday evening in early summer. Then Silja came out of the house in familiar working dress. She came straight to her father and asked him for something to do, though she knew quite well what there was to be done.

" Take the wood in and make a fire, and we'll get it over all the earlier," said Kustaa.

Their voices had exchanged greetings. The Saturday evening work passed smoothly for the couple, father and daughter, joined together by a warm mutual feeling. A feeling of deep human happiness, from which, as the years passed, everything inessential or disturbing had fallen away.

Not until they had returned from the bath-house, and Kustaa sat in his shirt-sleeves beside the back window, combing his still thick hair before a mirror, and Silja flitted about the range like a pale ghost of evening, did they begin to discuss anything. The father asked over his shoulder how she liked her lodgings, the family being unknown to him. If anything she said was not quite to his liking, he did not stop to explain it to the girl, but went on asking and commenting in such a way that the conversation between father and daughter revealed that both were of one mind. There he sat, her father ; the girl caught a glimpse now and again of his strong and fine profile against the window as she had once done in her childhood, while in bed with fever. Then the man got into the bed and said no more to his daughter, and did not even seem to be following her movements. Silence had settled down on the room ; one could almost feel the dignified evening thoughts of the man in the air.

Softly, as though gliding, and taking care not to rattle the door, the daughter went out into the yard, still wrapped in the spring-like twilight of early summer. The flowering bird-cherry bushes on the distant bank and along the roads beyond the lake seemed to be floating in that dimness. The birds gradually grew silent near the house, but in the crowns of the farther backwoods one could guess that some of the bigger songsters were giving voice in long, long melodies to the deepest meaning of the northern summer night, for which they had so cheerily come so far. There were nests already, and in them eggs—the depicter of the northern summer night soon finds himself under the spell of well-worn phrases. Under the pallid sky in the dimness flowers, the fading music of Nature, somewhere a solitary maiden—Silja Salmelus stood and moved, listening to and sensing the summer night.

She moved gradually to the end of the point of land on their own part of the shore, to the leafy verge of the bank, and sat down there on the trunk of a birch, bent near the roots. Her young mind seemed to expand and grow bolder. No one and nothing could disturb her there. Yonder in the house, within hearing, her father slept lightly, and no path led past here.

The water with its shores and islands rested as in a picture she had once seen. In the water the reflections repeated towards the depths all that rose to the heights on the banks. Everything the senses could grasp seemed to be gravely and eagerly assuring the consciousness of its goodness, to be whispering to the girl that if you still sigh for anything all we can do is to soothe your longing with what you now see. This direct message from Nature made the girl's eyes expand, as though they too, like the lake, had wanted to reflect in their depths everything in view. There was much the sixteen-year-old girl might have sighed for, something she might have owned and knew from hearsay had been hers, though she had never consciously missed it. That was perhaps why her eyes, having expanded, grew slightly moist and her breast heaved in a gentle sigh on this night on which she had come home from her Confirmation class to see her lonely father. Yes, he was lonely, the old man sleeping in the cabin. The thought lent support to her own melancholy; she felt herself his safeguard. Silja looked into her own being and saw that she was a woman.

The night grew deeper. Silja rose and took a few steps towards the shore, intending to climb back a little later to the house. She would have liked to stay too: in some way the landscape became imbued with a stronger life as a boat came forward from behind an island, travelling apparently from south to north. The rhythm of the oars revealed the rower's mood: how the summer night had taken possession of it, deciding the direction in which thought should run and thereby the interval between the strokes. The approaching sound did not disturb, only interpreted. Silja gathered a flower from the ground, without intending to do so, and looked sidelong at the oncoming boat. The rower let his oars rest, as though in answer to the girl's movement, although it was almost impossible that he could have seen her. He seemed after all to be no real traveller but only a lonely spectator of the night, a youth, apparently unknown, in clothes that were neither working-clothes nor holiday attire, that she could distinguish. A summer visitor from one of the distant villas, boating. Silja was quite certain she had seen him, some weekday in the village, on a bicycle. That was why she could make out his clothes at this distance. His nose was slightly hooked and his front teeth showed easily when he spoke to the baker's wife. Yes, it was he, right opposite her now, so that they might be looking each other in the eye. Silja made a few plucking motions at her flower, the brown eyes looked forth once or twice under the long lashes, then the girl began moving towards the house in such fashion that each step was like a separate little event, a confirmation of something. As she went the girl did not fail to note that the youth still rested on his oars, there behind her back. Not until the girl had been in the shadow of the foliage for some time, wholly invisible from the lake, did she hear the youth make a few strokes and then wait again for a moment or two, and when at last he started to row away the rhythm of his oars was unlike what it was when he came.

The night would by now be at its deepest. How long had she lingered near the water? As Silja came into the cabin she herself was aware that she brought with her in the folds of her dress a faint breath of the perfume of the night air. The flower was still in her hand. She felt like saving everything that had accompanied her from outside.

Sleep seemed unwilling to come even now, so she sat down at the side window, from which she had a view over the fields towards the village. So wonderful the night was, the first of its kind for Silja in her life so far. In the rear corner of the bed she could distinguish the white-clad figure of a man : father usually slept uncovered. Silja gazed in his direction and somehow the way in which she now looked at him surprised her. Father was an old man, who had been through much in his life, so she had been told. I am together with that old man cast here, he is my father. What does it mean ?

Her father slept on his back, moveless. Even his breathing was inaudible : there was something mildly terrifying in him. Silja remembered that her grandfather had been found dead in the threshing-barn ; no one had seen the manner of his end. Was father awake, although he said nothing ? Silja could not ask him, nor could she go nearer to make sure. She looked in turn out of all of the three windows. Everywhere the night met her, seeming now much emptier than a while ago. On the lake the reflections had grown dim.

At last came a movement from the bed and a faint sound as of choked coughing. Her father rose to a sitting position and then went over to the window giving on the point. Leaning against the window-frame he remained there moveless for a few moments. Then, sighing, he turned, and saw Silja at the other side of the room.

" Ah—have you come in," the old man said in a sleep-befuddled voice and went to bed again. Silja grasped that he had not seen her when he got up from the bed.

In the corner of the room the slender figure of the girl could be seen noiselessly moving, turning gradually white and disappearing into the bed. Sleep had fallen over the house. Outside there was no further sound of oars for long. Only a brief moment was left to the dawn of the approaching Sunday morning.

· 9 ·

IT was one of those Sundays before Midsummer, character-istic of which are their brightness and length. Man and his beasts of burden taste the delights of rest and warmth. Even an old man can move freely in his shirt-sleeves, for the sun finds its way nearly everywhere. The live things about the house too, ignorant as they are of what a Sunday denotes —the dog, cat, cock and hens and the swallows—respond somehow by their manner of existing to the prevailing mood of the humans. A person sitting on the steps has time to observe the ways of these creatures, whom he scarcely notices during the weekday round.

No cause for surprise, even if an old person should feel the urge to walk, merely to pass the Sunday hours. The young foliage of hedges and trees is so irresistible, so alive with the might of Nature, that admiration of it throughout a Sun-day is no shame even to a manly man. The most barren-souled farmer may set out to view and calculate his hopes of a harvest. To a poor cabin-dweller, with only an acre or two of land, who labours hard on weekdays in fields owned by others, this quiet bliss of a day of rest, costing him nothing, is still better suited.

The same expanse of water that had so tenderly mirrored its shores and islands during the night, now flashed and glittered in the light of the all-embracing sun. Kustaa walks on the point of land, in the direction he had perceived his daughter to move the night before. There was the curving stem of a birch, but it is not fitting that he should sit down on it, or stand around too long. He has no intention of doing so ; indeed, he is hardly conscious that he is being led by his observations of the night. No day is quite like another even in a very long life, but old Kustaa Salmelus has a feeling that this Sunday is a quite special day. Perhaps for the reason that the girl to whom he is so deeply attached, his only child, had been out of his eyesight a whole week for the first time and was now at home again, soon to depart once more. By the evening boat.

Even at this moment she was not actually at home. Most likely she was in the village attending to some question of clothes, in the sempstress's little room, where girls tried on their new dresses on Sunday mornings, or confidentially discussed with the dressmaker the cut and pattern of a coming new dress. In another week, maybe, it would be Silja's great day—what was it called : the confirmation of her baptism. Aye, when was it Silja was baptised, in the big room at Salmelus . . . and now the girl was ordering her Confirmation dress. The grey faces of the dead children crept into his mind.

Into the mind of a lonely old man all kinds of matters steal when he walks without any particular errand to the uttermost edge of his land and stands on the shore. He was in his waistcoat ; the blue sleeves of his shirt ended in strong wrists and male fingers pliable in spite of their age. If the man's mother had chanced to soar down with only such knowledge as she possessed at her death, she might have taken him for her husband Vihtori, of Salmelus. The colour of the son's hair and eyes, originally inherited from her, has faded in the storms and calms of life so much as to resemble the colouring of his departed father.

There he climbs back again to his cabin, Kustaa Salmelus, Vihtori's son. About ripe, he too. But now he looks whether the girl is not coming home by now. He is well able to lay the table for his meal, and has done so innumerable times during the past few years. Yet it would be very pleasant if the girl's hands were to do it to-day, seeing that she is at home.

She is coming. He can see her walking with another girl of her own age. They stop at the lane leading from the main road to the cabin. They sway and hop as they talk in a lively manner, take leave of each other and draw apart, but continue even then to stretch out their conversation, until they finally allow it to end in a few shouted remarks. Then Silja walks swiftly towards the cabin, but to the spectator it looks as though her thoughts were not speeding ahead of her, but lagging behind. Kustaa asks her :

" Who was that girl you came with and were speaking to ? "

Apparently there was something strange in the question, for Silja looks at her father with an air of mild surprise before uttering the girl's name.

" Oh, is that who she was. I can't tell them apart any more," muttered Kustaa, to get rid of the subject.

Silja laid the table, moving quicker at this task too than she was wont. She looked absently at the table and then in her usual manner at her father as though to say : you can begin now. The father came towards the table, and glanced over it, he too, before sitting down. He then looked at Silja, a slightly broader smile than usual on his face, and said :

" Well, aren't you going to give me any bread ? "

This was a queer Sunday, for all its beauty and brightness. Silja and Kustaa exchanging such remarks. The girl nearly looked irritated as she brought the bread.

Kustaa had the need to talk a little while he was eating, if there was a single hearer present. He had become used to it in the days when he was master on his own farm, and had inherited the habit from his father. At the table of a big household the talk easily ran riot if the master failed to rule it by his example. Thus Silja was used to hearing her father talk to her at meal-times of matters in general, of things not directly connected with the household. At meal-times he also uttered his little criticisms of people and happenings in the neighbourhood. And Silja, if she had ever given thought to the matter, could not have remembered a single sentence of her father's table-talk that could have harmed her. On the contrary, it often charmed her, and sometimes aroused in her a silent admiration for her father that made her gaze at his head unobserved by him.

Now her father went on eating, and not a sentence came from him. He did not look vexed, but seemed to be lost in thought, as though far away. Silja refrained from attracting his notice and tried to sharpen her attention, to avoid making any further absent-minded mistake in her waiting. Kustaa failed to get out what he ought to say—" I hear she has begun to run about at night "—for he was not absolutely sure it was true. He was already finishing his meal when he finally said :

" Eat, dear child, you too."

Even that sentence was not altogether according to their habit. In spite of its gentle tone, it somehow made Silja sad. It sounded as though it had been uttered by a very weak invalid. Silja was unable to begin her meal until her father had got up and gone over to the bed for his usual rest after a meal.

The day was already at noon. Ever brighter, calm and happy, it worked irresistibly on all Nature, living or lifeless. It tempted, led and satisfied people of different ages in different ways. The sun—symbol and exciter of all the instincts and passions attaching to human life.

When Silja had eaten, Kustaa, still lying on the bed, heard the girl say :

" I think I'll go to Mikkola for a bit."

Mikkola was the farm where the girl she had come home with lived. Kustaa did not know what to say, and the silence lasted a little longer than was natural.

"I suppose you'll take care not to be late for the boat, so that you won't have to walk," Kustaa said.

"Yes," came the girl's answer in a rather uncertain tone.

The girl went and the father was again alone in his sunny cabin. He lingered in bed, his wordless thoughts coalescing into an unexpectedly overwhelming mood.

The blissful summer Sunday still lasted. Several hours after noon it was still potent and full of happiness. Good-natured people who met on the road interpreted it to each other.

Silja stayed at Mikkola all through the middle part of the day. Kustaa made the coffee himself as he waited for her. Then he saw the girl coming along the road, slowly this time, and swinging a branch of flowering bird-cherry. Only a couple of hours remained to the arrival of the boat. Then the father would be left alone again for a week, the girl would go back to her class to prepare for her Confirmation on Mis-summer Day. A happy time, though Silja Salmelus would not be able to stand on this occasion before the altar where her ancestors for so many generations back had waited, with minds solemnly attuned to purity, for those marvellous symbols. This was a different parish, in an unfamiliar district.

One would have thought that old Kustaa's mind would have been uplifted and solemn these days. But for the most it was curiously confused, especially on this Sunday when Silja was at home. The reason was unfathomable even to the man himself. For was not the girl as fair and pure-looking as before, well-behaved and balanced? Even if she did pay a visit, what was there surprising in that ? Surely she could not be expected to sit indoors the whole day, on her holiday. And the only girl of her age in the neighbourhood was Mikkola's. To tell the truth, Kustaa did not know anything for certain against the girl. A few unwittingly overheard remarks, that was all. That Silja should stay out a little on a fine Saturday night near her own yard, that was only devotion. The child wanted of course to think over in solitude the thoughts awakened during the week by the parson's strong exhortations.

In some way, however, the band between father and daughter, firm as it had grown, was shaken.

It was by no means the first time that the father brewed coffee and set it on the table. Silja had often seen it happen, even after she had grown into a big girl, when she chanced to be unwell. On such occasions Kustaa would not seek female help from the village, but would leave his own work and do the kitchen tasks with fair skill. But to-day, when Silja entered the room on her return from her visit and saw her father setting out the cups, and the smell of freshly-made coffee reached her nostrils, the embarrassment of that morning, though now in a softer, more touching form, once more assailed her. Father looked so strangely old, a state Silja had hitherto not thought of connecting with her father. Something akin to pity flooded the girl's mind. She hastened to take over the task from him.

In Silja's departure that day to the big village there was much more solemnity than on her first departure a week ago. Then it had been an active Monday morning, and Kustaa had driven her there, as the steamer did not run that way in the mornings. On that occasion Silja had been homesick for the cabin, she felt defenceless among so many strangers. Now she could not help waiting for the moment of departure ; it was so

exciting to travel on the boat; there would be two or three
girls on board from the villages beyond theirs, from the direction whence the boy had come rowing last night. It would be
nice too in the yard of the house where she lodged; there was
a big level lawn, where young people were said to assemble for
games on Sunday nights.

Kustaa sat without making any remark, only looking on as
she made her preparations. His ear, too, was able to follow
her movements, for she was humming. The tune resembled
some sacred song, or was it a hymn, something anyhow,
picked up during the week. The girl bustled and hummed,
but did not look at her father a single time. Until while looking for something she asked him a very humdrum question in
the midst of her humming, as one might open ajar the
festival chamber of one's soul to shout some order to the
menials' room. At the same time she looked unconsciously
and without any shyness at her father, on her face a matter-of-
fact, hurrying expression. She saw in her father's eyes that
which made her stop to look, straight into the old man's
pupils, without being able to look away soon.... Her
father did not appear to have heard her question, that she saw
by the strange gleam in his eyes; in them was, as though in
answer, another and more solemn question.

Her father got up and went towards the bed.

"I feel a bit sick," he said. "Is there any water here?"

Silja left her own tasks and hurried to the water-pail. It
was empty. The girl hastened out. Kustaa was left alone.

And now the air in the room assumed almost the proportions of a character in the scene; to Kustaa it was as though
the air was watching him, as though it alone had divined
everything, as though in the air had been something with
which he would hereafter be called on to associate, abjuring
everything else. Sick in body he stared at the middle of the

floor, and again there came into his mind the memory of a similar stare long ago. He fancied himself looking in through the doorway of the barn at Salmelus, the old farm which he had nearly forgotten. He rose from the bed, turning first towards the window beside which hung the mirror. Some whim made him look into it ; he could not have said when he had last looked into a mirror as now, studying his reflection. He saw a man, but who ? It was the man who had once come to him looking like that and asked his opinion about something connected with the farm, during that last phase of his life . . . by that question and the pitifully moved glance that accompanied it, by those alone Vihtori Salmelus, long dead, had made over his estate to his young son Kustaa. From the mirror the same man now looked out, the same nose and mouth, the same questioning agony in the eyes. What would happen now ? What said the air in the room, and the floor ?

Silja!—she would come—and soon go. No, no,—he must know how to behave—as sometimes before—on certain occasions in his life.

The child bore the pail in silence to its place and then looked at her father ; he came towards her, a hectic flush on his cheeks, took the dipper and drank.

" Mustn't you be going now, dear child ? " he asked as he put back the dipper.

There it was again, that " dear child," out of use long ago, a phrase her father uttered for the second time that day. The long midday sojourn in the village, the many contacts with sky, land, and the glances and words of human beings, had caused the girl to forget the weight that had lain over the house that morning ; unconsciously she had fled mostly from that, but the weight had only grown heavier. Did not her father say a moment ago that he felt bad, that he was ill. Like old age, that was something Silja had been unable to connect easily with her father. She now looked at him as at some approaching disaster that could no longer be averted. Her father was aware before she was that tears were rolling down her cheeks.

" Don't be anxious, Silja darling," said Kustaa. " It'll soon be over. You see you don't miss the boat."

Silja's distress moved Kustaa so much that he wholly forgot his own condition; his body had to live through the last stage of its life unobserved by his mind. Silja had to go; the bows of the steamer might emerge at any moment from behind the farthest headland. Silja went, and Kustaa went to see her off, walking beside her to the main road. There he stopped, watching the departure of his only child, which he could no longer recall. The girl went, stepping daintily the path of that early summer Sunday, her aged father watching her elastic step from the end of the lane. The father had time to see another girl come at the right moment from another lane farther on to join Silja with expressions of joy. After the two girls had proceeded some distance, they met two youths, as Kustaa could clearly distinguish. The youths stopped and the girls stopped. Then the boys turned and began walking, they too, towards the quay. All this Kustaa saw before he went back to his cabin. For he still had time to get back to the cabin—there was even a witness to that—where he was subsequently found dead. Quite as his father had been found dead in the barn on the family estate.

Silja had time to settle down in her lodgings, and even to take part in the games on the lawn, before the news reached her. The boy from the village shop brought word to her, speaking as glibly as he had learned to do over the counter. To Silja, at that moment, it was as though in reality she had left her father for dead at the end of the home lane, though she had not known it. She looked at the people around her with wondering glance, as though they had known it and had notwithstanding enticed her to play with them. Even the shopboy seemed in no hurry to depart. Almost they seemed to be waiting for her to go, so that they could go on practising their dance. Silja too had tried to learn it ; she knew the tune and even the words.

There was no one to advise Silja what to do in her plight. The mistress of the house seemed to be more concerned with some other matter than the death of that Confirmation class girl's father. She was not quite sure how well off he had been, and now the money for the girl's lodging. . . . Probably she spoke about it to her own husband.

The road from the big village to the cabin was not very familiar to Silja, and it was late ; but she set off at once, going without another word to anybody. The mistress was left to wonder, and to comfort herself with the reflection that in no case could the girl have disappeared for ever, as her Confirmation class was still unfinished.

Silja fared along her road. It was Sunday night, and along the village road lounged groups of youths, who stared with cheerful impudence at the girl as she passed them. No one made any special attempt to molest her, her queer expression keeping off these starers, greatly as such loungers enjoy teasing the helpless.

It was nearly ten o'clock when Silja again stood at the end of the lane where she had left her father a few hours earlier. Without being aware of it, she paused here, as though she had only just understood what it all meant. She had walked the whole of the way home in a kind of protest against what the shop-boy had said to her in the yard. Now, faced with the short walk down the home lane, the act seemed to imply some measure of acknowledgment of the news.

Silja came into the yard and saw that the cabin doors had been locked on the outside. She went to a window; the curtains had been drawn inside. A small opening had been left in the middle, but nothing could be seen through it. Complete silence; not a walker on the road. The tender moods of the night before and the sunny joys of the day on roads and lawns were immensely far.

The master of Mikkola came slowly along the road. He saw Silja while some distance away, but did not quicken his pace. He drew steadily nearer, while Silja, a girl in her Confirmation year, stood pallid in the summer night on the threshold of her deserted home, in a yard that seemed to have grown cold. " Well, well, that's what happened here, poor child—you had only just gone when . . . " On ordinary occasions Mikkola was rather rough in his behaviour, but now he too spoke to the girl in a gentle voice, telling her at length how the matter had been discovered, and how it had then fallen to his lot to act, and that what he had done was to lay out the corpse on boards and send word to Silja.

Ever farther at an ever swifter speed receded her life of a few hours ago, her whole life in fact up to now, her childhood. In the mild and, to others, delightful summer night the cold winds of life blew on the orphan. Mikkola was now speaking to her as to a full-grown person, the first time Silja had been addressed as such. The man observed to her that he had not been in the house alone, but had first fetched a witness—so that no one would have anything to say. As he spoke he opened the locks on the door and went on ahead into the dim room.

Silja too entered the cabin. The dead spread around him a limitless potent silence. The curtains were drawn, so that at first Silja could not see.

Mikkola went to the big table. " We lifted him on to this table, as he had fallen just there, right against it—we

126

thought . . . " The man moved away again and drew aside the curtains, remaining a little apart from her.

Silja saw again the under side of her father's jaw, the curving nostrils and hollows of the eyes, as once before, at a certain decisive moment. The eyes were slightly open, as they had often been while her father was lying on the bed and Silja moved about the room quietly working, or said something that did not call for an answer. There lay the silent man, on his face the last faint shadow of the smile that he had needed so often at the turns in his life's road. He lay there undisturbed, as though smiling at the fact that Silja and Mikkola were watching him, perhaps waiting for him to change his position. He did not move, merely lay, on that table on . . . Apparently it was only now that the matter penetrated to the bottom of Silja's consciousness, for she now burst into a fit of crying, the note of which was light and musical as that of a child. Her father had once told her in a very funny way how she had slept her first sleep in the cabin on that same table.

The hard-natured farmer could find nothing more to say. He moved gradually towards the door, came back again, and began drawing the curtains. " I'll put these—so they won't come peeping—not that he would know whether they did or not, but it's better . . . " Mikkola muttered amidst Silja's slowly receding fit of crying. "Mm—I suppose you'll come to our place for the night. You can sleep with Tyyne— you won't be going back to the big village to-night—and we ought to make up our minds about when he's to be buried, seeing it's so warm—I'll do everything, unless you want someone else to manage for you—he's left enough money, there won't be any need to go to the parish, I know that—I haven't looked yet to see whether he's got that much at home, but there'll be some in the bank, and I can lend some of my own for the time being. . . . "

The grass wetted Silja's new boots, for the dew had already fallen. A midnight sound or two was heard, a stray scent breathed. Silja and the master of Mikkola, a queer couple to be together at that time of the night, moved past the sleeping houses towards Mikkola. Here and there in a yard a curious woman still waited, who, having seen Mikkola pass on his way to Salmelus's cabin, and guessing his errand, wanted to hear and see whether " the girl was taking it very badly that her father should go off so sudden."—" Solemn-looking she was, but she wasn't crying when she went past here," the woman would then report to her husband, already in bed.

The couple came to Mikkola, where the family was still awake. The mistress, and even Tyyne, with whom Silja had spent part of her day, were so embarrassed that they shook hands with Silja, and Tyyne spoke in a strange voice, as though reading the words from a book. Then Silja was given something tasty for supper, but she was unable to eat it, for tears poured from her eyes and her mouth grew dry when she tried to chew. So they all went to bed, Silja together with Tyyne.

The orphan's first night was an unlucky one so far as sleep was concerned. Tynne fell asleep almost at once and disturbed her bedfellow, who merely dozed occasionally, by her abrupt movements in her sleep. In its own way this helped to keep Silja's mind off the subject on which it tended to dwell. The sturdy farmer's daughter cast her leg over the much more delicately-built Silja, and pressed so hard that Silja had to struggle to escape from the weight, whereupon Tyyne turned altogether towards her and embraced her passionately, murmuring meanwhile to herself. Her breath was faintly nighttainted. Silja had never slept in the same bed with anyone else than her father, nor did she afterwards for many years. Now, as she lay awake, she thought of how near she had been to Tyyne yesterday, walking together and smiling in the sunshine. Of how they had met those boys on their way to the boat, and what Tynne had said. And what father had asked her and what he had said.

After that night Silja never felt any tie of affection for Tyyne Mikkola, who had been on the way to becoming her girl-friend. It was as though, at this first cross-roads of her life at least, old Kustaa Salmelus had stood guiding her in the right direction.

Weary, Silja went off in the morning to continue her Confirmation class, and Mikkola began to arrange all the practical matters connected with the death, which Silja would not of course have known how to arrange. Kustaa was buried on the same Sunday as Silja was confirmed, but neither event made any very deep impression on Silja or remained long in her memory.

The Daughter

. 10 .

SILJA did not stay long at Mikkola. To be sure, the master of Mikkola had been appointed her guardian, having been the first to help the child, but Silja, after her Confirmation, had hardly been a week in the house before the village women were hinting that Mikkola had had a stroke of luck in finding so suitable a ward : it had given him an unpaid servant, while all he had to do was to lift his remuneration as guardian. In the mouths of those yellow-teethed hags Silja's modest heritage grew into a quite considerable fortune, so that soon the solvency of Mikkola's estate had begun to depend on how much the master would be able to grab of that heritage for himself.

The outcome of this talk was that Mikkola packed off Silja into service somewhere else. In this way the girl came to Nukari, a small old-fashioned farm, where she was the only maid. There was not even a hired farmhand ; the master preferred an occasional day-labourer, in which capacity he now had a half-witted youth called Väinö, who was usually addressed as the Nukari bailiff. Väinö's bed was in the corner nearest the door, Silja's in the far corner. Sometimes in the dark, after both had gone to bed, wonderful conversations were held between those beds. Väinö, the " bailiff," unfolded his ideas of this world, and there were no all too strict bounds to the soaring of his thoughts. He would on occasion question Silja earnestly about the course of her life and compare it with his own. And then, as time steadily drew nearer the moment when sleep could no longer be avoided, the boy would begin to speak of marriage and ask Silja whether she would marry him when he had got on a bit.

Silja had not yet acquired full adult confidence, yet she felt that in this case she could lightly refrain from answering.

"Say, will you?" still came from the bed near the door.

"I'll tell you to-morrow," Silja answered and ostentatiously changed her position, as one settling down to sleep for good.

At that moment the mistress opened the door and came into the room in her nightdress. "Stop that chattering now, Väinö, so's you won't wet your bed again after tossing so much, and don't answer him, Silja."

The mistress went back and thereafter no sound was heard from the servants' beds. In her heart Silja could not help being pleased that the mistress looked upon her as a sensible grown-up person, but she would think too of poor Väinö. And finally of herself, her past childhood, her Confirmation class, her dead father, delightful even when he was aroused, whose living image was now beginning to fade, so that it was hard to conjure it up before her eyelids at moments like this while she waited for sleep to come. A posture only, or a movement, was all that revealed itself to her mind's eye, and then a mild wave of pain would flood her being that father was no longer the ruler of the room where she lay and had to have the courage to fall asleep. With a faint cry she would awaken to full consciousness, look in the dark at the window-panes, hear the breathing of sleeping Väinö, remember where she was, and sink back to real sleep at last.

Once Silja had to come home alone from a neighbouring village on a dark blustering autumn night. She had stayed longer than she ought, and when she finally reached the road, a nameless terror of the darkness and of Nature overwhelmed her, that resembled a little what she had felt on the ice-floe from which her father had saved her. Between the villages was a wood, where the road descended into a deep hollow.

Here the roar of the wind sounded high overhead, as though the darkness were a great bird, threateningly panting in the heights.

It was as though on this occasion too, father, in one of his postures, had been somewhere among that panting. . . . The orphan girl hastened on her road, and at the gloomy half-way point of her journey was nearly afraid. But as the wood grew thinner and the village drew nearer the vague disquiet changed into an equally undefined sense of bliss, that seemed to well forth dropwise.

She felt inclined to sing to outvoice the receding mutter of the treetops.

Her errand had been successful. Silja had been given coffee and treated as a responsible person. A young man there, whose name was Oskari Tonttila, spoke to her as young men speak to girls. Silja was, as a matter of fact, in her seventeenth year by then. As she approached the house, now humming audibly, she recalled all this.

When she came home to Nukari, high spirits reigned there too. Everybody sat in the big living-room, talking merrily. Silja's arrival was treated as an event of some importance; her warm happiness continued even inside. Hardly had she given an account of her errand to the mistress before cries and witty remarks were being exchanged. Among those in the room was a stoutish ruddy man, with a jewelled ring on his finger and a thick gold-coloured chain across his waistcoat. It transpired later that he was the master's brother, who had already been in America once and intended to go back there soon. His visit was in the nature of a farewell call.

He was addressed as Ville and he knew how to make that evening in the living-room, a rather dismal place, very jolly. His voice was a trifle shrill; when he sang he could make it rise higher than many women could. It was he who succeeded in getting the company to sing ; he even persuaded Väinö to quaver a few curious comic songs that his father had taught him and that people had already forgotten, but which the company, partly because of Väinö's manner of singing them, hailed with roars of laughter. Väinö alone was in an uplifted mood after his performance, especially as it turned out that the master knew the same songs and could join in with a verse.

Ville Nukari had knocked about the world a lot and was a good judge of people, old and young. He found Silja very pretty, although she was still so young and childish. He was friendly to Silja, and during the games and romps that evening took care to show it to her in words and deeds. When, after his song, Väinö began humming a dance tune, the visitor seized Silja for his partner and danced with her on the floor, the only couple there, while the others looked on. Silja discovered that she could dance the polka ; though Väinö speeded up the time, the dancers did not lose step, but spun at last like a whirlwind. Väinö got mixed in his tune first, whereupon Ville threw Silja high into the air and then spun round with her to a seat on the bed. His hand lingered a moment or two at her waist.

Ville Nukari did not, however, go so far in his behaviour as to scare Silja. When he said goodbye the next day and left, Silja came near to missing him. He asked Silja whether he could write to her, and Silja answered : " Write if you like." It was all she could answer. The result was a number of sugary letters, which Silja answered. One of the letters contained a very gaudy silk handkerchief, of a kind no one in the village had ever seen before. The matter became known, of course, as Silja had not the wisdom to hide the gift at once. It was something to build up hints on, though on the other hand it was a shade unnatural that a man in his thirties, who had knocked about the world, thus courted a girl only just confirmed, an innocent girl at that.

This connection with Ville Nukari was later to affect Silja's fate. She was in no such emotional relationship to him as people suspected after the arrival of that handkerchief. To her, Ville was in the nature of a relative older than herself, who liked her. When, therefore, Oskari Tonttila gradually began to make the kind of advances to her that young men make to girls, she had no idea that Ville Nukari's letters and handkerchief signified anything. Nor did Oskari, if indeed he had ever heard of the matter, seem to pay any attention to them. He danced with Silja at dances and escorted her home, keeping his hand on her hips as they walked.

To everyone there occurs in his or her youth some single event or longer or shorter periods of life, which, recalled at a riper age, awakened a sensation of nausea. They need not always be evil deeds or hidden crimes—unless, perhaps, they concern some act of pilfering in early childhood or an obstinate holding fast to some matter known to be a lie—but merely uncomfortable ballast of the soul of another kind. It is by no means rare that such wounds refer back to the beginnings of sex feelings. The awakening consciousness of sex turns sometimes to extremely surprising, even ludicrous substitutes. In most cases it is difficult to say who was the first object of the love feeling of any person.

While at Nukari, Silja Salmelus thus kept company with Oskari Tonttila, who was a little older than she was, at that time just approaching his twentieth birthday. He was a tall fair youth, who spoke little, except when he had been given a drink by someone ; at such times he was inclined to be rowdy and readily picked trifling quarrels. His parents lived on a hillside of little cabins on the outskirts of the village ; the father an ordinary morose big-boned block of a man, the mother too a fairly big woman who had borne over ten children. The children were sent out into the world almost as soon as they were able to cross the threshold, for old Jussi's wages did not go very far. Now and again, to be sure, they were to be found in the parents' cabin while moving from one job to another, and just at this time Oskari was living there, being engaged on part of a big cutting contract in the district.

Oskari was usually of a steady nature, though like his father, whom he resembled in every way, rather coarse. Returning once from some dance, he joined Silja, as he had joined many another girl on such nightly home-goings. As all the other girls had their escort and seemed in no way ashamed of it, walking as Silja could see very close to their companions, Silja did not know how to object. For that matter, Oskari did not say much to her, merely walked beside her and made clumsy attempts to pat her arm. They would walk along the dark roads, the company thinning meanwhile until as they came near to Nukari the couple were alone. At such moments Oskari could become talkative. In a queerly intimate and friendly voice he would ask about Silja's workday life and tell her about happenings in the village. He would light a cigarette, and so they would come to the farmhouse corner, where Silja stopped to say good-night.

" Can't I come inside ? " asked Oskari in that same good-natured tone, as though between them at least the matter was quite settled.

" No, for goodness sake, the master's ear is only a couple of yards off, and the mistress's still nearer." Silja could not help laughing at such a question. What would Oskari have done there in the middle of the night, even if it were permitted ?

Oskari lingered, nevertheless, a little while, drawing at his cigarette until the ash stood out and moving his weight from foot to foot, but with nothing more to say. It was almost as though he were merely waiting for something : for someone to pass by and see him where he was. The night, however, was silent, only a horse snorted loudly in the Nukari stable. As though the sound had been a sign, Oskari set off towards his own cabin, and Silja went inside.

So they became accustomed to each other, and the neighbourhood became used to their returning together from dances. By now Oskari was holding his hand on her hip and they were walking as silent as the other couples. An old woman tried to hint things to the mistress of Nukari, but the mistress was able to swear that at least while they were at home neither Oskari Tonttila nor any other man had visited Silja at night and hardly ever in the daytime. " And she's so sweet and innocent to the eye," added the mistress, " that I won't believe she knows anything about men yet."

" There's no guaranteeing 'em, however sweet and fine they are," whinnied the old woman.

As Oskari was not keeping company at that time with any other girl, the village girls found food, according to their varying natures, for conclusions and teasing. No other boy even tried to approach Silja, and she herself was still in full virginal unconsciousness, though her age was mounting by its two or three most precious years. Väinö's nightly speeches from his bed became, to be sure, tinged with a growing bitterness, and in the darkness he related more than one thing that he pretended to know about Oskari Tonttila. But Väinö's tales were about girls Oskari had known earlier and they made no impression on Silja, or if any, rather a good one. She found it not unpleasing that there should exist a young man, who saw her home and whose name was coupled with that of other girls and now with hers, as no one could in any case say anything bad about her.

So passed those years without anything else happening to them than that Silja allowed Oskari to keep his arm around her when they walked in the twilight—they were meeting by now oftener than at dances. When Silja and Oskari were with other young people, at dances in particular, Oskari was now much noisier and more talkative. He twirled about and cracked coarse jokes, for the girls too to hear if they wished. But as soon as he was alone with Silja, he was very gentle, both in words and behaviour. Once when he was, or pretended to be, mildly drunk, he had occasion to show fight on Silja's behalf. As they were leaving a dance, Oskari remained behind for some reason, whereupon a well-known young rough immediately rushed up to Silja in the yard and began firing off nonsense at her. "Hello! Here's our baby's mother!" At that moment Oskari came up and quickly put a stop to the rough's foolishness: "You're your mother's baby, and you'd better be quick and run off to her, or you'll get hurt."—The rough only had time to ask "How?" before Oskari answered "Like this" and knocked the puny rascal down with a well-aimed blow. The return of Silja and Oskari from the dance was spoiled, however, that time, as the rough's companions followed them at a distance, shouting and mocking. At the Nukari gate Oskari asked Silja to wait while he drove them off, but Silja uttered a short farewell and went inside. Oskari was left to settle matters with this unwanted escort somewhere else.

It so befell that this was their last real walk together. The following week Oskari went out into the world, to South Finland, where the Russians were erecting extensive fortifications and whence rumours came of fabulous day-wages. A clever man, it was said, could garner money there without having to work much at all. Oskari set off with a couple of other young men who were at a loose end just then. They were in brave humour, quite as though they were going to the war. They assured those left behind that here's boys off to the big works who can take care of themselves. To celebrate their departure they had a few drinks. The " Nukari bailiff," Väinö, had somehow joined them and had been given his share of the bottle. After which Oskari came boldly to Nukari with Väinö, the hour being still so early that there was no fear that the household would be asleep. They came into the living-room, chattering already in the doorway, Oskari lisping slightly as always when he had had a drink or two. Oskari explained that he had Väinö's permission to see his " steady," and Väinö babbled that it was all right to look so long as he didn't touch her.

This visit aroused in Silja a slight disgust, but it proved to be the last meeting between her and Oskari for over a year. Oskari travelled southward early the next morning, and when in the course of time he returned, their old footing could not be resumed. That this was so was due to Ville Nukari, who had meanwhile returned from America and found a post as buyer for a lumber firm. In that capacity he called once again at Nukari and stayed the night there. Unfortunately the master happened to be away in town, so that this brother of his was able to assume too much freedom in his old home.

The evening in the living-room passed almost as that evening had done long ago, when Ville came to say goodbye. All that was new was that Silja had prettily matured in the interval, and that the mistress teased her about her two years' courting with Oskari. This seemed to have a certain effect on the man who had been to America. He sought every opportunity for showing his superiority to the ordinary local men. He fetched a bottle from his travelling-bag and offered drinks to those who wanted them, not " distilled under any spruce-tree," this. And then after he had warmed up and the others too warmed and the talk became lively, talk mostly about America and dollars, the guest pulled out his pocketbook and showed them what they looked like. Silja came forward with the others to look, whereupon the visitor took one of the longish notes, with a strange picture on it of a man who looked like a woman, apart from the rest, held it out to Silja and said : " May I offer it to you for a keepsake ? "

Silja was somewhat nonplussed ; she neither took it nor refused it.

" Take it, take it, girl, while you have the chance," said the mistress, though in a rather spiteful tone.

" What use is it to me ? I don't want it," Silja answered, laughing outright, and as the visitor failed to take the note back at once, she put it on the corner of the table.

" I'll take it," ejaculated Väinö and was about to grab the note, but the visitor was quicker than the " bailiff " and put the money back in his case.

He passed the bottle round again. The mistress refused to take another drink and forbade her brother-in-law to give " that poor Väinö " any more.

" What's that got to do with the missus, so long as I do my work," roared Väinö in a voice that showed the effect of the drink.

" The missus wants you all to go to bed now, guests and home folk alike."

The visitor took another drink and then went to the parlour at the other side of the house, where a bed had been made for him. Väinö and Silja got into their own beds and the lamp was extinguished. In the adjoining bedroom the voices of the mistress and children died down, the last low whisper awakening no answer, the house seemed to be asleep.

As yet, however, hardly anyone but the children was really asleep. The evening had been so lively ; the drink too played its part in keeping them all awake ; thoughts ranged and flew over a wider area than usual. Someone may have remembered that the master was not in his customary place that night. If anything out of the common happened, the household would have to seek refuge in the master's brother, that fattish man, who was half a gentleman.

Then the door of the living-room creaked. Väinö heard quite well that the intruder did not come from outside, but from the parlour side. Feeling his way round the room the intruder muttered about something he had forgotten, and among the things forgotten was his good-night to Silja. He found her, sat down on the edge of the bed and, all in the same movement, stretched himself out beside her. The creaking and whispering continued, becoming louder, Silja's whispers in particular being clearly distinguishable. Väinö was in truth slightly defective in the head, but that stranger appeared to take him for quite mad. As Väinö, in his bed near the door, breathed regularly and audibly, the visitor thought he was asleep, possibly, because of the couple of drinks he had had, sleeping very deeply. Väinö, however, heard everything and understood all that was taking place in the other bed, and he was terrified now at all the speeches he had made to Silja's bed across the darkness. For if Silja had really been his betrothed now, a very dangerous duty would have been his : he would have to get up and drive away that scoundrel, first from Silja's bed, then out of the whole room. But Silja had never taken his remarks seriously ; hadn't she kept company all that time with Oskari, who was now somewhere out in the world ? Let her struggle or yield, thought Väinö, and continued to listen with ears cocked to what was happening in the far corner.

The visitor wrestled there about an hour, keeping silent in between. Väinö had time to think about that beautiful silk handkerchief that Silja had got in a letter. At last the sound of Silja's sobbing began to be heard from the rear bed, and as the girl tried at the same time to speak, the words came out loudly.

At that the door opened again and the mistress came in in her nightdress, a tiny lamp in her hand. She did not hesitate, but went straight to Silja's bed and said a few hard words to her brother-in-law. Silja tried, between her sobs, to say something in self-defence, but the mistress only snapped at her : " You shut up, I know well enough what's been happening."

This sentence then worried Silja for long, as it did not reveal whether the mistress knew everything as it really had been. From the way, however, in which the mistress treated her afterwards, Silja guessed that the mistress had heard everything or made a shrewd guess. The man was a relative of the house, so that the mistress had to adopt a different attitude towards him than she would have done if it had been some journeyman she was chasing from Silja's bed. So that in the end Silja had no bitter memories of the mistress of Nukari.

For when spring came, Silja left Nukari. Before that, however, certain other events occurred that are worth relating in the history of Silja's life.

. 22 .

APRIL had come. It had rained and been warm a few
days, the first starlings were whistling, someone main-
tained that he had seen a wagtail, and there were many whc
said they had heard a lark. But the ice was still strong. The
snow had indeed melted on the ice, and in places the water
on it was so deep that a gust of wind would raise ripples on it.
But the regular winter roads on the ice, those main arteries
moulded by struggle, sweat, hopes, quarrels, disappointments
and weariness, they still rose old and hard-trodden over all
the changes wrought in the ice by Spring. On them the going
was hard and dry. Especially for one on foot was it delicious
to be out on such a road, for if a load met him, there was
always enough room to step aside without being forced to step
down into the slushy depths. The boughs placed to mark the
road still stood upright as though in guarantee that the way
was open.

Along such a road Silja was walking one evening towards
the main village, northward. The sun was preparing to set ;
there was a suitable spot for it towards the north-west, where
the hills and rises left a shallow gap. But, as Silja walked, the
sun was still at least three fingers high in the sky : Silja remembered this old way of estimating measures from some
delightful occasion with her father, and now she too lifted
three thin transparent fingers as her father had done in the
backwoods meadow. The girl continued on her way, and
as there was no one to be seen on the whole expanse of ice, she
could give way to being herself. She walked with blissful
strides, her whole body seeming to dance in time to the humming that came from her lips. The sun turned red and set all

143

the wide landscape aflame. The guiding spruce and pine branches along the roadside, from which the winter winds and passing drivers had broken off most of the twigs, loomed gigantic against the glowing evening sky when seen close at hand ; their silhouettes seemed to rise and fall in her eyes in time to her cheerful stride. The wandering girl raised her head to catch the light of the setting sun on her face just as she wanted. Her eyes caught a momentary flash of what the reflected sunset must look like on her cheeks. Her lips went on humming the melody, to the rhythm of which her feet rose and fell.

Stored in abundance deep down in the young soul of the girl were experiences which at a chance moment like this, with the reflection as it were on her face of a similar mood in the early spring sunset, could find vent in a rare ecstasy. Like to thousands of others of her age at that moment in these and other villages and farms behind the walls of forest, she had already lived and with ever expanding senses tasted autumns and springs, winters and summers, known by experience the life of humans, animals and the growth of the soil, how they lived and increased, and what could happen to them without their being able to prevent it : things good, ugly, frightening, warming, and much more that the consciousness was unwilling to accept. She had seen the look on some maturer girl's face on the Sunday evening following the announcement of her banns with her coming husband, she had seen infants suckled, infants of whose existence a week earlier the only sign had been a stout-grown mother whose movements were heavy, she had seen blows exchanged, blood mixed at the slaughter of an animal, in the secrets of her body things had occurred, slowly maturing and such as took her by surprise and affected also her soul and set her meditating at idle moments while she tended the cattle. She herself had fought

144

and conquered. Yet the joint outcome of it all was that the soul now throbbed in ecstasy as though enkindled by the April evening sky. There was straight hard road before her still in abundance.

Then a sleigh drove towards her. The girl was so engrossed in her own mood that the oncoming horse nearly brushed her. Silja stepped aside : past her drove a man from a neighbouring village, who greeted her. Behind the sleigh, however, a light handsleigh had been fastened, and guiding this was Oskari Tonttila.

This unexpected meeting thrilled Silja enormously. The sunset glow was forgotten for a moment ; she no longer observed it, nor did she look back at the sleighs that had passed her. Her large and bright eyes were open, but for a few moments she saw nothing with them, but looked as it were into her own being. There something had been suddenly dashed asunder. Her humming had ceased.

It was not surprising that the girl should marvel so much at what had happened in her mind. For Oskari had been nothing more to her when he went out into the world than a friend, and even friendship had tended to cool. What then was this ? Why was she alarmed and excited by the knowledge that Oskari was again in the neighbourhood ? Why did it seem impossible, now that the matter occurred to her, that the boy would see her home as before, if they should chance to meet in the evening ? If it had been a dark autumn evening now and Silja had been walking along a forest road amid the roaring of the wind, she would surely have hastened her steps in fear. Even in the village she did not feel fully safe, and as she returned across the ice Silja was really near to dreading something. The sky now wore the blue of a late evening in spring ; a few stars were visible, but if one looked long there were very many. On the open expanse of the ice, where the sky could freely be observed, it was easy to note that many familiar stars were not in the same places as they had been about Christmastime, when one may have noticed them on some night trip. And as the stars, so something else had altered, no helping that. Silja was far from hoping that this time, on her return from an unsettling expedition over the ice, a loud and merry company would await her in the Nukari living-room—no— And when she did arrive, the house was quite silent. Silja accounted for her errand and then went to bed, rather more slowly than usual.

. 12 .

SILJA did not meet Oskari again until the following Sunday evening. Her thoughts dwelt indeed incessantly on the returned wanderer; involuntarily she remembered him while at work, while preparing to sleep and while getting up in the morning. And still she marvelled at her own self and the fact that the man had become so important to her while he was absent.

Then Sunday came. One of those damp spring Sundays in April. The ice could no longer be crossed; open water showed here and there, and big ice-floes drifted and revolved. One might see a biggish stretch of the winter road turned upside down and stranded on the shore; the thick streaks of manure, soaked empty cigarette boxes and other rubbish, all aroused in the beholder a spring melancholy. Winter had gone. From the eaves on the northern slope of roofs water dripped all through the idle Sunday, the drops boring a hollow in the hard ice below. As evening drew nearer the weather turned colder, fine icicles began imperceptibly to form at the corners of the eaves, drops ceased to fall into the hollow made by them, which now froze hard. And in the morning the world smelt of frozen earth, and a lively sun shone on the bluish icicles, the red catkins of the alders and grey walls.

But before the morning had been the Sunday night. Oskari Tonttila was living in his parents' cabin, whither he had come from down Helsinki way worth plenty of money. Old Jussi lay on the bed, which was really too short for him, so that the back of his head rested on the wooden end-piece. He lay there, looking and listening, and opening his mouth too whenever any subject discussed by the others had generated sufficient heat. The speakers on this occasion were Oskari and Miina. They talked about the village girls, of whom one had had a baby and another was believed to be in a similar way. Silja at Nukari was mentioned, and at that Jussi growled from his bed, as one might do who had been too late for the preceding conversation : " You have to take good care with them—or you'd soon have some other man's brat to feed."

Oskari was standing just then on the floor of the low room ; he took a few steps in his creaking topboots and went to look out through the window at the melting lake, leaning his elbows on the sill. But the remark interpolated by the old man just at that point of the conversation remained disturbingly in his consciousness. He cast a question on the subject over his shoulder, and got a still coarser answer from the old man, aimed this time straight at Silja.

" Well, who's been getting at the girl ? " Oskari asked in a slightly harder tone.

Miina, his mother, now began speaking in angry jerks as she brewed the coffee :

" That rip lay there one night, that brother of the master's, Ville. They say he's a lumber foreman or some kind of forest-buyer now that he's back from America."

" Who said so ? "

" Väinö was there, who sleeps in the room. It's true all right—the missus drove him away next morning."

Oskari went to another window and took up a similar position there. He whistled softly and made his boots creak. Then, gradually, he began moving about on a series of little tasks that revealed his intention of going out. Miina knew from experience that on such a trip Oskari was likely to be away until the small hours. In similar fashion other young men were leaving huts and cabins ; they could be seen here

148

and there on the road, sometimes meeting and hearing from each other what was on that night and where. They would all return in the small hours, behind them the dances and fights of that day, the whole passionate contents of the Sunday night, the dashing break in the daily grind. Now and again, once or twice a year, it would happen in the parish that a man who had gone forth on such a Sunday evening failed to return. At such times there would often be two missing : one carried to the table of the operation room behind the church to await the coming of the district doctor and his assistant, the other hustled to the cell in the corner of the gaoler's cabin. So the darkening, sighing, ominous latter half of an April Sunday is always full of opening and concluding stories. One sees, hears and feels them everywhere. Whether, like a sentimental farm-maid, one sits beside the window, looking as much into one's own heart as at the twilit road, or moves outside on one's way somewhere. On such a spring evening as this, when it is no longer winter and not yet summer, and the shadowy countryside teems with the noiseless progress and expectation of those thousands of little happenings, little events, which, after the long light day of rest, hasten as it were to their places, to begin, continue and end in earnest, in the shelter of the twilight and night.

From a small beginning a dance emerges somewhere and gradually develops into full festivity. Towards the end of the week a doubtful rumour spreads, its originator unknown. Even the inhabitants of the farm mentioned only hear of it from some outsider. They wonder mildly who could have said that there was to be dancing at their place on Sunday evening. No one has asked me for the loan of a dance-floor, the master says dourly.

But when Sunday afternoon begins to darken, people gradually assemble at the house. They are all acquaintances and sit decently on the benches. Impossible to drive them away. Ever new people come; one of them carries an accordion. It is tried out a little, just to hear its tone. A low, repressed lilt of a polka steals out. A couple of girls from the oven corner take the floor together, the accordion grows bolder, the dance is in full swing. Not until an hour or two have passed do heads appear in the doorway that are eyed at some length. Oh, indeed, so he's here too. Looks to be drunk. Keep an eye on him.

The dance is like a big living being, whose course cannot be determined by the dancers. Sometimes it complicates or speeds up the little fate-like entanglements of the young in no small degree.

As we have seen, the strange effect of that meeting on the ice continued to work on Silja all through the week. Unconsciously she waited for a meeting with Oskari some evening and easily found pretexts for being on the road in places where he was likely to be. Then on the Sunday she heard that there was to be dancing that evening at Pietilä, and she spent the whole day in such a fever that the mistress's patience was tried. She began to hint that she would not allow Silja to go there. The girl turned silent, but hurried through her tasks just the same.

"All right, you can go, off with you, off with you, God's creation, it's more than anyone can bear to see you in the house in such a state." There was a friendly note in the mistress's voice, and both smiled as their glances met. The girl's spirits rose again.

But there were still many hours before it would be polite to go, and Silja did not yet know of any companion from the vicinity. In reality, there was only one companion in her thoughts. She hoped so intensely to see Oskari before evening that little by little she began to be convinced that she would see him, quite as if they had arranged to meet. She began to dress herself in the living-room, shy of her surroundings. A flush burned on her cheeks and her eyes shone. Bustling about the room, the mistress was drawn to watch the preparations of her young maid at some length. She watched the expressions on the girl's face and the flexible movements of her young body, that unmistakably revealed the pitch of her mind. There was both pity and disgust in the mistress's voice when she said :

"Now, girl, don't be in such a fever, it bodes no good for you—and watch out for yourself, as you're still that babyish."

Silja no longer heard the warning ; she was off on her way. Without hesitating she walked on towards the Tonttila cabin, with brisk steps, as one sure of her errand. The highway led at first between fields, then rose in a gentle slope to a sparsely-wooded pasture, where all the fine symptoms of the April night were as though condensed. The sky flamed again between the west and north-west, but was not so largely and openly visible in the pasturage as it had been on the ice ; here it filtered through the birch-tops, which were promisingly naked. The delicate crowns and bunches of twigs showed dark against the sky ; they too seemed, like spectators earlier on the scene, to be regarding the evening glow. Silent and moveless stood the innumerable tree-tops, yet in some way they imparted to the young walker on the road, whose distended eyes rested on them the whole time, an assurance that they were governed by the same mood as herself. A beautiful Sunday evening, promising events which the later spring could further develop. New food for bliss grew in Silja's soul on this road too.

The trees thinned again, and the road ran once more between fields, narrower and more densely-fenced than those Silja first passed. The back wall of the Tonttila cabin came into view; the old window in the wall appeared to be casting an ingratiating side-glance at the comer. It was Oskari's home; here lived his mother and father, who had perhaps heard that Oskari and Silja had sometimes kept each other company before Oskari went out into the world. In those days Silja had occasionally seen old Miina in the village and had not been able to detect more in her glance than a certain curiosity about herself. And the mistress at Nukari had once said to her, half in spite, that Miina Tonttila would be content to get her for a daughter-in-law, seeing she was rich. By riches the mistress meant Silja's tiny inheritance, the value of which was known to the inhabitants of this village, too, much more exactly than it was to Silja.

The road finally carried Silja to a spot opposite the Tonttila dwelling; the side window of the cabin now regarded her from the hillside a few yards away. Silja felt that she would go into the house; something had pushed her too far for her to draw back now. Something seemed to be continually trying to intrude itself on her mind, something that seemed to grow more urgent the farther her journey proceeded, but what it was she could not say. She now walked slowly, hoping that she had been seen from the house and that some one would come out. But no one came, and no one within seemed even to notice the presence of the vacillating spectator. In a window of the neighbouring cabin a head could be discerned spying on Silja's movements. They knew there.

At the end of the path leading to the Tonttila cabin Silja paused again, but then went on into the house without further hesitation. In the porch she sensed the thin smell that has its own individuality in each separate cabin, seized the latch of the door, that had worn in a manner characteristic of the grasp of the inhabitants of the cabin, and entered the living-room, the order and furnishings of which had become permanently

152

established by the joint work of the strong-willed mistress of the place and the passing decades.

In their established places were now the master and mistress. Jussi was still in the position from which he had recently fired at his son certain coarse remarks about their present visitor, Miina had her coffee ready and was wiping the pot. Silja's greeting was answered by a whine from above the coffee-pot ; the old man in the bed said nothing. There was no need for him even to turn his head, for his small eyes could take in everything, but quite fortuitously a slightly mocking expression was lent to them by the fact that he had to look at Silja across his cheeks and nose. A silent throb of laughter shook his diaphragm.

Silja had time to feel a little embarrassed before a new glance came from the region of the coffee-pot and the sound, in a whining tone, of the words : sit *down*, the latter word faintly emphasised. The visitor could now, if she liked, draw her own conclusions regarding her hopes of any longer conversation with the family.

" Oskari doesn't seem to be at home ? "

" No, he doesn't "—and the coffee-pot swung from the range to a wooden tray on the table.

" Does Miina know where he went ? "

" I keep track of no one's wanderings, and I don't ask."

" Would he have gone to Pietilä ? "

" Perhaps he has—and perhaps he's gone to look at forests —maybe to buy 'em."

Silja was surprised at first, but then understanding rose in her consciousness, as though something heavy and fat had thrust its way from dark recesses to the surface. Silja grasped Miina's hint and, what was truly wonderful, felt at the same time something befree itself and expand within her. So this was what had secretly weighed on her mind as she came along the road. This was what had fettered and pushed her onward: and now even Oskari seemed suddenly to withdraw very far from her, as he had already withdrawn from this house. Together with that relative of the Nukaris these people all seemed to be in league with each other and bound for somewhere together. What am I doing in the room of these strangers? How could I, Silja, come here in this way? Why, I am running after a man who has held his hand round my waist.

"It's poured out for you," came Miina's voice from the table, and as Silja did not immediately grasp that the invitation was intended for her, the voice grew more commanding: "Take it, take it, before it gets cold, or isn't it good enough for you?" Not the briefest glance accompanied the words.

In the same way as one should answer the good-day even of a gypsy, so shall hospitality be offered to a person from one's own village if he happens to come while the coffee is on the table. Silja went towards the table, her dress, shoes, hat and her whole form and being moving there in the middle of the floor of the Tonttilas' living-room and coming to a halt at an old chair. Miina and Jussi could not help seeing it, wherever their eyes might be turned. Silja drank coffee, the taste and odour of which was characteristic of this dwelling, with something of the general smell of the room in it.

The presence of the girl there was in some manner extraordinarily audacious. Jussi and Miina, an old couple frequently at loggerheads with each other, were now jointly amazed, though they said nothing, either by word or glance. She was in her full senses, their guest, well dressed and clean-looking, but in it all there was something either senseless or shameless to come here asking for Oskari, a woman half a stranger.

154

"No wonder, either, if they do get brats, there's no blaming the man for it," announced Miina after Silja had gone.

Jussi said nothing to this, but on the present occasion there was affirmation in his silence. In their own way they were content, with this cabin of theirs, their brats, their habits. Oskari was welcome to stay away until morning.

Silja thus left, her mind strangely and peacefully frozen; her progress was again a similar half-automatic movement to what it had been when she came, though much had since altered.

Hardly had she reached the highway, when she heard giggles behind her. At first she did not turn her head; it was something that belonged to the situation, as though someone had been waiting round the corner for this retreat of hers. Then she heard low-pitched remarks that seemed to draw nearer. . . . "Forests"—these voices too were probably saying. And now, for the first time, Silja saw before her the events of that night, which she had hitherto never once thought of clearly and from the outside. In all probability Silja's instincts had assured her that during those night hours in her bed she had gained a valuable victory, that after that night she was, as it were, a more worthy person, definitely grown up, one who knew this life and was capable of faring along its paths. Now the incident again rose into the forefront of her mind—in the measure in which the impression gained in the Tonttila cabin gradually became fixed—rose and swelled, but in another colouring as it were, acquiring the form to which those other people, in their own separate ways, had moulded and magnified it. Silja saw the incident also as it actually had been, but it did not move her in any way. Her sense of victory, which had hitherto been half unconscious, now grew and gave confidence to her whole being. She seemed to be undergoing a series of awakenings, her spirit stood erect and felt its power; the young woman began to divine the right living of the life that thus continued.

Oskari, to be sure, had not been in the cabin; Silja had not yet met him eye to eye. But that was a trifling matter. All the experiences Silja had lived through with that young man, these too were now included in the distasteful atmosphere, the thickest centre of which was yonder in the cabin. It was as though it was only now that she was escaping from the clutches of the man from America.

Silja looked behind her at this point and recognised the two who came there; their names were Lempi and Iita. They were maids from a neighbouring village, on their way to the dance. After a moment of hesitation Silja waited for them to join her.

" Were you visiting old Miina ? " the girls asked innocently. Probably, though, there was also a spice of mockery in the question. Silja answered :

" Old Jussi's there too."

" Yes, and what about Oskari ? " said one of the girls, half closing her eyes.

" No, that was Oskari who went past us at Siltaa Hollow," the other girl blurted out.

The dance was in full swing when the girls arrived. In reality it was a kind of entertainment; a charge was made at the door, and between dances there were other items on the programme. For the exchange of letters between boys and girls a box had been hung on the wall; envelopes and paper were supplied at a table in the rear. The atmosphere was a little dull, as many of the merrier lads had not turned up yet, and this delay made it certain that when they did appear they would be intoxicated.

Oskari was nowhere to be seen. A less-known acquaintance came occasionally to ask Silja for a dance, but neither managed to dance well. It was as though her feet kept on asking her at every step for advice about the next step.

Gradually, however, the public increased in numbers, and at last, when it was past nine, Silja saw Oskari in the doorway. A slight intoxication glittered in his eyes; obviously he had been present for some time, but had kept in the shadow. He now seemed to be teasing Lempi and Iita, who burst into laughter every now and then, their bodies inclined backwards and their knees bending.

In spite of everything Silja felt a little confused when she stopped in the vicinity of the group after a dance. She cast a glance at Oskari, but Oskari was just relating something. "... What is there funny in that—she came to ask whether old Jussi Tonttila had any forest to sell. Didn't you know that she's joined one of the big—Hey, Silja, which firm is it? "

Both girls turned to look at Silja. In Silja's eyes was a characteristic dark flame; and her lips had curled into the fine beginning of her most beautiful smile. Then, calmly, she moved away, and the delightful glow on her countenance soon enticed the best dancers to her side. The whole time, however, she sought a suitable opportunity for escaping without being observed.

The opportunity did not come until after midnight, when the post was distributed; at that moment everybody's attention was turned in one direction; all were listening to the names being called out by the distributor. Silja was out already in the lane and there was no sound of anyone following her.

After those present had received their letters, a few were left unclaimed, and these were sold by auction. A journeyman bought a letter addressed to Silja Salmelus. Having read it in the circle of his companions he left it on the oven-top, where, with the due comments added, it lay until morning.

In its original form the letter ran : " What kind of prices is your firm paying for timber cut in bed at Nukari ? It would surely be nice to keep your ladyship company, but I have to go into the forest for the night, not having any American dollars myself to buy with. Well, so long then with best wishes from yours truly."

This Sunday night in April had seen its own stories acted. So far as human beings were concerned they were drawing to a close ; dawn was breaking, an exceedingly fresh April dawn, bright with colour as the evening had been, but somehow merrier and more childish. The fine scent of frozen earth was delicious to the lungs of those who had left the hot dust of the dance-floor. A wagtail, morning-chirpy, flashed its tail on the pigstye roof at Nukari as Silja approached it. It was not afraid ; its whole being bespoke a cheerful confidence, and it did not fly away until its own, doubtless very important business called it.

Silja felt a sense of well-being, liberation and freshness. Far away were both Ville and Oskari. Her mind found it hard to realise that she had paid an astounding visit to Tonttila the day before, and thrust the matter away from her, whence, nevertheless, in the course of time, after Silja had entered into entirely new conditions, it sometimes returned, or intruded in a distorted form into some dream.

Just now, however, Silja was as happy as the spring morning. The sun drove away even the idea of sleep. It seemed also to drive out all memories from the room, none of them being related to sunlight : even Väinö was not to be seen in his bed, the lad having apparently gone home on Sunday night and stayed away. Ever stronger grew the sun ; its rays already fell on the table, soon they rested on the end of Silja's bed. When was it that she had felt something

158

resembling this? Long ago, in the far-off days of her childhood, after the happy conclusion of some good event. Her dead father—his life seemed to have been put together of such events from which he always emerged a better man. Silja felt that she had gained something; that she was richer and in her existence better guarded, as though her dead father, the cast of whose face she no longer remembered, were still living with her and they had together, by a wordless agreement, decided how this life was to be taken on different occasions. Just now it was to be taken sunnily.

Silja really felt no need for sleep, nevertheless she stretched herself fully dressed on the bed, to enjoy this special morning hour with greater freedom. There she day-dreamed, of something new and different that was to come into her life. She would leave this place and go somewhere else, everything would open out . . . spring was coming . . . and after that, summer . . . when it would be like that and that on village roads and the yards of farms, and people would be stronger, in some way better than they were here . . . The sun shines . . .

It shone on Silja's eyelids, which, unnoticed by her, had closed. Like a red, dimly perceived intoxication it worked through them on her uncontrolled consciousness.

Until the mistress came from the bedroom and poked her in the thigh—something she had never needed to do before. " Get up, get up and change that frock, unless you want to work in your finery ! You must have had a time, sleeping that soundly," the mistress said.

" What have I had ? " asked Silja in a thick voice as she opened her eyes.

" What you went to look for last night, I suppose," the mistress answered.

The sun shone already in a large way, its light killing everything evil that it directly touched. No hint by the mistress could affect Silja ; happily she set about changing her dress. She had just had time to undress, when some instinct made her look out of the back window towards the road, where a man was walking. The man was Oskari. Silja's mind involuntarily encompassed in one brief flash the path it had taken Oskari two hours to tread. Back of the road, in the direction from which Oskari was coming, was a room whose door opened readily : Silja had heard talk of it and coarse laughter. That girl had been at the dance ; she had even read out some sugary stuff. Oskari looked tired and disgusted and did not even turn his head towards the Nukaris' window as he passed. It was not pride ; the man really looked as though he had forgotten that the house existed.

That was the last time Silja saw this first actual " courter " of hers, whose company she had submitted to and finally desired, chiefly because other girls had similar suitors and wanted them. The sudden encounter on the ice in peculiarly favourable circumstances had enticed Silja into the wrong path altogether, an expedition whose memory remained to reproach her mildly from the depths of her consciousness. Perhaps, after all, the mainspring of her emotion on the ice had been the struggle she had had to fight that one night, silently and in the end victoriously, in her bed at Nukari. As Oskari Tonttila had previously been awkward and matter-of-fact in her company, at moments almost childish, Silja had perhaps unconsciously rejoiced because of the opportunity she had seen of telling Oskari of her victory and, by so doing, as it were of sharing her joy with him. Only Oskari had not been big enough for that. Now Silja could rejoice in her sole possession of her victory. Perhaps the rising flood of life in her this morning was due to that—unknown to her, as so many other moods are at the decisive moments of life.

The mistress of Nukari was usually sympathetically inclined

towards Silja, as most people had to be. But this morning Silja affected her mistress disagreeably. The mistress eyed Silja's clothes, as though to read what those skirts had experienced during the night. And though she failed to observe anything, her distaste did not diminish. The mistress of Nukari was still in the prime of her womanhood. True, when she laughed one saw that some of her back teeth were missing, and her hair had lost its lustre in many childbeds, but the form and movements of her body were still full of life, and did a good-looking stranger come her way, there was thrill and melody enough in her speech and laughter. Yet Silja's morning mood irritated her.

Moreover, after that night the girl began to want to go to dances oftener than before, and would be seen returning now with one, now with another of the village youths. After the dance at Pietilä and Oskari's second departure into the world Silja felt indeed a quite special desire to dance, and enjoyed the willingness of the young men to dance with her and escort her home. None, however, of these escorts appeared to become attached to her in earnest; they were content to see her home. And as they were not permitted to come in, there was nothing more they could attempt, even as a matter of habit.

Actually, Silja was longing to get away from the neighbourhood. In her blood, wherever it may have come from, was the inclination to escape into new surroundings whenever anything of special importance had happened to her. Often chance came to her aid at such times, and this was the case now. The feminine nature of the mistress of Nukari once having conceived a faint dislike of the girl, the dislike failed to disappear, and it was far from being diminished by the fact that the master sometimes defended Silja, being aware that at any rate the girl did her work as well as before. The master, a man still strong and hale, was turning into an old man.

Silja's youthful freshness really appealed to him. But if he chanced to say a word in that direction, he was sharply reminded of his brother Ville's former designs. " The Nukari brothers seem to have the same tastes."

The mistress began therefore in all quietness to arrange for her sister, who had just been confirmed, to come to Nukari as her " assistant," as she said. The news was broken to Silja in good time beforehand by the mistress, and as the old women of the village soon got wind of it, Silja had no lack of offers to find her a place. She did not mind much where she went, and thus she came to Siiveri, over the boundary of the parish, a much bigger and more prosperous farm than little, old-fashioned Nukari.

. 13 .

IN one respect Silja Salmelus was in the right state of mind
and at a suitable stage of her development when she came
to Siiveri. She had lived long enough and seen so much of
the conditions under which a country servant-girl, especially
if she was fatherless and motherless, had to live, in by far the
most cases, that her nature had had time to adopt a firm and
definite attitude towards them. Her own experiences had
indeed been slight, and innocent compared with what opened
out to her now on the big farm in a large village. At Siiveri
three maids were usually kept, whose accommodation was a
room attached to the kitchen beside the cattle-yard. The
village lads called the room " the Maidens' Rest." The male
farm-servants had a room in the stable building. The family
lived in the " house."

Who knows all the fancies that a young backwoods girl
straight from her Confirmation class can spin around a situation on one of these big farms ! At her own home there is a
single cow, which by the laws of nature runs dry at its own
fixed seasons. If this occurs at the worst possible moment,
when the father's earnings have dried up much as the cow's
supply of milk, all that the children have to moisten their
bread with is salt fish and the reeky salt drainings from the
fish. Father and mother are grouchy, the children may not
play, as it only makes their appetites grow. There is hardly
anything they may do ; the only breaks in the monotony
of the winter day are when they scurry round the corner of
the house on their necessary errands, look to see what has
come, and observe in it tiny white worms the length of a
flax-seed. . . . Then the child scuttles back into the cabin,

boots flopping, and the warmth of the cabin is the highest enjoyment known to the child, as shivering, it crouches to sense it at the mouth of the plaster stove. So they grow up, attend a class or two of an ambulatory school, then the elementary school for a year or two, some of them, then, finally, and best of all : their Confirmation class. Best of all because it brings them the liberty, and also the compulsion, to find work as a maid. If, on an occasion like this, a girl succeeds in getting hired to a big prosperous farm like Siiveri, she is overjoyed. While preparing for her departure she sings the few ring-dance tunes and jingles she has been able to pick up in the confinement of her home.

There she enters on her work, companion to a couple of older maids. To be sure, the food is not much better than that at home, but such as it is, there is enough of it, and that means much. When the skim milk, still warm, is brought in from the cream-separators in the dairy, the maid has the same freedom to fill her stomach with it as the pigs and calves. And such beings as she, fresh from the cabins with their only half-stilled pangs of hunger, drink deep of it, and put on flesh. Her hips, arms and bosom are soon firm and solid, her wages can be stretched to pay for a new dress, sewn by the village dressmaker, as for any grown-up person. Attired in this she goes out on Sunday evening ; the older, hail-fellow maids have nothing against this young one accompanying them : there's company out there for her too. Company is indeed forthcoming even for this daughter of the cabins, now well on the way to filling out, and no farmhand or day labourer either, but a youth on a level with the times in the matter of pence per hour and card-games, slightly-built, neat and nearly white of face. His parents have rooms, not a cottage or cabin, but rooms. This youth comes and sits on the grass beside the newcomer Saima and begins to keep her company, talking so smoothly that even the indecencies in his talk flit past so neatly that a girl like her, used to rough and mostly angry language, hardly notices them. She is merely amused—to have beside her a young man quite as the big maids have. The youth turns the talk to her feet, her shoes and stockings. He admires them in the silliest manner. But then he wants to see what colour her garters are.

" They're speckled," the girl says laughing, but the glib-tongued youth says that he will never believe a " woman's " word unless he can make sure with his own eyes.

" This time you'll have to believe," says the girl, but by now the youth is trying to lift the hem of her skirt.

The girl defends herself, and in the end the boy scarcely saw them, but he has succeeded in establishing cuddling relations.

Some time later there is perhaps a dance in the youth's home, in the " rooms." The youth, Viljo, is slightly drunk, just enough to make his thoughts, words and deeds move at their easiest. He begs for a dance with the girl with the speckled garters, but she is unwilling, as she really cannot dance the dance then being played. The youth is deaf to her protestations and pulls her by force on to the floor. They have hardly gone half a turn before the girl is hopelessly muddled. The youth casts her aside and takes a new partner, one of the big maids from the same farm. The young maid slips out as unobtrusively as possible, goes home, to her own particular " Maidens' Rest," and goes to bed. For a little while her thoughts stray hither and thither ; she is vexed at her not being able to dance that dance, but finds comfort in the reflection that she will learn it yet, she can practise it with Sanni in the cattle kitchen. Towards dawn she awakes. Sanni, her bedfellow, has come home and lies there beside her. Sanni twists her body and tries to force Saima nearer the wall. Not until then does the young girl notice that the extra space is needed for a third person, who, breathing hard, is insinuating himself into the other side of the bed. " Mind that girl doesn't wake up," whispers the stranger, who turns out to be Viljo. The couple then gradually settle down, draw a deep breath and fall asleep for a few moments, locked in a tight embrace.

Entirely different is the life here from that at home in the backwoods cabin. The girl learns in time to dance and all that comes after a dance. In the summer the maids sleep in old storehouses ; when the doors of these are closed, it is dark inside, and even a beginner loses part of her shyness, nor does a hearty lumberjack scruple overmuch, but takes what he wants. So the girl lives the life of a maid, and in time becomes the wife of a cabin-dweller, who asks nothing about her previous experiences. So long as she looks after the brats, the cow and the rest of the household, she gets her due.

Siiveri was just that type of farm, where a young maid is subjected to the experiences described. To Silja nothing in particular was allowed to happen, but she too knew what it was to be squeezed nearly out of the bed she shared with another maid, when extra space was suddenly needed. Sometimes the master came into the room unexpectedly and drove away the maids' followers. " Make love, but do it so I won't hear you," he said to the maid standing before him in her chemise, shedding tears and affirming her innocence. The master of Siiveri knew enough about these matters ; he had not been the bachelor master of a farm, to whose sort maids' doors always open, for nothing ; he had also been a pupil at an agricultural school and attended forestry courses.

Silja's bedfellow was Manta, whose age was probably approaching thirty. She was a real maid and held herself to be a maid, could swear on occasion and was able to counter the lewdest thrust with her own tongue. Actually she was a warm-hearted woman. Her eyes, nearly black, which glowered, big and moist, straight into any eye, flamed when anger or joy shook her maid's soul. She would yell as she walked, shout: " A rook is no bird and a maid is not a human being " ; or, if the quality of any food was being discussed : " If humans won't eat it the pig will, and if the pig won't eat it the maid will." She accepted the low status accorded to a maid with cheery insolence.

Nor did she deny herself the joys of this life for the reason that her lowly status compelled her to enjoy them in a coarser form than her better-situated sisters.

Because of certain traits in her appearance and nature she had very few chances of becoming any man's wife, but there did not lack those who consented on occasion in the dark of night to embrace her : men of wandering nature whose own attitude towards the world was like Manta's. Manta had been a maid over ten years now, and in the neighbourhood no one knew, or cared, much about her past. To Silja, whom Manta regarded as still inexperienced, she would sometimes vaguely hint things, as to a child still unable to understand everything. Even in the life of the maids on a big farm such quiet and tender hours may occur ... when Manta's big cow's-eyes stare slightly crosswise into the dimming sky and she sings something about " wavelets in a pool " and " love everlasting " and near her, absorbing everything, is a slenderer, miraculously still virginal little maid ... for instance on Saturday nights, after the bath, half-dressed, while hair is being combed.

Nukari had been a good school for Silja. Although everything was much bigger here, the fundamental current of life was nevertheless the same here as in the smaller circumstances there. As Silja had once won an exceedingly ordinary battle while at Nukari, and since then had grown stronger, she managed very well here too. Near the farm was a house where a girl of Silja's age was living at home. She did sewing work and had literary interests ; some of her poems had been printed in a religious journal. Silja became acquainted with her over the ordering of a dress, and the two were soon good friends, or rather the sewing girl began to display a quite special affection for Silja.

Servants were not very much interested in religion in those days. Most of them had surrendered to the general spirit of the times, the chief trends of which were easily ascertainable in print and by the spoken word. It was therefore unusual for anyone from the " Maidens' Rest " at Siiveri to turn up at Holy Communion. This miracle, however, occurred, after the sempstress had succeeded in persuading Silja to accompany her to Communion Service. Since her Confirmation Silja had not given any thought to the matter, and as she herself had not felt any call, this second and last Communion remained very vague in her memory.

One effect it had, when it became known : the young people of the neighbourhood began to look on her as religiously inclined, and the coarsest type of youth no longer made advances to her. At the most one of them might twit her with her association with the sempstress—Silja and Selma Rantanen are each other's sweethearts—and one of the coarsest of them all, the drunkard son of a neighbouring farmer, who had vainly attempted to gain Silja's favour, shouted to another youth who was trying to interest Silja : " Why trouble yourself for nothing—she's Christ's bride "

It all ended, however, in a curious manner that made Silja, in accordance with her nature, again begin to long for a change of situation and locality.

At Siiveri too the maids moved into the storehouses in the summer, as it was cooler there. Silja continued to sleep as before with Manta, who was being regularly visited at that

time by a local youth, one of those whose parents lived in
" rooms." On a neighbouring farm there was a young man
learning farming, who liked to run riot at week-ends, and as
he was a fine young fellow and a stranger, the village girls,
maids and farmers' daughters alike, showed him great favour.
It so happened one night that he was drinking ale with Manta's
friend of the moment, and after midnight, the two went together to visit the Siiveri maids, Manta's sweetheart promising
to guide the stranger to Silja's side.

" To be sure, she's a bit offish, but you'll get round her all
right," the guide told his friend.

" You let me get started . . . "

They drank a lot more ale and then staggered off towards
Siiveri in the early summer night. Hushing each other, they
stepped across the yard and knocked at the storehouse door.
As it happened, Manta had not been home all that night,
having gone off on a visit to some hamlet. Silja was awakened
by the knocking and explained matters through the door to
the thick-speeched seekers. Manta's friend, however, refused
to believe her and demanded to be let in, and with him came
that apprentice. Having satisfied himself that Manta was
really not there, one of the men left, but the apprentice flopped
down on Silja's bed and stayed there. Manta's young man
probably knew the true state of affairs all along and invented
the search as a ruse to get Silja to open the door and thus
admit his friend.

The young man did really remain there, for he fell at once
into a deep sleep. Silja spoke to him and tried in every way
to revive him and make him go away. But the man merely
lay there, lay and snored as long as the drink ruled his nervous
system. About five o'clock he awoke, licked his lips, seemed
to recall something and made a few half-hearted attempts to
take Silja in his arms and then went away.

A small matter, in itself trifling and insignificant, but destined to have its own significance in the maid Silja's life. The departure of the apprentice in the morning had been observed on the farm, and was not suffered to remain the secret of those who beheld it. The master too heard about it, but as the young man had once been his guest and was otherwise a good fellow, Siiveri did not grudge him the favours he thought the visitor had enjoyed in Silja's storeroom. He said nothing about the matter to Silja. With the apprentice he chanced to come face to face at some celebration, on which occasion the young man frankly told the master that he had been in the young maid's storeroom, but had not the faintest recollection of how he came there and what he had done. He woke up in the girl's bed, that was all he remembered. He asked Siiveri several times what the girl was like, whether she received visits from many men and whether there was any need for him to fear infection. " Damned nuisance when one can't remember anything. . . . " Siiveri was able to set the young man's mind at rest.

The religiously-inclined sempstress too heard about the matter. To be sure, it came to her in the form of a rumour, but there was little need to fear that so simple a matter could have been exaggerated by being spread as a rumour. All that was in question was that that apprentice on Sorola Farm had been seen coming out of Silja's storeroom at five in the morning and that Silja must have spent the night with him alone, as Manta did not come home until about nine. No more need be said. Who so wished, could help out his hearer's understanding by look or word.

Selma Rantanen, that pious girl who had been attracted by Silja and looked on her as a friend, was thus among those who heard the news. On the same occasion someone who happened to be present hinted wickedly that Selma and Silja had gone to the Communion Service together and were generally regarded as virtuous girls. " Still waters, still waters . . . "— Selma Rantanen no longer sought Silja's company. Later that winter Selma wrote a story about the first step astray of a young farm-maid. She read it aloud to the church sewing-meeting and then sent it to a lay, but pure-minded weekly, which published it in the spring.

Silja was tired of Siiveri and the whole village. She relapsed into that dreamlike state in which she cared nothing for her surroundings. She took pains with her dress and outward appearance, and even increased her wardrobe beyond a modest sufficiency, so that one person, seeing her growing store of linen, remarked that she must be preparing her trousseau, probably in hopes of that apprentice. Silja also paid increased attention to bodily cleanliness. As the farm bath-house was heated only on Saturdays, Silja would heat water in the cattle-kitchen boiler midway in the week, lock the doors, undress and wash herself. The master once happened to pass the kitchen window while Silja was washing herself. He saw the blind in the window and boylike peeped through the crack. He saw the young girl's body in the red glow of the fire, looked awhile and then crept away, his mind keyed to a curious, rather sickly sentimental, pure pitch.

Silja stayed all that winter at Siiveri, and nothing further occurred to give rise to talk about her of the kind that had been spread in the summer after the apprentice's night visit. In midwinter, life in the " Maidens' Rest " became quieter. Manta, Silja's bedfellow, was pregnant, and as her condition became obvious, her follower ceased to visit her at night. Those who slept in the other bed were sobered by Manta's fate and were not quite as ready as before to admit those who knocked. In addition, events occurred out in the world of such gravity that they were felt even in the maids' quarters.

Thus Silja was left in peace, to sleep that sleep of her life that could be deeper as she worked by day than when she awoke in the night. Little by little, the familiar longing to escape into new conditions grew. Soon this hope of hers was fulfilled.

It was a Monday morning in the latter half of May. All the signs of nature pointed to the best sowing-time : buttercups were in flower, the bream spawned, larks trilled passionately as they rose towards the pale sky. The soil of the fields fermented, it was at its brightest and spongiest ; one became aware of it through the soles of one's boots. The porous soil awaited the steel of the plough as a dam excited by desire awaits the sweetly violent clutch of the approaching sire. It lay waiting for seed that it could turn to shoots and in time to ears and stalks.

The byre doors were open, and from within came the sound of restless cattle and occasionally a commanding bellow.

The men followed the master to the fields, the mistress bustled with the maids in the byre. In the work of each group there was a special savour that day.

For although in Nature everything was as it should be, the mood of these humans was altogether strange, hitherto unexperienced by them. It had been that, all through the late winter, ever since the days the Czar was dethroned and all kinds of noble things happened, to the prosperity of the fatherland. But in the fatherland and its inhabitants were other aches than Czarist oppression, and these aches were not cured by the revolution ; so the revolution had to continue. And it was being continued in this village.

On the biggest farms in the village unrest had been evident

already at the end of the previous week : farmers from the adjacent hamlets who had been to the village on business looked grave as they unharnessed their horses in their yards. Each thought of the place nearest to his, where labourers had held their meetings and sung their songs, thought of the fiercer cottars in the neighbourhood, remembered some wandering worker to whom they had been curt. And along the roads near the houses the Saturday evening hubbub of the young people was quieter than usual, though there were many of them standing at the roadsides. Only a half-daft maid here and there emitted a full-throated bellow of laughter, which seemed to grate as it echoed in the evening.

The master of Siiveri was in the prime of life ; his wife, of a family well-known in the adjoining parish, was a fine woman with a ready tongue. It was pleasant sometimes to hear the badinage between master and mistress. They were a cheerful farming couple who managed their land and cattle with youthful vigour, and sensibly. The master knew the right proportions of artificial fertiliser and manure, the mistress was capable of working out her fodder schedules in accordance with the milk supply. Both were well acquainted with the level of country wages at any time, and the mistress knew how to organise the feeding of the hands in such a way as to strike the lowest possible limit of cost. The maids, who always stayed on longer than the men, were given a stray tit-bit or two on the side, but the wandering labourer who worked for a daily wage had to be and was content with salt fish and skimmed milk to vary the taste of his bread and potatoes. " The pigs grow fat on it," the mistress of Siiveri would retort if a cheekier wanderer than usual had the impudence to be sarcastic about the richness of the farmer's table. They were a stout-hearted couple, each able to extract from the chief centres of production, the cattle and the workers, all there was to be got, and avid for both visible and enjoyable wealth and healthy egotistic happiness.

For farmers of this type the spring season of 1917 was a very uncomfortable and disturbing time. They were proud too, and sensitive to all kinds of humiliation, and it was just their kind who got most of it at that time. Artturi Siiveri was redder than usual when he led his men to the fields that morning : in the usual state of affairs he would scarcely have taken part in the work with them, but now he went, in his pocket a loaded pistol. One of his men had already absented himself; he had been seen about with those ominous gangs on the Sunday.

A gang of this kind was waiting now at a suitable distance beside the road. " Wouldn't it be better to let to-day be a holiday," came a mild remonstrance from the gang, but Siiveri drove past with his men and field implements without answering. They went into the fields and began their work. The men standing on the edge of the field raised their red flag and struck up a song. One or two of them began hitching up their belts. From the field the master of Siiveri was heard shouting at his horse, as a man shouts at his own well-fed property, of whose obedience he is sure.

Meanwhile the peace of the byre too was being disturbed. The work of cleaning out the cattle-stalls was halfway when a committee adorned with red ribbons arrived, which had already been to stop the dairy and was now going the round of the byres to spread the information that as matters were not so and so, then neither were they to be so or so. The leader, better dressed than the rest, offered the mistress a written resolution to read, but was told that she would accept no other resolutions in her own byre than those made by herself or the bull. But there was Manta too to be considered, Manta of the big moistly protuberant eyes and a soul that feared nothing and was ready to laugh aloud even at a funeral. She now snatched the paper from the spokesman's hand, saying: " Let me put a receipt on it "—and before anyone had time to move she had passed it under her skirt with a grandiloquent gesture and was handing it back to the spokesman with the remark: "It's got our stamp on now, and be off with you." The next moment she had buried her pitchfork in the pile behind the nearest cow, the loaded pitchfork rose, the mistress did the same, and the committee found it wisest to seek the open air.

There, however, a graver sight confronted all of them. Excitedly gesticulating, another group of people approached them from the direction of the fields. In its midst the mistress at once recognised her husband, who was being carried by the enraged gang. The mistress rushed fearlessly at them, shouting: " Have you hellhounds killed my husband ? " For the master's face was bathed in blood, the sole patch of skin visible gleaming deathly pale. " Which of us is the killer ? Here's the slaughterer's tool," panted one of the men, and held out Siiveri's pistol.

After this event Silja had to leave Siiveri. The master was like a man raging drunk ; he walked about the house, refusing at first to let the mistress cleanse and tend the marks of his treatment. He went out and shouted roughly to his own men : " As there's a strike on, go to hell the lot of you." The strike-leaders had already left. In vain the mistress tried to appease the master's fury, the insult had penetrated too deep into the heart of this proud-spirited farmer. Seeing the maids he shouted the same words to them, and when they appeared not to take him seriously, but shot glances at the mistress, he seized a chair and threatened them with it.

At that Silja gathered together her belongings and took them to the cabin of an old woman with whom she was on friendly terms. Manta did the same, after which the two maïds set out southward along the warm smooth highway. And that was the last Silja saw of the master of Siiveri. Her things reached her by travelling journeymen, and the master of Siiveri was killed by the rebels the following winter in a particularly cruel fashion. Silja heard of it at Kierikka, where she was then in service.

Before that, however, she found employment in another place, towards which she was now walking along the road. Neither she nor Manta had any definite goal; mostly it seemed to them that this was only a slight disturbance in the day's routine, a wonderful walk thrust on them by those red-ribboned men. When they came to the next village Manta already proposed that they should call at a certain farm where she had been in service before. The farm had not a good reputation; it was owned by a widower with all kinds of little scandals to his name. Manta hinted at them as she marched with swinging movements through the gate into the yard. Silja followed unwillingly. The talk soon led to a decision that Manta should stay—" let the strikers say what they like, I'll stamp their papers again if they come here." Silja went back to the road and continued on her way in the same direction as before. Occasionally she met idle, defiant-looking groups of men at the roadside and on village greens.

She herself was slightly astonished to be walking on, ever farther and farther towards where the sun was then shining. Behind her, there where she had come from to this place, the country would have been more familiar. But in the most familiar place of all, the home cabin, were new and entirely unknown inhabitants, with whom she had no connection whatever. There ought to be still a little money due to her from her guardian, which he had promised to account for as soon as she was of legal age, and that she supposed she was now. But Silja had never been much interested in the money ; it was as if she were feeling for it in her father's pocket—on that late Sunday night when she saw her father, on her return from the big village, lying on the bare boards of the table. Or rather, as if the " guardian " had been at those pockets and then given Silja what he thought fit.

It was past noon when Silja came to the main village of the parish, the farthest she had ever been in this part of the country. She stopped at the baker's shop and asked for something to eat. The kindhearted woman who served her noticed the girl's beauty and at last asked where she came from. Conversation thus being opened, the baker's wife soon knew everything and was able to relate that here in the main village too, farmers had been carried off their fields and strike-breakers beaten. The woman then began to deplore that she had just engaged a new maid, otherwise she would have tried to strike a bargain with Silja. " It's altogether another matter with me, you see, being as it were always in people's view. I'd be happier to take someone with looks and not an ordinary dung-sweeper. . . . I'm sure cattle work isn't quite suited to your nature either, seeing you've kept so pretty, eigh, he-he. . . . But just you wait—now wasn't that professor at Rantoo just saying that they wanted—yes, he was. What if I were to telephone to him. What wages do you want ? " the mistress asked as she started off into the house. Silja told her what she had been getting at her last place.

Soon Silja heard the mistress explaining over the telephone that the master had fallen into a rage and driven everybody off the farm, bleeding in the head—no, that was the master, the master, no, no, not this girl—her head's sound enough, and a pretty head it is—what, the rest of her ? Yes, yes, neat and pretty—You look out if you take her, he-he-he.—The woman laughed inside, and Silja too smiled.

"He's such a joker, that professor, though he's over sixty," the woman said when she came back into the shop. "He's pensioned now, a widower, lives mostly all through the winter alone in his villa, but he gets so many relations visiting him in the summer that he has to take a maid. . . . It's over three miles from here, but let me see : there's generally a boat from there in the evening to fetch the letters, so that if you wait here a couple of hours you won't have to walk. . . . Aye, the professor said that he trusted me enough to buy a pig in a poke, and to send the girl on. . . . It's what I just told the professor in fun like, that it isn't the first chit who comes along 'd do for a situation like that, the same as in my house. You'll be sure to like it there—if only all those poor misguided people would know enough to stop their foolery," ended the woman on a soft low note of pity.

Silja had not paid attention to half of the woman's good-natured chatter : her thoughts ran already on the journey by water before her. She crept from the shop and walked towards the quay, from which a beautiful lake landscape, opening out cape by cape towards the south, could be seen. Somewhere there she would be going. A distant speck on the surface of the water seemed to be growing larger ; nearer and nearer it came, all too slowly in the watcher's eyes. The urchins on the quay said it was the post-boat from Rantoo way.

"Does it call at the professor's villa ? "

"Yes."

The spring sun was still high when Silja Salmelus, newly departed from Siiveri, was slowly floated, on her seat in the silent postman's boat, towards her new situation. Her mood was exceedingly solemn, as sometimes in her childhood when she was on her way home from school or a long errand after an unusually happy Saturday. At such times the loveliest mode of travel is by water. The shores blossom and the transparence of the green lends to the air around a special appearance. The road, too, along which one floats, is new and virginal for every traveller, innocent of the tracks of any preceding voyager. No dust raised by others, no annoying intruders from the roadside; and those who chance to be making the journey together in the same boat are in some manner humbler to each other when resting on the mysterious element. For the moment they are removed from the soil of the earth.

For a while Silja almost forgot whither she was bound on this journey, until the postman, opening his mouth for the first time of his own accord and motioning with his head, told her where the roofs of Rantoo could already be seen and that they would soon see the professor himself on the path. Suspense caused the passenger on the seat to tremble. The title of her new master gave food for speculation, and for the first time for long Silja remembered her own family tree and that her name was Salmelus. As she moved over the calm water in the fine spring evening, the girl's imagination tried for a moment to form a mind-picture of the old house which she had never seen within the period of her conscious memory. It was as though in her excitement she sought support from it, trying to become once more what she had been born.

THE villa was on the shore. The postman rowed to the little landing-stage, where an oldish man, obviously the Professor, was waiting for his mail. He peered at the girl from under his thick eyebrows. He was dressed in country fashion and in some indefinable way presented a generally shaggy appearance, which would not, however, have misled anyone into taking him for anything but a gentleman.

" Well, well, are you the one Mrs. Pietinen telephoned to me about. She told the truth, anyway, so let's go up and settle our terms at once. You'll find it nice to work for me, as soon as you understand my habits. You see, I'm one of the common people too, from this very neighbourhood, and I'm a bit old-fashioned in my ways. For instance, I call pretty girls like you by their first names as soon as I see 'em for the joy of it, and if my temper's raised I do the same to old women. Just now I feel like jumping to the moon and calling the whole nation by its first names. Come up here and get something to eat, and then you can look around a bit to get the hang of the place. Do you let young monkeys into your room at night ?"

" They don't try to come," Silja was able to say at last in the spate of his conversation. At the same time she involuntarily cast a pretty smile straight at the old bear.

" Oho—do you think I haven't eyes in my head, even if they are getting old ? Yes, that's one thing that I don't allow. I'm cock of the roost on this island. For that matter, if you get hold of an honest sweetheart, I'll even pay for the wedding, but I can't bear that stealthy cuddling at night. Well, no need to feel anxious, we'll get on all right. You don't look suspicious to me."

So Silja entered the Professor's service, where the battles of agricultural labour did not affect her. The following day she took steps to have her belongings brought to her from Siiveri. The Professor saw to it that she received the remainder of her inheritance and that the accounts balanced, and seemed to derive a malicious joy from pressing the master of Mikkola hard. " I don't think he was quite innocent of roguery, that good guardian of yours," he once expressed his thoughts. " I know those noble farmers, those hardworking sons of the soil. They can pull at a coin until it is oval, even out of an orphan's hand."

That came later : but this first evening at Rantoo Villa was great and wonderful to the lonely girl. She was moving along the track of her life, her youth still in the ascendant, her life still with its own resources for a further expansion and rise, and an increase in its devouring fire. A summer was to come that burned deeper and fiercer than any summer so far. Something mysterious, that felt sublime and blissful, was in this place, in its master and even in the surroundings. Silja did not meditate on it, and if anyone had thought of explaining it to her, would not have believed it, but everything this new master said to her on this first evening and later, was as though Kustaa Salmelus, long dead, was pouring forth through the mouth of this entirely different person the words which during his life he had with such entirety left unspoken. There was something in his speech that Silja's life needed for it to acquire the full vitality of a complete being, if only for a short time. Was she again living in the atmosphere of her home cabin, what though everything was on so much larger a scale ? To this house too, a path led from the highway, only broader, straighter and more level. At the end of the path was the " cabin," two-storeyed, to be sure, and painted, but with

windows of exactly the same pattern as those in the home
cabin, and inside—true, there the Professor ruled, who spoke
in a straightforward and firm voice, just as her father had often
acted straight, and, mostly, silently ; yet Silja felt from the
first moment in this house as though it was only now that she
had found the support and shelter that she had suddenly lost
on the death of her father. Silja remembered to-day the
ominous weight of that Sunday. . . .

" Go on, go on out and look at the grounds a bit," said the
Professor in the evening, " you'll see for yourself, what's
what."

Silja walked in the grounds and came to a birch-clad point
of land, at the tip of which she stopped and remained looking
at the calm evening-lit lake and the reflection on the opposite
shore. The note of a cuckoo sounded, and the crowns of the
distant trees were such that one could guess the thrush was
holding his evening litany there.

Whither had she come ? Had the emptiness that had
hitherto been part of her life suddenly vanished ? Was it
true, this sudden strengthening, expansion and purification of
her life, that almost made her limbs tremble as sometimes a
sudden excessive effort while she was working had done ?
Or had all the evil she had so lightly passed by during the
five years of her orphanhood now taken on this shape to bring
her irrevocably under its spell ?

Silja walked back to the " cabin." The Professor stood
at a window gazing out at the summer night, he too. Silja
came almost on tiptoe, and when the Professor spoke to her
it was in a voice soft and as though humbled since the day,
and in his sentences was none of the earlier luxuriance.
Having come a little way past him Silja paused, for one more
moment. Face to face with the summer night. . . .

When Silja went in, the Professor quietly joined her, told

her where her room was and then turned to go, but came back again to say : " Why, I haven't heard your name yet ? "

It was long since anyone had asked her that. She felt as if she were whispering it to this strange summer night that was now beginning.

" Well, good-night, Silja," said the Professor and went softly upstairs.

Silja had felt herself alone when, on the night following her father's death, she lay beside Tyyne Mikkola. Nevertheless, the room on that occasion was familiar, so also the girl breathing beside her. Indeed, since then she had always been alone, alone on the stormy road in the autumn darkness, alone while she walked beside Oskari Tonttila, alone while defending herself against the lumber-buyer. Lonely had been the path that brought her to this wonderful place. And most of all was she now alone in this little neat chamber, after the old man who felt so queerly familiar had disappeared upstairs and the house thereafter became silent.

The sense of loneliness was now stronger then ever before, perhaps for the reason that the circumstances of this world loomed just now so crushingly close to her consciousness, and that among those circumstances were so many new and unexpected. The whole of her stay at Siiveri with all its details floated at the very surface of her consciousness, how she had pretended to sleep at night and yet had heard and understood, the strong sweaty life lived in work, dancing and what came after, all, all, right to the bleeding head of the master that morning. Had it really been to-day ? and had it any connection with the fields, such as those she could now see from the window ? Her father had been a farmer, a master . . . from that idea her thoughts took a new turn, it was almost as though she could remember the old Salmelus farm, something in connection with it that pained and crushed her, in which her father was implicated. Her eyes closed, the surface of her consciousness half-slept, but deeper down the agitation continued : a picture formed there at random, in which her father was mixed up somehow with those red-ribboned men and something dreadful happened, beside which the blood-letting of the master of Siiveri was an ordinary refreshing incident.

At that point the agitation within her grew, her whole body twitched, her eyes opened and consciousness welled forth to take in again the summer night. The strangeness of her sur-roundings now seemed softened, and helped to calm her. The thought recurred to her, as something new, that in the upper storey a man lay sleeping who surely ruled this house and the whole circle of its interests like—like a wise father. It was good again to be alive ; even the room seemed more familiar now that her eyes had been closed for a moment, permitting her to awake in it. . . . The friendly chatter of the baker's wife in the village came into her mind : it felt like a memory of yesterday. Silja stretched her limbs, stroked back her hair and let her hands remain behind her head. Sleep did not seem willing to come ; this special deep solitude enticed her to regard herself in what seemed an impermissible manner, to think of the parts and forms of her body, of herself as a woman . . . at an age when many already had a child. . . . For that, a man was needed, and what happened was with the consent of both : inexplicable mystery that one could consent to. . . . Instinctively her arms withdrew from behind her head and stretched out sideways, while her head sank still farther back, until her neck felt strained, and for once her thoughts dwelt on what was terrible to her, but now almost bewitched her, on a sturdy, strong-limbed man, such as her eyes had often chanced to see, even unclothed . . . and on the miracle that one could consent with him to. . . .

184

The girl rose from the bed in her night-linen and went to the window. From it she saw the birch-clad point belonging to the villa and behind it a stretch of water, the view she had gone to see earlier in the evening. The sky, a few fields and behind them a dim group of buildings in the village were also visible. She looked out again towards the point and the lake, and a sadness, poignant and sweet, never before experienced, filled her mind. Her surroundings seemed to be tactfully drawing aside. Would she go out to the birch-clad point? Was father asleep in the cabin? What was it happened quite newly in the vicinity of that point? Had a very young man, with such and such teeth and such and such clothes, come rowing and rested his oars, a beautiful youth whom she had seen before? He had come—five years ago, and not until now had she remembered it. So many disturbing matters had arisen in between and effaced it altogether from her consciousness. Her father had died before she had had time to live the following evening. Now, however, father seemed to be alive again, the night was once more safe, so safe that one could venture an encouraging gesture while standing at the tip of the point, an inviting gesture to the rower to come and talk to her, perhaps land, and sit beside her.

The night already looked at her with the air of an accomplice, aware of her secret. The brown eyes of the white-clad woman glittered towards it under long lids, as the last stars in the nightless spring sky of the North may glitter if one stares hard enough.

Tears, for the first time in those eyes, for such reasons.

And then in the morning began Silja's life and service in Rantoo Villa. She awoke to the sound of the Professor coming downstairs—at a much quicker pace than he had mounted them the evening before. Silja was startled by the idea that she had slept too late ; she jumped up and hurriedly pulled on a frock. As she entered the kitchen she heard the clock strike five. At the same moment the Professor poked his head out of the doorway of the adjoining room and said :

" Ohoo, are you too up already. You ought to sleep more —make you grow. I've got some tackle in the lake yonder. I'll be gone a little more than an hour, so that you needn't have got up before six. But you can make yourself some coffee, now you're up, I shan't want any until I get back. There'll probably be an old woman coming here in the meantime; she's from a cabin over yonder called Kulmala, and she's a cousin of mine. She'll show you all the places I never bother about; she's done a bit of cleaning here and cooked for me a little while I've been without a maid. Well, I'm off—make yourself some coffee."

Silja could not resist the temptation to watch her master's departure from the parlour window, so completely had he captivated her. Watching the big man, still upright in spite of his age, walk down the path to the shore, Silja unconsciously raised her hand to her breast, so full of gratitude was her mind, purified by sleep, of gratitude that extended almost to the dewy path trodden by her master. If only I could—if only I could do my work well—and everything would still be like this even when other people come.

The " old woman " came, a neatly dressed, oldish, but still robust woman. " Ah, so my cousin has already found himself a helper," she said in a friendly voice and stared with little, good-natured eyes. Silja had to tell her name and where she came from ; they drank coffee together, Silja rather shy about playing the hostess, which she need not have been, as Sofia took out the cups from the right cupboard. So they became acquainted, and then went over the house together. The time passed so quickly that the Professor returned from the lake with his catch to find no coffee awaiting him. In their inspection of the house they had entirely forgotten him.

" Confounded women," roared the Professor, and Silja was near to bursting into tears. But the Professor said, pointing to Sofia with his thumb : " Don't let that old woman tempt you from the path of virtue, which path is that you learn my habits and fulfil my commands." Silja grasped, however, that the relations between the cousins were affectionate and close. From the kitchen, whither she had rushed to make new coffee, Silja heard them talking in low matter-of-fact voices.

" Come and see us, Silja, in the evening when your work is done," said Sofia in the doorway as she went.

" Yes, you do, that's one of the things you have to learn here. This Kulmala woman, you should know, is a flighty widow who collects all the young men of the village at her place, so that there'll often be male company left over for a guest."

" A good parson preaches his best sermons about himself," Sofia retorted, laughing with screwed-up eyes.

After Sofia had gone the Professor related her life-story.

" She was a pretty-faced girl too in her youth and went into service in Tampere with a rich old bachelor who fell in love with the pretty country maid, found his affections returned, of course, but went that summer to a health resort, where he suddenly died. Luckily, Sofia was engaged to him and was able to prove it in court, so that when her boy was born, she got an allowance for him until he came of age. Some time in her life she got married again and even went to America—but now she's a widow again, owns the cabin in which she was born, a daughter over ten, a piano brought from America, a little land, a cow and some chickens. So now you know, in case you go there, and you're welcome to go. I go there myself now and again. She often has the bit of work on her land done by the neighbours all coming there together, and then there's dancing : if there's to be any work done at all on the land this summer even that way—or even dancing. Well, well, is that coffee of yours still warm ? "

The day passed brilliantly. The Professor had, indeed, his own habits, but he asked very little of Silja, so that she was sometimes nearly worried when he tried to do all kinds of tasks that a servant could have done. The following days too went off well. Guests were expected, but in the end only Miss Laura, the Professor's daughter, arrived with a quite unknown girl who came with her on a few days' visit. No word came from the son-in-law's family, and the only references to his doings were couched in a slightly mysterious form.

Near Rantoo, however, was Rauhala, an old farm-house from which the land had been sold, leaving only the big grey main building on the outskirts of the village, and in this the former mistress received paying guests. Five or six visitors were usually there, from various places, who stayed their appointed time and then made room for others. The old mistress was a good friend of the Rantoo family, and when she arranged any festival for her guests, she always invited the Professor's folk, and thus these, especially Miss Laura, were on familiar terms with the summer residents at Rauhala.

Then one evening Silja went to Kulmala, on an errand of no particular urgency for her master. The road led at first through the yard of a farm called Kamraati, dipped under the branches of an old crab-apple tree, and there was the roof and chimney-pot of Kulmala before one. As it was the only chimney in the house, a friendly curl of smoke nearly always issued from it. A few fathoms further along the old-fashioned hedged village road, and one stood at the Kulmala gate, at one side of which, at this time of the year, an ancient gnarled bird-cherry was in flower, at the other an astonishingly big alpine currant-bush. Then came the yard, with the house at one side. Amidst the bushes of the yard three narrow characteristic paths had been worn : one to the byre, one to the storehouse and one to the village road. Silja stepped through the doorway into the porch, where Sofia came out to meet her. For the first time, the girl's glance shone in the Kulmala porch and soon in the living-room, where blissful and significant events were later to befall Silja. At this moment a home-like twilight dwelt in the room. Beside the living-room was a kitchen and a little parlour, where Sofia offered what refreshments she had. The piano had been carried into the living-room for the summer. The girl Laini, a fair neat-featured child, played a few familiar dance tunes and songs on it by ear. From the kitchen range a puff of smoke occasionally burst into the room. The window had to be opened, and a near neighbour walking on the road paused to hear Laini's valse tunes.

Silja sat in the rocking-chair and enjoyed herself, sensing the friendliness of the atmosphere. Her reddish frock, gleaming hair and brown eyes delighted Sofia, who had been told Silja's real origin. Every sentence spoken was of a nature to provoke a smile, when a tiny dimple would form in the girl's left cheek, appear and vanish, varying according to the talk and the smiles. She sat gracefully leaning against the arm of the rocking-chair, her dress revealing the forms of the youthful body now in the full blossoming of its womanhood. As there were no other people present, she could be and talk as she wished, without being afraid to disclose her own true self.

Soon after this visit, summer visitors from Rauhala, who enjoyed coming to Kulmala, began to sit in that same chair. Sofia would sometimes shout to them to come in, if they happened to be walking on the road. One of them was musically inclined and began to teach Laini. The others

would watch Sofia milk her cow and tend to the calf. In July
the moonlight already began to be noticeable. On such
nights the atmosphere in the Kulmala yard was especially
effective. The old master of Kamraati would perhaps talk of
former times. " You remember it well enough, Matti," he
would interpolate to the Professor, if the latter happened to
be sitting beside him on the bench in the yard.

In the early part of July a young man arrived at Rauhala to
spend the summer. His first name was Armas; his surname
Silja only uttered once, although this young man came to
mean more to her than to any other person in the neighbourhood—and more than any other person in any other neighbourhood.

The Professor's daughter, Miss Laura, was a fair-haired
erect maiden, always with the same expression, one hard to
interpret, in her eyes. She never lost her temper; her yellowish hair, curling at the temples, awakened the impression
that every emotion had already been experienced on her behalf
by previous generations. No one had ever observed her sigh
in connection with any young man. But this time it chanced
that the young man at Rauhala called Armas obviously
awakened her interest; even Silja could not help hearing how
the young lady spoke of him every now and again at the
breakfast or coffee table. Before long the young man himself
appeared at Rantoo. He was lively and youthful and the
Professor enjoyed talking to him.

It was in these circumstances that Silja first saw him. She
had to take something into the room where the family and
the guest were sitting. The young man sat at the piano and
was trying to play, and Miss Laura stood near him singing.
At the moment when Silja came into the room something
went wrong with the music and the young man spun round
and looked at her. Silja curtseyed lightly as she had been

taught to do to visitors. She wore the same dark ruddy frock of which the professor said that it fitted her a good deal better than was permissible in a maid.

When Silja returned to the kitchen, she was like one half-witted : Sofia had happened to come with her, so that there was a witness to her condition. The girl twittered and talked at random. Sofia, an experienced person, believed she understood how matters lay. Silja got rid of the things she was carrying and, totally unaware of what she was doing, threw her arms round Sofia's neck and hugged her fiercely. The next moment she was back at her work. " It's so lovely to be here," she said to Sofia, as though wishful to lay the blame for her recent behaviour solely on her delighted mood. As she helped to wash the dishes Sofia related, as it were offhand, what she knew of this summer's guests at Rauhala. " Young Mr. Armas is good-looking and nice and jolly ; have you noticed how his teeth flash when he talks, and smiles ? I do believe Miss Laura has her eye on him.".

The visitors left, and Sofia helped Silja until everything in the house was in order again. Miss Laura came into the kitchen specially to ask her to do so. Supper had been eaten and the table cleared before Sofia left. As there was no obstacle to her doing so, Silja went with Sofia, without even asking for leave, so excited she was by the events of that day. Sofia understood what was in the girl's mind and good-naturedly suffered her arm to be taken. To herself, however, she decided to warn Silja against getting into such a fever, as soon as a suitable opportunity occurred.

After that evening there was one sole purpose in Silja's life. She carried out her daily tasks, if anything with greater care than before, and stayed up late if by so doing she could gain on her next day's work. She devoted special care to Miss Laura's needs, gazing at her long and gravely whenever she happened to be near. But not many minutes would pass without her looking out towards the path that led from Rauhala. She could be quite assured that no one went from Rauhala to Kulmala without her knowledge. Armas would sometimes pass down the road, now alone, now in the company of one or more ladies. Occasionally he would escort Miss Laura to the gate at Rantoo and then turn back. But it was only when he went on farther out of view that Silja felt impatient with the work she was unable to leave. And even when she had seen the young man return and go into the house where he lived, she would set off, as soon as her work was over, along the village road and follow it—not in the direction of Rauhala, but in the direction of Kulmala, where she had seen him moving.

Once, however, it chanced that Silja went to Kulmala without expecting to meet anybody ; she was on an errand. Sofia was just laying cups and saucers on a tray, on which was a clean white cloth. That meant an honoured guest, and Sofia invited Silja too into the parlour. " There's someone there," Sofia said glibly and opened the board-door leading from the kitchen into the parlour. Silja was on the point of entering the room, in the belief that some farmwife or other was there. But, in the rocking-chair sat he whose first name was familiar to her—and who had this time reached Kulmala without being observed by her.

Silja saw him there before her quite near, his lips just beginning to open in a smile : but at that she drew back into the kitchen. This gave Sofia occasion to tease them both. She urged the young man to fetch Silja into the parlour. He rose indeed from his chair and came, first into the narrow kitchen and then, failing to find the girl there, into the living-room. There too he could discover no one at first, but soon the young man heard the sound of stilled breathing from a closet beside the kitchen door, and on his trying to open the closet door he found that someone inside was pulling hard at the clasp. There was no need, however, for any great effort on his part before the door opened and the girl was nearer to him than ever before. Sofia bustled in the kitchen and pretended not to notice the playful wordless struggle. The young man felt the scent of the girl's hair, the touch of her arms, breasts, shoulders and hips, and caught a glance from her eyes, and in it all there was just so much violence that the relics of age-old instincts in each of them were satisfied.

Silja and Armas had met, and nothing smaller than death could efface the traces and consequences of that brief moment.

Soon Silja was in the parlour : she had to declare her errand to Sofia, which was only to ask Sofia to take her place for the evening so that she could go to the main village to the dress-maker. . . . Yet the whole time her eyes flashed and tiny bubbles of laughter broke into her speech. The young man had remained in the living-room and was banging at the piano. It was obviously not real music, but merely the fierce, in-stinctive fall of his hands. Silja squeezed Sofia's arm and hurried away.

From this moment onward for some time to come it would be vain to speak of any outward development of relations be-tween Silja and Armas, so far at least as Silja is concerned.

And yet, how beautiful an ordinary country church is on a Sunday morning in midsummer, when the heavens are calm and cloudless and all the growth of the earth is attaining the height of its luxuriance, at the moment before Man sharpens his scythe to mow it down. On such Sundays people flock to the church who do not take much interest in religion during the week. In snowy-white shirt-sleeves the master bustles near the stable-door, shouting to the stable-boy who leads out the horse, before going to the shed to draw out the trap, the newness, neatness and polish of which he pauses to admire. He throws the harness over the back of his mare, now in her prime ; soon the breast-strap has been tied, the tail-strap and girth adjusted, the reins secured to the bit— every action carried out swiftly and instinctively, so that the master is able while harnessing the horse to shout directions, if need be, to his men. He drops the reins and rushes to hasten on his wife, who emerges finally in her silk dress and hat, prayer-book and umbrella in hand, shouting, she too, a command to the cow-girl standing listlessly near the byre, and coming to the trap climbs into it, a little clumsily and as though critical of the whole outfit, the master's sole concern as they are. The master steps lightly into his seat on the right, and so the couple set off at a steady jog, between fields, their own and those of other farms, soon those of another hamlet, up and down the low hills. As they draw near a cross-roads, they see through the shimmering morning heat and over the level green of a rye-field the approach of a similar couple from another farm. The horse and those in the trap are easily recognised, but there is no call to start shouting to each other, even though the two traps ascend the next rise one close behind the other. Yonder the church can already be seen on its hillock, over the village fields. The number of vehicles grows, the church bells ring. . . .

A steamer has brought worshippers by another route. Young summer visitors seized with the impulse to see the parish church and congregation. They have come by the lake-steamer, but have decided to return through the woods, by the path skirting the narrow waterway. . . . The church bells ring, a different rhythm now from that a moment ago, doubtless the parson's chime. . . . The congregation moves towards the doors ; from the graveyard come those who had something to take there, a group apart for the moment, these. Farmhands from the neighbourhood and younger lads who seek their company mingle with the crowd and enter the church, or at least that part of it from which one can easily escape after a little while. The village cobbler, he with the hanging moustaches, a public character, known to be a leading spirit in the events of this summer, goes past the church with an expression of solemn indifference. He has been to the Post Office, on Union business.

Roses bloom on the overgrown graves ; the sun heats the black silks of the farmers' wives until their cheeks glow and they try to pull down their silk shawls as low over their foreheads as the seemliness of the occasion will allow.

In church the air is cooler and moderately fresh ; only faintly can a refined nose perceive the human smell characteristic of this people, imparted by successive generations to the interior of the church. The sound of fidgeting too is low, for there is less coughing in summer than in winter. Only the long spell of coughing of some old man is clearly heard, coughing that no longer depends on seasons, but is a reminder that the flame of life in the cougher is burning low and tends to splutter as it nears its extinction.

The organ quavers through a few runs of its own, pauses and bursts full-toned into the morning hymn, in which the congregation joins—the young people clearly and correctly, sure of the melody, the old people stumbling as well as they can after. Verse after verse of the hymn rolls out, until after the closing verse the organ does not stop, but hums gently a while, as though trying to withdraw its influence over the spirit of the congregation. The clergyman is at the altar.

The church is cruciform ; on one side of the main aisle sit the women, on the other the men, facing the altar ; on each side of the side aisles the worshippers face the main body of the church.

By the time the litany has well begun the mood of the congregation has become settled. A young gentleman, a stranger to the locality, gazes from the men's pews beside the side aisle at the congregation. Straight in front of him are the women, whom he can watch in profile, as with varying expressions they follow the altar service and respond in the litany. His gaze wanders, to be sure, hither and thither among the women, to do which he need not turn his head or attract attention to himself, nor do those he looks at observe him : but he has laid note, already during the morning hymn, to one worshipper and felt an emotional tremor pass through his being, an accidental encounter divined beforehand. The girl wears a simple headdress, a white summer kerchief knotted behind her head, so that the ends hang down to her shoulders. Under the edge of the kerchief, along her brow and temples, brown locks, whose glint already seems familiar, are visible ; the face seen in profile is pure and devotional, the red of the mouth and curve of the upper lip giving it almost a child's expression.

She bows down now for the confession of sin, the words issuing in a solemn booming from the altar. One sees shoulders and bowed heads, clumsy and stiff, backs scarcely able to bend, worshippers straightening out to reveal the same immovable, frozen expressions as they wore when bowing down in confession : but the gaze of one man is fixed on a girl in the women's pews, and in the eyes of this man the girl's face appears to have become still purer than before during the confession, as though Sin itself in departing from her had left new beauty behind it. . . .

The light mood of the young man surrenders to the atmosphere of the sunlit church ; the solemn rhythm of words and the organ hymns and amen-accompaniments, all uphold in his consciousness that one single picture, in which his sensitized faculties can see no blemish. The glances hitherto exchanged in everyday circumstances, even the sweet wordless playful struggle, recalled in this place to memory, were all prized fruits of life, honey held forth a single time and no more by life's dearest flower.

So, in the life of a clean young man, moments crystallise, like pearls from the generous hand of Life itself. They fall into the depths of the soul as an everlasting treasure, where, by those who have kept them clean, they are good to delight in afterwards. But there are many ways of keeping clean and of defiling ; the same method may sometimes preserve, sometimes impair their purity.

Such is the church built and cultivated by Man during the morning of a fine summer Sunday. In the afternoon the devotional mood of the morning wears away as the Sunday itself. The fresh night draws nigh, when other paths are trod.

. 15 .

SILJA and Armas : the summer still before them.

There is a spring whence, at the Professor's express wish, his drinking-water is brought—he used to say that this little act of magic was the honour paid by him to the true superstitions of his ancestors, from which long occupation with science had divorced him. He explained also that it was excellent spiritual discipline for young maids to set off, after their work was over, with bucket on arm, for a walk down a birch-shadowed path of unsurpassed beauty. They might linger on the errand, so long as they brought the water home before midnight : whether they sat alone by the spring, reading " he loves me, he loves me not " from grasses, or with their sweethearts, was not his concern.

Silja too had to find the path : on her first occasion Sofia only gave her a general idea of where it lay. A person at Rauhala could see when the water-carrier went, first along the highway, then down a lane up to a little wooden bridge, under which a brook ran, subduedly foaming. At this point Silja lingered already on her first trip : she had been fully instructed in the Professor's views on this task. Below the bridge was a boulder-bestrewn rapid where the water mildly roared, and overhanging this, intricately interlaced, grew numerous bushes and tall reeds. The sight interested the girl ; she wormed her way through them until the soft jungle suddenly ended in a tiny meadow, in which were the ruins of an old mill. The clearing was closed on all sides ; the only view was the lush undergrowth that began again lower down, and the only sound that carried there was the murmur of innumerable little branches of the brook. A spider had fastened on one of

198

her sleeves and some white sticky substance on the other, but both were as something secretly whispered to her. . . . Having dreamed to her fill in this wonderful spot, she rose to continue her way to the well, deciding to come here again on similar walks in the future.

This resolution she carried out ; and then one day—in the week following the Sunday when she had been to church—she left her empty bucket under a bush at the roadside. The bucket, however, was visible, and was espied by one who a little earlier had seen the girl come in this direction with the bucket on her arm. He took the vessel and hid it more carefully, and then paused a moment, straining all his senses. The deepening evening seemed to be demanding a share of his attention : the meadowsweet glowed richly, the smell of moss from the brook mingling with its strong perfume to create an impression the like of which he could not remember ever having experienced. And as he listened to the babbling of the rapids, he began to imagine the presence of countless other sounds of nature behind it, each from its unknown source adding its own note to that dominant melody.

Perhaps, in that leafy jungle, a faint impression of a trace remained at the place whence the beautiful child had plunged onward. A desirous eye easily guided the pursuer along her tracks. There she sat, her dress more workday than on that last occasion, but at the same time intimate as the beginning of this summer night. The young man crept behind her back, the ear of the solitary sitter catching perhaps a rustle, though she did not turn her head. Her heart beat furiously. It revealed who the intruder was, who now revealed himself. In the eyes of the intruder, when the girl's glance finally met them, was a mischievous gleam, as though he had been younger than he was. That glance and those features Silja had seen before, in some past summer.

She remembered now. The memory came as a sweet immaterialised anaesthetic blow dealt by the summer night. Her companion too remembered—when at last, later, they began to exchange words.

"Oh—my water—what time is it—it can't be midnight yet?"

It was very near though.

The generous hand of life had dropped many pearls for each of them to preserve.

They went to the spring together, up the gentle rise of the last part of the journey, along the birch-lined path. On each side fine white blossoms, of a kind Silja had never seen before, glowed on long stems in the grass. She was almost afraid of the path; the flowers were a kind of enchantment. How was it possible she had not noted them before? They blossomed a little ago—one for each of us—and now a new one will flower somewhere—

The girl bent down to regard one, but did not pluck it. The youth jumped away from the path and brought one, holding it against the girl's face to admire it. The thin fine perfume of the night-flower harmonized with the girl's expression, in which, after the first kisses in her life, was a quite special gentle assurance. She took the beautiful white cluster from the young man's hand and bore it in her own hand at her bosom, as one may sometimes see in old paintings.

Midnight had passed before Silja undressed, alone in the neat little room that was her very own. Again she went to the window and looked out towards the birch-clad point, as on her first night here after the Professor's footsteps had died away upstairs and she, Silja, was left in her own potent loneliness for the first time in this house. Sleep was loth to come now, too, but the eyes that gazed out into the night shone with

200

a different glow. Nor did they gaze into emptiness as then, nor did her mind seek her former cabin home and the youth who rowed past on a night long past. Her gaze and mind were now turned thither where she had taken leave of her love —Armas. Nothing else existed now. Not a thought of how the Professor might be sleeping upstairs ; Miss Laura was an unimportant young person whom she happened to know. No, they had all withdrawn somewhere, she alone was living this summer night, still, a little—after all—hungry for her friend over there. She did not miss him much, knowing that she would soon be with him again. He is there, in that house, in that room, and I am his.

Once again, settled in her bed, the girl thought daring thoughts, still more tumultuous than on that former occasion. She touched her own forearm with her lips, seeming by so doing to be savouring anew those recent kisses. Cautiously her instinct guided her imagination, which sought rest from its present fever in her previous experiences. At certain mind-pictures her whole being rose in opposition—Oskari Tonttila—the visit to his home—dances—and something else from which her thoughts fled in panic whenever it threatened to come near. . . . Her mind found shelter in the blossoms of the white delicate night-flower which she had laid beside her on the pillow. It was of finer texture than any flower in the gardens Silja had seen, and surely no perfume in the world could equal that which it exhaled.

How delicious to awaken like this, awaken to life and every kind of blossoming in life, awaken while others slept, after having in some fashion been asleep all one's life—even in one's waking hours.

As once before on that first night—which the present night in this room greatly resembled—Silja awoke after the lightest touch of sleep. Now too she got up and went to the window.

But this time the sun was already rising, and again she could think of " yesterday." Only now the thought of " yesterday " was calming. The early morning, in which only the birds and the sun-touched air were awake as yet, announced that a new day had begun which, sunny though it was, would contain its share of everyday, at least at first.

The girl went back to her bed. On her pillow she saw the night-flower, now a little faded and tinged with yellow in the light of the dawn. She took it, broke off part of the stem and then put it between the pages of one of her books. Sleep came.

. 16 .

So passed the early part of the summer. Night was at one time almost non-existent, a mere holding of the breath, as it were, by the heavens while evening gave way to morning. The young and happy needed sleep only as the slightest break in their days, and very little food either. For many young people, and older ones, it was the last beautiful summer. To be sure, there are always some living their last summer, but in the case of this summer there were special reasons. Everyone had his or her premonitions, but no one knew.

Midsummer too passed. The human mind still tried to imagine the nights were white. Here a girl sat by a window reading, as midnight drew nigh, the letter she had received that evening. She even took out her writing materials and set to work on her answer; it was still light enough for that, though July had begun. And so expressive was still the nocturnal light that the writer got no further in her intention than the opening phrase: " I am writing to you in the delicious summer night . . . "—before she was lost in memories of her distant friend, fancying herself walking with him this same night there where they had once . . . and the dawn was reddening in the north-west. The young lady is on a holiday here and has hoped for more experiences than have come her way, by these hopes betraying her friend. But her hopes have remained unfulfilled, and now she tries to compose a pretty answer to her friend's letter. Only longing disturbs her. Dawn comes glowing, a precious day and night of summer and youth has gone.

A week later, when she reads a new letter, the dusk surprises her and this time there can be no thought of writing an answer. The leaves have grown darker with the nights, bats fly around the old building.

Around Rantoo way the summer has been quiet and peaceful, and even from the middle of the parish come tidings of peace. On the small farms where the workers are old friends, the haymaking passes off easily. The master tries to be merrier than usual, as though by these means to lead his own thoughts and those of his men away from the burden of the times.

Ever further the summer progresses. The rye pales, and on southward slopes shocks begin to appear. The material for bread was safe, no small matter that summer. As the sickle swished into the ripened stalks life felt safer, warmer. ... Here and there young reapers, with the fire of those mysterious times flaming in their eyes, refused to work a minute over the agreed time, although a quarter of an hour would have seen the rye all harvested. But on most of the reapers such behaviour on a fine harvest-time evening in an ancient field made an unpleasant impression. ...

The Kulmala kitchen is small and faces the north, so that Sofia already has to use a lamp as she busies herself with coffee-making and other preparations one Sunday evening at harvest-time. In her field a merry reaping-bee is in progress. A girl comes every now and again from the field to confer with Sofia, anxious lest the musician should fail to appear. Someone sets off on a bicycle to seek him. There is not much space in the kitchen, the big coffee-pot is nearly in darkness on the range ; but Sofia is able to judge its boiling so well that not a drop brims over, only the scent of coffee steals into this first lamplight of the autumn. One of the girls is helping by now to set the table, taking down the cups from a familiar shelf. Through the open window the voices of new-comers can be heard, among them the Professor's voice.

Sofia glances out of the window and sees her cousin stepping out briskly beside the young gentleman from Rauhala. The old man has a wonderful red hat on his head.

"Are you a Turk or something?" Sofia asked as she met him outside the door.

"Is there anything left to reap?" asked the Professor in turn and continued his way to the field, from which came the swish of sickles and shouted conversation, merged into the familiar noise of a reaping-bee.

The Professor had not brought a sickle with him, but at the first expression of disbelief in his ability to cut rye he snatched the sickle from the hand of the nearest worker, and grunting with the intensity of his efforts began reaping swiftly and skilfully. Beautifully the first swathe grew along his path and he went on with the second until the others all began watching him, upon which he stopped. An old cottar, of the same age as the Professor, remarked, addressing the crowd: "We've reaped together, that man and I, in earnest and all day long—I'll bet the Professor remembers the time we worked in the Hillu fields, when he was still a young man." His surmise was confirmed, and the sickle went back to its younger owner.

"Do you fancy you know something too?" the Professor shouted to the young gentleman, who was neatly tying a sheaf, which he lifted with an easy motion into the middle of the plot, where the next shock was to stand. This too was no small marvel, for he was of gentle birth.

"When did that Silja manage to slip here?" the Professor went on almost at once, as the girl threw down beside him a sheaf she had just tied. The Professor had begun in earnest to build up the sheaves into shocks, as there did not seem to be anyone regularly on that job. The smile in the girl's eyes was all the answer he got. The atmosphere of the field was intense and happy. Here and there backs straightened and eyes sought the gate, where Eemeli Kukkonen could already be seen with his accordion. Farther down the road the Professor's daughter was approaching with the young lady who was spending the summer at Rauhala. Sofia came from the yard towards the field, apparently with an invitation to coffee. Some of the reapers went, but others stayed, for the rye was nearly cut. "Don't go yet, it'll get dark if we start coffee-drinking in between." But down on the house steps someone was testing the accordion's tone and the trills fired the minds of the young so stiongly that many of them were too impatient to go on working. Finally Sofia alone remained in the field to glean fallen ears and straighten a hastily-made shock or two. In the house and beside the steps the voices of the coffee-drinkers blended already in a steady murmur. As the widow drew nearer the house she heard a rhythmic thumping emerge from it in time to a trill-embellished valse. She looked once more behind her at the darkening field, at the rows of shocks that had arisen as in a twinkling, sighed deeply and entered the circle of din made by the reapers.

All the doors were open. The shyer lads stood about and skylarked in the darkness of the porch, and to these Sofia uttered a merry exhortation. On the back bench of the living-room the Professor was sitting with the owner of the neighbouring farm, who had arrived unobserved at the house. The young gentleman from Rauhala was dancing with Miss Laura: Sofia paused to watch them. Was there anything between the two, as people were whispering? If there was, it was something pretty much settled by now, for Sofia could not see them talk much or even exchange glances. Now the young gentleman was bowing to Silja. A beautiful girl, that Silja; her eyes looked so good, especially in the lamplight.

Indeed, she looked very lovely this evening; Silja herself

206

felt it somehow. This was the highest harvest-festival of her life. No doubts about anything, she felt it anew from the arm that wound itself about her body and in winding seemed to be sensing the feel of her back and waist. This youth had recently been tying sheaves; chaff still clung to the lapel of his coat, and from his skin came a faint male scent. They danced well together; instinctively, in the darker parts of the room, they pressed closer together until each was aware of the existence of the girl's breasts. The music stopped, one could crowd through the door into the yard, still maintaining one's hold of one's partner.

The red full moon peered through an opening in the woods as though playfully spying on someone. When it first appeared it was impossibly big, only to shrink and turn paler as it rose in the sky. The dark green of the earth's surface could still add its own tinge to the moonlight; the atmosphere was warm and intimate. Silja Salmelus gazed out of her dark eyes, moonbeams entangled in her lashes and flashing reflections from her pupils.

The ale-barrel was broached, the crowd grew livelier, each member of it occupied solely with the person with whom his or her conversation was proceeding. It was easy for couples to vanish and appear again. The first rest was already over. The accordion-player had had his coffee and ale; taking up his instrument again he began a fine new valse.

The Professor's high spirits had risen higher. He listened to the tune for a while, then frowned, got up and went over to the musician. " Give it here, and I'll play," he said, and the next moment he had drawn the accordion to him as, earlier in the evening, he had seized a sickle.

" Now there's another tone in the old musical-box," chuckled the farmer beside whom the Professor had been sitting. The Professor played to the full extent of the bellows, and the young gentleman happening to dance past him just then with Silja, he winked at the youth and broke audibly into the words of a Swedish song.

The floor filled, everyone wishing to be in the dance when it was the Professor who played. By now the old man was singing loudly and infectiously; he went on while there was a single couple left out on the floor.

Silja and Armas did not exchange a word during the dance, but they clung to each other closer and longer than before. " Let's go . . . " whispered the youth's voice in the girl's ear.

No one was in the yard or on the steps when they went. There was only the moon to stare and keep on staring. It was cooler now, a fine smell rose from the dry clay of the drive, something moved in the dim grass, a mouse or a disturbed grasshopper. The barn was on a hillside, behind a cluster of low bushes. They were quite certain no one had seen them come here. The Professor had apparently stopped playing, for a couple of laughing remarks in male voices were wafted from the steps over the yard. The men had girls with them, but these made no sound. They went off somewhere towards the brook, none of them remembering the existence of the barn.

It was a warm night, the sun had had time during the past few weeks to charge young people with the whole strength of summer, the blood throbbed through full veins, and with it awoke in every nerve all the instincts placed there by Nature, almost to pain and bliss simultaneously. The cooler night held in condensed form the relaxing fire of the day. Young betrothed people sought out each other, and those too, whose glances had recently been kindled, the one by the other, walked the silent bye-paths, avoiding those who, so they believed, had never known anything like this and were therefore likely to envy them and spread base rumours ; such were, in particular, the oldest women, and men at the worst period of middle-age toil.

Hundreds and thousands of couples crept thus, nor were they aware of what they were doing. For in fulfilling the raw command of Nature their souls sank into a deep and pure childlike half-sleep. During those decisive moments the rough and foul-mouthed farmhand, who had at last succeeded in persuading the poultry-maid from the manor to accompany him, lived through the same experience as the pure gentle youth in whose embrace a noble and innocent human flower emerged from its bud. None of them remembered at the moment what Nature's aim had been, in guiding them so far. To them it was Life, the finest perfume of young delightful life, up to the penultimate moment of its climax. After it had happened, Nature drew as it were away, after-moments not being its concern. The couple might doze in each other's arms for a few moments, drawing a veil between what had been and the approaching everyday dawn.

" Let's go and dance again," Silja said, passionately clinging to her lover's arm.

" Will there be anybody left there now ? " the youth replied in a slightly cooler tone.

They went into the yard.

Down the steps came a young reaper, too young yet for such gatherings, his brain fuddled with ale, his face grey and uglily contorted. The boy hurried off and vanished. Sofia came out too and whispered to Silja and her companion where she had hidden the ale, not wishing to keep it freely available after a few of those lads had gone at it senselessly. She was giving them small beer now—" But there's plenty left for you, just try."

They went, delighted to be going together on this little secret errand. Unconsciously Silja still clung to the young man's arm, as though never more intending to withdraw her hand from it, and he had not the heart to thrust it away, so deliciously it quivered there. Indeed there was no one left to fear. The Professor and Laura and the guests from Rauhala had already gone. While they were going they had looked for Armas, but had then decided that he must have left before them.

Silja drank the ale as though in defiance, her mood seemingly still in the ascendant. Her glowing eyes sought those of her companion over the tankard with such power that the young man seemed inwardly to shrink. A polka tune still burst from the house. They went in to dance. In the dust the red of the dawn was already discernible, the musician's fingers fumbled, the keys clapped more loudly than before. A quite young farmhand, who had danced hard all the evening and not got drunk, was still dancing, though his collar had stuck together into one limp band. He danced with all of the women in turn, and politely begged for a dance with Sofia too. He did not forget Silja either. Armas watched them dancing and was strangely moved—what a perfect gentleman the boy was, so faultless his behaviour.

When Silja was free again, Armas motioned to her that he was going for another drink from a certain tankard, and Silja followed him. The girl's eyes glowed deep and unfathomable ; the youth's white teeth broke into view as he licked his lips after drinking. Then they went back to the house, a good deal more warmed than they were a while back.

" And now, Kukkola, let's have the Professor's valse," the young gentleman shouted with a queer boldness.

The tune began, and everybody danced as before. A couple of middle-aged cattle-maids for whom there were no male partners left over, danced together. They were out on a spree merely by the act of keeping awake. For them it was experience enough to be able to go straight from this house, without a wink of sleep, to the morning milking in the cow-yards and then, with the sun already flaming high, drive their cattle to familiar pastures, through a familiarly worn gate, past and over familiar cattle-tracks.

When the valse ended these same maids gave what turned out to be the signal to break up. They fetched their shawls and went in full view of all, the blameless young farmhand going with them as escort. There were no more dances after that. Eemeli Kukkola rolled his eyes a little and made ready to go. Sofia led him to the hidden ale before he left. The day was clear and bright, permitting thick folds of dust to be distinguished from the shining streaks of uncovered floor in the living-room.

Outside the daylight was still more clearly evident, or rather the early morning, which has almost a stronger individuality than the day. The time when the Professor, Miss Laura and the summer visitors from Rauhala were here seemed immensely distant. They were wholly unrelated to the life that now reigned, diminished in scale and intimate, around Kulmala. Armas was especially aware of this when he noted the growing boldness with which his girl clung to his arm.

Actually this was something both of them were experiencing for the first time. The young man had naturally danced with many girls before this, and many of them had taken his arm, but in it all there had been nothing like this. Silja had no thought whatever this night, but sped forward along the flower-bordered track of her life, speeding all the quicker for that she was now at its summit. Her soul was full of the glow

of emotion, her body had, as well, known something unfore-
seen, miraculous, ecstatic, painful—something beyond which
there was no going, beyond which one had no desire to go,
nothing shameful, nothing to deny—so long as one could
hold on to that arm, so long as one could trust as now, fully
trust. . . .

It was still some hours to their usual getting-up time.
Silja longed for an opportunity to rest together somewhere in
peace, to sit closely-held, to approach each other. The new
and miraculous she had experienced still drew her. It was unlike anything she had even imagined before, anything she had
ever heard of during the many everyday hours of her life;
not that she had ever stopped to ponder over the meaning of
what she heard: such phrases had recoiled harmlessly from
her. Thus her experience of the night had no connection in
her consciousness with anything she had ever heard mentioned.
It had no connection anywhere, neither with the past nor with
the future; it was merely life on this blissful night, for which
everything in the past had been, and from which onward the
future was a blank even to the imagination.

"Let's go that way yet, there's such a beautiful rock
there."

They passed quite close to a solitary sleeping farm. Silja
knew the way. They followed the garden fence, climbed a
rock mound, which gave excuses for helping each other, came
to a smithy and went on through a lush pasture, until a belt of
bushes thinned, showing a rock cliff that fell steeply before
their eyes down to the shore. From the top of the cliff the
crowns of the spruce growing along the shore could almost be
touched. On the opposite side of the narrowish channel a
long narrow bay opened out, at the end of which the sun was
just rising. The sight joined together in strange fashion these
two playthings of Fate. The place had been known to the girl,

and here she had brought her lover in this dawn when her past life was in any case over, happen what would.

It was easy to feel that here was peace undisturbed, that not even chance could bring anyone here at this hour. Only the sun rose and saw. The young man and the girl—the young woman—knew already what would happen to them here. No uncertainty, no fear, nothing—only the miracle revealed by their now merged lives.

They were never to learn whether their arrival together was observed at Rauhala or Rantoo. Miss Laura, who did in fact see it, was too high-minded to disclose it to either of them.

But when the day began the atmosphere of Rantoo Villa, hitherto so fresh, seemed in some way to have become vitiated. Even the Professor's wings drooped a little, as he himself described his condition, adding his opinion that it was due to his staying up past midnight and then being unable to sleep at once owing to the ale he had drunk. At the breakfast-table, just as Silja was bringing in a dish from the kitchen, Miss Laura remarked in a careless drawling fashion that the young gentleman Armas—her own words—was said to be leaving by the day-steamer. The dish in Silja's hand shook a little, so slightly that it would have been impossible for anyone to swear that it had trembled. Perhaps Silja's steps, as she went back into the kitchen, were quicker than usual, with an effect of acceleration, but the door did not close any more loudly than usual, and no sound came from the kitchen.

Most noticeable of all was perhaps the very fact that nothing was heard from the kitchen, although the serving would really have needed continued attention. When the bell rang for her, Silja came in as one asleep and empty-handed, although the signal was for her to bring in the next dish.

" Well, are you too dance-befuddled, like me ? " growled the Professor.

" It wouldn't be surprising if she were, seeing that she came home at four," Silja heard Miss Laura answer.

" If this wasn't Silja's first dance, I might lose my temper, but I'll let it pass," the Professor said.

Miss Laura made no reply—except by her silence.

. 17 .

SILJA was inwardly very well aware that her life at Rantoo could never again be what it had been as recently as the previous day. Even though she were to remain, life would never be the same, even where the villa was concerned. The sooner she could escape and be alone, the better. The breakfast dishes gave her the solitude she needed.

It gave her the opportunity of sinking while she worked into that frozen stare that seemed to encompass the whole of her being, so that it neither knew nor sensed anything, but merely existed. Somewhere outside of her a voice seemed to be whispering : you have shared the same fate as so many others of whom you have heard in your everyday life ; exactly the same thing has happened to those others—and then the man has gone : as this one is going, unable to see you any more, perhaps afraid. The consequences, Good God, what were they ? That, and that, shrieked the outside voice which seemed to emerge from the rattle of the spoons. It shouted and shouted—much more as well, everyday truths such as the time one had to wait before one could be sure.

The girl stood stiff and dazed beside the sink, listening to the rattle of the spoons, which went on embellishing and flashing forth new aspects of her situation. Armas, Armas, where are you ? Come and keep me from falling into this bog !

But Armas has told those people that he will be leaving to-day, in two hours he will be going somewhere—where, of that Silja had no idea, not having thought of asking. How had it been possible for him not to tell her he was going then, on their moss-grown rocky couch ?

There he was coming now, turning towards Rantoo and entering the yard. Naturally he could not chose the kitchen door, but had to enter by the main door. Silja caught a flash of his fine profile through the window. He looked paler than usual and wore a travelling cap and another suit. His face was less merry, but as pure as before.

The family received him in the big living-room. From her place in the passage Silja could hear what was said without having specially to listen. A letter had come for him while he was dancing with the girls in the evening, with the news that his mother was seriously ill. He had to go. The steamer would be here in an hour.

"Well, shall you be coming back here?" the Professor asked.

"That'll depend on how matters turn out."

He then said goodbye to those in the room, seemed to be recalling something, and—"Oh yes—I have to say goodbye to Silja too," she heard him say. He was coming towards the kitchen.

He had time to see a moist flaming glance and a familiar beloved form that dashed out of the kitchen door and slipped into the cellar. The young man returned to the living-room and said something about the girl not being there; would Laura please give his regards. On Laura's face was a very still smile as, standing quite near, she looked past the speaker and made no answer.

Thus passed the young man from the Rantoo circle and nothing certain was heard of him afterwards—until the next summer, when similar tidings and worse came of so many others. From what she had seen from her window that morning, Miss Laura drew the conclusion that he had invented the letter about his mother's illness and that all he wanted was to escape. When, long afterwards, she heard that his mother had really died three weeks after his departure, she was ashamed of her suspicions, although she had not disclosed them to anyone.

Silja, who was left to bear all that had happened during the night in her soul and body, saved her happiness by that little flight. The gentleman who came to say goodbye was only a distant shadow of the beautiful youth with whom she had walked in the twilight while the night-flowers bloomed and had lain at last on a mossy bed in the red light of dawn. When Silja heard his voice in the living-room, her instincts arose in fear. Her own soul quickened and enlarged everything; it clutched the treasures it had acquired and fled from anyone who tried to draw near. The whole of this villa, which up to now had been like her own distant home, more indeed in these most intimate matters of all, now seemed to have become an ordinary coarse farm where the master swore, the mistress scolded and the village men made advances to the maids. Worse—because it had once been so good. Silja felt that she would have to go away very soon, that every moment made her life here harder and harder to bear, for each moment added to this new life of her soul. It could not be beaten down, for then it would have cried out everything aloud under its own pressure. Silja felt that she could not even control her eyes. When the family went down to the quay to see Armas off, Miss Laura glanced into the kitchen and saw there Silja, the maid. Silja could not help looking straight into Miss Laura's eyes. In that brief glance was a humble plea for support and help, and also defiance. An unconscious long-drawn exclamation broke from Laura, and her own glance revealed admiring, almost envious surprise, and deep disgust. By that exchange these two young and in no small degree noble feminine souls were joined in lasting acquaintance.

Happily, Sofia happened to call while Silja was still alone in the villa. Sofia came, as level-tempered and good-natured as ever. She began familiarly chaffing Silja about what she had noted on the night of the dance, watching with understanding the expressions in the girl's eyes and bustling about in her former manner. But when she heard that the young man was probably just then stepping on board the steamer, she was seriously surprised and stopped her teasing. Silja said no more, not even about the illness that was the cause of his departure, though she had heard of it. She guessed the direction of Sofia's thoughts and, almost as though deriving some consolation from it, let the atmosphere remain charged. In any case Sofia's sympathies were with her, Silja.

Silja had almost to fight down her tears when she asked Sofia to take her place for the evening, as she had business in the main village, the dressmaker and other matters.

Sofia hastened to consent a shade too eagerly. " Do go, my good girl, and stay all to-morrow if you want, I'll do all the work here ; as I've done it often enough before—you go. . . . "

" I'll go now then, at once, before they come back from seeing the boat off."

Sofia looked long at the girl, looked as at something well known, a repetition of something in her own youth. Instincts almost of motherhood awoke in her towards the unprotected girl. Not, however, that she could bring herself to think hard thoughts of him who was leaving. She could not imagine that a young man like him would leave such a beautiful girl to her fate—and if matters began to look as though he intended to do so, she would discuss the matter seriously with the Professor, who would set everything right. The worst obstacle might after all be Laura, although there never had been anything between her and the young man ; that at any rate was plain.

Silja went. When the party came back from the quay they were surprised at first and then a little disconcerted. There was no deceiving old Matti, the Professor, in these matters at least. He growled out something and made a weary gesture as though warning anybody not to try any explanations on him, for they were not equipped to be his enlightener, as he was wont to say to the assembled family. He climbed upstairs and one could hear by the beat of his footsteps that he was not to be interrupted. A few minutes later he was seen to go down to the lake with his specimen-cases and nets. It was his customary round whenever anything happened ashore that disgusted him. He would stay on the lake for hours, then remain as long upstairs with his instruments—until the bath-house had been heated, and then go from his bath to bed.

Laura, too, let Sofia do what she liked. The young lady gave her relative to understand that she had no desire to discuss the whims of servants or to hear any hints about which partners had danced most with Silja on the preceding night. On her face was the self-satisfied, rather absent air that revealed nothing. Quite as though she had her own plans about everything, and everything was proceeding exactly as she had planned. She might make, at the most, some trifling addition to Sofia's suggestions for supper—merely to show that the events of the day had not put her out in the slightest degree.

It was a perfect summer day in August, but it is unlikely that anyone at Rantoo observed it at its golden height.

One, however, of the recent inmates of Rantoo was aware of the beautiful August day from its zenith to sunset, for it was her sole companion from the moment that she left the familiar paths of that summer. Silja walked on in the sunshine without any destination, seeking only for high ground from which the longest view of the lake could be obtained.

At one side of the village, behind well-known houses, was a hill where short yellowish grass grew, criss-crossed by cattle-tracks. One could just as easily avoid the paths and walk anywhere ; the ground was free from twigs and the air light to the lungs. From this vantage-point she saw the steamer moving southward and the Rantoo family returning home, Miss Laura's familiar red sunshade glowing as though it had been a giant flower plucked from the roadside that she was twirling. She walked some distance in front of the others. And there went the steamer, an everyday occurrence at this hour, yet strangely solemn now, as though this time there could not be the usual tobacco-smoking old men and lumber-jacks on the foredeck. Silja turned her glance away, studied with eye and ear her surroundings, as one preparing for some action, and then cast herself on her back at the edge of the open hill-top, bending her head backward so that the sun shone on her face from below.

The surrounding peace rushed into her consciousness with an effect of a hissing noise. Among the stunted young forest up here there was no individual tree upon which a fugitive soul might fix its attention. Not a single bird's nest in the forks of the bushes or on the yellowing ground, not a little piping mother came to cry out her distress to the human intruder, not a flower at the tip of any stalk to attract a blue butterfly. Only the leaves of the alders, dark above and grey underneath, but otherwise unconscious of their purpose. They too never reached the age of blossoming, but were cut for brooms or to fill a manure-heap as soon as they began to rise above the height of a man. These alders never flowered, only sent forth shoots from their roots, ever new shoots.

Somewhere on this hill cows and calves came to graze, per-haps a few sheep too. But now not a single bell tinkled. On the western slope was a series of springs ; there grew green birches and even the alders could not be prevented from attaining to the dignity of trunks, so that in the spring catkins hung from the branches, like fragments of an old-fashioned gold chain. Pollen smoked in the air at such times, and in winter one saw elongated seed-pods. There the cattle now lay, having eaten juicy grass and drunk sweet water from the springs, lay collecting scented milk for the children of the dwellings below to drink and the women to churn—in those dwellings, where strong couples who had found each other lived and multiplied.

The sun shone on the face of the lonely outstretched woman so fiercely that she was compelled at last, dazed, to turn on her side ; a fit of shivering made her at the same time instinctively crouch into an attitude resembling an embrace. She crushed ever harder her own breasts, her body straightened, arching out backwards, and she moaned aloud.

Evening was coming—where could she go ? and with whom should she go ? She could not be alone, after last night. Where ? where should she go . . . ? She knew nobody, and even if she had known however many, she could not accompany anyone, there. . . . Only him who had gone.

No one who had chanced at that moment to come along one of the cattle-tracks and see her could have helped being alarmed. But no one came, not even a cow or a sheep. The woman fought, fought her fight, until her moans turned into open and fierce weeping, which lasted for a while. Then her crying abated. The day was by now clearly inclined towards evening. She rose into a half-sitting posture and on her face, in the red-streaked cheeks and expanded pupils of the dark eyes, was again a calm, almost ecstatic expression. Everything was over, and she felt that a new phase of life had begun. All that was left to her was to guard with wisdom this new state, lest it too should collapse through new contacts.

Her mood held; the evening promised an exaltation of even giddier height than that she had known the previous evening. When at last she got up and began to walk away, in the direction where the sun had tended, a violent fit of shivering and a feeling of faintness assailed her. She circled the hill until she had come to its western side, where the springs were. Stooping, she drank from the hollow of her palm the cold iron-tinged water, which sweetly caressed her dry mouth, but provoked a new and severer fit of shivering. She felt that she would soon be in need of her bed. What was to become of her? She could not go back to Rantoo, not on any condition, she would sooner stretch herself out at the foot of yonder tree. Pain, increasing in volume, drove her nevertheless stumbling forward, until she saw beneath her the roof of the Kulmala house. Laini, anyhow, would be at home.

Silja descended to the gate, where the Kulmala cattle were waiting for the evening to fall. Laini was in the yard and saw her curious arrival, watching with staring eyes as Silja brushed past her into the house, without the usual words of greeting or explanation. And even afterwards about all Laini could do was to go on asking questions—" Why did you come from that direction? —where have you been?—weren't you at home? —didn't you see mother?"

" Yes, I saw her and I was there, but give me something now —have you any milk?—can you heat it for me?—I don't feel well."

It was hard, however, for the girl to do anything: it was so amazing that Silja should come down to the house from the hill. As the child went on obstinately questioning her, Silja finally said in a weary tone: " Never mind," and stretched herself out on the bed in the living-room, on the edge of which she had sat yesterday between dances. She lay there at full length, shivering violently now, trying to turn the counterpane over her for cover. Her eyes were closed; occasionally an agonised moan came from the mouth shadowed by her hands and the coverlet. Even Laini grasped that it was no use her asking Silja anything else. She left Silja alone and hurried to her mother at Rantoo. As she passed through Kamraati yard she had time, however, to tell the mistress of the surprising event, and so when Sofia hastened home from Rantoo, the neighbour was already in the Kulmala living-room and able to whisper what she had observed of Silja's condition. " It looks to me like there was something wrong in her head, for there's no sense in what she says; she talks about reaping and tying sheaves and says the end of the straw has to be put under the loop and not left standing up."

" No, let everything be as it is, and let me keep it," said Silja at that moment, opening her eyes and looking at Sofia, the mistress of Kamraati and Laini. " No—there's nothing wrong with my head, but it's so hot—and cold," she added.

" What am I to do with her ? " sighed Sofia. " I can't take her anywhere in that state."

" Do let me stay here, for the Dear Lord's sake, He'll give you too what you pray for—I can't go there—dear Sofia."

" Do you think she has anything on her soul ? Ought I to send for the parson ? If she dies where she lies, it'll be the everlasting loss of our souls as well. . . . "

The Professor came hurrying down the path and burst into the room all in one rush.

" Confound the girl, to go wearing herself out dancing like that. Let me feel her—ooh, what steam she has up. Has she said anything ? "

" A little, all mixed up—the missus here wonders whether we oughtn't to bring the parson to see her."

" Aye, and why not the sexton with him, it's all he's got to do during the week, watch for corpses—and pay the ground money and grave-digger and bell-ringer," stormed the Professor, rather more coarsely than he intended.

" Well, everybody can't afford to be as careless of their souls as the Professor, who trusts in his worldly wisdom."

" Leave other people's souls, at least, in peace. What is in danger here is a body, so if you want to be sure of escaping perdition, run off home as quickly as you can and send that farmhand of yours, Taavetti or Jerobeam or whatever his name is, for a doctor. I'll pay."

Grave of countenance, but with deft sure movements, the Professor arranged a compress for the girl and started placing it himself around her. The girl wound her arms trustfully round the old man's neck as he lowered the naked upper part of her body on to the compress. Soon everything was in order, the last pin fastened and blankets drawn over the patient. The girl seemed to calm down and fall into a doze.

The women had looked on attentively, and the mistress of Kamraati, in spite of the recent encounter, could not help whispering the old proverb about whoever was clever at one thing is capable at another. The Professor laid his hand lightly on the girl's forehead and then gave an order for her to be left in peace. The old man was quieter now himself and made pushing movements with his palms to get the women out of the room. In the porch he opened his mouth once more and said : " And now I'm telling you, Sofia, not to let any old women in there to crow. The girl's best medicine just now is peace. Keep some pure water and fresh milk handy in case she wants them when she wakes up. The compress can stay on until the doctor comes. After that he can do as he likes."

The Professor was off already along the road, his pace suited to the present occasion : it was easy for anyone who knew him to guess his mood from his pace and the way he held his arms. Just now his left hand was in his coat pocket, his right in the armhole of his waistcoat and his head calmly erect ; obviously he was pleased. He felt a quiet pleasure, as though his aged blood had warmed without the aid of wine, at having been permitted to give effectual help to a fellow human being, a young, good, beautiful, unprotected being. A hard fate, but she'll bear it—I sent a message through my hand to her brain to hold out, thought the old man to himself as he walked, smiling softly at his own fancy.

Silja's soul moved in strange regions, seeming to float away, with the cool eternity for sea, into regions of blue and gold. Far away in the distance was the port whence she set sail : yesterday's reaping and her arrival at the dance, all part of this same voyage.

Soon she found herself lying somewhere in the cool of the dawn, with something pressing on her so that she felt a sharp sting on the right side of her chest. "Not so hard, darling"—Sofia caught the words as she bent over to awaken Silja to be examined by the doctor. He stood gravely waiting, and although Sofia was shy on Silja's behalf because of that remark, he seemed not to have noticed it, but began his examination when Silja staggered to a sitting position.

Most pleasant it was when the Professor came back some time afterwards and began changing her compress. The room seemed more than ever to resemble the old home cabin near Mikkola and the Professor was like father—soon she would see the moonlight and hear the frost crackle.

It is summer though outside, somewhere in front of the house is a birch-clad point of land, it is a beautiful and blissful Sunday night, a young unknown man is rowing on the lake. . . . The Professor noted that the girl almost hugged his neck when he lowered her on to the bed. This time he sent his secret message to hold out to the girl's nerves and subconscious mind while he was thus holding her—her head resting on his left palm, his right palm aware of the beating of her heart within its cage.

Silja's illness took its normal course from the following day onward. In the daytime she was fully awake, recognised the room as the Kulmala living-room, tried to take what was fed her. The evenings and nights she spent in those lands of blue and gold, where the islands were golden, the water blue as the finest silk, as was the sky. She fared onward there, arrived somewhere where great honour was shown her, the crew of her own vessel completely outshone by the beings who did homage to her, there where she had come. She sought their king and was directed to the presence ; she bowed and curtseyed deeply and looked where she was told to look, but saw only a medley of gold and blue that seemed about to take fire. At that she tried to divest herself of her shoes, but a being beside her pointed to her feet, and she saw that she was already barefooted. And her feet were quite flawless and white, although she had believed she had a slight lump on one foot and had been ashamed. But now that she saw the beauty of her own feet she took heart and said to the king who was a medley of burning blue and gold : " Behold, I am what thou hast made me—am I a flourishing branch of the vine ? Do I flower ? And is my beloved mine ? He clings to the branch which is I, and kisses the flower that is within me—his breath strengthens me, his spirit dwells in the circle of my flower. . . "

Sofia tried to give Silja the medicine ordered by the doctor. Silja awoke to full consciousness.

" I dreamt that I was finishing my Confirmation Class— someone was preaching."

A special kind of gravity spread over Sofia's face : such talk was disquieting from a sick person. What was she to do ?

226

The Professor had forbidden her to speak of spiritual matters. " Even in church your soul is not as pure and ready as Silja's," was what he had said. A thought occurred, however, to Sofia—it can't hurt the girl if I read her a beautiful hymn from the hymnbook. She asked the girl which hymn she liked best.

Silja made no answer, but when she saw the big hymnbook in Sofia's hand she cried : " Don't read about that dreadful destruction of Jerusalem ! "

" My good child, I hadn't thought of doing so."

But Silja had closed her eyes and seemed to be suffering, and Sofia, her desire to read gone, did not repeat her offer. In her next stupor, however, Silja saw blue-grey and in its midst her father, who was confusedly, almost unwillingly, telling something about her, Silja. Then he caught Silja's glance and drew aside, seeming to set her free—to go there where she usually wandered.

One evening Silja—she had just been looking at her transparent hands and remembered that that was her name and that someone had said it was beautiful—one evening, thus, she had taken her medicine and felt calm. Her hearing seemed to grow acuter, and she heard Sofia talking outside over her tasks. Her sentences were short and matter-of-fact ; she was teaching Laini rather sharply. Silja also heard carts passing along the road and her ear told her that they were laden with grain ; it was easy to tell that by the heavy, but muted rattle of the wheels. The clock ticked on the back wall, a fine new-fashioned clock with turned and polished pinnacles and an exasperatingly slow beat. The day must be some days after—after—after she set out on this journey. When was it she set out ? Wasn't it that night and the Sunday before her father's death ? That was when she set out, but had she taken the right direction, seeing that she now lay here and was unlike all those others who had also set out some time,

Sofia looking after her house, the men driving the loads of grain.

Everything seemed a mistake, a wrong step. The living-room displayed its walls and furniture, built and made by Sofia's grandfather, so Silja had heard ; the Professor's mother was born within these walls. Shall I ever have my own living-room ? Haven't I a husband, aren't I his wife, after we have . . . Where is my husband ? No, my husband is not he who went. He danced with me the whole night and loved me with all love, as I him—but he who went was thin and pale.

An immense wave of longing swept through the girl ; she herself did not know what she longed for, she only felt within her something that strove agonizingly for fulfilment— once having entered that path. Terrible that she could not undo that departure. If she could get it all back again, she would press it all so close to her that nothing, not a thought, could come between. There would be no agony or pain then. Only being, and everything would be fulfilled.

That evening Sofia walked across to Rantoo and told her cousin that she hardly dared to continue with the responsibility of nursing the girl alone, as the patient had again been so restless that it didn't look as though she would last long.

" Wait a bit," said the Professor, " when was it she fell ill ? Let's try to get someone to help you. Meanwhile you go and give her what was ordered."

And then Silja paid her last visit to the land of burning blue and gold. Again she wanted to meet the king who was merely a burning spot in that wonderful country. In the fire, how-ever, there was red to be seen this time, a dark red like con-gealed blood. And again her feet were flawless, and white and clean as those of an infant straight from its bath, and she walked on them towards the king. . . .

But it was no longer a king; the fire turned dim and from behind it came a well-known sweet whisper, and unseen arms were laid around her: " I am here, this is my soul, but you must still return to earth, to wait for me, until we meet again." And everything grew cooler and faded, seeming to melt together into cold streams. As though a play were over and the dawn come.

Day was in truth breaking; it was morning, a calm and peaceful August morning, when Silja opened her eyes and saw around her the familiar living-room. But now the cracks in the wooden walls were like a greeting from a distant land of childhood. Beside her bed stood a very clean-looking, ruddy-cheeked woman in a blue dress, with a kind of white cap on her head. Silja gradually understood that the stranger was there for her sake, so intently was the woman's attention fixed on her; Silja's awakening seemed to be matter of great joy to her, though she hid the feeling so well that one guessed it only from the friendly beaming of her face. She spoke to Silja rather as though addressing a child. " Let's have a nice rest now and be happy. Soon the sun will be high in the sky and bring us quite a new day."

As Silja lay in her bed half-asleep, one part of her mind still seemed to be looking backward there where the whole of it had been a little while ago. It was hard for her at first to think of all this as illness, rather was it something into which she had been rushed this summer, though it felt as if all her life had been shaping for this end. Closing her eyes she could still see shining gold which now resembled the back wall of a church: the bright frame of the altarpiece, the cheerful numbers of hymns on an oval frame beside the sacristy, all seemingly in movement as the organ began to sound. Silja had time to examine the vision of a church wall—it did not belong to the church where she had been confirmed—it was something far more distant in time, a place where she herself was walking up the aisle with her father and a quiet woman who was probably her mother. A sister and brother of hers had died and been buried to the sound of church bells, though all that Silja remembered of it was that walk along the church aisle. For that matter, she had been to church this summer too, to the parish church here. . . .

The day continued to be absolutely calm. The sun shone brightly, yet the air remained so crystal-clear that every individual noise could be distinguished. There had already been one slight frost that had silenced the ceaseless summer rustle of nature, that sound of a myriad tiny living things, each inaudible in itself, but together capable of filling the warm air of high summer. The rhythmic beat of flails now began to be heard. Silja asked Sofia whence the sound came. Sofia explained volubly all she knew of the day's work on the neighbouring farm, quite as though she were seeking by her words to caress and encourage the convalescent girl, and to lead her back to sight of and contact with the incidents of life. It was a great joy to her that the girl was recovering, seeing that she had had to remain in the house.

Later in the day came the Professor, whom Silja had entirely forgotten. This time he did not come to the bedside, but sat in the rocking-chair, gently swaying. He spoke openly as he was accustomed to do, but in a controlled and intimate voice. " Well, my girl, you were so close to the gate of the Beyond that I bet you've never been so near since you were born. Now you'll have to lie nicely still in that bed for a bit longer and try to work up an appetite."

Then for a time all was quiet again. Silja was left alone. From the yard came the clucking chatter of hens and occasionally the louder cluck of a cock. A sooty thresher called at the house to see Sofia. He smiled as broadly as a nigger, seeing

230

Silja on the way to recovery. Silja remembered that he had been one of the merrier dancers when. . . . Her tired mind instinctively avoided recollecting where, preferring to seek shelter in those wondrous excursions to the land of dreams, a land that grew, alas, dimmer as health returned.

Gradually Silja began to long for such solitude where nobody and nothing connected with this place could intrude. During her illness something seemed to have been burned away from what came before, her past was as it were shut off behind that devouring veil of fire, and her returning life could build only on what had been strong enough to endure the fire. For this reason Silja longed to be somewhere else, where a new period too of her life could begin.

She followed obediently the instructions of her nurse, as one biding her time: and really she had no idea where she would ultimately go. In her eyes was a level smile, an inheritance from her father, though there was no one here to recognise it as such. The face, eyes, hair and whole being of the girl all displayed a special fragility and ethereality; the thin flush on her cheeks seemed to have in it an element of shyness. If Silja had not been obviously convalescent, there might have been cause for alarm in her appearance. As it was, Sofia used to look at her long.

Nevertheless, the day came when Silja walked across the floor and gazed through the windows at the familiar scenes of that summer—even at Sofia's field, whence the rye had been cleared away. That was where they had been reaping—and tying sheaves. . . . From the side window she looked out into the yard and saw the gate and the beginning of the path that led—there. . . . She was still very weak, for she felt almost giddy, looking up at the clear autumn sky.

Cloudy days came too, and on one such day the Professor arrived, lively and bustling. He came to say that they were off to Helsinki the next morning, he too. He asked Sofia to come as before and take the keys and gain an idea of how everything had been left so that she would know if anything was disturbed.

"Who knows all the changes there are going to be here?" said Sofia.

"Who indeed?" sighed the Professor, "but what I do know is that this girl of ours has only changed for the better." He got up and began taking leave of Silja. "Goodbye, Silja, and thanks—it was short and pleasant, your stay with us, and I would really have kept you on after you got well, but for the fact that I'm moving into new conditions. Aye, well. You stay here with Sofia until you're quite strong. You can afford it all right, your illness hasn't cost you anything. Then look for a situation on some quiet farm, where you can breathe the air of a cattle-shed, that's what your lungs need. Goodbye, dear child."

The old man was off along the road, and Sofia had to dash after him as best she could. She had only time to whisper to Silja what the Professor had already hinted: that the old man had paid her every penny that Silja's illness had cost.

When Sofia returned in the evening, she brought with her Silja's wages, from which nothing had been withdrawn. The old man pretended to have forgotten it while he was at Kulmala that day. It was clear, however, that he had merely wanted to prevent any protest by Silja; perhaps the girl's look of gratitude would have moved him too much.

"There are not many fathers who take as good care of their daughters as the Professor has done of you while you were ill. But Matti has always been a bit different from other people; his blood is still warm for all his age, and no one ever knows all that's in his mind."

. 18 .

COLDER and colder grew the autumn, until one morning the ground was covered with rime. Mankind enjoyed the treasures gathered for them by the summer; their food was now at its strongest. Bread, milk, butter, potatoes, and meat and fish too, were all at their freshest; the power of the summer sun still dwelt in the forage fed to the cattle, and the bread of mankind tasted of new grain. Everybody felt strong and hearty; young couples who had found and known each other in the heat of the summer, now planned marriages. Even the land acquired new strength, for it was well manured and the sky rained sufficient moisture on it for the beginning of a new growth the next spring.

For Silja a situation was found of the very type the Professor had recommended. At the farther side of the parish was a quiet farm called Kierikka, and one of the village old women got Silja taken on there. She could go as soon as the cattle were taken in for the winter.

On the morning of her departure she went, accompanied by Sofia, to Rantoo to fetch her belongings. The house was deserted, and as no fires had been lit for some time, it was also chilly. They went through all the rooms, stopping to look at familiar thresholds and corners. Sofia chattered softly as though to herself, Silja answered only by expressions and looks; to her it was as though they were moving in the weekday silence of a church. It was only now that she was taking farewell of the past summer. For her this was the beginning of the solitude for which she had patiently waited since her recovery in order to assemble her memories.

She came at last to her own little room, where everything

233

was as she had left it that sunny day of departure. How long ago was it ?—nearly a month now. In this cool air it was easy to think of days and weeks as they had actually been. One could recall whole months, recall the distant day in early summer when she had come to this house and stayed in it alone with the Professor. Even he had gazed out then at the summer night and been reticent and spoken softly. Silja began to feel as though the Professor too had just had to part from his own home, as she would be parting in the evening.

Stuck behind the lintel of the door was a twig of rowan, its peeled stem yellowed and the leaves dried. Silja looked round to see whether Sofia was watching, and then threw the twig into her basket with her clothes. On the cupboard rest were her hymnbook and Bible history : she remembered what was between the leaves, but did not look. No, not until she had reached the final silence and solitude. . . . What kind of sleeping-place awaited her ? At least there was no other maid where she was going—and if she was not allowed to have a light at night, she could look at them in the moonlight. The moon was nearing its fullness. She had to leave this place quickly.

Sofia heard Silja coughing in her room. She began to hasten their departure, remarking that it was not healthy for Silja to stay too long in such cold rooms, weak as she was.

" What, when I'm starting work as a maid this very day ? " Silja shouted back in answer.

Sofia came to the door. " I'm sure you've had a good time in our village this summer. I suppose it feels sad to have to go."

"There'll be other joys perhaps at Kierikka," Silja answered in a rather strained tone.

" Not of the kind there were here—but perhaps the Lord will send a new summer, and then you can come back here,

234

you know," Sofia went on as she busied herself with some trifling task.

Silja stood at the window with her back towards Sofia, as though she had stopped to wait for something. Sofia had an impulse to lay her hand on Silja's shoulder in passing, when the girl suddenly turned round and hugged her, and it felt as though she were silently sobbing. Sofia understood and had nothing to say; she let the girl remain where she was as long as she liked. She patted the girl's shoulder again. "Don't you worry, Silja dear, we've all got our own troubles in this world, you're not the only one in anything—even though you will be alone, at first. You thank your luck that you will be alone, many have had to go through worse."

"How do you know what is going . . ." the last words were lost in the folds of Sofia's blouse; the girl was like a child on Sofia's ageing breast.

"Well, I do know that—and I'm sure a person of your age knows that much about her own condition," Sofia said in a grave voice.

"I—I haven't thought of that at all," sobbed Silja, "it's only life altogether . . ."

"There's cause to think of that too. It's little you know of this world, you dear child. You wouldn't know anything until you held in your lap what I and many another have held. Your life will soon be on a right footing, at your age, for you are pretty and a good girl and will soon find a husband, if you only get better and stronger."

The girl still tried to express her feeling that Sofia had been good to her and even now, when there was no one else. . . .

"It's easy to be good to the good," Sofia replied.

A noise had sounded from the yard as though a horse had been pulled up there, and now, while Silja was still sobbing on Sofia's breast, someone could be heard tramping up the

kitchen steps.   Their moment of emotion thus came to a
speedy end.   Sofia went to look who had come and recognised
the owner of Kierikka.   Silja followed her into the kitchen
ijust in time to see a man, past middle-age, shake hands with
Sofia.   The man explained that he had been told at Kulmala
that the girl was here in the villa, so he had brought the trap
along.   " I suppose that's her," he ended.

" That's Silja Salmelus," Sofia assured him.

The farmer made no motion to shake hands with Silja, but
started pondering aloud : Could it ... could she be the
daughter of that Kustaa who had to leave Salmelus Farm,
which—Aye, Roimala it was who got it.

A solid and stolid sense of everyday had entered the room
with this topbooted farmer.   It dominated the atmosphere
now that he was the only man under the villa's roof.   Silja
felt as though some impertinence was being committed towards the Professor, as though an improper spirit was spread-
ing through the chilly atmosphere of the room, and as though
she too were helping to spread it.   No more feeling of a silent
empty church.   Soon, however, they were outside.

" As there's nothing in this house to offer a guest," Sofia
suggested, " we might all go back to Kulmala for coffee."

The farmer protested that he had no time.   " Let's get the
girl's things in the trap and start off," he said.

The things were therefore hoisted up and a start made.
Silja was already in a mood not to care whether she entered
Kulmala again.

Kierikka's movements were rather indolent ; obviously he
was not in the habit of working every day.   His head was
always in the same attitude, whether he was lifting or setting
down a burden, and his breathing became heavy at the slightest
effort.   His nose had an appreciably high bridge to it, but as
there was a scar very plainly visible at the highest point of the

bridge, his nose looked as though it had a growth on it. Sofia had previously told Silja that the Kierikka family used to be a rather proud lot, but that their prosperity had waned under this present master and life at Kierikka was now something of a struggle to make ends meet.

Kierikka seemed much more at home driving than he had been at lifting Silja's belongings; it was easy to see that he had done more driving. The reins, to be sure, were of common hempen rope, and boards were missing here and there in the body of the trap, but the man's manner of driving was that of a big farmer. He sat on the right side and when they came to forest he looked now and again at the maid beside him with little, rather impudent side-glances.

" Did your father leave you anything, or was he quite cleared out ? " he asked once.

" I forgot to find out from the Professor, he looked after that matter last," Silja answered.

" Ah, you're quite a fine young lady, with a professor for cashier, he-he. He's a lively old man even at his age."

" Oh he is," Silja admitted impulsively.

" Did you find that out too ? "—and again came the quick impudent side-look, and the flash of the scar on his nose.

Luckily Silja had not fully understood the farmer's question and the look that accompanied it, so that for the present her impression of him remained that of an ordinary farmer.

They came to the first of a cluster of backwoods huts. The ruts in the road were occasionally so deep that the hubs of the wheels touched the road surface. Near the hut was an oldish man, who screwed up his eyes as he answered good-day and added : " Kierikka's still taking girls for rides, I see, instead of turning over a new leaf."

" Well, Mikko, would you grudge me what you have had yourself," the farmer answered, adding to Silja, after they had passed out of the man's hearing : " There's an old scamp for you—lives in his hut with a woman, and neither the priests nor the Levites can do anything to stop him. Babies keep on coming—for the parish to feed, when all's said and done."

They drove past low-growing sparse forest, meagre fields with stopped-up ditches, grey ramshackle dwellings in which, as often as not, one room was still only half-built, or a window opening stopped up with shingles. Forty years ago the builder had intended to add a room to his hut, but still there was only the hut, that too with rags and shingles in the place of panes broken long ago. Silja had never seen anything like it, having always lived in more fertile areas. Even the cabin where she had spent her childhood with her father was of another class than these backwoods huts beside the muddy bad road. Her removal day. . . . Far different her road now from the lake along which she had fared last May to her summer's fate.

Could Kierikka be somewhere here, among similar surroundings? No, it was not; the master had only taken a short-cut through this backwoods community. Soon they were back on a properly sanded highway, along which, at regular intervals, mile-posts rose like fingers. Even a couple of telephone wires followed the course of the road. Beside this road too was an occasional ramshackle dwelling, but in some way the good road seemed to ameliorate the impression of misery. They could at least look on mile-posts and hear the humming of telephone wires.

The forest grew sparser ; houses were more frequent, and some of them displayed the windows of her childhood : two large panes side by side, and above them a third of like size placed horizontally. Rags and shingles were to be seen only in an occasional bath-house window. Here was a bigger house with an orchard around it. The farmer let his horse

238

drop into a walk, and Silja began to think they had arrived at their destination. It proved, however, to be the next house. First came a storehouse built of stone on the left side of the highway, badly cracked, for its foundations had given way. Over the door was a long stone slab on which, in old Gothic letters, the name *Kalle Kierikka* had been cut. A little farther on was a cow-house, also of stone and in a better state of preservation than the storehouse. Silja had read the name over the door and knew where they were without asking.

The farmer took his task so seriously that he drove into the yard through the main gate, although he could have reached it via the cow-house. Between stone pillars an iron gate was suspended with the word "KIERIKKA" in wrought-iron letters in the centre. They drove through the yard to the porch. At the other side of the yard was another building, the guesthouse, in which no one lived; fine white curtains showed through the windows. The two buildings had originally been painted different colours, but time had worn the paint down to pretty much the same tone in both. Mud was everywhere in the yard.

The present master was not the Kalle Kierikka whose name was over the storehouse door. Kalle was the master's brother, who had lived and died nominally a bachelor; during his rule the farm had remained on the whole as prosperous as before and even acquired a certain outward splendour, as wayfarers could note. The present master's first name was Hermanni; he had not troubled to repair such of his brother's works as began to decay. Silja was first shown into the living-room. The walls had once been plastered with clay, which had since fallen away in many places; apparently the foundations of the house too had moved. The beds obviously hailed from the time of the former master and were a kind of sofa, the bedding being hidden during the day under a board cover that formed a seat. There was one such bed near the door and another behind the big oven, against the door to the kitchen. Silja grasped that the latter one would be hers.

The mistress was much more talkative and livelier than the master. Twilight had already advanced so far that a tiny oil dip burned in the kitchen when the master and the new maid entered the living-room, from which one could look into the kitchen. The mistress was busy there, her skirt tucked in at the waist, showing the topboots she wore. She had obviously begun the evening chores for the cattle and was therefore slightly out of humour at first. She scolded her husband for returning so late.

"It's not through wind and clouds we've been driving," the husband defended himself.

But the mistress had already turned to her new maid. "Well, it's the first time a girl has been brought to us from a fine place like the Professor's. Wonder if you know what you have to do in a low farmhouse like this. Do you know which end of a cow the calves come from ? "

"I've tended cattle nearly five years," Silja answered.

"Oh, well, you ought to know your job then," the woman went on in exactly the same tone, which Silja was to find out was her usual manner of speaking.

Silja had seen farmwives before, and was therefore not surprised at her reception by the mistress of Kierikka. She was aware that she looked delicate, and that the woman might have good grounds for talking as she had done. The mistress could not be expected to know or to understand the wonderful exception formed by the past summer, which weighed more in Silja's experience than all that had gone before.

A tall, reedy, dull-faced farmhand appeared near the living-room door and went through a series of habitual movements :

240

took off his topboots and placed them in the arched aperture under the big stove, fumbled in his hanging cupboard, lit his pipe, but uttered no word. Silja gleaned from the mistress's remarks that his name was Aappo, that he had been at Kierikka a couple of years and had no intention of leaving.

Silja also made the acquaintance of the cattle and even milked three of the cows. She had milked a few times at Kulmala while she was convalescent, so that she was not wholly unaccustomed.

The effect of it all was that although there was a bright moon that night, as Silja had expected, she was unable to keep awake, but fell at once, in her bed behind the stove, into a deep sleep. When the moon reached the part of the sky visible through the nearest side window from Silja's bed, its beams fell on the hair and profile of a young woman, a delicately-drawn nose, mouth and jaw and a pale cheek, all resting on the girl's left hand. The thin coverlet revealed to the moon the contours of her body, which seemed to repeat on a larger scale the curves of her face. . . .

The moon of heaven was indeed the only witness who had known the girl throughout her young life. It had occasionally watched over her sleep at Salmelus, when the cheek and profile of the girl still displayed the round curves of childhood. It had gazed on her later, over a shining surface of snow, the first time she had been near the gates of Death, whence the loving care of a father had recalled her. As a pale summer moon it had seen the ripening maiden on various paths, and had never disapproved of what it saw, but looked back un-flinchingly whenever the girl—or her companion—cast a glance at it during a moment of happy silence. Once—not so long ago—the moon had been half-hidden in foliage, there too as though turned away—and on its way elsewhere. It had disappeared without seeing any more of Silja on that occasion, and for many nights it was absent, until returning once more, it peered forth, narrow, and turned the other way. It wished to follow what was happening to Salmelus's daughter; it swelled and watched her recovery, noting again on some evenings an old man near the girl's bedside. And now the moon was full, as the girl had hoped it would be when she reached her final awaited solitude. But the poor body was tired and slept; the moon did all the looking while it dwelt in the part of the sky from which the bed could be seen. And after that it threw its beams nearly the whole night long into the air of the room to keep Kustaa's daughter company while she slept.

For that matter, the moon had seen Kustaa in his youth, and also Hilma, still beautiful as she moved about the Plihtari yard. If the moon had been a sentient being it would surely, gazing on the sleeping girl and remembering all that had gone before, have drawn a deep breath, perhaps a slightly tremulous one. But after all, there is nothing sentimental about the full moon, which merely throws on the sleeping and waking alike the stream of light poured on it by the sun. Until the sun itself arrives and does it directly and powerfully, more powerfully than any act is performed on the earth.

Silja slept at once so soundly that she failed to hear even a howling from the road. The highway passed quite close to the Kierikka main building, only the width of a fathom separating the road from the edge of the highway ditch. A few of the village lads were aware that a new maid had come to Kierikka and wanted to show their interest at once by a serenade outside the house. The song they sang was not, however, one of the familiar country airs, but spoke of the proletariat and blood sacrifices, " if needed." The master was still awake and told the mistress that he had met two men with red rosettes marching in step as soldiers do, and that they

242

omitted to answer his greeting. The same fellows were now probably yelling outside.

"Not they, it's that Kalle Mutkala and Vihtori Lovela, I know 'em, who've scented a new bitch," and the mistress turned over, disgusted, and went to sleep.

But the master crept into the living-room, where, having established that its two inhabitants were asleep, he went to the rear window and looked out along the moonlit road. He was in time to see the two young men his wife had mentioned ascending the adjacent rise. Nevertheless the type and tune of the song had awakened evil apprehensions in the master's dull farmer-soul. He turned his back on the windows and looked as it were at both of his servants at once, letting the impression gained by his mind from them sink of itself into his consciousness—and then walked back to his bed. Once there, he still lay awake a few moments, and a slight indefinable fear was not far from his mind. There's so many of these poor people that nothing'll help us if it comes to a tussle. They'll take us farmers' property all right—ran Kierikka's thoughts, the while his breath already came loudly as in sleep.

Silja had thus failed to hear anything of the song, and was unable to understand what the mistress meant by her coarse hints the following day. She went on learning the work of the house and made the acquaintance of the food and drink provided. They were unlike those in the Professor's house, but in the food itself and the manner of eating was something that hinted that one could eat much ; the human beings ate in the living-room and the cattle in their own quarters was another thought that occurred to the mind. And as a matter of fact human and cattle food were spoken of in the same breath here. The same soil provided both.

It became a problem where Silja was to keep her clothes. "There's never been a maid here with so many clothes," the mistress said roughly. Yet she could not help admiring Silja's fine dresses and wealth of underclothing, to the extent that her nature admitted of admiration. Finally, Silja's clothes were stored in the family's private storeroom. The mistress was quite pleased to permit it, as soon as the situation had become clear to her. Gradually, Silja became aware of the consequences to her. Though she was much slimmer than the mistress, many of her clothes could be worn at a pinch by the older woman.

Then one night during the month of her arrival, Silja lay awake, as she had tremulously imagined she would do at once. The night was at first quite dark, but after Silja had stared at the darkness about an hour, lying moveless on her back, the horizon beyond some place unknown to her was strangely illumined, and a little while later the moon rose, big and red. As if it had heard the girl's prayer while still below the horizon, it was shy and turned its face away, to the right. It seemed to be casting side-glances—as much as to say—I know—I have no advice to give, but I do know.

Notwithstanding the size of the moon, the moonlight was so dim that Silja had no desire to get up and look at anything. She no longer even looked at the moon. With her head bent slightly backward she lay in the same position and same state of mind as on the hill beside Kulmala that day when a steamer left and she fell ill. She lay hugging to her bosom what she had found in the land of shadows, amid the blue and gold, in the shade of a burning bush, when someone had whispered to her words she could no longer remember.

. 19 .

OUTSIDE in the everyday world November came. Foggy silent days when the rooks hopped along the cattle-house eaves avid for the remains of slaughterings, and the jays, more timid cousins of the rooks, flew around the barn, screeching and flashing the gaudy surfaces of their wings. Not many signs of work were visible on the farms ; here a load of fodder might be seen moving, here a master on his way to the storehouse. According to old custom, all farmhands were holding holiday week. . . . A hundred years and more, life had been like this at this time.

Yet life was different. One noticed it perhaps less around Kierikka, which lay in a remote corner of the parish, but in the centre of the parish the change was obvious enough. The workers were again in a ferment, as in the spring at sowing-time, and now the masters too were organising. They founded bodies of guards and exercised. Only one farmer in Kierikka village joined them ; a man recently arrived in the village and of an active character. Kierikka " couldn't be bothered " to exercise, but treated his neighbours to thin platitudes suited to a master. They contained a moderate amount of old farmer wisdom, a mild annoyance at the working classes in general and especially at those who went to meetings—and a phrase picked up somewhere : " It's like this, agriculture can't compete in this country with industry." To such a sentence not one of the old men round that way could even think of an answer.

In the main village the Red Guard disarmed the Farmers' Guard, which it called the " Slaughterers' Guard," held its members imprisoned and extracted from them a solemn

245

declaration that they would never again oppose the aims of the workers. Pale and weary for lack of sleep, wealthy farmers signed their names to the declaration with trembling fingers and were allowed to go home.

All through the parish arms were being taken away from farmers. Kierikka had to give up an old muzzle-loading rifle that had not been fired for at least twenty years ; it could not even be loaded, for the children had broken the moulds for the bullets. It was confiscated, however, Kierikka merely remarking as he took down the musket from his wall, " You'll bring it back yet, remember my words." " We will, we will, when the people has calmed down again," the old tailor, a famous reader of books, assured him. In his younger days he had spoken at Bible meetings ; now his head nearly shook under the weight of this new ideal and the rise of the proletariat.

In the neighbouring parish a whole shipload of Russian soldiers had been around, and a well-known farmer and a commercial traveller passing through the parish had been killed. The master of Kierikka did not believe the story about the Russians. " The Russian soldiers won't meddle in them matters. It'd have to be a bigger thing to get them moving," he said importantly. " Well, they've been this time, and that's a fact," argued the cottar who had dropped in to talk matters over.

The master of Kierikka was not—any more than the mistress—a reader ; the only paper that came to the house was a tiny parochial news-sheet that adhered to a policy of strict neutrality. And the only part of this sheet read at Kierikka was that which contained the advertisements, after which a conversation would begin about who knew the farm at the other side of the parish which was advertising a cow for sale—in which matters the farmhand, who had worked on

246

most of the farms in the parish, was the biggest authority. The result of this slight interest in public matters was that the inhabitants of Kierikka were able to remain rather long in peace of mind and body in spite of the troubled times.

When fighting broke out in January the farm was not seriously disturbed nor were undue burdens laid on it. The horses were often requisitioned, but as the Kierikka horses were a poor lot and the best one, the mare, was in foal, the Reds frequently passed over Kierikka and impressed horses from the other farms. Kierikka had nevertheless to furnish grain and other food.

Then, in the early part of the war, events occurred at Kierikka which would have brought it prominently enough to the notice of the Reds, if they had known exactly what occurred. The Reds had their sentinels, armed to the teeth, in the most curious places. Nevertheless, during those first weeks it was very easy to slip through, almost under the noses of the guards, as, shivering in the cold and with thick fur caps drawn over their ears and nearly over their eyes, they drew at their cigarettes, so that one could see the stationary glowing tip a rifle-shot away. Many were weakened by hunger when they joined the Red Guard, and the strong and fatty foods they ate in enormous quantities dulled their otherwise poor and unpractised power of observation. Thus it befell that two men, strangers to the district, came into the Kierikka living-room one evening. They related, to be sure, that they had come from Tampere and were on their way to the front, but their story was unconvincing. They were obviously not workers. They pretended to be tough, but could not hold their cigarettes as a real rough holds his, moreover in trying to do so they revealed the delicacy of their fingers. Their story, too, was rather vague. One of them said that they had been advised to call at the farm, to which the mistress hastened to

247

say that she didn't know of anyone who could have sent strangers to call on them, and began winking her eye at the master. "And if it's the front you're thinking of going to, why headquarters aren't far off from here—there'll be someone coming from there for the evening milk any minute, so you can go along with them."

The others present in the room were the master, a neighbour and Silja. The younger of the strangers looked most at Silja, looked indeed so warmly that his glances were observed. "We're rather in a hurry," the young man said, "so could that girl come and show us part of the way?"

"You can have her for a little while, provided you don't take her altogether," the mistress answered with ill-tempered coarseness.

"We'll be seeing you again," the men said as they went.

"I'm sure I don't want to set eyes on you again," the mistress said as the door closed behind them.

Silja had put on a warm coat and a woollen shawl over her head when she set out to guide the unknown young men. She seemed to read a request to do so in the eyes of the younger of the two. And after they had crossed the open yard to the stable passage, this young man seized Silja fiercely by the arm and whispered : "Listen here, girl, you are pretty and look kind, surely you are not a Red at heart."

Silja could not help laughing and in some way admiring the passion in the young man's voice and movements. "There's not even a red cow in the byre any more, since headquarters took it," she said, with an intimate laugh.

"Hear this, girl. Do you know that our life is in your hands? Help us, for we've got to get through the front Kuuskoski way, and I'll bet there's a Red with his gun on every path."

"That there is ; the first one's over there, by our barn,

even now; but it's only Ville Teliniemi, and he won't eat you."

"Don't joke, but tell us some other way to get to Kuuskoski, some way through the forest—and some place, if you know one, on the way, where we can rest and get food."

Silja offered to bring them food from the house, but the men thought it safest for them to go. So they set off, the strangers on skis a little distance on one side, but following Silja, who walked along the road. She guided the strangers past a few houses, the men-folk of which were all away at the local Red Staff headquarters, until in the shadow of a barn in the forest she stopped and sat down on the step. The men made a detour to reach her, and Silja then explained as well as she could the direction they ought to take and carefully described a cabin where she had once been, whose aged owner she knew.

"Tell him Silja Salmelus sent you, and he'll trust you." She told them they could count on getting food there and further guidance.

After the men had repeated their directions, the younger and more passionate-natured of the two suddenly seized Silja and imprinted a firm kiss on her lips. "If this ends well and I ever come back here, I'll marry you, God help me, I will."

"Don't promise too much, I've got someone," Silja said, looking in the direction she had told the men to go. "Now you've got to be off, and I too," she said, adding—amazed at her own words—"give my love to Armas." The excitement of the moment and of her own soul found vent in this sudden and unconscious remark.

The young men scarcely heard the last sentence, or perhaps took the final word to be "army." They were off in the direction pointed out by Silja, who walked back to Kierikka, her mind aroused to a new warmth. It was wonderful how life kept on bringing her such sudden events: something began—acquired momentum—and wore out. The girl hurried along the winter road, the sensation of the hug and kiss still alive in her consciousness. Her bosom glowed, the snow and ice seemed to vanish, it was a summer night again on Kulmala hill or on the path to the spring, bordered by night-flowers. The stranger who had arrived from the unknown and gone on into the unknown—had taken from her a kiss to carry there where she guessed her friend of the summer night to be. He was surely there. He was there and would come thence and they would meet again, a much better meeting than this past summer. Behind them was now a joint waiting and expectation ; they would seek each other without further thought, without shyness. On the finest night of the summer they would go straight to the verge of the remotest forest meadow, to the brink of the woods. . . . It was delicious to wait in any circumstances, when what one awaited was—this. And when waiting called forth its own sweet symptoms in which, in the midst of the January forest, was blended the scent of a meadow in summer.

The girl's mind glowed on the dark road. The snow gleamed white—and along the snow at the wayside came two men on skis, with rifles slung across their backs. When they saw Silja, a sharp command rang out: " Stand ! " Silja did not realise at once that she was expected to stop in her tracks, but took a few more paces, whereupon one of the men unslung his rifle and presented it at her. She stopped calmly.

" Where've you been ? " the man asked.

" I was over there—walking."

" You've been guiding one of them slaughterers—you tell the truth now, and it'll be better for you in the end."

" I've nothing to tell. Let me home, there's the work to do yet."

" We'll show you your home—if you weren't a woman, you'd have sung your last hymn. You come along with us to headquarters, they'll blow the whims out of you. Forward march."

The men changed their minds, however, so far as to call at Kierikka on the way to question the master and mistress. The mistress began rattling off : " Two tramps called here all right, but they weren't given anything in this house, for I says to them, you go to headquarters, that's where they know all about matters, I don't know anything, and he asked that Silja to show them the way, I do believe they were making eyes at each other, or so I took it to be, and I said Silja could go, go on and show them the way, but I'm sure I don't know what road they went and don't care to know. . . . "

" Best take Silja with us to headquarters and the master can come with us so's we can find out whether you've had such callers before."

" What good will I be there, when I don't know anything about the whole matter," the master grumbled.

" Well, this trip won't take you long, and we haven't time to go into the matter properly here. Come on now," the older man said in a commanding tone.

The local Red Staff sat in their usual cloud of tobacco-smoke, looking calmly patient, as those may look to whom power has been given. These few cottars and labourers, whose forefathers, and they themselves in their youth, had laboured hopelessly year by year without bettering themselves whether they worked hard or lazily, for them this sitting about at headquarters was a real achievement in their lives. They had food, rest, tobacco, and pleasant talk. It was for them a mighty and thrilling experience, especially in the early days of their power, to order many formerly stiff-necked landowners to do practically anything. It made the quieter ones almost giddy at first, awakening in them a queer feeling that they had entered a path the end of which would be terrible, whatever happened. The same feeling attached to arrests of acquaintances and their examination at headquarters.

The Staff knew Kierikka and were well aware that he would not harbour Whites. He wasn't capable of such deeds, nor would he put himself out to undertake them—he never wanted "to be bothered." And as regards Silja, they grasped that if she had meddled in such matters, it was pure childish ignorance on her part, so that all that remained to do was to frighten her.

"Tell us straight out now what men they were and where you took them," Rinne, the headquarters boss, said to her in a gentle tone.

"I don't know who they were, and I was to show them the way to headquarters."

"That wasn't the road you took them."

"You can get here that way. They said they wanted to go round by the forest."

"Ho-ho, that I do believe they did," Rinne laughed. "Well, how far did you take them?"

"To Kivilahti's barn. They asked me to show them the way first to the nearest member of the Staff, and doesn't Kivilahti belong...?"

"He belongs somewhere, anyhow. Well, what else did they ask you?"

"They didn't ask me anything—at least I don't remember."

"Silja can stop here for a bit then, and perhaps her memory will improve. You, Kierikka, can go home, but you look out that your maids don't get any more sweethearts of that kind, and if they do, be quick and report it to us, or the blame and the consequences will fall on you."

252

" The girl won't have to be very long here, will she ? We'll be in a bit of a fix at home . . . we've not been unfriendly towards you."

" That's nothing to boast about now. Everybody's got to be as they're wanted to be this time. You go and keep a lookout for any slaughterers dodging round your yard. . . . And as for the girl, I daresay you'll get her back in the morning. We only want to find out what those slaughterer lads did to her in the barn—whether there's any hay sticking to her back—and that kind of thing."

Rinne spoke now in a rather harder tone. At the bottom of his heart he despised men like Kierikka, who could not even be looked on as worthy opponents, and secondly, he had an old slight grudge against the man.

" You hop off home, old man, and leave the girl here, seeing that you thrust her on slaughterers," said a stranger who had the appearance of a townsman.

Kierikka went. What else was there for him to do.

When Silja was left behind, no one seemed to pay any special attention to her. Rinne and the rest of the Staff went into the next room, after motioning to Silja to sit down on the bench in the living-room. Behind a table sat a man ready to issue permits of various kinds, elsewhere were seated a couple of horse-drivers from the village and a few members of the Red Guard whom Silja did not recognise. These made lewd remarks to Silja now and again, but she refused to heed them even by a change of expression. After trying the coarsest words they could find without awakening the faintest tremor of disgust on the girl's face for their pains, they desisted.

Rinne's wife, a friendly even-tempered woman and a cook much in request, invited Silja into the kitchen for a cup of coffee.

"She's a prisoner and can't go anywhere," said one of the lewd-mouthed men.

"I know this prisoner and can keep watch on her," answered Rinne's wife. "You come along, Silja."

At that moment the telephone bell tinkled and in the next room Rinne began speaking:

"Is that the Vuoniemi Staff—Rinne speaking from Mahanala Staff Headquarters—Want to report that two slaughterers will probably be trying to get through your way to Kuuskoski—they were seen here at Kierikkala this evening —stale news, did you say?—escaped—what were your sentinels doing . . . shot?—what the hell—a sentinel shot and no one heard at barracks—the Devil's own Devil."

The voice stopped. Silja had heard and guessed everything. Rinne was heard to go into the living-room and ask where the girl had got to.

"She's being treated to coffee by your wife," answered an unknown voice.

The door opened. "Silja Salmelus here," came Rinne's sharp command, in his voice not a trace of his recent light humour. The girl's heart contracted; she turned pale and staggered, uppermost in her mind Armas, whose name she had cried, and another, whose shadow had passed over her. In spirit she sought and found support—and followed Rinne. This time they did not come to a halt in the living-room, but went straight on into the back chamber, where the Staff were sitting.

The men looked grave, but of any special energy there was no trace except in Rinne. His moustaches, which he was continually twisting upward when he spoke naturally, when he also pronounced most words as they were written, were now left to droop in peace. He said in an unfamiliar, yet controlled voice, speaking partly to his companions, partly to Silja:

254

" This Silja Salmelus has helped two men to cross the front, two dangerous enemies who shot one of our sentinels on their way. Do you confess to doing this ? "

" I confess what I already confessed, that two men came to the farm and the mistress told them to go to headquarters if they wanted to get to the front. When I went to show them the way they said they would rather go round by the forest and asked where the nearest member of the Staff lived, so I showed them the way to Kivilahti's place."

" What arms did they carry ? "

" Neither of them had any arms."

" How do you know they hadn't pistols in their pockets ? "

" I know they hadn't, because I—I'd have felt them."

A faint smile showed on the faces of the men. Silja felt that she had said a great deal in favour of the two strangers—some instinct of self-defence had brought that impossible insinuation to her lips.

" The girl's been what she has been to them, but hasn't helped them, not to her own knowledge she hasn't," one of the men said.

Silja's expression did not alter any more than it had done in the living-room. An absent air was on her face ; almost she seemed to be turning over pleasant memories in her mind. Even when she was spoken to she did not come back to reality at once. Rinne said :

" Aye—the best punishment for her would be to hand her over to our boys to be what they wanted her to be to them, but a good Red soldier wouldn't want the leavings of a slaughterer."

A noise outside put an end to Silja's examination. A group of Red soldiers had arrived from somewhere. Rinne went out to hear their errand. They asked for someone to drive them to Kurkela's place. Silja heard the request plainly ;

Kurkela was the one farm in Kierikkala whose master had joined the Farmers' Guard. Rinne whispered something to the men and was shown a paper. The strangers appeared to find it hard to lower their voices, which creaked as in a heavy frost. "Yes, it'll be done to-night. Who's going to drive us there ? " she heard one of them say. "Take the girl in yon room," one of the men who had been there when Silja came was heard to answer. "She's just been caught helping slaughterers," another added in a judicial tone. "What's the good of a girl like that, we'll put her against a tree . . . " "No, we haven't concluded her examination yet," Rinne answered in his learned style, and a laughing voice added : "We examine our own girls here." "Where's Teliniemi ? " Rinne's voice rose over the hubbub. "Here, captain," came the cottar's answer. "Take one of the horses on duty and drive these men where they want to go. You're under their orders."

The party set off, and Rinne came back into the back room. Over his recent grimness of feature a peculiar shine seemed to have settled, and he was twisting his moustaches again. One of the men asked him who the strangers were and received an answer in Rinne's choicest language : "Who they were did not become quite clear to me, but my impression is that they were travelling inspectors of the Slaughterers' Guard."

"Doubtless they were. And now what about this girl who hugs slaughterers so tightly that she knows what there is in their pockets—what are we going to do with her ? She's a working girl, though one of the benighted sort, I'll admit."

"That's so, she hasn't been mixed up in anything, I'm sure of that. Let her go as soon as it gets a bit lighter out-side."

"Very well, but she's got to join the Union and have her poor brains enlightened. Where's the membership-books—
256

have you the money with you to pay your entrance fee ? "
All this, said in a kindly tone, showed that the visit of those
men and the peculiar solemnity attaching to their departure
had transferred the Staff's thoughts to other matters than
Silja's case. Bigger things would be happening in the
neighbourhood that night. When Teliniemi returned from
his drive, they would know. The time was still so near the
beginning of the war that very few had so far been in direct
contact with bloodshed. The maid of a shiftless farmer faded
to insignificance, when a big landowner was to be . . . these
cottars, good-natured at heart, did not pursue the thought to
the end, but felt the need to take all the more enthusiastically
the part of this poor girl. In Rinne's eyes and soul a silent fury
burned, for he did think out matters to the end, so far as
Kurkela's fate was concerned, but he too had no more direct
interest in Silja.

His wife came from the kitchen. " Stop all this talk now,
Silja hasn't done anything wrong, a poor maid like her—
come with me into the kitchen, Silja, and I'll make a couch for
you where you can lie down until it's morning and then rush
off for the milking so that we can get our drop too—and don't
you ever get mixed up with such lads again, however they
may tempt you."

Silja lay down on the couch pointed out by Rinne's wife,
but did not sleep. From the living-room came the sound of
voices and the clicking of rifle-sights, but after three o'clock
it became quiet there. The Staff slept in the back room.
Once the telephone rang. Rinne answered in a sleepy voice,
peeped into the kitchen and then went back to sleep. A little
later a sentinel came in and set about awakening his relief,
who grumbled and protested, so that it was some time before
he could be induced to rise. At last Rinne's wife awoke and
made coffee, in spite of Silja's offers to do it for her. " Oh

yes, and then there's your permit forgot, we'll have to wake up one of the men to write it for you."

Others beside the clerk awoke. A couple of the most lewd-mouthed of the men who had sat on the benches the evening before awoke and sat up.

" Well, militia-man, aren't you going to see the girl home, after licking your lips all evening ? "

" Yes, God help me, I am," and the man spoken to jumped to his feet.

" You going unarmed ? " a third put in seriously.

" I've got all the arms I need on this trip," the rough said, slipping his arm under Silja's—nevertheless he came back and thrust a pistol into his pocket.

Silja did not know the name of her escort, but remembered having seen him at a dance. He was a tall fair man, inclined to jerk his legs and shoulders as he walked.

" Well, where are we going to cuddle ? "—and as Silja made no answer, the man drew out a cigarette holder, blew down it, and failing to dislodge the cigarette-end, placed the holder in the cup of his left palm and struck sharply against it with his right palm, when the fag flew into the snow. He blew down the holder again and stuck it in his mouth while he chose a cigarette from a packet and replaced the packet in his pocket, after which came the fitting of the cigarette into the holder, the lighting-up in the shelter of his palms, and finally the flick of the match-end. Every movement was carried out as though the man enjoyed doing it and was proud of his ability to do it as smoothly as any other rough, no matter what part of Finland he came from.

In the south-east the sky was turning yellow. Silja walked as in a strange new world into which she had fallen the previous evening in the Kierikka living-room. At her side walked the rough, emitting faintly improper remarks that were as though smeared with some kind of fat which made them slip out easily, with an effect of friendliness, between puffs at his cigarette. Silja listened and at some could not help feeling slightly amused, so that she smiled, which of course spurred on the rough.

They walked on until, beyond the last house in the village, they came to an old log-barn with a doorless opening facing the road. Here the rough proceeded to action. He stopped and made Silja stop, the girl still unaware of his purpose. It soon became clear enough.

" Come on now and let's warm ourselves in the straw," and he began pulling Silja there by the arm.

Silja looked at him in surprise, but as the man went on tugging at her arm and was now reaching for her other arm, she shook herself free. At that the rough changed his tactics ; he snatched her into his arms and carried her into the barn.

He failed to observe a sleigh coming slowly from the direction whither they had been proceeding, the driver's rifle leaning against the back of the sleigh. In the twilight the solitary driver caught only an impression of movement near the barn. He secured his reins and, reaching the barn, opened the safety catch of his rifle and with the weapon held out before him stole to the door-opening. From within came the sound of a wordless, but fierce struggle.

" Who's there ? " he yelled, his voice unnaturally angry because of the darkness.

" Reds, from Mahanala headquarters—is that Teliniemi ? " the rough answered, clambering out of the barn, but still holding the struggling girl by the wrist.

" It is—but what the devil are you scrapping here for ? Let the girl alone, if she doesn't care for you."

" Well, what happened on your trip ? " the rough asked, as though wishing to change the subject, at the same time releasing the girl, who shook herself angrily before proceeding on her way.

"It's over now," Teliniemi answered, looking straight ahead. Silence reigned for a moment, until the rough asked:

"Where did those fellows go?"

"I drove them to the station."

"Ah—I bet they were a hard crowd," the rough said and sat down beside Teliniemi.

"So long, girl, and good luck to you," he shouted after Silja.

In the south-east red had crept into the yellow of the sky by the time Silja reached Kierikka. It was not worth while going to bed, so she sat down and waited until the mistress should appear for the milking. The fatigue of the night had vanished, a queer supersensitive alertness possessed her. She felt unusually well. Since her departure from the house in the evening life had tended steadily upward. She could not have explained her sensations, nor did she dwell on them. Something that had slept for months had awakened, and Silja knew that it would never sleep again as long as she lived. She waited.

. 20 .

THE next morning she heard that the master of Kurkela had been found shot on the ice beside the road. The matter had been reported to the Staff, who had promised an investigation. Silja told nobody of what she had heard and seen at headquarters.

The Red reign lasted seven weeks in this parish—long enough for the quietest inhabitants to become used to it. Here and there a local member of the Red Guard would sit in all peace in the living-room of a farm and talk to the master without any special hate on either side. The farmer might even risk a few remarks against the Reds so long as he did not lose his temper, and even then a cottar long acquainted with him would only warn him. When the Whites came the farmers generally did all they could to save their own men and dependents. For during the first few days after the parish was captured, White soldiers from other parts of the country would go to houses pointed out to them by some local inhabitant, and if they found the man—or woman—against whom information had been laid, would lead them out and shoot them behind the house without further ado. The judgments of the " court " sitting in the main village were also of a summary nature. The great flood of prisoners created a lack of accommodation and other troubles, compelling the court to hasten over its work.

The Kierikka family, after that visit by the master and Silja to the Red headquarters, did not come into any contact worth mentioning with the revolutionaries. The farm lay a little aside of the route leading from the station over the ice to the front, and Kierikkala village as a whole saw little of any other evidence of the war than the local Reds. Thus Teliniemi sometimes sat in the living-room at Kierikka when he came to fetch a horse, talking of the situation at the front, to which the distance was about ten miles. Teliniemi was a likeable open-hearted fellow, who knew very many people. He knew of happenings round Siiveri way : the master of Siiveri had been killed—he was found dead at the roadside with a bundle of old bread-ration cards in his mouth. He knew also that Oskari Tonttila was dead. Oskari had been ambushed while taking a few soldiers to the front. The men had turned the sleigh as quickly as possible and reached safety, all except Oskari, who fell. He had been buried last Sunday.

Of such matters Teliniemi sometimes spoke in the evening in the Kierikka living-room. Occasionally he would glance at Silja and with a wink make sly hints about what might have happened to her if he had not chanced to come along. " He'd have worn you out in the end."

" I'm not to be worn out unless I feel like wearing out," Silja would answer in a similar tone, but the girl's smile revealed to Teliniemi that she was grateful to him. To questions by the Kierikka household Silja would only reply : " Teliniemi's always inventing things."

Towards the end of March the atmosphere in the parish, which had gradually become settled, again became disturbed. Orders came in an ever-increasing stream, some of them quite incomprehensible—as for instance the one that no lights whatever were to be shown in houses after dark, because, it was said, signals might be given. Goods were also being commandeered which had not earlier been in request. Thus one day two men, one young and the other old, came to Kierikka and said they were collecting sleigh-rugs. There was only one rug in the house, and that a tattered one, but it was taken. " There's no arguing when it's an order," said the older of the two, a bald-headed old fellow with a tangled beard, deadly in earnest.

" Anybody's good enough for a ruler now, like that Jussi Toivola," Kierikka remarked when the men had gone. He had happened on one of his trips to see the old man before, though he lived at the other side of the parish and in one of the remotest backwoods. Kierikka gave a description of Toivola's hut and of the man himself, finishing up with the opinion : " You can say that a rifle has had far to seek there for its bearer."

The excitement in the air of the village became ever tenser. If anyone had chanced to study the expressions of the Kierikka maid Silja during those days of suspense, he would have laid note to a warmer glow behind her lashes and a higher flush on her cheeks. No one, to be sure, had time to study the expressions of a farm-maid in the prevailing excitement, but of all those in the village, Silja was probably the one who waited for the coming decision with the most passion. For she awaited, hoped and believed that it would bring with it more than a mere change of soldiers and officers. All through those days and nights, wherever she might be moving or resting, she felt that the two youths she had guided were already waving to her across the din of battle. They motioned to her and to someone beside them, as if to say : he's coming, for whom you are waiting and to whom you shouted a greeting when we left you. And the more fear, on the one hand, and emerging malicious triumph on the other, met and clashed around her, the more Silja forgot what was at stake for these others. Her own mind was filled with a swelling beautiful hope. The passage of time seemed in her consciousness to be carrying her nearer to some former distant sunny hour, the turbid sleep of the interval fell away from her.

She began, more frequently than before, to stare in the

direction whence the new was expected to come, and sometimes forgot her work, so that the mistress had occasion to say: " Are you so sure that there'll be any bigger blessing for you from that source, seeing that you are on tiptoe that way every minute ? "

It so happened then one evening, after two separate groups of Reds, each unaware of the other's existence, had been to the farm and demanded horses within half an hour of each other, from which the conclusion was drawn that matters were going badly with them at the front, that Silja was standing at the north end of the yard. She set out along the path in the direction in which all her instincts drew her. And now a stealthy movement became apparent farther down the path. The dark apparition of a man stopped at a bend in the road. Silja too stopped, then went forward a few paces.

" Is that Silja ? " came a low fierce whisper that sounded familiar. Hearing her answer the man came forward and began to speak, breathlessly :

" The front has given way at Kuuskoski and the Reds are in flight. Some were caught by the Whites and I suppose they were shot. I can't go very far, as things are in a bad way at home. After a few days, when the worst's over, they might spare me. I've got to hide somewhere near home— they'll shoot me at once if I'm caught, as it was I who drove the men to Kurkela when the master was killed—but all I did was to drive the horse, which you can witness to if needed— you saw me that night when I came back. Listen, I'll hide in the straw in Kierikka's old barn—you take word to Emma to set some bread and hot milk somehow near the door, I'll get them all right. . . . You will, won't you, good, kind Silja, and if I ever get out of this fix, I'll remember you all my life. . . . Let's go now at once before anyone comes to look for you."

264

Overcome by terror the cottar, once so merry, stole along the road, stopping every now and again to listen. Near the house he begged Silja to go on ahead as though she had not met anybody.

That was the night of the great flight on this sector of the front. Then came the next day, when there were neither Reds nor Whites in Kierikkala village, and those who remained in the village knew the greatest fear. None dared to show themselves much. The mistress of Kurkela, however, was seen to drive towards the main village, dressed in black and with an expression of silent solemn anger. She was off to meet the Whites as soon as possible, apparently to report the murder of her husband and other happenings in the village. The mistress of Kierikka was one of those who saw her go, and felt an evil twinge in some corner of her soul. She too was mistress of a farm, but the woman in the sleigh seemed at this moment to belong to a higher class.

Silja, too, saw the mistress of Kurkela drive past. A few minutes later, without a word to anyone, the girl went to the Teliniemi cottage and in a low voice gave Teliniemi's message. The situation in the cottage was truly desperate, as the cottar had hinted to Silja on the dark road. Emma, his wife, was in the last stages of pregnancy and one of the children had diphtheria. The tear-stricken woman said she would do her utmost and thanked Silja for daring to do them such a service.

21

Soon after this visit Silja was drawn into a situation that was a counterpart to her adventures after the twilight walk seven weeks earlier, when she played guide to the two mysterious young men. Kierikkala village had not long to wait in that dreadful suspense when not a shot was fired or a single rifle even seen. The Whites' foreposts were soon established in Rinne's house, whither the leading farmers in Mahanala hurried to give their accounts of events, to complain about the loss of their property and to lay information against the most notorious " Reds " in the locality and tell where these lived or might be expected to be hiding. The sunburnt North Finland soldiers appeared to care little about material losses, but paid close attention to reports of murders by the Reds. And if any woman was denounced as a specially virulent agitator, a couple of men would set off at once to arrest her and take her to the main village. Rinne's wife had fled from her home, but had not accompanied her husband very far, and coming back was taken straight from the highway to the temporary prison.

The White soldiers were of course told that Kurkela had been murdered and that at least Teliniemi had been with the killers. The maid Silja at Kierikka may have been their guide too, for she had been seen at the Red headquarters that night and had further been seen to leave in the morning accompanied by a well-known Red. A search was consequently made at Teliniemi's home, where everything was turned upside down. From there the search party went on to Kierikka, whither other representatives of the White forces, on the same errand, had preceded them.

Many farmers who had kept noticeably quiet while the revolutionaries were in power, and even fawned on the Red leaders, now became transformed into enthusiastic "purifiers" of their neighbourhood. Very quickly they procured white armlets and rifles and went off, two or three of them together or accompanied by soldiers, on a round of the cottages and huts. In this way the master of the farm—Santala his name was—where Silja and Manta had first stopped on their departure from Siiveri, was now eagerly occupied, despite his ugly reputation, in such work in the company of a couple of beetle-browed northerners.

Santala may have been related in some way to the Kurkela family, for he and his followers were especially keen on investigating the murder. He too had heard the foolish report that Kierikka's maid Silja had acted in some capacity as guide on that nocturnal mission of bloodshed—the rumour was all the more silly as it was known that Teliniemi, a local man, had driven the murderers and that no guide was consequently needed. Santala came, however, to Kierikka and demanded to see Silja in the commanding tone he had picked up during the past few days.

" What do you want with her ? " asked the master.

" We want her for a bit, to explain how she piloted them murderers to Kurkela," Santala roared importantly.

" She hasn't piloted any murderers," the master of Kierikka answered in a rough voice. Kierikka may not have been a flourishing farm, but the family's reputation was clean, and this fact Kierikka always remembered when he met Santala, and his tone was accordingly arrogant.

" We know all about it," Santala said in a spuriously amicable voice and with an upward glance. " That girl was at Rinne's headquarters on the night."

" She was, and a tight place she was in too, having helped a couple of Whites to cross the front."

" Helped them, I dare say, to Rinne's headquarters, so that they were killed on the way. Do you think we don't know where Silja was told to guide them? We know another thing too, that you gave the Staff a cow so's they'd be on your side —or it may have been a pig."

Cursing, and in the plainest words, Kierikka referred to Santala's past, the mistress continuing the attack by turning to the two soldiers.

" You'd be ashamed to go about with a man like that if you knew what he is, but as you're from some other place, you can't know—his papers is such that I can't soil my mouth by letting out all that's in them papers—we know the Santala crowd, we do."

" Now then, woman, stop yelling or you'll get a bullet in your belly," Santala said, slightly abashed.

" Not from any gun of yours," shrieked the mistress and began in truth to relate Santala's sins.

Silja happened to come in just then, and Santala hastened to turn attention to her.

" Aha, Silja, come on now to the main village and account for your doings," Santala broke out shrilly.

" I'd like to come, if the master'll let me. I'm expecting friends from that way."

" Don't pretend, lass, you know well enough where your friends are after you had guided them to Rinne's Staff."

The soldiers who had accompanied Santala began to have enough of this fluctuating battle of words. They saw that Santala's well-meant errand had somehow gone wrong and that the matter in hand was by no means clear yet. In brief words they ordered the master and Silja to come with them to the White headquarters in the main village. The master harnessed the horse, and one of the soldiers shared a sleigh with him and Silja; the other drove behind in Santala's sleigh.

"Aye, let's hope the young gentlemen you helped are there now, and that slimy wretch Santala'll have his nose knocked out of joint once more," the mistress shouted when the sleighs were in movement.

"Now, mistress, less noise," one of the northerners said sternly, whereat the mistress slipped quickly into the porch.

As they passed the old barn the soldier asked Kierikka: "Any knowledge, master, about where Teliniemi is?" It was wonderfully awing to hear a rifleman from hundreds of miles away inquire in such a serious way for an insignificant cottar whom he had never heard of before or seen.

"All I know is that he must have gone with all that fleeing crowd."

The morning was sunny and warm. The snow melted almost in one's sight, and the nearer the party came to the middle of the parish the worse became the road. In the open spaces around the church one saw indeed wheeled carts. All along the road the party passed armed guards and patrols, with whom Santala, from the rearmost sleigh, kept up a running fire of remarks. "Any Reds about? We've got some rather doubtful coloured ones in that first sleigh."

Then they passed the building where Red prisoners were housed. Behind the house was a pine-wood, and there executions were carried out in the evenings and sometimes during the day.

Before them a man was driving a cart which seemed at a distance to be loaded with fir-twigs. The man drove at a walk, and as the road was almost bare here, the Kierikka party was compelled, when they came up with the cart, to drop into line behind it.

The cart was not, however, loaded wholly with fir-twigs; in it was something else which the branches were intended to hide. At the back of the cart tiny rivulets of blood could be seen. Silja's eye too caught them, and slowly she became conscious of what was under those twigs. Unconsciously she had followed the course of the cart for some time, since its first emergence from the clump of trees behind the prison. Her mind refused, however, to accept the reality of what she could distinguish between the twigs : a glimpse of a woman's skirt that Silja believed she had seen before. The cart was driven by Taavetti Kannusmäki, a decent cottar with a child-less wife, hard-working and thrifty, a man liked by the farmers because he did not mix in politics. He had now been appointed to this special task.

Silja was not to remain long in her vague state of mind. Santala soon made everything clear in a loud voice, as Taavetti Kannusmäki explained matters to him in a mild, low tone. Santala had bounded out of his sleigh and run to the cart-side.

" Come on, Silja, you too, and see what has become of your friend at headquarters. Here's Rinne's wife on her way to the ideal state. Who's that other one ? " he asked Taavetti Kannusmäki, and Taavetti answered gravely: "It's Kivilahti."

" Ah, has that old fox fallen into a trap at last—well he won't come commandeering any more pigs from me."

Kierikka was deeply disgusted, but said nothing, only coughed loudly. Even the soldiers seemed to have had enough and hastened on the horses.

The Commandant's headquarters were crowded ; a long queue of all manner of persons were waiting their turn to be admitted into the back room. Excitement was reflected in each face, for everyone regarded his own errand as important and urgent, so dissimilar as all their errands were. Here a farmer was trying to get in a good word for a Red cottar of his, here a woman wanted to know if the Reds had left a roll of such and such cloth anywhere—if so, it was hers. Beside the porch door sat a rifleman, with a hand grenade dangling from his belt. He was a farmer's son who had managed to reach the Whites and to return fighting with the victors. He was being interviewed by a few acquaintances, who gazed at him respectfully, almost humbly.

Here stood now the master of Kierikka with his maid and that Santala fellow with the twitching eyes and white armlet. Kierikka felt his position deeply and could not refrain from answering his neighbour in the queue, when the latter demanded to know his errand: " I've no idea at all—it's that Santala's raking up."

On Silja's cheeks an eager flush burned and behind the lashes one caught the moist suffering gleam in her eyes. Her strange sense of waiting, which had grown in intensity each day and night that passed, seemed to have receded now that she was in the centre of events. She could not picture meeting him in these circumstances. If she wished for anything at this moment, it was that Armas would be prevented from seeing her here, standing in this line. Somewhere far off she seemed to see the beautiful carriage of his head and his arm rising in salute, somewhere whence he very much wanted to come and meet Silja, to go away with her, somewhere—to some new summer again, away from this smell of human beings on these roads, where the bodies of shot prisoners were carted.

Neither did she think much of the two youths whom she guided one evening—curiously enough, because that very action was the cause of her being here. That too seemed to have no connection with the present, for in that too was the scent of summer, imparted by the kiss the younger of the two had stolen beside the barn. No, it was not anything one could think of on this highway.

Silja found, however, one of the young men.

The parish Commandant, one of the local gentry, did not fully understand this case of the master of Kierikka and his maid, or lacked the time at present to go into it. So far as the master was concerned he had no doubts whatever, a solid old farmer could not have been so closely allied with the Reds as to make it worth while dragging him here, and the Commandant snorted angrily at Santala when the latter went on babbling about a pig that had been taken from Kierikka to Rinne's headquartets.

"Didn't you take them a pig too—but perhaps they were better able to spare one at Santala seeing that you were left," roared Kierikka.

"I did, but only between bayonets."

"Well, that didn't make any difference."

"Kierikka can go home for the present, but the girl will have to be taken to prison," the Commandant decided. He gave an order to a soldier.

"I'll take her, as I'll be passing there in any case," whispered Santala.

"I've given my orders," the Commandant said sharply.

They had passed out of the house and were turning from the gate into the road when a bespectacled gentleman in a tall white lambskin hat and light-blue, short fur coat came smartly towards them. Quite by chance he stared at the woman whom a soldier was apparently escorting prisonward. He stopped abruptly, gazed long at Silja and said at last : " What the Hell—where are you taking that girl ? "

"To the prison, Commandant's orders, Captain," the soldier answered.

"Wait," said the gentleman and went with quick steps into the Commandant's room, not by the door through which the public were admitted, but by the main door. A moment later the Commandant came out bareheaded and called Silja back.

The faces of the two farmers, Santala and Kierikka, lengthened at this unexpected scene, but for different reasons. Kierikka believed he could recognise the gentleman as one of the two men whom Silja had gone out to guide—and remembered how his wife had behaved towards them. The Devil only knew what trouble the man might make : perhaps that pig had been given away a bit too easily, and he had happened to say, half in fun, that they'd have to look after his house, seeing that he was giving them a pig. All this the master of Kierikka had time to think of in self-defence. Santala, again, was perturbed because the man addressed as " Captain " had not paid any attention to anyone but the girl, with whom he seemed to share some old and pleasant memory. Who knew what the girl would tell him now.

Silja was the only one who enjoyed—after all—the encounter. She had at once recognised the Captain as the older of the two strangers, this one had not said much to her at the time, the younger one being so much livelier. He appeared, however, to have impressed her picture on his memory.

" Will you go in through the big veranda there ? " the Commandant said to her as he vanished inside.

The Captain rose to greet her as she entered, and then said to the others present : " Fancy you sending a darling like this to prison camps ! This young lady's advice was good and accurate, and if I'd made the same promise as my friend, I'd have to offer now to accompany her to the parson—as it is I'm sorry to say I'm engaged already. And Fredström is no use either, for he's lying with his head shot to a sieve somewhere between Tampere and Vilppula. It was touch and go for us that time, and if the Red we met at a fence hadn't been such a fool, the Devil knows what would have happened to us. But we offered him a smoke, and the next second Fred-ström snatched his rifle and thrust the bayonet through his stomach. He fell without a sound and we made off at the Devil's own speed. We were in a bigger fix after that with the first White outpost before he would believe that we weren't Red scouts. He would insist at first on shooting us and then marched us off with our hands up. But this girl was plucky enough that night, thanks once more to her. Isn't that the master of the house himself? Why, so it is. Listen here, you: you've got a confounded shrew at home for wife; she ought to have been brought here and not this girl, who deserves a medal, and if I go on living will get one."

The whole case was taken up again, and this time Silja spoke much longer than she had done recently. She described her arrest on that evening, then related what she knew of the master and mistress—that they had not to her knowledge had any dealings with the Reds. A pig had been taken to the Red headquarters, but she believed the master had been paid for it. She then related the rest of her experiences and what she had heard that night at Rinne's house and on her return. She told them her impression of Teliniemi and—remembered her plight in the barn. She stopped and was obviously embarrassed, so that Santala had time to emit an expressive " Ah ! " Then, taking courage, she described the whole incident in a tone that sounded as though she were blaming Santala.

" And who might you be? " the Captain asked Santala sharply.

The Commandant replied in a disgusted tone on Santala's behalf, whereupon the Captain said: " Wouldn't it be the wisest thing to let Santala go back to his farm and stop there ? "

" Yes, you can go home, Santala, and we'll send for you if you're wanted again."

" That Teliniemi seems to be a fine fellow—where is he now ? " asked the Captain.

The general opinion was that he had gone in the great flight. Silja said nothing, but when everything had been settled—the master of Kierikka recommended to pay the price of the pig to the White funds, as he had been friendly to some extent with the Reds and many others had had their pigs taken for nothing—Silja asked to be allowed to speak to the Captain alone.

" I'm going your way, and we can talk as we go. Let's be off now."

Kierikka was told to come on behind with the sleigh, while Silja and the Captain went on ahead on foot. Blushing and stammering, Silja finally told him all she knew about Teliniemi, described matters in his home and his cheerful nature, and expressed her deep conviction that he had not taken part in the murder of Kurkela. And then she begged the Captain to arrange matters so that Teliniemi could safely emerge from his hiding-place, which Silja knew.

The Captain looked at the girl in surprise, no longer as warmly as a little while ago.

" I cannot promise anything definite, the court decides about such matters, but the fellow will have to be brought out of his hole in any case, or . . . " He did not complete the sentence, but Silja understood what he meant. Tears came into her eyes as she begged the Captain to do all he could for Teliniemi.

" If everything turns out to be as you say, I don't think he'll be in danger of his life. I don't believe he'll get off altogether though. I'll get a couple of soldiers and when you've shown them his hiding-place they can bring him here and then I'll speak for him to the Commandant. That's all I can do."

He acted on his decision at once. They had reached the prison building by then and the Captain beckoned to the nearest guard, to whom he gave an order. He also stopped

Kierikka, who had just reached the spot in his sleigh. From the building came two riflemen, strangers to the district and sulky-looking fellows. The party set off slowly along the half-melted road, the horse straining, the runners of the sleigh squeaking in the sand and lurching forward every time they came to a film of ice.

A conversation began between the farmer and the two soldiers.

" You local men will have to clear out these forests when we advance ; there might be Reds hiding in 'em."

" They'll come out, I daresay, in their own good time," Kierikka answered.

" Aye, but you oughtn't to keep them there, eating un-necessarily," one of the soldiers said.

" They'll eat when they're in prison, won't they ? " Kier-ikka remarked.

" Who said they had to be taken prisoner ? " the northerner answered darkly.

" That's it—they'd only escape," the other added.

Silja, her cheeks still glowing, heard this conversation. They had not proceeded more than two or three hundred yards at the time. From her seat beside the master on the driver's bench, Silja seized the reins and pulled up the horse. She must see the Captain again, she shouted, something important had been forgotten. And the next second she was running along the road to the prison, before her companions had time to say anything. " What's come over the girl now ? Such a fret she's in."

Silja found the Captain and spoke to him more passionately than before. " I'm not going with those men to take Teli-niemi, they talked of such dreadful things that I'm sure they'll shoot him as soon as they lay their hands on him. If you won't come with us, I won't show those men the place. Your life was in my hands once and you were allowed to live, now you save my life."

" But there's no one threatening to take your life."

" Yes there is, for I won't tell where Teliniemi is hiding unless you come with me and give your word of honour that Teliniemi won't be killed, at least until the whole matter is cleared up, and that they'll believe what I say."

The young soldier laughed as he looked at the girl's glowing cheeks and shining eyes. Impossible to suspect such a person of any wrongful intention—and as the question was of a married cottar, there could not be any secret affair of the heart at stake. The Captain thought for a moment, then said : " Well, as you attach such weight to the matter, I suppose I ought to give you something for my life. Wait here, and I'll arrange it."

After he had come back from the building, and before they reached the waiting sleigh, Silja stopped him again in some excitement and mentioning the name of her friend of the previous summer and looking up through her lashes, asked whether the Captain had heard anything about him.

" I know that he'll be nearing Viipuri about this time, if he's still on his feet. . . . But what interest have you in him ? "

Silja delayed a moment to find the right words before answering : " He spent last summer here." She did not look the Captain in the eyes.

They came to the sleigh, and as there would now have been five passengers, the Captain sent one of the soldiers back and sat down in his place. So they drove on towards Kierikka, and there was no more talk of cleaning out the forests. Now and again the Captain glanced at Silja with a smile of sympathy, and she answered his glance confidently and trustingly. Kierikka and the soldier were as though of a different company.

They drew near to the place whose secret inhabitant Silja alone knew. She was nearly trembling with excitement and sought the Captain's glance of her own accord; almost she sought his arm. In her mind she pictured a happy home-coming in the Teliniemi cabin. The sick child would surely get well.

"Does our agreement hold ?" she asked again. She was as though intoxicated, so that the master looked at her suspiciously, astonished.

"Quite certainly it does," the officer answered in a merrier tone than she could have wished.

They drove on a little farther, until outside the barn Silja again reached for the reins and shouted : "Whoa."

The horse stopped, Silja sprang down and beckoned to the Captain, at the same time motioning to him to keep silent. She then crept into the barn and whispered : "Teliniemi— listen, Teliniemi—this is Silja—come out—don't be afraid."

The straw began to heave ; a hand, then a topboot and finally the whole man emerged into view. Teliniemi looked round him, blinking his eyes and brushing straw from his clothes. His eyes roved from man to man, from the officer to the strange fierce-looking soldier with the white armlet, then to the master of Kierikka and lastly, again, to Silja. For one tense second he stood motionless, then, before anyone had time to do or say anything, he snatched the knife from a sheath at his belt and waving it in one sweeping movement and looking with endless scorn at Silja, said : "You, a creature of the slaughterers, fye, woman." The powerful stroke cut through both the jugular vein and his windpipe.

"For God's sake, Teliniemi, you're not going to be killed," cried Silja, and the Captain rushed forward to prevent the suicide, but too late. In gradually waning spouts the man's heart poured his blood into the straw.

278

"I believe, old fellow, you were guilty after all," the Captain said, watching the last spasms of the death struggle.

"No, he was not guilty. Oh Emma and the children," Silja sobbed and set off running, her hands pressed to her face and heedless of the others, towards the house.

After that she never saw the Captain or the soldier again. The two went straight back to the barracks to their duties, and that same evening came the order for a general advance, when the fighting troops moved forward on Tampere, where fierce battles still awaited them.

So the front was gradually drawn farther and farther south of the parish. Another fortnight or so and there was no front left. The Reds were defeated, the fallen buried. But throughout the summer the courts still dealt with the prisoners, and in many prison-camps the rifles of firing-squads cracked. Some, more fortunate, began to trickle back to their homes. Death proved the executor for many prisoners ; they died of starvation, and varied were the tales told by the survivors. In these tales a savage coarseness was wedded to a surprisingly apt humour, downcast minds preferring thus to cloak their deep-sown bitterness.

22

Silja Salmelus suffered as though she too had gone through a disheartening flight, followed by internment in a prison. At least two months after the war she still lived in a kind of stupor. Dreadful dreams tortured her, so that she often preferred to keep herself awake rather than submit to sleep. Her dreams were chiefly concerned with Rinne's wife and Teliniemi and were, especially those in which the cottar appeared, sometimes very curious.

Silja never learned exactly what Emma Teliniemi thought of her after that terrible event. Emma suffered other calamities about that time : soon after the death of her husband her sick child died after a series of severe choking attacks. She had money brought home by her husband as pay for his services in the Red Guard, but, to begin with, a strict order was issued for the return of all such money to the local White headquarters, which still existed in the main village, and then, when Emma in her distress tried to use her money through secret channels, she found out that it consisted of notes printed by the Reds, and was therefore worthless. People went about in those days with a list in their pockets on which were marked the numbers and other signs by which the revolutionaries' notes could be recognised. This final misfortune broke Emma's spirit. Her child came prematurely while she was all alone, and she nearly died of loss of blood. While she lay in this helpless state an equally destitute neighbour happened to call and was able to send word for help. A Sister of Mercy finally arrived and did what she could : procured relief for the woman from the parish and made a desperate attempt to set things right in the house. But in the parish were many such cases of distress, to all of which this charitable Christian had to attend, so that Emma Teliniemi was often compelled to be alone at home in her helpless condition. Her weakness kept her confined to bed much longer than would otherwise have been the case.

During this period Silja came to Teliniemi one Sunday at noon. The Sister of Mercy was elsewhere at the time, luckily for Silja, for she was thus able to demonstrate at once her desire to help the woman. Emma had become curiously soft after her illness and misfortunes ; she looked long and gently at Silja, her head moving slightly in time to her breathing. Silja too stood still and looked, yielding as it were her eyes to the gaze of the older woman. And so it befell that both began to cry before either had had time to say a word about the event that had so deeply affected them.

" I'm so sorry, I'm so sorry," Silja sobbed. " I trusted that officer so fully and thought that it would be better for Teliniemi to be set free from his dreadful plight, as it was quite certain that his life wasn't in danger. Oh, why didn't I prepare him."

" There's no trusting in them, Silja," panted Emma. " You too, Silja, guided them and helped them to cross the front— yes, Taavetti knew that you had guided those Whites, though nothing worse happened to you for it, and it was those same men who cruelly killed old Lehtimäki while he was on sentry at the cross-roads. There's no trusting those who rise against the poor and gain the victory—it's all over for us," ended the woman, looking with tearful eyes at her infant.

Nevertheless, she willingly permitted Silja to pick out dry swaddling cloths from the line and according to her directions change the baby's cloths. In the afternoon the Sister of Mercy came back, but declared she would have to spend the night with a pneumonia patient. Silja thereupon said that she would come to Teliniemi for the night, after the evening tasks were over.

She kept her word and watched through the night, more strictly than she need have done, until the Sister of Mercy returned. But as she walked on the Monday morning to Kierikka, she was so weak that she went on for some distance without knowing she was walking, until she suddenly started and stopped. The same thing occurred to her while she was milking: she had to make an effort to keep herself from collapsing under a cow. The mistress too noticed it and remarked that Silja, as a person in another's employ, was not committed to such help, let the parish see to that, the taxes were big enough . . . there was no getting any work out of a girl who stayed up nights, " especially if she's a weak little body like you."

Silja stayed awake many another night after that, although she did not go to Teliniemi again. She lay awake in her bed, with the nights growing gradually lighter, as though drawing nearer by degrees to lonely sleepless souls. The days too grew brighter, the usual delights of spring and summer seeking to console and refresh oppressed human beings. On Silja, however, they had a queerly fatiguing effect, so that the mistress was moved to complain to some neighbour that her maid, formerly a moderately good one, was becoming slack and inattentive.

Neither Silja nor anyone else could guess as yet what was in question. True, Silja coughed occasionally, but as it was not a proper hard cough, no heed was taken of it, rather was it looked upon as a little trick of vanity, a mannerism such as people sometimes acquire. As in Silja's expression there was at the same time a brightness that might have been a reflection of the waxing spring, and her beauty thus increased in sensitiveness and fineness, her tiny cough could easily seem almost

282

an affectation, the more so as it was followed by a little tinkling noise. Indeed, the peculiar trait of purity in Silja's being grew ever plainer and more striking, keeping step as it were with the change that was taking place outside, where the littered yard and roadsides grew green and were purified as the refuse of winter soaked into the earth and fed the new growth. There was something transparent in her apparition. No one here in Kierikkala had ever made any special attempt to gain her affection, but now she seemed to withdraw ever farther and fade away from the people around her.

In the night her body tended to become too hot. Silja thought it was the warmth of the room and the weather, but if she cast aside her blanket, cold shudders would go through her. So she would draw the blanket over her again and cuddle down in her favourite attitude as a child and try to imagine the world around her non-existent. All the more intensely was she then aware of her own immediate existence. The curled-up embryo-like attitude of her body seemed to bring with it a corresponding state of consciousness; who knows whether pre-natal impulses may not have quivered deep down in her subconscious mind at such moments. At least she felt that she had never been younger than just then—or older. Time was merely existence at that particular moment. Behind her closed lids and in the region of her mouth and breasts was all experience, simultaneously : her childhood and father, youth and its pure and beautiful phases—those approved of and pre-served by the soul—and finally all her late experiences. The same response was awakened in her soul whether it was Rinne's wife or Teliniemi that came into her mind, or the youth who had kissed her on the threshold of Kivilahti's barn. . . .

And lastly her mind would release to its surface the only memory that it had again avoided since that recent passionate day of exaltation and tragedy. When the rising warmth in

the cells of her body called forth a state close kin to sleep,
when the surrounding everyday world was sunk in a deepening slumber and the twilight spirit of the spring night opens
ajar the door of the soul, although bodily eyes are closed—
then he would return, looking from afar as though seeking,
as he had once done from a boat on a Sunday night during her
Confirmation period, return and love her as he had done five
years later, breaking nothing, but strengthening . . . and then
stand looking from beyond her latest experiences, asking as it
were if she understood. . . . I do, I do ; in a new summer,
this one, perhaps, that is nigh—or else there beyond this
world, in the fire of blue and gold where your spirit embraced
mine and spoke incomprehensible, unendingly kind words.
Soon the rye will wave, soon the night-flowers blossom, of
loving, as you once smiling hinted. Come !

And sleep bore her farther. For a few hours it sought to
bring rest to the cells of her body, which some alien influence
had come to disturb. As the other functions of her body relaxed, her skin ejected through its pores those disturbing,
wearisome intruding particles, her temperature fell, her
breathing grew more even, her lungs coughed. She awoke
for a minute, noted that she had perspired, and remembered
that she had not used to do so. It was morning ; the clock
was striking a half-hour, inpossible to guess which. But the
light in the room was wonderful, quite different from what
it had been in the evening. From the bed beside the door
came the harsh breathing of the farmhand—this was the
living-room at Kierikka, different in every way from her little
room in Rantoo Villa, on the window-sill of which when she
thus awoke, were meadow-flowers in a tumbler, and a branch
of mountain ash stuck behind the lintel of the door reached
out for her attention. Different also from her home cabin,
where the breathing audible was her father's. The only de-

light here was the silence, the total absence of all that belonged to the daytime.

And during that brief moment of wakefulness the only person in the world for her became visible even while her eyes were open. He came and wanted to abolish all that lay between, came and implanted himself in her soul so sweetly that her eyes closed irresistibly, and with her new mood came a new calmer morning-sleep, happy as in her earliest childhood, when her consciousness, even while she slept, knew how to await the caressing pat of her father's hand as a signal to awake. But her father's pat always came exactly at the moment when her sleep thinned of its own accord, and if vestiges of it lingered in any limb, father would unerringly pounce on that very limb and by rubbing it and squeezing it with his fingers, grunting as though it was he who was being massaged, drive away the sleep from it so that she could jump refreshed from the bed and run straight out to the steps to greet the sunlight.

On this morning of early summer the cows were her awakener. Actually it was the mistress who had to arouse her, keeping up meanwhile the half-friendly grumbling she had latterly adopted : "It's downright curious how you're getting to be like that in everything."

This morning, and then on many other mornings, it was really difficult for Silja to get up for the milking at her usual time, five o'clock ; the distance was fairly long to the dairy, so that the milk cart had to leave early. Whereas Silja—this spring she could have slept in the morning even to eight o'clock. She never could do so, not even on Sunday, when the farmhand slept as late as his sense of shame would let him. He had taken the horses to the far pasture, where they could stop until Monday morning, for at Kierikka no one went to church except once each summer to Communion Service when the rye bloomed.

Thus they would fare forth morning after morning, the slightly bow-legged mistress of Kierikka, her angrily-good-natured head poked forward, and her delicate long-lashed maid, who had been born, long before all these later matters and events, the daughter of a bigger and more dignified estate than this; they would walk to the cattle-yard, where the cows, some standing, some still reclining and chewing the cud, awaited them. The surface of the cattle-yard was covered with fir-twigs, except for little seas of filtered mud, so that the milkers had to carry with them a pail of water and a rag, for complaints had sometimes reached them that the milk from Kierikka was dirty, and that meant deductions from the milk money.

Silja had arisen unwillingly, but she soon felt better, for the air at that early hour is fresher than at any other time. Certainly its divine appeal was also due to the fact that the air of the living-room was more than usually stale in the mornings. To be sure, the room was fairly large, and ordinarily no more than three persons slept in it—besides Silja, the farmhand and just now a day-labourer—but even the master, who had a chronic cold in the head, joked about the air when he came into the living-room in the morning.

Once on her feet and her lungs filled with air purified by hundreds of millions of flowers and leaves, Silja was in fairly good condition for work until breakfast-time. At some moments she would even attempt a low-pitched fragment of song. But at breakfast the mistress would notice that Silja hardly ate anything. In a way, of course, that was all to the good of the house, for there were enough maids who ate so much that their keep became a serious factor from the employer's point of view, but neither did it seem right that Silja

286

should breakfast on a dish of skimmed milk brought by the milk-carrier on his return from the dairy, milk used at Kierikka as at other farms chiefly for the pigs and calves. True, such milk was always on the servants' table, but no one could say there was nothing else beside, food that kept a working body in trim for work, such as potatoes, pickled sprats, margarine, and above all, strong rye-bread. Of the latter there was really no lack, and a farmhand and a maid were entitled to eat all they wanted. The most niggardly master or mistress, even in that summer of food crisis, might not speak of the bread-devouring feats of a servant except in joke. And there was no doubt but that the farmhand who lay at night in the bed beside the door made the best use of his ancient privilege. If the sprats happened to be a bit yellow with age or the margarine rancid, the man would eat a whole rye loaf, washing it down with skim milk.

The mistress would say to Silja:

"Eat, eat, girl. No one's going to do any work on the scrap you eat. Then in the evening you'll be like a wet rag."

Silja did as much work as she could, also in the evenings, although the blood raced in her ears in a quickened throbbing and memories of former times began to recur to her now even while she was working, as they had first done in the evenings in bed while her temperature rose. Something would now whisper to her already in the afternoon that hers was a state from which there was no return.

Silja clearly realised that she would not return, even to her past life at Kierikka upon which she had entered so unthinkingly the previous year. For her nights began to be more and more unlike what they had been before: the evening rise in her temperature was sharper, her perspirations and coughings towards morning also grew worse. Even the farmhand noticed it, being driven occasionally by thirst to get up in the small hours after a spree at some cabin or other. If anyone happened to tease them in the daytime about their sleeping in the same room, and Silja, instinctively finding it the best way out, said to him : " How about it, Aappo ? " the farmhand would answer, with a self-satisfied shrug of his shoulders : " Shut up, I wouldn't have you, you're in a consumption, I can tell by the way you cough at night."

Midsummer drew nigh. Silja began to take note of the month and its separate days ; she would look at the almanack and calculate what day it had been last year : this Sunday was Saturday last year, such and such a Saturday. And the more the mistress found cause to rebuke her for her inattention or lack of strength, the longer became the moments Silja dwelt in the surroundings and incidents of the previous summer. What the times and events were she lived anew in those hours before midnight, when sleep would not come and heat wearied her body, no one ever learned. She began, however, to feel a growing antipathy towards the farm and to wonder that she had been able to live there over a whole winter, almost from summer to summer. Ever more sharply defined became her memories of Rantoo and the summer there, almost as though she were suffocating here, and there was fresh air. The thought of a return to the neighbourhood of Rantoo was a fixed point in her consciousness, of the kind one cannot let go of for a minute. She began to hint to the mistress that she would like permission to go and see the place where she was in service the summer before. If she were to set out early in the morning, she could be back in time for the evening milking. It would be nicest of all if the mistress would let her go on Midsummer Day.

" You're going nowhere on Midsummer Day," the mistress answered. " We, master and I, are going to Communion

Service that day and you're needed at home to cook the dinner."

The mistress said this in such a tone that the subject seemed to be closed. A little later, however, she said of her own free will : " But the day after Midsummer is a Sunday, and you can go then if you've a mind to."

So the day of Silja's summer excursion, which was to be her last, was definitely settled. The expectation of it gave her strength ; although her temperature now rose in the evenings to an obvious fever and in her midnight dreams the Professor might appear with his mouth in a broad grin and pull her hair, and although her morning perspiration was more exhausting than before, she would get up briskly in the morning and hasten out of the stale air of the living-room into the freshness of the summer morning to milk the cows. She did not wish any harm to the house, though she had as it were betrayed it the whole time, by coming there and settling there with no thought for it—enough that she could come and stay. This place denoted indeed a new move southward, but for once she wanted to return northward, at some moments perhaps farther north than Rantoo, to Siiveri or even to her father's former cabin.

So far north she was never more to go, but even a brief visit Rantoo way had in it much that was beautiful and significant. On that particular morning there was no need to awaken Silja ; she was already milking the first cow and singing when the mistress arrived at the cattle-yard.

" My word, how pleased we are at our journey. Wonder if it bodes any good," remarked the mistress, who always found it hard to stomach the joyful agitation of another person.

As it turned out, it did not bode any good, but at least in the morning everything was as pleasant as could be expected on the day after Midsummer. The weather was dead calm, the air dry, not a trace even of dew—which caused the master, as he sniffed the air from the porch, to remark that it would rain later in the day. Just now, however, the sky was cloudless and shimmering with heat; one could hardly see where the sky began, so full it was of a mild glow. After Silja was really clear of the house—the dreadful barn behind her—the sun, air and the flourishing earth were for long her only company. Under her feet was the forest cart-track, now covered by level green grass beautifully scored by wheel-tracks and the line of earth trodden hard in the middle by horse-hoofs. In parts the road was so lovely that she had to sit down on it. And as she sat she enjoyed a real Sunday morning feeling. She had changed every stitch of clothing on her, and in her clothes lingered the clean smell of the storehouse. She noted it herself and was reminded of closing-days at school in her childhood.

When she came through the forest to the next village, which already brought a foretaste of her journey's end, it was pleasant to observe that the girls there were also dressed in bright Sunday summer dresses as they ran about the yards on little tasks in preparation for church-going. Some of them were known to her and smiled as they bade her good-morning.

A dry cart-track rounded the foot of a hill from this village to the village dominated by Rantoo Villa. But there was also a foot-path straight across the hill, and this path Silja began to ascend. The climb tired her, it is true; she felt again that painful fit of exhaustion and weakness of the knees; her mouth grew dry. On the hill was a cabin occupied by a widow and her daughter; Silja had often been there to buy eggs for Rantoo Villa. Here too a sense of Sunday was in the sunlight on the grey wall of the cabin. Behind a screen of apple-tree branches a familiar window had a beckoning air. An invisible cock crowed loudly in honour of the good Sabbath morning. Lower down the slope the lid of a well was visible, surrounded by thick spring grass. Silja remembered that the Professor had praised the water from the Kukkula well, declaring it to be connected in some way with his beloved spring —the one near which night-flowers grew. Silja stopped at the house to moisten her dry throat and rested for a moment on the steps, talking meanwhile with the widow and her daughter of the events of the previous summer and the past winter. She heard that the Professor had been at Rantoo all through the revolution, whilst the young lady had been first in Helsinki, then after many adventures had succeeded in getting to Rantoo towards the end of the fighting to be with her father.

" Yes, and that young gentleman, that ' merry and beautiful ' one, as we used to call him, nothing certain's known about him. Some say he fell and others say he was badly wounded. I haven't met Miss Laura at all to ask about him ; she'd be the one to know, for they were said to be keeping company last summer."

This dwelling was not on the highest point of the hill. But from its yard could be seen the spruce which formed the farthest landmark of the hill. Silja went on, along a path that grew ever more familiar, until she came to the part of the hill that she knew best. It was a little opening, the trees and bushes here seeming to withdraw from around the visitor to afford him an opportunity to see the landscape. The most peculiar feature of the place, however, was the hollow rumble that even the lightest step drew from the ground. The grass that grew here was always withered, so that it was hard to imagine when it could have grown. Across the grass led a narrow path, familiar to all its users, who would often stop at the first hollow echo beneath their feet and stamp with some force to awaken a louder sound, as children are tempted to go on awakening an echo once discovered. The excellent water from the Kukkula well had refreshed Silja so much that she too stopped to stamp her foot and listen, smiling meanwhile to herself.

Her beaming smile may also have been directed at the view opening out below. There, in its former place, was Rantoo Villa, the same colours, the same contours of corners and eaves. The same birch-clad point was confined by the water glittering in the sun, the point that Silja had often compared with the similar point of land below her former home cabin, the one from whose tip she had looked forth, sensing the silence, on a night during her Confirmation period. From the reverberating summit of the hill she saw again the point at Rantoo. Tucked away in the bight of the point, invisible here on the hill, were the bath-house, the bakery, the bricked-in cauldron for boiling the wash in . . . she knew exactly what they looked like in this sunlight, the smell of the iron cauldron, when one went there on some errand or other on a Sunday morning such as this.

The path led downward, to the barnyard of the nearest farm and thence to the village road, which continued the descent between fields of green and red-streaked rye. Ever more familiar became the road; sharply defined memories began to attach to ever more frequent sites. Reaching the bottom of the hollow Silja observed that the hill at Kulmala was higher than she had pictured in her day-dreams. How high, seen from the hollow, the opening was where grew that same ever yellow stunted grass, the opening from which one could so easily follow all that was happening in the Rantoo grounds and on the quay. Silja knew it well—it was from there she had looked out when—the steamer left. . . .

The ground rose again, and Rantoo came into view from a new, still more intimate angle. There was the cross-roads where she had to decide whether to go to Rantoo or to

292

Kulmala ; Silja stopped. In the whole expanse of field no one was visible ; only from the Rantoo windows could she be observed, and that eventuality held no fears for her. She did not, however, continue along the road to Rantoo, but turned to the left and was soon in the Kamraati yard. On the steps of the servants' quarters sat a couple of men, strangers to her, and old half-daft Kalle Kärkelä, whose only son Silja knew had been shot after the war. The old man stared at her out of little lifeless eyes until she reached the old apple-tree from which the Kulmala building was already visible, himself like an unconscious symbol of deepest melancholy.

There was still the gate, whose latch was so well-known to Silja, to be opened and shut ; Silja knew the exact tug that sent the latch clicking into its place. The bird-cherry and the alpine currant-bush still kept watch, a year older, but as sunny—and as useless—as before. A few steps along a level path, and she began to hear the sound of a piano.

Laini was playing something majestic, pressing frequently the pedal that caused the chords to hum fiercely, so that one caught only a vague idea of her melody. The girl was so absorbed that she did not see the visitor until Silja was well in the room. Greetings were exchanged and the two girls looked at each other, each finding the other altered during the year that had elapsed since they first met. Laini had seen the makers and the making of war and had developed during the winter into a big girl. To her, Silja was a memory of the previous summer. The sight of Silja further recalled to her mind in a new light matters which she had observed then, but had not understood at the time. There was a sense of unfamiliarity on both sides.

Sofia was not at home, but was sure to come soon. She had gone perhaps to Rantoo.

Silja did not know what to say to Laini, and Laini was

equally helpless. The girl only stood about, moving occasionally to a new spot, and Silja's inward condition was very
much the same.

" Have you got a cough, Silja ? "

" I've had it all the spring," Silja answered, roaming now
from window to window and looking out at the landscape.
The field where Sofia's rye had grown last summer had now
been sown with hay. Silja went out, to look at it more closely.
Laini disappeared into the kitchen.

In the growing heat the chickens kept up the same low
murmur as before. The fence around the cattle-yard was as
before, the same gate ajar and slightly askew. From the
cattle-shed came the smell of dry dung and fir-twigs ; the
milking pails were on their shelf beside the cattle-kitchen door.
Alone, Silja gazed at them as she leant on the garden fence. No
one came to keep her company, until a swallow skimmed past
with a faint squeak as if confirming the truth of what Silja saw.

All this was exceedingly commonplace and belonging to
that moment ; it brought back to Silja hardly anything of
the past, except the fact that she was not what she had been.
The vague perspiring fatigue was on her again. How distant
everything was, how different life had been last summer and
now. This was the end—at least she would not find here that
for which she had longed.

For that matter, what else had last summer been than
longing ? Now that she thought of it, her feeling was that
she had not gained everything, only a faint foretaste. There
had been no continuation after the beginning—hardly indeed
a beginning. . . . Why had she been what she was and acted
as she had acted ? Why had she not risen and followed,
clinging fast to what she had ? And why had last winter
wrought such dreadful changes in the way of the world that
there was no going back to what had been ?

294

Surely the most melancholy moments of this last phase of Silja's life came to her then as she leaned against the Kulmala fence, while Sofia was still away and Laini inside the house.

Oskari Tonttila came into her mind—and all the little events she had shared with Oskari. Calmly, almost affectionately, Silja recalled them. Even the visit to Oskari's home that had been one of the events her conscious mind refused to accept, even that was now a satisfactory memory in its own way. Oskari was dead, and his individual worth was now safe and unalterable in Silja's consciousness. As she moved about the Kulmala yard occupied with her memories Silja felt that she herself was wholly forgotten, that it was by some mistake that she still found herself in this new unfamiliar summer.

The feeling did not leave her any more that day. Sofia came home from Rantoo and was at first overjoyed to see Silja, welcoming her warmly and scolding her for not having been to the village before. Yet at the same time a touch of strangeness crept into her behaviour ; she was no longer the Sofia of last year, whom Silja in her gratitude had hugged so passionately when they went to pack up her belongings in the villa. Sofia obviously withdrew farther and farther as the day wore on, friendly as she was. In her face was a species of helpless pity whenever she looked into the girl's eyes. Silja did not fully understand the reason until she was again on the forest track, on her way home, and the grass was red with blood that she had coughed on to it.

The same expression was in the Professor's eyes when Silja went down to Rantoo with Sofia later in the day to see him, and strangely enough, the Professor was unable for once to speak out what was in his mind. In other ways too, the Professor was another man, saddened, much quieter and much aged. When he shook hands with Silja on her departure he was clearly moved : the old man was indeed attached to this " child " whom he was well aware he was seeing for the last time. Much had collapsed for him during the past months, and now this girl whom he had nursed last autumn, whose arms had been round his neck while he arranged her compress, was going. . . .

Silja met Miss Laura too, and Sofia did not forget her station, though she was compelled to ask a number of exceedingly transparent questions, for Silja's benefit ; in this respect she was still the same Sofia as last summer.

" Young Mr. Armas," the term was Miss Laura's as she proceeded to relate, with her own unchanging expression on her face, all that she had already told Sofia, which Silja, because of the alien expression on Sofia's face, had not cared to ask, and Sofia had not had the heart to tell Silja unbidden. " Young Mr. Armas—yes, he was still in hospital with his dreadful wounds. The poor boy had gone through much. First the death of his mother, soon after his departure last summer, and now, probably—well, he had lost a leg and nearly the whole of one lung. . . . "

Silja grasped ever more clearly that everything for which she had instinctively sought reinforcement here, was actually at its weakest here. She would have to go back, for that for which she longed existed now in truth only in her own soul. There she might seek to cultivate it.

. 23 .

So this Sunday, long and bright as it was, slowly began to acquire an atmosphere of evening in its brightness. The march of the shadows in the Kulmala yard was something Silja could read very well; the farther noon was left behind, the more insistently did the gateway clamour for her departure. Sadness lay in the realisation that ultimately she would have to go to Kierikka and stay there. Her visit had already been so long that no protest was made when she rose to go.

Rantoo was again long visible as she walked the path that skirted the wide slope of the hill. A sandy cart-track took her through the ploughland, the villa receding meanwhile behind her back, so that when she again stood on the hollow-sounding summit of the hill, after climbing a zigzag stony path, she had to turn round to see the beloved area. The sunlight that had fallen on it yonder from the right in the morning, now fell from the left. Return was impossible; the place had as it were accompanied her so far on her way, but now seemed to have said farewell and quickly turned away. The fields, the path and house-roofs were now part of this village, unrelated to Silja. It was as a stranger she stood there, her heart beating, an agonised perspiration on her throat. Better for her to hasten on, beyond sight of the village, to rest on the forest track, where the air was cooler. Her body still trembled after the exertion of the ascent; even to walk downhill made her knees ache.

The last stages of Silja's beautiful summer excursion were its climax. On the summit of the hill she had made up her mind to rest at a certain spot on the forest track; she reached the spot and sank down in the grass as one who has reached her final goal. And in one sense she had reached it. Several persons had commented on the persistence of her cough—" a summer cough can't be got rid of before winter "—but here beside the track a patch of red suddenly appeared in the green grass. It was the first time it had happened to her, and not very much blood came this time ; soon it had sunk into the grass, but not before she had had time to reel under the endless panic and agony of a premature death. Not until now did the excitement awakened in her by her journey relax. True, her hopes when she set out in the morning had not been high, but what hope she had had was fled, dissolved on those sunlit village spaces which she would surely, after this, never see again. Fatigue had ended in this hemorrhage.

Was Silja ever to achieve the life which all her senses had reached out for throughout her youth ? Was a mirage-like memory to be the sole fruit of her hopes ?

So it would seem. Silently the girl sat there, leaning on one elbow, on her face an unthinking ecstasy. No danger while one could control the coughing. Keep your mind on matters of to-day. . . . Yesterday was Midsummer and to-day Sunday. How nice that two such days should come together in the midst of summer. Yesterday had not been a holiday for her, to-day was. Can it be a whole year ago that that happened— and that ? Like a story it was, what she had heard from Miss Laura, the Professor's daughter. Now was the right time to think it over. Her glance roamed back from the past to the present and became fixed on the darkening drops of blood on the grass, seeming to be absorbed in the way in which the blood withdrew into drop-form on the blades. But only her eyes were thus occupied. Her thoughts dwelt on her lost friend, on the young man and his amputated leg and mutilated lung. She thought too of the proud carriage of his head,

298

which her imagination saw only as ennobled by those trials. Not yet recovered, and impossible to say when he would recover, after the hours he had lain on the ground wounded.

Now, however, it was summer, the snowdrifts had vanished, flowers bordered the remotest paths, amidst which one could sit at one's ease. In delicious unawareness they have sought the same path, a merry humour bubbles in their talk and eyes, until a tiny clearing invites them so prettily to sit down that there is no refusing. . . . And when one came to the point of sitting down together, one had come to many other things, so blissfully warm. . . .

It was warm, yet the tired girl who sat beside the track shivered, shivered and suffered from thirst. Perhaps it was not really warm any longer, for the sun had sunk to the level of the tree-tops; its rays were broken by the crowns of the mighty spruce which stood everywhere in close-knit ranks, strong and aged, unmoved by stray sitters at their feet. The day that was closing for human beings seemed to have ascended to the level of the last fine branches, beyond reach, the mighty forest the last to claim it for its own. The eye could already discern in the immediate vicinity a twisted low juniper with threads of spider-web like fine harp-strings between its roving crown and roots. The surface of the road too was as though more sharply defined than a moment ago; when she gazed on it, it seemed to wear an expectant look, an air of waiting, as the Kulmala gate had done in the afternoon. The afternoon—had the afternoon gone? Yes, it was evening. She had kept company for hours with byegone and distant times. No one had gone past . . . or had they . . . She had been to Kulmala and had heard music.

Silja was humming even now. Perhaps not aloud; but all her being sang, a long song that gradually crystallised into a new hope, a wider hope than this Sunday visit had been.

As the young man had not been there, neither in the Rantoo yard nor the Kulmala house, her heart soon forgot that it had sought him there. It returned definitely and finally into itself and found there what it sought. . . .

Her heart found him and was secure in its possession of him ever afterwards. They were always together. They never went anywhere, no one should unnecessarily notice her friend's injuries. They were content merely to exist together, which was all the easier as her brain had no exact knowledge of where her friend was in the flesh. The long spell of rest beside the forest track ended with her rising, sure and confident of herself. The blood on the grass, shrunk almost to vanishing-point, was part of a distant past. Never had she been more sure of her life than at the moment of her rising from the ground, although her body felt as though it belonged to someone else and the shivers and thirst still continued. She would have to live and grow stronger now, seeing that her friend seemed to be coming nearer, growing as it were in size, every moment. He had had his own trials since he left her in the summer, last summer, a little while ago : events had occurred in between, but they receded now. His departure had been a kind of delusion, something Silja could not understand. Therefore it had happened that he now lay somewhere crippled, whilst she, the other human factor in this matter, wandered on this twilit road, on her way to Kierikka, to a house of soiled clothes, crumbling walls and dully quarrelsome people. Different the ways into which they had drifted, hers no less than his.

The forest thinned again and the track grew more even, to turn finally into a lane fringed with barns and sheds. A villager joined Silja here and asked where she had been ; he was mildly surprised at the talkativeness of the usually silent

300

girl. Why, she was mixing up this summer and last, talking of the war and the fallen and the badly wounded. She seemed to be curiously exalted, her cheeks glowed, her breath came in audible gasps. " I believe you're a bit tired after your walk," said the villager finally, the beginnings of vague suspicions in his mind.

Silja had delayed beyond the time agreed on with the mistress on her departure. The mistress had begun the milking alone and made no answer when Silja asked her whether a certain cow had been milked, or should she milk it. Perhaps the mistress had not heard, or had quarrelled with the master and was therefore untalkative. Silja took a milking pail and stooped down beside the cow ; it appeared to be unmilked. She tried it ; the first drops tinkled against the side of the metal vessel. But there the milker's strength gave way ; she fainted.

" God bless us, what's come over her," the mistress panted, in great distress because of the difficulty of getting her full pail to stand up straight, so that she could go to Silja's assistance.

A little milk may have spilled over, but the mistress was now at Silja's side. The girl's throat was hot, but her hands were very cold. Not a word came from the girl ; her head drooped lifelessly.

" For God's sake, come here, some of you. Where are you all ? Hermanni . . . " The mistress shouted as though the whole household was jointly neglecting an urgent duty, as though everyone ought to have been waiting at his post that Sunday evening for this event and the cry of a watchful mistress. But not a single blessed one of them—no ears, no eyes, in the whole lot of them—even the children, where were they ? Children ! . . .

Silja was already opening her eyes. She reached out for the fallen pail and tried to get up to continue her milking.

"Don't," said the mistress, "I should say you've done, poor body, all the milking you'll do in this world."

The girl recovered so much that the mistress was able to help her towards the house. The master had just bestirred himself into the porch. A look of unwilling embarrassment spread over his face, as though the mistress, by supporting the girl, had somehow got the better of him, emerged perhaps after all the victor of some preceding squabble. The mistress did not hesitate to keep up a withering fire of grumbling remarks as she passed him and to leave his questions unanswered.

After that milking, Silja was no longer able to work. On the Monday morning she felt better, having slept as those sleep who, after long efforts, have reached their goal. But when she tried to rise, everything went dark around her, and a sudden thirst gripped her throat. She had to sink back on to her bed ; her moan carried to the kitchen, where the mistress was already moving. Elsewhere too, the farm was awakening ; from the yard came the lowing of cows, and in his own corner of the room the farmhand was smacking his lips.

The mistress came into the living-room and turned her little eyes on Silja. The mistress was put out by any break in the everyday routine, and a sick servant is not an everyday occurrence. On the other hand, one had to be kind to an ailing maid. So that now the mistress of Kierikka would utter a very mild phrase to Silja in an angry voice—and hard words in a gentle voice. The cows began lowing again, for the usual milking hour was already past. They lowed straight into the mistress's consciousness. She grasped that the milking could not be done that morning in the customary manner, and said :

" I suppose we'll have to have Santra Mäkipää here in your stead for to-day."

By this remark the mistress wished above all to make it clear that the farm was not going to nurse Silja in bed for
302

nothing. The mistress was perfectly aware of the state of Silja's means : three months' pay untouched and—the slow brain of the mistress had time to think of that too—an unusually large wardrobe. Remembering these, the mistress was careful to say " in your stead."

Silja cared little what arrangement was made ; all she wanted was to rest. The bed was soiled and the bedding frayed, but outside the day was fine and one felt it even here in the room ; work on the farm seemed to proceed especially easily that day. The children were constantly running in and out of the living-room, leaving the door open for the scents of nature and the sounds of human toil to stream through. Kierikka was almost like a home to Silja all through the long June day. The holiday that had begun for her yesterday continued to-day.

She heard discussions between the master and mistress. They were debating, with much arguing and contradicting, how long Silja could be taken care of without help from the parish. She heard the master point out that the girl came from another parish and that their own parish would not give her anything ; there'd only be trouble if one tried.

Then the mistress came in to talk to her. She pointed out first that Silja's illness was probably a mortal one and that she ought, while there was still time, to make her peace with God.

And then a few words would have to be said about worldly matters too, to make sure they were agreed about them. If Silja would consent to this and that—and that—and then that —perhaps they would manage somehow. . . .

Santra Mäkipää was soon sent for : she came, full of importance and her own hurries. To Silja, however, it all felt very insignificant. A matter of much more importance was that she was now lying in bed, as her friend was in some place unknown. It would be pleasant to tell each other how each

303

had thought of the other while in this state. Silja felt as though she had been promoted in some way, brought nearer to her dear absent friend, here, in this new summer, never more in the old, which she had newly, yesterday it was, visited on a summer Sunday.

This first day of illness in bed was thus like a solemn holiday. In the evening, to be sure, sleep would not come ; it was so very warm, though the farmhand had opened the door. Thirst assailed her, and as Silja had forgotten to ask the mistress for water, she had to get up to fetch some. The night was light, she knew the way to the bakery water-barrel. She had never happened to go there at that time before or notice that in the white light of a midsummer night Kierikka, with its inhabitants asleep, was as pretty as other houses. An old family estate with rooms built long ago, in other days.

Sleeplessness began to be almost like resting, and although her mind imagined that her friend was coming to join her, her intelligence was capable of enjoying her fancy as a flight of the imagination. In all her consciousness there was no room for disappointment.

So Silja rested. The novelty of the situation had the effect of inclining the mistress to give vent to what faint Christian feeling was in her in little benevolent deeds. She brought Silja real unskimmed milk to drink, milk that was carefully saved from the dairy ; occasionally she brought real coffee and sugar, which she had succeeded in obtaining in exchange for flour, unknown to the master. The coffee caused a pleasant temporary perspiration. Silja would have been quite content with her lot if she had not had to sleep in the living-room, the many drawbacks of which were much more obvious to her now than when she had been able to move freely. It was really curious that she would soon have lived a year of days and nights in these surroundings. Her bed had been equally frowsy the whole time. Now, moment by moment, she seemed to be awakening to a cleaner and finer life. Impossible that she should be like this when, some time, that indefinite visitor arrived for whom one could not even begin to imagine an outward form, but whose nearness was as certain as life itself.

One day towards the end of the week, when the sun shone again after a rainy night, Silja managed to stagger outside unobserved. She found that she could bear moving about, although her breath did seem to grow hotter. She gazed in amazement at the sights of the house and yards, as though seeing them for the first time. Someone had emptied a pail beside the bakery door. The cows had been in the yard and left their traces, which now displayed wheel-marks.

Through the opening between the houses she could look out over the village, right to the lake, where the sunlight was transformed into glitter. The eye soon grew dim looking at it ; it tired her. From the fields came the shout of a ploughman to his horse, from somewhere so near that she recognised the voice. Marvellous that she should be thus idling about the yard on a day of hard work, and that no one in passing shouted an order to her. Although her life grew more beautiful day by day and as though clearer, although it rose to incomparably higher heights than the lives of those others who laboured yonder and bade others labour for them, yet she herself was in a state that precluded any effort on her part. Somewhere at the bottom of her consciousness knowledge of this conflict between achievement and endeavour vaguely oppressed her.

She went on and came at last to the bath-house, where luxuriant nettles hid altogether the rotten lowest tiers of logs. The window of the adjoining room was almost on a level with the nettles, but the sun shone on its greenish panes, patched with shingles. It would be nice to go right into the bath-house at this early hour. Her childhood came into her mind. But the window of this bath-house looked north, and its damp smell had a raw flavour.

In the little adjoining room, however, there was sunshine and a sweetish smell such as old unpainted wood sometimes has. Silja went in and sat down on a low stool that had been cast at some time into the room. Other furniture lay about in jumbled piles and there was even a four-poster bed, age-old and lacking a bottom.

The mistress had seen Silja moving near the bath-house, and as the girl failed to reappear, she came to look for her, opening the same doors as Silja had done. The woman's little eyes showed the irritation that a person of ordered habits feels when she sees something done, however trifling, that she would never do. What had made the girl come here? The mistress could not help casting a quick glance around to see whether there was anything there worth—well, hardly stealing, as nothing of that kind had ever been observed in Silja—though for that matter who could know everything that might come into the mind of a person, whose life was obviously ending : she might be looking for something with which to bribe Santra Mäkipää to take her place for a long time and perhaps keep her afterwards when she could no longer hope to stay at Kierikka. The mistress's mind moved indeed slowly, but it made this journey during the time needed for her eye to complete the sweeping glance.

" I thought," Silja said, " that this would make a sick-room for me."

Her ear really heard her mouth speak these words. No such thought had been in her mind ; she was especially affected by one of her words : sick-room. Yet now it began to seem to her that it was just what she ought to have thought and said.

"Who's going to feed you here?" the mistress asked, taking up a pail, from which the hoops clattered down as she did so.

"All I need is a little milk," Silja went on. "And I'd be out of the house in case this disease were to be bad for others, as you have children."

An unthinking vacant look appeared on the mistress's face. She made no answer.

"There's a bed here too, without a bottom," continued Silja. "We could let Santra clean up a bit, and I'd pay out of my wages, as long as they last . . ."

"I'm not going to have any Santra ferreting about here. I can clean it myself if it comes to that. Wonder what the master will have to say to it all. Well, come away now anyhow."

The mistress made off, walking much quicker than Silja.

Silja was allowed to move into the room adjoining the bath-house, which was cleaned and put in order, Silja helping as much as her strength permitted. The room looked so nice that the mistress could not refrain from saying: "I wouldn't mind moving here myself." To which Santra Mäkipää answered as she went: "You'll be getting this back quick enough, mistress, from Silja." The remark revealed her sympathy for Silja.

The fitting out of the room had been a task of such solemnity that when everything was finally in order, its intended occupant found it rather wonderful that she should really be settling there. Silja was so tired, however, that she lay down on the bed at once, as for a rest. She lay there fully clad until evening. When night came she undressed and went to bed as usual. But in the morning she no longer got up to dress herself. She was thus definitely condemned to a sick-bed. The story is nearing its end, the event from which it started and which gave rise to the whole narrative.

The most delightful days of summer were passing, the hay was ripe for cutting, the rye was beautiful and rich, still upstanding. The sun shone, the air smelled of sunbeams. The nettles under the window of Silja's room had risen so high as to be visible through the window, and imparted a mysterious greenish tinge to the atmosphere of the room, oddly in keeping with the regular coughing of its inhabitant. Very soon the characteristic outward signs of her illness had become visible in her arms, they seemed to have grown longer between the joints, the wrists and thin fingers still thinner. Her expression too became ever purer and more ecstatic; the roses on her cheek-bones glowed against the milky-white of her skin, the beautiful long lashes were more noticeable than before, as though some calm wide-reaching dream needed their shadow more than ever.

As her appetite was very poor, she grew rapidly thinner, never, however, to such an extent as to present a disturbing view to the eye. So long as she was able to rise from her bed, one might have perceived through her thin linen, as she moved cautiously over the floor, the fine femininity of the lines of her body. And on her face was an eternal smile ; that, if nothing else, might have revealed whose daughter she was. Though here in this place, as in her previous one, no one had ever seen her father. They were used to thinking of Silja as a farm-maid, taken into service from such and such farms. And now she was dying. The mistress said it as a certainty while pouring out coffee for the cupper-woman in the kitchen, and to Silja herself at her bedside. The mistress also talked to her dying servant in a religious strain, and Silja listened sympathetically, yet in some way amusedly.

For Silja was looking at the same time at her own neat apron, suspended over the mistress's dust-grey skirt. The mistress had forgotten to take it off, and now, observing it herself, she said : " I took this apron of yours as my own is in the wash."

" You did right to take it," Silja said.

There it was, a clear promise and an exhortation. The next time the mistress gave the cupper-woman coffee, she explained the matter at length, happening to have on one of Silja's skirts by that time. She added a remark about the need for some kind of return for the expense of engaging a substitute, even if one were to charge nothing for keeping an invalid maid.

" I suppose this girl too had no wages left owing to her," the cupper-woman asked, well aware of the exact amount of Silja's outstanding wages.

" They wouldn't go very far, even if a few marks were owing to her," whined the mistress and poured out no more coffee for her guest.

From the ramshackle window of the bath-house room the sound of coughing carried to the grass of the yard, where the drab-faced Kierikka children spent their days. Sometimes the master would stroll about there. His heavy footsteps would cease and a faint air of male boredom appear on his face as he attempted to weigh the nature of the coughing. The master never went to see his maid. Not during the whole period of her illness. Nor, on the Sunday when she was buried, could he " be bothered " to attend the funeral. The cottars and the mistress went with the farm horses.

There was no longer any Silja then, but on this day she still lived. In noble solitude her spirit celebrated its highest festivals in that ever-diminishing agglomeration of material, her body, which, nevertheless, to the beings that battened on it, flourishing and multiplying, was an enormous world. Those elongated beings absorbed and execrated the substance of her body. And as their vitality increased they broke into two separate beings, a process now proceeding at a furious rate all along her lungs and windpipe as far as her throat and elsewhere too in this lovely creation of nature, which, as an individual constant pattern, had existed and grown for twenty-two years. A senseless destruction of material life. With the evening, fever rose in the body, its surface shivered with cold, until the night hours drove forth the heat through the pores in the shape of perspiration. From dawn onward through the morning the forces of life and death jointly rested. And as the outside world and eternity were then at their most beautiful, the spirit could celebrate anew its solitary festivals.

The senses, servants of the spirit, were disturbed in their functions by the teeming infinitesimal life that went on in the body, but the noblest senses, the eyesight and hearing, were fully active. Rather were they refined to a higher pitch than before. And behind them the brain was alive, every impulse of the senses seeming to open into its innermost core, which was notwithstanding boundless, having no dimensions.

In the apertures between the roof-trees of the bath-house porch the swallows nested, twittering from dawn to eve. Not very distant was the high beam of the well, on the peak of which one of these most delightful companions of the sick girl was nearly always perched. Her hearing had become so much acuter, or so much " distorted," that it seemed to distinguish in the twitterings a rational speech. Tone harmonised with meaning in this speech, and it was not the doggerel in which healthy people mock the note-sequences of swallows. Thus the swallows were her closest companions, who kept her mood lively without ever hinting at her special state. They were content to cry out behind the door, though sometimes one of them would perch on an unexpected place, the cross-frame of the window, and remain there for a moment upright, its white under-side gleaming towards the beholder.

310

It seemed, however, to be engaged on its own private errand, an aside from the day's routine, and appeared not to notice the sick girl. The greetings and remarks of the birds came by invisible paths.

Light, however, came as a vision. It filled all the air near the panes, sought out a bubble in the glass for a prismatic display, or a larger flaw which, strangely distorted, magnified or reduced the spot of nature behind it. Its chief abode was the sky, which the bedridden girl could see where she lay. Her mind hung as it were on something up there, reaching ever higher, into the very heart of the lightest blue, where she finally imagined she saw herself receding, receding, until her eyes grew dim and a faint giddiness made her head reel. Her ear too lost for a moment the twittering of the swallows. Many are the obstacles on the path of a hopeful human being who imagines herself to be living the richest realisation of her hope.

For was it not essential that she should be permitted to reach the only human spirit remaining to her ? All others are far withdrawn from her : the mistress who comes to tend her and gazes at her with little pitying eyes, dressed now entirely in Silja's clothes, the children who accompany their mother and stand there staring, every opening in their faces agape, as the mistress looks to Silja's needs ; from far off comes the voice of Santra Mäkipää, uttering something that sounds like : " Isn't it Silja's wish too that I should get the same wages, seeing as how you've got money coming to you —I'm only asking because it seemed to me by the mistress's talk that it was her idea that I ought to show some charity towards you. . . . "

Everything receded, only one drew nearer. Soon they would be able to meet, at first in the daytime in the sight of others, then a second time in the evening on a leafy path, along the sides of which, under the birches, fine white night-flowers with curling blossoms gleamed. There on feet that seemed not to touch the earth they walk. . . . Silja was unable to think of her feet, they were as though missing; they were said to be swollen . . . and vaguely she recollected that something was lacking in her friend's feet . . . and lung. With the turn of her thoughts in that direction giddiness overcame her again; her body shivered, the evening was growing late. I am here, in this room; the mistress was here a little while ago. This is a dull kind of farm, to which I came without thought of where I was coming. And in the winter I helped men who went to war, first those—and then Teliniemi. . . . Pain of body, agony of spirit, semi-consciousness. Until the night waned—impossible to count which night.

One of them, however, was the last, and it gave way to a beautiful Sunday morning. To a morning that had as it were awaited its turn behind all other mornings.

The sun had risen some time after three and climbed gradually to overlook hundreds and thousands of yards and windows, paths and porches, and even to peer into rooms where human beings slept in their beds. It looked also into birds' nests, in which to be sure there was no atmosphere of Sunday, for in them every morning, especially the sunny ones, is equally holy. It shone on the world of insects and reptiles, and when a little insect flew joyfully into the morning sea of light, a swallow dashed ecstatically to seize it. Refracted in many ways the sunbeams penetrated below the surface of the lake. A tiny living being rowed itself eagerly forward, bent on its own sustenance and the multiplication of its species; the next moment, with pretty lithe movements, a little fish, delightful denizen of the sun-illumined water, had snatched it. Past them flitted a big fish, into whose mighty jaws a smaller fish here and there vanished.

Somewhere an old clergyman chanced to awake, so old that he had become childish and soft, especially just after his morning sleep. He looked out of his bedroom window for a time at the exceedingly beautiful calm morning, standing there in his nightshirt, and thought of the glory of God in Nature. Then, with a tender sigh, he padded back to his bed. His corner room was at that point of the rectory where the stone foundation is highest. But under the Kierikka bath-house, as we have seen, there was no stone foundation ; if there ever had been a corner-stone, it had sunk long ago in the soft earth. The bottom logs had rotted, the window settled askew . . . yet the sun shone through it on the bed of the dying maid inside.

During her life Silja, now dying, had seen as much of the sun as others in her country. That, again, which was now concluding its work of destruction in her young body, cannot endure the direct touch of the sun. What if the light of the sun had been able to penetrate as a living breath to all the hidden cells of this human being and there work what it was able to work on her skin ! But the sun shines not into the grave, and the tiny rod-shaped beings within her were representatives of the grave. For a grave too is life.

Poor Hilma, Silja's mother, fell under the onslaught of those tiny beings. Her many sorrows had lowered her powers of resistance. Silja had hardly known any deep sorrows, only passing states of agony which easily assumed a poetic glow. In her, material seemed to crumble away of itself, as though humbly withdrawing to leave more room for spirit. Her beautiful love filled her mind as long as consciousness existed in her. And the greatest miracle, the merciful providence of Nature, was that she was never permitted to exclaim in spirit : " Now I die and shall therefore never attain to the goal of my dreams." On the contrary, her extinguishing spirit knew at the end a complete unity with the spirit of her friend. A beautiful male spirit it was, and so much Silja's understanding strayed at the final moment that she never knew whether it really was the spirit of her friend in whose shelter she crouched, or whether father, seen at the height of his manhood, took her in his arms and held her close, looking meanwhile ahead, a proud victoriousness in his glance. Sweet it was in any case . . .

So ends the tale of the last flourishing of an old family tree that happened to end at that time ; they are always ending. But these " trees " are not like the trees of the forest. There is no real death for a family ; if we could look unhindered through time, we should see " branches " of every family still alive. Surely the Salmelus family too battles, gains and loses, lives at the highest level of its manhood this very year in which our narrative ends. In the widest sense of all we are all members of the same family and can therefore respect each other's struggles in all time. You too, the farthest reader in point of time of this narrative, may respect our battles.

This natural stress of battle is only a sign, the meaning and significance of which we are permitted, indeed constantly compelled, to study.

CPSIA information can be obtained
at www.ICGtesting.com
Printed in the USA
BVHW072012061021
618316BV00001B/49